Gerhard Holtshauzen was born in 1982 in South Africa. He works as a freelance writer and editor, and has been writing stories in old diaries since he was ten years old. He spends his free time glued to the screen of his computer, watching movies or enjoying the company of family and friends.

He lives in Pretoria.

The Changed Agenda

Gerhard Holtshauzen

The Changed Agenda

Vanguard Press

VANGUARD PAPERBACK

© Copyright 2009
Gerhard Holtshauzen

The right of Gerhard Holtshauzen to be identified as author of
this work has been asserted by him in accordance with the
Copyright, Designs and Patents Act 1988

A CIP catalogue record for this title is
available from the British Library

ISBN 978 184386 415 8

Vanguard Press is an imprint of
Pegasus Elliot MacKenzie Publishers Ltd.
www.pegasuspublishers.com

First Published in 2009

Vanguard Press
Sheraton House Castle Park
Cambridge England

Printed & Bound in Great Britain

DEDICATION

To my mother

For never once doubting or questioning the imagination that runs my inner world, and now hides in plain sight on paper. This would never have worked without your support.

PROLOGUE

Darkness

It wasn't absolute, though. Gas lamps alongside the streets gave enough light to warn anyone about any slick spots in the street, and the light also served to banish the ultimate gloom of the fog that lay thickly over the cobbled ways. That, and the gloom could hardly devour the heights of Big Ben, the clock staring down at the fog-covered expanse of London at night.

He ran fast, dragging his friend after him. It was hard going, but Eric was a large man, tall and well-muscled, a fact hidden beneath the tweed suit that he had decked himself out in for the evening. He hadn't thought that they'd be running for their lives again so soon. Their enemy was relentless, he knew, and he should have known that nowhere was safe for too long. Eric halted their near-heedless chase abruptly, causing his friend to crash against his side. He fell down, and Eric helped him up again, sparing a moment to cast about them, looking for telltale signs of their pursuers. In the smog that permeated the London streets it was hard to tell, but there were ways to discern beyond sight. Eric narrowed his eyes and looked at his friend. Aidan showed no signs of change, not even here. His eyes were glassy and almost colourless, drained of their blue lustre. His face was still slack and devoid of any feeling or emotion, and his body was dead weight in Eric's arms. Eric placed a hand on Aidan's face, tilting it so that, under normal circumstances, Aidan would have looked him in the eye.

"I could use some help," Eric whispered, and dropped his hand. Aidan seemed unwilling, without active protest, to support his own body, so Eric heaved him into his arms and continued running. The strain would show soon, he knew, and this was hardly the time to let any strain get to them. He ran off, taking a side street, knowing the dangers inherent in such an act. But he feared no thieves and murderers marauding in the black of night. In fact it was safe to say that any such delinquents would fear Eric.

After a while, he reasoned that they could always try a train. It had worked before, if only because the pursuit had been far behind. Eric doubted the same would go again. He and Aidan were hunted, and he was losing ground fast because he was basically carrying his own weight as well as that of his unresponsive friend.

He made it to a station more to the outskirts of the city. Once there he all but sagged to his knees, allowing Aidan to gently roll from his grasp as he let fatigue overwhelm his body. He let his mind wander, hoping against hope that they would be safe here. But he couldn't sleep, or allow himself any restful luxury. He couldn't leave Aidan unchecked for long, even though the probability of his friend waking up or making a response of any kind was scant, even non-existent.

He bundled the both of them into a nook inside the station. Getting in had been easy, as well as evading the drowsy police officers skulking about to prevent break-ins or people trying to take up residency in the station at night. Only then did he close his eyes for an hour, still making sure he was wakeful enough to become alert if the need arose.

An hour later he knew it had been a mistake.

He sensed the arrival of their pursuers. He lifted Aidan in his arms again and broke free of the nook, rushing outside to the tracks. He hoped a train would arrive, but he doubted it. It was too early, even though the sun was rising far in the east, and casting the foggy station in a lurid, raw morning light. For a second he swore loudly, and berated himself.

"I could really use your help," he sobbed to Aidan, whose posture showed no change. Snarling, Eric placed Aidan on a bench, strode some distance forward and waited. There was nothing for it. He couldn't run anymore, and he couldn't leave Aidan alone. He owed him too much. So here they would stay, and he would fight.

It was too much to expect their enemy to come face to face at the onset. Instead, a dozen thugs emerged from the fog, their hulking forms draped in trench coats, their faces obscured by the dark, and the bowler hats drawn down over their foreheads. They had a myriad of weapons in their hands, from cudgels to chains and knives. Eric calmed his breathing. None of these weapons could harm him. But they could slow him down, and disadvantage him, if only slightly. He wondered if these were hired or subjugated thugs. He probed for their intentions, and found nothing lurking behind their faces but blind subservience. No will was left, nothing but the guiding power of a dark presence. Eric almost sighed with relief. Killing them would be a mercy.

"What's going on 'ere?" a nasal voice called. Eric started, as a police officer materialized on the platform, buoyed up by both the belligerence of power and the annoyance at having a quiet night's calm disturbed. The thugs didn't stop their measured advance on Eric's position, prompting the officer to bark a warning.

"All of you, stop where you are! That's an order!" The next instant, the officer flew forward, and then collided with an invisible wall with a sickening crunch. Eric could hear the bones break, and he could see the blood spurt from the lifeless body that had been the officer. He lamented such a loss of life, but it could very well be him next. One thing he could ascertain from that display was that his enemy was close. Probably watching everything, biding his time. That was what the thugs were for.

"Are you a coward? Do you fear me?" he screamed into the gloom. "Show yourself!"

Nothing was forthcoming on that count. Sighing, Eric regarded the thugs. Those on the outskirts of the line slowed down, and the three in the middle raised their hands, weapons brandished, charging forward. Eric assumed a defensive stance. As the first thug, knife raised, moved in, he unleashed his gift. It was a gift, but it was also the reason he was being hunted. Energy whined, manifesting as a slim but long blade that danced between virulent magenta fires and darting specks of dense black. The blade sang as he swept it down and then up, slicing through the thug's arm and severing the hand holding the knife. The man made no sound, a sure sign of mental domination, as he went down. Eric moved past, ending the misery of such a subsistence, dragging the energy blade across the man's throat. The second thug also met the blade, and Eric dispensed with disarming the man, shoving the blade forward and extending it, watching it punch through the man's chest where his heart was. The third thug managed to get past his guard and nearly surprised him with a very heavy blow to the head from a club, but he compensated, lifting his free hand and manifesting a flat surface that deflected the blow. The surface coalesced into a massive double-edged axe with a long handle, and as the remainder of the thugs closed in, the blade in the other hand became a whip of whining energy, lashing out and decapitating two while the axe sliced three other bodies in half. The other four had their eyes punched out by the angry tongue of the whip, even as the axe became a massive sword that severed their heads. As the bodies tumbled, Eric stood still, heaving in gulps of air. He was tired not so much by the fight as by the fact that he had been running the entire night. But the adrenaline told him he could still keep going. And now that the thugs were disposed of, the master would show himself. Eric turned to the sound of hands, slowly clapping.

The man whom he knew as his enemy – no other name had ever been ascertained, except maybe 'the Frenchman' – strode from the fog, clapping his gloved hands. He had a small round bowler perched on over a high forehead, and dark eyes glittered in a narrow face that tapered to a strong chin and a cruel, smiling mouth. Low laughter rolled from the man as he casually walked closer.

"Well, well, un bon surprise, oui? But not an unexpected one," the man drawled, French accent heavy. "I merely wanted to see if you were still capable of resisting." The man looked down at the mess of his ruined followers, the smile actually widening, as if in fondness. "I see the constant running hasn't dulled your skill."

"Speaking of dull," Eric breathed. The weapons still muttering angrily in his palms extended into long links with large round protrusions at their tips. Eric lifted his arms, even as the spheres grew large blunt studs. "I'm going to cut your heart out with one of these."

"Oh, so crude," the Frenchman said, momentarily frowning, but still not losing the smile. "I admire your spirit; it is a matter of joie de vivre, n'est pas?" He laughed, a low, melodious and above all condescending sound. "But there is no need for this." Eric started as one of the weapons lashed back, striking him against the side of his head. As his vision danced, he narrowly dodged the other monstrous sphere. He tried rolling to one side, and found himself rooted to the spot. "Such an exquisite gift you have, mon ami, and used with such expert control. But it has never been a matter of your control, but of mine." Eric rocked back as the second ball met its mark, smashing into the side of his head. He felt the blood run down his face, even as the gash – a mortal one, but not for him – began sealing. "And then of course there is your regenerative body. Unparalleled," the Frenchman said, voice couched in rapturous interest. "I have always wondered just how capable this compensation of yours is."

Eric, still dazed, felt a burning in his hand. He knew the Frenchman was manipulating the energy, and though he knew what the shape was, he had no control over it. His breathing increased as the energy became a jagged blade, and screamed loudly as his arm was jerked about, the blade slamming through his chest. Missing the heart, mind, but the pain was excruciating. His screams rent the early morning air, and he hoped more police officers were in the vicinity, not that it would help much. The Frenchman's renewed laughter assured him of it.

"No, no, such a thing would not do. I have taken care of our other friends in blue, yes, the foolish Englishmen and their little whistles. A throat can only swallow so many shrill metal objects, yes?" Laughter again, always continuous laughter.

"What do you want?" Eric grated through the pain, teeth clenched to keep from screaming again.

"I? Is it not obvious, hmmm? I want to study you, take you apart eventually. Make you suffer, most assuredly."

"Why?" Eric demanded, feeling hope crumble.

"Because I can," the Frenchman replied amiably. He looked past Eric's rigidly held form, and grinned.

"Ah, a friend. I've heard of your catatonic little protégé, hmmm. I think I shall let you watch him die, and then maybe your spirit will be broken enough to make this more amusing, oui?"

"No," Eric whispered, trying to look around. He didn't have to, as the same unseen force that held him unbending suddenly spun him around, forcing him to watch as Aidan was lifted from his position on the bench, floating on nothing. His progress halted abruptly, and then before Eric could make an outcry, he was thrown over the side of the platform, to land heavily in the middle of the tracks.

"Ah, do you hear it?" the Frenchman asked, chuckling. "The morning train. Such a sweet sound. I have never seen what happens to a body run over by a train."

"Damn you, stop!" Eric yelled, tears of pain and rage rolling down his cheeks. No amount of struggling would dislodge the unseen force that held him immobile. The shrill screech of the train echoed clearly over the crispness of the morning air, and the plume of steam soon came in sight. In helpless frustration he watched it approach. On some impulse he turned his head.

"Aidan! Aidan get up!"

"He can hear you, but he won't respond. That is the nature of such things," the Frenchman said happily.

"Now do be quiet, I wish to watch this without your screams – however welcome – interfering." Eric continued yelling at Aidan to get up, but his friend remained unresponsive. The train rolled into sight. "The moment of interest. Watch carefully please," the Frenchman said. Eric tried to squeeze his eyes shut, but they

16

remained open, held thus. He raged, he yelled, he screamed, but the Frenchman didn't mind, and Aidan didn't hear him.

But then he did.

As the train rolled closer, slowing down – it wouldn't matter, it would still run Aidan over – Aidan's eyes seemed to glitter. Their lustreless hue suddenly became a vibrant sky blue, even at a distance, and his face contorted first under pain, and then a frown.

"Aidan get up!" Eric yelled again, and Aidan did so, gingerly rising as if he had all the time in the world.

"What is this?" the Frenchman demanded, smiles and laughter lost. Eric was summarily dropped, falling to his knees. For a single moment he remained where he was, and then he shot forward, hoping to make it in time to get Aidan out of the way. Aidan regarded him with wide eyes, eyes that showed shock, horror and then, strangely, understanding and commiseration. And then his eyes became lost in colour, the light blue of a glacial winter sky, radiating light and power enough to blind. Eric held an unwilling hand in front of his eyes to shield from the glare, barely registering the Frenchman's enraged yell. He could barely make Aidan out anymore, but as the fog light of the train illumined the tracks where Aidan stood, he was sure he could hear something like the sound of air drawing inward, a low whine, a hissing of wind. And then the glare faded, and as the light returned to normal, Aidan was nowhere to be seen.

"Mon Dieu, mon Dieu, quel catastrophe!" The Frenchman yelled. Eric wanted to laugh, but he had no energy left. He was forced to listen to his enemy rage. "I have heard of such things! Oh, my friend, you have much explaining to do." Eric was heaved to his feet again, surprisingly, bodily, by the Frenchman, who raised him to eye level. It was moot; Eric didn't have the energy to land a punch, never mind break free.

"I can't tell you what I don't know," Eric remarked, but he didn't bother to keep the elation from his voice. Elation that Aidan at least had escaped. The Frenchman's return smile promised unimaginable misery in reprise.

"Ah, but that was what they all say. And you, my friend, can shrug off almost any wound. I have seen it. It will prove amusing and exciting to devise ways to torture you, so that it hurts and is lasting, yes. Hmmm."

The blow that ended Eric's consciousness was another unseen device, but at least it brought welcome darkness and bliss. At least for a while.

It was hardly as easy as she had thought it would be.

Even she knew that when dealing with certain people, prudence was required. When dealing with him, one had to be downright paranoid, or suffer for it. Which was why she was abandoning this course of action. She had already lost too much in the efforts of getting close to him, or close enough to make it worth her while to persist in keeping an eye out. But the problem was that he knew far better how to watch out than she did.

She stepped over the body of one of her minions. Rarely her actions were this costly, especially not to her own side. Her black garb trailed like an ethereal shimmer of night-dark silk behind her, the hem dragging through blood and other unmentionable organic elements. She didn't care right now. If she did, she would have died a long time ago, and not be here, close to the top, with little by way of resistance save for him. She ducked into a niche and allowed herself a slight laugh. That she would be as intimidated as to refuse to say his name. But then, he seemed capable of hearing it spoken, no matter where you were, and then to direct his attention and his cohorts at you.

It took precious little energy to duck beneath the hand that reached from outside her hiding place to snare her. She grabbed hold of it, swung around underneath it and forced the owner to dance forward as she pivoted to bend the arm behind his back. He made no sound – extremely professional, even under extreme pressure of pain, the followers of that man – but she knew she was causing pain.

"Did he send you to me? How did he find me?" She settled for the domineering tack. He struggled, but she pulled tighter. Even then he refused to utter a single sound, and she wondered if perhaps he wasn't mute. It was too little to hope for; his hold on them was too strong, even for her to break over time. But she could extract it, at cost, with little damage to herself.

All it required for her to do was to kill the man who was still squirming in her grip.

"Answer me!" she demanded. When he didn't, she lifted her other hand behind her back. She luxuriated in the feel of the radiant power that allowed her to extend parts of her body, and felt the three nails of the middle three fingers grow to abnormal lengths. They would be as dark and immutable as her guise, and for special effect, she forced their edges to a barbed perfection, and felt the small agony of transmuting some of the blood closest to her nails into a virulent poison, something even one such as this man would die from within seconds of injection. She then lifted the hand closer to his neck, stroking the Adam's apple with the fingertips just beneath the nails. "I am warning you," she whispered, voice sultry. Still no answer. She sighed, forced to unwilling admiration for her prey, but she was as ruthless a killer as they came. Gently she nicked the fragile skin over his carotid artery, administering a very slight dose of the venom. At once she felt him struggle in her grip, as he entered into the throes of incoming death. "Last chance."

"You don't have an antidote, so the point is useless," he grated, a typical muscle-brained oaf, but nevertheless indomitably ensorcelled within the will of his master, who could turn even ones such as he into obedient, tame, completely loyal pets, of no mean skill. She hissed in affront, decided that killing him would serve better in the long run than questioning him here and now, and made a liberal swipe across the front of his neck, opening the skin and the trachea with negligible ease. She let him fall, and he was dead before he hit the ground.

She hurried after that. Priding herself on patience was one thing, but waiting for the axe blow to fall was another, and she had to deliberate on what her next move would be. It was easy getting out of buildings such as this, with their narrow corridors leading as often as not to dead ends. To the untrained and the careless such structures resulted invariably in their deaths, since a high-speed chase made for hasty, foolish decisions, based on whims and availabilities, and these fools often entrenched themselves with no recourse or chance of escape. But she had other skills at hand to facilitate her escape.

He had outwitted her, but she doubted he was able as yet, or powerful enough, to keep her and to contain her. Birds of a feather, and hated foes.

It was with little trepidation that she entered into one of the small hallways. She took four turns right, one left and then three right again, where she ducked beneath a crossbeam that would have dissuaded another from going further. But then, they didn't have her skills. She halted before the small, dark hole that was all that remained of some maintenance chute. It was hardly big enough for a child to go through, let alone a grown woman.

She slipped through several moments later, finding herself on the other side of a dank, grime-covered wall. But she was also inside the entry foyer of what she now discerned as a one-time hotel, long since abandoned.

And she had a reception committee.

She counted twelve men, only half of them similar to the bullnecked freak she dismembered back there. The other lot were more like her own people would be; cold, ruthless and calculated. Slimy, oily, even, but totally dedicated to the pursuit of inflicting pain on others, and enjoying the destruction of flesh and peace of mind. One of these saw her, and smiled a cruel grimace. He had oriental eyes, just like she did, but where he stared at her with anticipatory black amusement, she regarded him with uncharacteristic blue eyes. This alone should have caused him to back down. But then, these were the minions of her enemy, and driven by him they had little by way of willpower to refuse what he presented them with: the chance to kill, maim or murder. Brandishing short knives and varying forms of short cudgels, they rounded on her. The leader of the small group lagged behind, since it was he who would deliver the customary jibes and ultimatums. She waited patiently.

"End of the line," he said, a slow drawl that nevertheless betrayed the intelligence behind the words. He seemed like a lawyer, a very corrupt one, who meted out injustice as easily as he could warp the system to shield the criminal. The man even looked like a lawyer, which meant he seemed arrogant and decked out in contempt.

"Really?" she asked, walking closer until she was at the head of the fan-shaped set of wide stairs that led down to the reception area where the men waited. The lead man didn't answer again, but the others hefted their weapons, and stepped closer as well. "No courtesy for a lady?" she asked.

"You're not a lady," one of the less intelligent brutes replied, leering evilly. It happened to be a very piercing remark, and one that managed to actually affront her, but she knew they were much too ignorant to know better. Yet for a single moment she lapsed into indecision, and then she resumed her course. One step at a time.

"Do you boys know who I am?" she queried, leaning to one side on the railing to emphasize the femininity of her being. The idea was lost on the brute who had so offended her, but not on the rest. They too grinned, except for the oily lead man. "Do you know what I am?"

"We know," he said then, and he pulled out a gun. Its length glinted in the lurid light cast from flickering street lamps and other ambient glows from outside. This he held close to his shoulder, completely unfazed by the underlying threat in her question. "You cannot pass." She noted the looks of puzzlement the lesser thugs shared with each other. This was an unusual tack for their boss to take. Where was the lingo, the cruelty, the inviting camaraderie? It brought a grimace to her face. So her enemy didn't share on every level.

"And what if I must? Do you think you can stop me?" she challenged, voice deep and husky. Once again she affected a very feminine pose, meant to confuse the idiots. It worked, as far as she could tell. The blithering moron who had so slighted her leered again – he seemed very good at it – but this time it was lasciviously. She granted him a mock kiss, a fleeting notion of indulgence, and then she acted.

The battle was over before it progressed scant seconds. The outcome was that the floor was strewn with bodies, all of them mangled, their appendages twisted at grotesque angles from normalcy. Only the leader remained, and both his legs were broken, as well as the arm that didn't hold the gun. He regarded her as she resumed 'looking' female, and she delicately squatted next to him. He would be dead within a few more minutes – she had aimed a very decisive venom-congested nail into his wrist. But she would watch him die, not hasten it. "Now, tell me what I want to know."

"You will not survive my master's wrath," he said, nearly choking on thick black blood as it threatened to well past his clenched teeth.

"Your master better watch his back," she cautioned. This time though she would not fail, or act in half-measures. Carefully she retracted a nail, changed its state and extended it once more. The serum she concocted had been forged in the depths of her being, where even she spoke only absolute truths, and if it could garner the undiluted truth from one of her own kind, it worked even better on other people. They just died much faster. She eased the nail into the same slash she had opened on the man's wrist. His eyes bulged momentarily, and then they glazed over with the altered process of mental function. "Now, answer simply and quickly," she commanded. "Why is your master so keen on controlling this part of the city?"

"He looks for something," the man replied, completely uninhibited, totally unbiased.

"Do you know what it is?"

"No."

"How did he find out about my activities here tonight?"

"He sensed your intent long before he made our orders known to us," came the sure-fire reply. The very basis of its truthfulness unsettled her, but she pressed on.

"Where is your master now?" She waited for the final answer, but the man remained lying on the floor, staring at her, eyes widening with more than unnatural candour. She frowned, and noticed too late the black runnels seeping from the edges of his eyes. He lifted the gun, but as she recoiled she noted where he pointed it.

"I will see you soon. Until then." The voice was not his own. He pulled the trigger. She dodged back as bone and viscera, brain and grey matter exploded to the side, the super-accelerated bullet taking out more than half his skull. She frowned again, this time in genuine distaste for the extreme goriness that festooned the side of the reception desk.

There was nothing more for her to do. Straightening, she lifted the lapels of her garb and pulled it shut over her mouth, leaving only her upper head exposed to the outside, before exiting through the front door.

CHAPTER ONE

2061

The bluff overlooking the ocean held two occupants.

It was early morning, and the air was crisp and cool, a fitting addition to the overcast white sky of late autumn. One of the occupants was standing, a defiant cast to his frame. He was idly throwing rocks down the defile, not paying much attention to his friend, who was seated a few feet back, contentedly puffing on a cigarette. Both of them were clad in warm clothing.

"We've been gone for some time, Luke. Think we should head back?" the standing one asked his friend.

The seated one, identified as Luke, shrugged. He rose slowly, stiff from sitting down for so long, and stretched. He was more well-muscled than his friend, as well as slightly taller. Long blonde hair hung in a ponytail down his back, and he stared at the world through sea-green eyes.

"Nah, let's enjoy the quiet before the others get here."

"I bet they're here already," Luke's brother said. He went by the name of Daniel Hirsch, Danny for short and 'Danny-boy' to those who knew him well. In contrast to Luke, Danny was lean and trim, as though most of the fat normally found in a human body was scoured from his frame. He had tightly curling jet black hair and a face that hinted at amusement. By his stance and the way he walked he appeared the more physically active of the two, and he held himself in an agile way that spoke of fitness. He threw the last rock from him and turned around. "Hope they brought suitable entertainment."

"Nathan will have taken care of it," Luke said, eyes twinkling mischievously. He took another cigarette from the near-depleted packet and stuck it into his mouth. Danny quirked a brow at the gesture.

"We've only stood on that bluff for twenty minutes and you polish half a packet. Pretty serious stuff."

"I admit, I chain-smoke," Luke said, grinning lopsidedly as he maintained the cigarette on his lower lip. "I enjoy the smaller things in life."

"I know you too well," Danny remarked, and snaked out one fast arm, swiping the cigarette from Luke's mouth and casting it over the edge. Luke regarded him critically, frowning. Danny grinned and mocked an apology, but beyond that showed no sign of remorse. "When do you intend to quit?"

"I don't," Luke said. Danny shook his head.

"I don't get it. I smoked for five years and my lungs started feeling like dirty bags, but you smoke for how long? Seven, and you don't even wake up coughing!"

"Robust health," Luke said, and grinned when Danny treated him to a critical glare. "The Hirsches are known for their iron constitution."

"You lie pretty badly, even when you joke. Judging by your brother's disposition, bullshit is also a Hirsch thing."

"Hey!"

Daniel grinned flippantly and waved away the deeper implications. It went without saying that he himself counted as a Hirsch, mainly because he had been living with the Hirsch family for the last nine years. His own parents had died when he was six, and the Hirsches had rescued him, aged eleven, from a foster home – possibly the eighth – and had seen fit to adopt him into their already close-knit family. Since then, he had virtually become part of the family, not merely by default of paperwork. To Luke he was an adored younger brother, and to Nathan, a close companion stuck halfway between brother and closest friend.

They began descending the bluff, making for the roadside where they had left the car. "But you don't smoke the way you do without picking up health issues. It's a miracle you still find enough cigarettes to smoke – government clamps down on smokers nowadays."

"When you're desperate enough, laws don't really matter," Luke replied and withdrew another cigarette. Danny watched his brother and rolled his eyes, throwing his hands in the air.

"I hope you don't end up on a hospital bed someday, your lungs liquefying, and I have to stand there saying 'I told you so!'"

"I'll be able to afford cloning, I guarantee it!" Luke countered. "Stop worrying!" When Danny merely shook his head and raised his brows, Luke halted. He knew Danny very well, and he knew the expression that came over Danny's face when he had stated his wishes, or his opinion, and it went unheeded. Sighing, he looked at the cigarette in his hand. He frowned, pursed his lips and threw the thing away from him.

"Sometimes I hate you," he said. Danny, noting the lack of a cigarette, spread his hands and gave a disarming smile.

"No you don't, you hate it when I'm right!"

"It's the same thing with you!" Luke snapped back, but not unkindly. "It can't be healthy for one person to know another that well."

"What are you talking about?" Danny asked. He had reached the passenger side of the car, waiting for Luke to unlock the vehicle from the driver's side. "I know what you've told me. Where is this coming from?" The locks clicked open, both doors sliding upwards. Danny climbed in first, watching his older brother. Luke seemed upset, somehow. His face yielded the set look that Danny identified with deep thought, or preparation for some or other heady revelation. Daniel, surprised by the switch from Luke's amiable disposition of before, was nonetheless powerfully intrigued: he treasured moments of confidence, because to some extent he was a superb mediator when it came to problems; he loved sorting other people's issues out, but he would never admit it openly. "Well?"

"You know how you're always going on about mental control, and how much you think you have of it?"

"I know how much I have of it!" Danny all but crowed. Between his friends, he was known as a brain, mostly because everything he did was calculated and deliberate, and backed by a cartload of stability, information and assurances that buoyed him up irrefutably. Arguing with Danny was delaying the inevitable: eventually everyone saw things his way. Luke admired him immensely for it, and was even a little jealous, because Danny seemed to go through life without questioning the underlying currents of everything around him. It was a prevalent testimony of his refusal to back down from anything: life had hurt him and abandoned him, and he vowed in actions to pit every single grain of victory out of triumphing over it.

"Whatever, the point is that I have to tell you something. Something important about me." Luke was flustered, Danny realized, and he steeled himself accordingly for whatever revelation was forthcoming. Part of his charm was that he could field almost any problem, his own or his friends, and he didn't hold with judging. This was why he knew more about Luke than most people did, and why he was more than a little disturbed by Luke's behaviour: he'd never seen his brother so distraught.

"Shoot," Danny said, which he usually did when Luke averred to telling him something, but was too cautious to do so without encouragement. Luke gave another long sigh, and then looked up.

"I haven't been completely honest with you. I mean, we've known each other for nine years now, and you are possibly the best friend I've ever had –"

"You're gushing, and I'm becoming self-conscious," Danny interjected. He frowned, startled, when Luke stared at him with a glare that he'd never experienced before. It held a veiled frustration that was unexpected.

"This is serious, Daniel," Luke said. Another warning: Luke never used Danny's full name. "Pipe down or I won't tell you."

Danny nodded, aware of the inferences. With Luke he shared many misgivings and personal hopes, and it was automatically implied that continuing on the path of idle banter in the face of the seriousness now was courting conflict and a loss of trust. So he nodded tightly, embarrassed, and stayed quiet. "There is something about me that I've never shared with anyone but my family. My blood family."

Luke halted, sighing again, as if gathering new strength. Daniel, knowing well enough by now that blood was the only thing that was denied him the ultimate position of true family among the Hirsches, ignored the unfortunate overtones, chalking it up as Luke being seriously vexed by whatever he was about to say.

"You and I always joke about stuff that people can do. Bending spoons and reading minds, people catching fire without warning, stuff like that." He paused, and Danny noted the hesitation was a gap for him to add his agreement.

"Yeah, so? We do that all the time," Daniel said, squaring his shoulders and leaning back into his seat.

"Exactly. But we don't believe stuff like that, right?" Luke challenged. Danny shrugged.

"Never seen evidence of it before," he added. He started as the car locked itself, the lights going on as it came to life. He cast about him, wondering what was happening. He knew about remote access – his own car had it – but this was a little weird. He looked at Luke, who was still staring at him, both hands on his lap. The car's engine whined, the low electric hum speaking of departure. "This is a trick, right? Where's Nate? Hidden anywhere?"

"Danny, this is no joke. I wouldn't do that," Luke replied wearily, as if he was somehow resigned. Danny frowned mightily, trying to figure out the ramifications behind what was happening. As if to exacerbate his feelings, the car surged forward, moving fluidly into the road. The steering wheel moved perfectly, the electronics admitted to everything being flawless and without lapse or shortfall. And all the time Luke was watching him, hands in his lap, feet tucked back beneath his seat. Realization of a kind dawned, as did the denial.

"No way. No fucking way!" Danny exclaimed.

"Way," Luke said, voice sounding final and undeniably firm. The car surged forward faster, even as Luke's usually dulled aquamarine eyes flared luminous blue.

She knew more about that mystery than anyone else gave her credit for.

Persephone lay back in her couch, luxuriating in the feeling of being alive. She had an inherent distrust of humans, but she kept them very close to her, with regards to that old human saying. Her most trusted servants were human, and they served her with the same fervour and adoration as any human would usually serve one of her kind. Strongly muscled men aired her with ridiculous feather fans, an affectation she assumed with regards to her status as a near omnipotent being amongst these futile little insects. *She missed being close to him.*

He had cast her off when his supposed destiny became known to him, and he had discarded her like a dirty dishcloth, but not before she had learnt more of his intentions and the facts behind them than he would have cared to admit. Now she harboured that information against the day he would try to turn against her, like he had against so many of them. And his anger was always fatal. She would just make sure it never came at her, and if it did, that she had the leverage to remain one step ahead, and alive.

"Bring me Sirtis," she murmured silkily. She heard one of her many doting slaves move off to comply. Within moments of her command Sirtis was brought before her, a lovely human specimen with an oval face, dark brown eyes and a strange shade of reddish hair. Sirtis was one of the few human beings she had entrusted with some of her closest secrets, a rare occasion that warranted the woman's absolute servility and the added contractual clause of certain death under treasonous circumstances. Sirtis had been groomed to experience extreme amounts of pain – Persephone had learnt those lessons of control well from him – and would die before she snapped under torture. It made Sirtis the perfect person to oversee Persephone's matters in regards to ferreting out information that was crucial to Persephone's survival.

"Have you found anything new?" she asked.

"Not quite. I have no idea as to whether your former love has found out anything else about the Cortez Incident. I doubt it, but he still has many of his people posted close by, in case something crops up. That, and there has been word of some or other new Changed in New York."

"That would appear beside the point, Sirtis," Persephone crooned in her bored voice. "Surely you have something more enticing for me."

"There is a New York Changed," Sirtis began, daring the wrath of her mistress.

"What about it?" Persephone demanded, pouting.

"She has skills, it seems, similar to our mutual friend's, or at least to some extent." Sirtis turned her head slightly to emphasize the latter part of the statement, and Persephone smiled slightly.

"I will look into it. After all, how powerful can this Changed be?"

Marianne Sirtis watched Persephone leave the room.

She would never admit that she sometimes loathed working for the woman. It was hard seeing her as anything but a woman, a seductive, merciless one that could slice through social gatherings like a hot knife. She was alluring, the paramount female figure carried off with little by way of facial make-up, wearing designer outfits that flattered her entire being. The only thing that alerted you to the danger were the dead eyes that only livened up with the azure gaze that dominated them when Persephone used her powers. Otherwise, the dense brown, almost-black orbs held little emotion.

Sirtis had been a struggling Harvard graduate, one who had trouble finding a job that was fitting for her age. She was still young, barely twenty-five, and despite her apparent genius she suffered from the well-known beauty backlash that usually assailed the women who were both intelligent and pretty. And she knew she was pretty. Wild red hair framed a face with prominent cheekbones, full red lips and dense, agate eyes. Dressed in figure-hugging, tailor-made business suits, she reminded of tenacious, ruthless lawyers. To some extent Marianne could play that part, but her major had been politics, and though she still yearned to play her part in the workings of the government, she had seen the undercurrents that she had found, with growing horror, were dominant throughout the Americas and several other key, major Asian and European cities. She served one of the Changed, a remarkable feat, for all she couldn't brag about it. Who would believe her if she told someone that her boss was a megalomaniac bitch with the ability to exert massive mental control on her employees, or rip holes into buildings and cars simply by lifting her chin?

By and by the job wasn't bad. Apart from that one hellish episode where she had first been treated to meeting the man Persephone once loved, which was followed by her ordeal with extreme pain – to inure her to interrogation techniques employed by the other xenophobic Changed – she had pretty much achieved her goals in life. She needed no husband, wanted no children and desired no comfortable life in some rural county. No, she wanted wealth, money and power. She had money in excess, which she stashed across the entire world in trust funds and three engorged Swiss bank accounts; she could be considered wealthy as well, since she moved in circles that not even the most exalted lawyers and statesmen managed; power she also had, albeit a power that came with obeisance to a single mistress. But she managed.

What bothered her now was the task ahead. She'd had to weigh choices very quickly, and the one she alighted on promised pain in the near future. The other had promised death. Telling Persephone about the new Changed one in New York, and the supposed – but very plausible – allegation of some link with Persephone's former love, would mean that contact with other, powerful Changed would happen quite soon. Sirtis had been taught the ropes of covert operations, even personal participation therein, from the best people that Persephone could find, and she knew enough to know that fighting the minions and the attention of the other Changed was like navigating an underwater minefield with a submarine the size of the Statue of Liberty: conflict was inevitable. And Marianne knew exactly which Changed would find her first.

Her other choice had been to conceal the discovery from her mistress. Of course, the slim chance was there that the entire episode would have been ignored by Persephone, but there was also the chance that she could just summarily invade Marianne's mind again. It was rare for her to do so, since Sirtis was one of Persephone's favourite people, as far as favouritism extended within the Changed's mind, but not unheard of. When that happened, everything that could possibly be concealed would be laid bare, and when that happened, Marianne's life would come to a very abrupt end: the wrath of the Changed were terrible, and Persephone rarely left more than a few traces of body fluids and blood after she had her way with those who opposed her.

Marianne waited for Persephone to be some distance from the room, no doubt making ready to go and find the New York Changeling. Sirtis then stood, left by the back way and used the elevator that would take her to the labs provided so easily through Persephone's money. The Changed had entire forensics teams working here, with affiliations rooting into police departments and law firms. Some of the city's greatest detective minds worked for her, and they didn't even know it. This was the beauty of the Changed hierarchy, with them hidden in the shadows, pulling strings.

Marianne took a seat at one of the all-surround computer terminals, watching the translucent screen play with riotous colours. She commanded an interface to the scan terminals located throughout the city, hoping to catch a glimpse of the Changeling. Of course, Persephone would be doing the same thing, but she would be using a neural net, which enhanced her skills of telepathy to the extent of an entire city's expanse.

Sirtis sighed. Sometimes she felt sorry for the new Changed, the ones that had just realized their skills, and then had to compete with others of their kind who were more skilled and adapted to the destructive bent. She always wondered exactly why the Changed refused to play a peaceful game between themselves, instead of entrenching themselves in a city of choice and annihilating any other Changed who so much as breathed within that radius. At times she had weighed the possibilities of her aiding one of the newer Changed, but the disadvantages were too incredible to ignore. Discovery was the key.

For that reason, she had begun work on something very dangerous, which she kept in safety on her own computer systems at home. The data was encrypted, and she imbibed a very potent and equally risky substance called Neuronull, the illegal drug that submerged certain memory patterns. A smart drug, and one that protected her from Persephone's more focused probing. The drug was filled with tiny low-level AI nanites that could be programmed to block very specific memory patterns, effectively rendering the sections of neurons affected dead to scanning and recall. Effective duration of the 'nullification' could also be adjusted, but not flawlessly. If Neuronull could have been used to safely block her mind from any probing, she would have used it, but the drug induced massive hallucinations after excessive use, resulting in a terrifying, insane death. As it was, she could only use it to block off the most treasonous of her recollections. The device she was working on was amongst these.

It took just three days before Persephone became suspicious.

"There have been hints about dissent in the ranks of my people," the elegant Changed woman said, walking seductively across the marble floor of her antechamber. She wasn't looking at anyone, but seemed to be enjoying herself with an air born of petulance and self-assurance. She was a furnace of power; she knew it and she broadcast it for everyone to see. Marianne waited, showing nothing, relying on the fact that she knew that Persephone wasn't nearly as strong a telepath as she thought she was: the data banks were very interesting concerning the workings of other Changed, ones worth mentioning and taking note of. Ones that Persephone were right to fear. This fact alone would not serve to make her feel better, or remain aloof of Persephone's mounting rage. Fortunately, three other close aides of Persephone's were with Sirtis in the room, watching the woman pace about, her stride growing more unrelenting as her temper began fraying.

"My lady, if you are talking about a Changed loose on the streets, we had no warning and the man simply vanished before we could –" one of the other aides, a slender and dangerous-looking man began.

"It is not my funding I am worried about!" Persephone snarled, even managing to make that sound almost petulant. "Sometimes the servant that is closest at hand is the one that strays the most." Her lazy eyes casually went from staring the now cowed man in the eye to lingering on Sirtis. Persephone smiled.

Sirtis had nothing else to do but to remain silent. There was no way Persephone could trace anything to her.

The Neuronull capsule had had hours to complete its dissipation by now, and the nanites were already beginning the reversal sequences, causing a light headache as acute memories began reintegrating.

But Sirtis still knew of a plan, and that was dangerous. Perhaps now, fatal. Persephone rose from her lounging pose with the grace of a panther, chin up, head tilted slightly to one side, a seductress and femme-fatale in one, always. Marianne did the only thing she knew could always delay Persephone, if not dissuade her. Swallowing pride and mortification, and hoping her face didn't betray the shame she always felt at such gestures, she bowed low, body perfectly balanced for perfect servility, even forced.

"If my lady has seen fault with my performance of late, please, punish me." A bitter draught to down, and one that could bring out either the vicious, destructive power of the Changed, or the strangely incongruous softer side, the one that sympathized with the plight of the human servant, if only for a while, and with little remorse to show for treatment thereafter. She waited.

When she felt Persephone's long fingers trace a slow caress down her cheeks, she relaxed slightly, knowing that though the soft side had been triggered by her response, anything was still possible. The Changed stroked down to her chin and tilted her head up to look into her eyes. Again the twinge of doubt, of feared discovery. But the eyes remained liquid brown and dense. Had they turned iridescent and blue, Marianne would have measured her existence in the few milliseconds it took to lose consciousness as the pain engulfed her and her body was ripped to shreds.

"Not you, my dear," Persephone drawled. "You are too valuable for me to cast aside. But I deplore your lack of control over those you keep close to you."

"My lady?" Marianne asked, keeping her voice neutral. Persephone turned her head in the usual languid fashion, eyes fixing balefully in the direction of the door. It opened to let two massive men – mindless henchmen – in, dragging a limp form between them. It was a woman, her face and body beaten black and blue, hair bedraggled and wild. The lab coat she had on could once have been called white.

Persephone assumed a smile, and this time there was nothing coy or misleading about it. It held all the feral intensity of a shark realizing its next meal was within reach.

"This is Linda Randall, one of your own, specially trained associates. I heard Linda was working on something forbidden. Of course, Linda didn't remember much at all after her punishment." The two men dropped Linda to the floor, where she lay, damaged face almost featureless apart from two dead eyes, staring listlessly upward. "Sometimes the death of the mind is more interesting, than the death of the body."

"I am sorry for my laxity, my lady," Sirtis said, voice leaden. In the rare cases like this, it was best to show absolutely no signs of emotion at all, whether remorse, regret or glee, since Persephone would eventually tie the response down with some or other snippet of info, to snare even her most trusted aides. The woman was devious enough for three. "What will you do with her?"

"I? Nothing. I will leave the sordid details to you." Persephone drifted back to her couch, but this time she crossed her legs and spread her arms along the back of the seat, regarding Marianne with a slight smile. "I've had her mind destroyed – you would never know if she was hiding something critical, so I gathered it would be a suitable penalty. I want you to destroy her consoles as well and to have all data erased. I will send someone to check up on the process, just in case dear Linda had accomplices." Marianne nodded, and waited for the slight wave of dismissal before she pulled herself erect and marched from the room, as if nothing had happened. "And Sirtis," Persephone added, halting Marianne's swift turnabout, "make sure this drug, this device, that Randall was working on, all of its components, is destroyed out of hand. I will not have my people turn against me in such a way." Sirtis nodded curtly, not wanting to remain overlong.

She even shut her ears to the sound of Persephone berating the other three remaining aides. She didn't want to know what about. Her close brush with death just now, the potential death that could have been hers in an instant, had alerted her once more that to know very little was more profitable to life than knowing too much, or everything.

It was only once she was inside the chamber which she had been allowed as an office that she breathed deeply and forced herself to calm, before she became hysterical. Linda's death had been an unfortunate necessity; Persephone could be devious, and the regrettable reality was that Marianne had to play by those rules.

Linda had been a good scientist, and a good acquaintance – Marianne didn't fool herself by thinking she had friends – but the very fact that she had been the closest, next to Marianne herself, to Persephone's inner circle of followers had doomed her to this test. And though Linda had been killed – she might as well have, being nothing more than a vegetable now – she had passed the test, or rather, Sirtis had.

It had been simple, leaking the info on the project Marianne kept safe on her machines at home, and slowly but surely Linda had pieced the little bits of info together. Of course, many days and nights of ardent working till late had seen Linda grow loyal in commiseration to Marianne, and it had never even been a question of betrayal, when Linda had finally confronted Marianne about the more detailed technicalities of the project Marianne had been working on. And Marianne had been forthcoming about purpose, onset and progress, but not safety precautions. Now Linda was out of the picture, and whatever ideas Persephone may have had about those in high ranks out to betray her had died with Linda's mind. Effectively, it removed Marianne herself from any scrutiny at all.

She didn't know whether she should sigh with relief or with remorse.

It would take just a little more effort by way of caution to secure whatever extra data Linda had compiled on her consoles, before wiping it all out. It would of course be extremely harder, with the threat of Persephone sending someone to watch the process being done. But Marianne would manage. She always had.

She was almost certain that soon, she would be able to wrest herself from servitude.

Persephone watched her aides retreat, taking the bloody body of Linda Randall with them. She hadn't been in a very destructive mood today, or else she would have mutilated at least one of the four people she trusted most next to her. Such examples served as their own warnings, their own lessons in obedience. But today, she had settled for a verbal tirade, a tap on the hands backed up by the threat of painful death at her hands, should failure become a question. She sighed, because in truth she had quickly gotten bored with the whole charade of verbally abusing her aides. She turned around and made for her couch again, and spoke as she did so.

"You can come out now," Persephone said to no one in general. Immediately the sky darkened, as if someone had thrown black sheets over the windows, causing the entire room to be plunged in a thick, cloying gloom. Persephone smirked, marvelling at Amorphia's intransigent approach to meetings with others of the Changed. The woman was entitled to use her powers, even flaunt them, but not in front of her betters. Certainly not in front of Persephone.

"I think she lies," said a silken voice, heavy with its Oriental accent. Amorphia herself had always been Asiatic in her origins, but no one knew when, or exactly where. The woman was a wild card, a force of nature that brooked little or no query as to its explanation. Instead of a comfortably stealthy disguise, Amorphia's unique powers doomed her to a life of shadows and sightlessness; her unusual alabaster-white skin, the preternatural smoothness of unblemished cheeks and icy indigo lips, all features which no cosmetic brush or pencil could conceal. And the eyes that betrayed her as Changed, the icy, winter sky gaze that faded from sight when the use of their gifts did, failed to comply, in Amorphia's case. No, her lusciously slanted eyes remained unerringly crystalline in that aspect. But then, Amorphia had one of the greatest powers of the Changed. The woman could dissolve her body into thick, inky smoke at will, pass through any space and fill any vacuum. She could change her form, but not her features; she was barred from shape shifting, from turning into someone else with the cunning accuracy of a normal morph – normal being used lightly. As she rested warily next to Persephone's couch, her upper body alone manifested, the rest a massive shroud of shapeless billows, as though she was reaching out from some smoky realm.

Persephone regarded her with carefully concealed disdain. She also took care to keep the long, black-lacquered fingernails in sight. Trust was for fools, and the dead.

"Her mind remains aloof from Randall's death. No, Sirtis is mine, fully and completely."

"There are ways to conceal things, even from you," Amorphia said, lilting voice betraying a spark of taunting. Persephone wished to snarl, and Amorphia dissolved into thin air, reassuming her full, sleek shape on an opposing couch, some distance from Persephone. No doubt the woman feared Persephone's wrath, but not enough to refrain from barbed commentary.

"If she were using such a thing she would forget even what she herself wished to remember," Persephone countered. Her right hand drifted to one side, a languid gesture that brought a thin, full glass of wine floating through the air from its tray. It was a small thing, but a certain display of whatever power she held, and a warning to Amorphia. But it was a wasted effort, Persephone thought. Amorphia would notice, but wouldn't care; the amorphous chit had to rely on her own gifts with the persistence of moment-to-moment indulgence. That, or she flaunted herself to such an extent as to make Persephone's own affectations look threadbare. "But it would be prudent to remain watchful. You brought the Circuit?"

"Of course. He awaits your instructions." Persephone nodded, pleased. The Circuit was a minor Changed, a man so close to human to be almost unnoticeable, save for one key element: he was a psycho-cybernetic access, capable of sending his mind through circuits and machinery, and to either cause havoc, spread destruction or restore order. Or watch and observe discrepancies, which was why Persephone had commanded his services. He was, despite his gifts, a scruffy character, one that had maintained his humane characteristics and resorted to execrable habits and vices. It was through these vices that he was so easily controlled. If anything untoward was happening beneath her nose, Persephone would soon know of it. "But I fear his services will not come cheaply." The last remark had obvious undertones. The Circuit was notoriously immune to telepathic or empathic wavelengths, due to his highly organized mental defences.

Persephone knew that she could always murder him with the brunt of a thousand telekinetic sledgehammers, but what would be the point of it all, then, crushing him for insolence and losing his unique skill? Oh no, she would have nothing to do with him, working rather through her underlings. After all, humans could be quite brutal sometimes, and the Circuit wasn't immune to physical threats. The only other thing to be concerned about was a very mundane matter, and one that could be borne. Still, Persephone detested such scruffy creatures, beings that had given in to their cravings and lusts and had discarded propriety and cleanliness for aloofness and the disregard for anything remotely acceptable by the standards of human existence. She had never seen the Circuit, but Amorphia's description of the Changed was one of stringiness, untidiness and irreverence. The latter was the one that would determine the odious little man's survival or not. But while he searched the confines of the networks that ran like a massive hub from Persephone's skyscraper citadel here in New York, she would indulge his whims and demands – within limits, of course.

"I think you need to return to your city soon," Persephone said to Amorphia, staring at the dark-clad Oriental being from over the top of her champagne flute. Amorphia smiled, but her eyes remained free of the warmth of the gesture.

"Oh but I enjoy it so, here. Chinatown amuses me, the similarities, the vibrancy amidst your clammy, stodgy American culture. Why go back?"

"If you enjoy such vibrancy, perhaps New York isn't the city for you," Persephone added, and her voice grew frosty.

"Are you so afraid of others that rival your power that you resort to the cheap tricks you use to cow your servants?" Amorphia challenged, all smiles gone, replaced by a haughtiness easily rivalling Persephone's. "You forget who fell from grace, Persephone. I will not fall when you ruin another solid plan."

"Who said anything about planning?" Persephone queried, leaning forward, face shrewd and cold. "He does not forget, but forgiveness is another matter. And you, Amorphia, have come quite close to ruining your own end of the deal. Or didn't he send some of his goons after you?" Amorphia's clouded expression made Persephone smile, and she knew she had scored a hit. "I will not interfere if he decides you are no longer necessary."

"Had I been as afraid of him as you are, I would have found your words intimidating," Amorphia said, eyes glowing blue. "But I am not as the others. I am not flesh and bone. His power can work against me for only so long." With that she vanished altogether, her features seeming to balloon and then expand into dark smoke that coiled backwards and seemed to compress into a tight bunch, before dissipating into nothingness. Persephone, rattled by the frankness of Amorphia's words concerning the Changed who led them, settled down, paying the departure no more heed. She hadn't considered how hard it would be for him to get rid of Amorphia, and for the brazen fool to flaunt her own might in the face of his was enough to make anyone cringe. Disturbed, she drained the wine before pouring herself another glass.

CHAPTER TWO

The Taking

Nathan opened his eyes.

He wondered again whether he had to check on Daniel, but then thought against it. He felt a little conflicted nowadays; he was a nice guy and he enjoyed the fun things in life, the more laid back matters. He was everyone's friend, and he often doubled in keeping the peace when the need arose, but he wasn't used to all of this checking-up business even though Danny was his brother. Nathan sighed. Even after nine years it was hard for him to give Danny any label whatsoever, and fitting him neatly in between friend and youngest brother was as close as he could come. It had never really caused problems of any kind, these distinctions, before, but now, the family was in a crisis situation. And with all the recent stuff that happened, everyone was really concerned with Danny's condition.

They kept him safe and they held him secure, in his own suite within the Hirsch household, where he had lived for the last nine years, when he wasn't sleeping in his dorm rooms at the university. Nathan still remembered that evening, little more than a week ago, the eeriness of it. Danny had walked in on Nathan and Joanie, having wondered what the two of them were up to, staying out of sight when they knew he was home from his Classics Trip to Turkey, and they hadn't come down to say hello yet. Nathan couldn't remember hearing Danny climb the stairs. He had simply, suddenly stood there, a look of utter shock on his face as Nathan idly toyed with the wispy energies flowing and undulating above Joanie's splayed hand, and as Joanie's face registered indecisiveness and Nathan knew his own face had assumed a default sheepish 'busted' look. Nathan had been the first to start talking.

"Uh, hey Danny, me and Joanie were –"

"Danny we can explain." Joanie almost implored at the same time.

Nathan knew what he was capable of. He and Joanie both were different, from the normal people walking outside going about their everyday lives. Nathan had known since the day he turned sixteen, when the sensations of bursting energy felt like it would claw its way out of his chest and his fingertips. That was how he had eventually become drawn to Joanie: same place of study, and a simple stare from across the room, and he knew they were more alike than he could imagine. With him it was physical: speed, agility and the one he kept secret from his parents, which was levitation. Joanie shaped energy, and she could read minds, which still freaked her out completely. However, both parents, though very alarmed at first, had become more or less accustomed to the idea of their changed sons and Nathan's similarly different girlfriend, and had moved on with life as if little had changed. And they loved Joanie. But even Danny didn't know, and keeping it from him had been the hardest thing in the world to do, a situation only alleviated when Danny, a proto-genius of sorts, had left for university aged fifteen, two years earlier than most people, and been out of the house for the better part of the times the others were there.

And then there was Nathan's brother, Luke.

"If you'd just let us explain," Nathan had started, but Danny had backed away slowly, an incomprehensive look on his face.

"Why is this happening?" he had said, eyes wide, face a rictus expression of mounting discomfort.

"We didn't tell you because we didn't think you'd—" Nathan began, taking solid steps until he was next to Danny. He then got treated to a venomous green sideways glare as Danny interrupted him.

"Understand?" he challenged, and Nathan smiled lopsidedly, fielding the barb: Danny was the most understanding and accepting of the bunch, the one everyone kept close in confidence. "You didn't trust me." There was such a volume of resentment in those words that Nathan felt like screaming.

"I know and I'm sorry about that. But we've never told anyone about any of this!" Nathan protested.

"I know about Luke," Danny said softly, the reproach still strong in his voice. The simple statement rocked Nathan back in shock. For a moment he was violently upset and angry about his oldest brother's lapse, about the breach of trust the two had sworn about keeping their secret from anyone without such differences. But Nathan quashed the urge to yell angrily, and when he looked back at Danny's unremitting dark green gaze, he frowned, willing to field the stare and answer any questions Danny had; Nathan felt, at least now, that his adopted brother was owed that. Biting down on the well of emotions he felt, he reached over to Danny and placed a hand on his arm. Danny recoiled, an almost violent reaction, body shivering as though he reviled the gesture. Nathan breathed deeply and thought quickly of what else he could add to defend his position. He started by explaining why even Danny couldn't know about it, despite the fact that they were all so close to each other. Danny listened, face thunderous, and after a while ripped his arm free from Nathan's grip. But he remained standing there, listening, and Nathan, relieved, went on, stopping for breath before he came to Joanie's part in the telling.

He was about to continue when a gasp from Joanie ripped him from his thoughts.

Danny was no longer looking at Nathan, but rather at some unknown space near the ceiling, face a new mask of horror and uneasiness, as if something was bothering him. Nathan was hardly empathic, but there was something unsettling Danny, and it wasn't the discovery of him and Joanie's gifts, not anymore. Danny's mouth worked soundlessly and he began casting about him, his motions frantic.

"Danny what is it?" Nathan asked, puzzled by the sudden change. When Danny didn't answer he placed both hands on Danny's shoulders and rotated Danny to face him. "Hey."

He noticed it only then. Danny had dark green eyes, dark enough to look almost black in some cases, but here, where the room wasn't very well lit, the green was brilliant now, an incandescent pulse that seemed to give off light rather than reflect it. Even as Nathan continued watching the eyes changed from their glowing green to a luminous dark blue.

"What are you doing to me?" Danny demanded shakily, and tried to break from Nathan's grasp. The eyes flared between Daniel's dark but warmly welcoming green gaze and a disarmingly unreal flare of glacial actinic blue that remained in place and grew whiter and lighter as Nathan watched. He was still staring, mesmerized and horrified at the same time, when he felt the suddenly mounting pain in his hands. He looked down, distracted, and saw oily grey-blue wreaths of smoke coiling from beneath his hands where they held onto Danny's shoulders. With a cry of alarm he broke free, the vengefully darkening smoke streaming now, and he glared, strangely angry, at his brother.

"Oh he's changing!" Joanie yelled.

Daniel ignored both of them, and instead threw himself towards the wall that curved around to the stairwell. He fell heavily on his side, but righted himself and began crawling quickly on elbows and knees for the stairs. To the sound of Joanie's shallow breaths of mounting terror, Nathan shook his hands to get rid of the smoke and the pain and darted forward again.

"Danny, what –"

"You stay the hell away from me!" Danny flared, eyes venomous green once more. Nathan halted, momentarily thrown and hurt by the exhortation, but decided to ignore it.

"I know what's happening! Danny, you're..." he began, realization dawning and enhancing his insight, but Daniel shook his head vehemently, as if to block out Nathan's words.

"It hurts," Danny whispered; face crumpling under a seizure of pain that slowed his progress to the stairs.

Nathan hovered above him, afraid of touching Danny again but also caught between that wariness and the desire to help him. But Danny was going through something which Nathan had also endured, although he couldn't remember anything this violent. His changeable mood showed as his face reverted to the uncharacteristic mien of anger. "I need to go," he said, and tried to get up.

"You can't go, where will you go?" Nathan challenged, aware to some extent of his brother's discomfort, but deeply unsettled by the brutal insistency in Danny's voice. He acted on split-second reflexes, born of the agility and speed that were his main gifts, and ducked back as Daniel simply vanished in a fiery wake of scalding, friction-burnt air molecules, leaving a fierce tug of crisp cold air in his vacant place. Nathan sprang erect, wonderment filling his face.

"Outside!" Joanie yelled, having run to the window.

"Teleporter," Nathan breathed, stunned. "That's a neat gift." He rose from where he had landed in his attempt to escape the burning blast from Danny's teleportation surge to make sure Joanie was alright, and then resorted to high speed, watching the house's various rooms recede into blurry, seamless flows of night-dark hues that sped past him, before he reverted to normal speeds and virtually disgorged himself into the driveway up front. Danny was sitting there, eyes wide, staring at both splayed hands as though to find out whether they had changed somehow. His breathing alerted Nathan to the fact that Danny was hyperventilating. He tried to reassure his friend, but Danny's upper body twisted around and he fixed Nathan with a glower that conveyed immense anger and fear. Nathan was no empath, but again his senses saved him; even in high speed, as he dived for some cover, he felt the blast of something unseen hammer by overhead, a certain violent stroke that would have pulped him had he been any slower. Behind him, the bushes withered as if blasted by scorching wind. He swore loudly, aware of the implications of such an attack, and sprang to his feet, prepared to field or avoid another assault if necessary. Instead, Daniel was once more oblivious of Nathan, his entire body limned in a soft, almost misty light. His hands were over his ears, and his mouth was open as if in a soundless scream. Before Nathan could do anything Danny rushed forward, still on his knees and in his pose of torment, sliding smoothly across the pavement as if it were a polished surface. Nathan winced involuntarily as Danny practically prepared to ram the gate, but instead he moved right through it as though it wasn't there. The yard alarms triggered, and Nathan did wince then, aware that this fracas would demand explanations in spite of his parent's uneasy support of him and his brother's differences. And if they found out Danny was also like them, now. With almost all subterfuge expended, he looked up to where Joanie was standing. She opened the window, and he called up to her.

"Get Luke and my dad!" As an afterthought, "and make sure my mom knows what's going on!" Joanie was already turning away, and Nathan turned back to the immediate problem. Danny was no longer just outside the gate, but in the middle of the street running past the house. He was standing there, panting, body drenched in sweat and hands clenching and unclenching. He was once more staring at nothing, but his eyes remained a measured, stable blue now. Nathan knew what that meant: he, Joanie and Luke evinced such coloration whenever they engaged their gifts. But Daniel's eyes held something more, like a toned-down form of barely controlled power. They flared again, beacons of energy that provided light rather than reflecting it, a scary possibility to Nathan's awed appraisal.

The sudden addition of strong headlights from a car broke the reverie. Nathan ran for the gate and stared beyond it, and saw how close the car was. He swore under his breath, and knew that he wouldn't make it in time to avoid the accident practically unfolding before his eyes. The screech of brakes worsened the feeling, and Nathan picked up speed, hoping he might at least try to avoid the fast-pending accident from taking place. One heartbeat, he was up on the gate. Another beat and he could be at Danny's side, hopefully grab him and roll both of them to safety from the car that was now scant feet away from crushing Danny to – Danny rippled. For a single instant Nathan could swear his brother was looking right at the car with total awareness and calm, and then he seemed to become insubstantial, and with a tauntingly slow tilt of his head, geared himself sideways, out of harm's way. Nathan watched as Danny seemed to smear horizontally through the gate and back into the driveway, where he rematerialized fully in a rolling bundle of flaccid limbs. Nathan jumped from his gate vantage and spared a glance for the surprised car, and was immensely thankful that the alarm lights on proximity alert outside the house dimmed just then, dumping the entire driveway in the cover of darkness. He waited, breath bated, for the car to move off, before making for the prostrate form in the driveway. His parents, brother and Joanie cannoned from the front door of the house, concerned and loud with their demands to know what had happened.

Since then Danny had been catatonic.

He ate mechanically when they brought him food, and he went to the bathroom of his own free will to wash himself and to do the necessary things, after which he would return to his blank pose on his bed, staring ahead at nothing and registering nothing whenever someone spoke to him. So they kept him here, secure and safe, because they didn't know what else to do with him. He was their adopted brother, and Luke, Nathan's senior by three years, had an almost slavish devotion to Danny, and he had in uncharacteristic adamancy insisted that the family wait until Daniel regained coherence, before doing anything else. The demand was, strangely enough, upheld by their parents, who despite misgivings allowed Danny to remain, and not taking him to an institution, as their dad had ventured, trying all options.

Nathan tossed and turned. Seeing Danny in such a state, when he knew how Danny normally acted and went about doing everything, was harrowing, especially since Nathan knew what kind

49

of person Danny was, and how much he enjoyed life, everything and everyone around him despite his inherently dark and unsettling personality. Danny was the composed one, the collected presence that remained unperturbed and undaunted by the worst times and things in life, keeping his cool and maintaining his balance. Now he was a nearly mindless automaton, unresponsive and uncommunicative.

With a muffled snarl of frustration, Nathan rose from bed.

The Hirsch house was doused in silence and nightfall.

Nathan ambled from one room to another, working more from time-honed awareness and recognition of the objects around him than some other form of gifted foresight. He descended the stairs that led to his and his brother's bedroom suites and arrived in the kitchen. From there he gravitated on feather-light feet through the guest lounge and into the guest bedroom suite where Daniel had stayed for the last two weeks.

He stopped before entering the bedroom. He was still a bit dazed and asleep, but by this time his senses, though not necessarily attuned to empathy, were still fine-tuned and trustworthy. And as he prepared to place his hand on the handle, he knew that something was wrong in Danny's room. Not just about the vapidly vacant consistency of Danny himself, but about presence. Nathan frowned. He wished there and then that he had an empathic bent like Joanie, despite the trials and pitfalls such gifts invariably added as w – Luke.

More so than Joanie, Luke was a strong telepath, a gifted and dedicated empath in spite of the torments of mental acuity and focus. Luke could sense the thoughts of other people several blocks away if he tried hard enough. Luke would know if something was wrong with Danny, even if he couldn't access Danny's thoughts – Luke never could, even when Danny had been normal; too much rigid self-control and mental discipline, and after Danny's breakdown, Luke didn't even want to try: he'd said it was like having your senses stripped away and being stranded in a black void.

Nathan hovered between racing back to wake his brother and opening the door and finding out what was going on Danny's room. Wracked by indecision and hounded by a mounting sense of dread, he bit down on his lower lip and ducked about, careful to stay silent as he engaged a little haste and flowed through the gloom-ridden house and back up the stairs. Luke's door was slightly ajar, and he slipped inside and bunched down beside his brother's bed.

"Luke, wake up," he whispered, gently but insistently shaking his brother by the shoulder. "Hey!"

"What?" Luke asked, opening his eyes and mumbling into his pillow.

"Something's up, something's wrong in Danny's bedroom!" Nathan replied.

"So check it out," Luke rejoined through his sleepy haze.

"Luke something's wrong!" Nathan insisted, coming closer and almost hissing in his brother's ear. When he drew back his brother was regarding him with a frown. Then he squinted, raising an eyebrow as he noted the slightest luminous sheen to his brother's eyes.

"Premo?" Luke queried. It was an unpredictable aspect to Nathan's repertoire of gifts, but not a completely surprising one; seeing as Luke was a full-range empath, he never doubted his middle brother's assumptions concerning such things. Nathan's mild premonitions were a different twist to his bevy of physical gifts, and though they were rarely stable and couldn't be controlled or forced, when they did occur they were rarely wrong. Luke stared beyond his brother and engaged his own gifts, mind surging free to the soft flare of light blue in the eyes, and he sent his awareness outwards, aiming it at Danny's room. Nathan waited, impatient, wondering what was taking so long.

"Someone's in Danny's room," Luke said softly. "I can't read… him… her… whoever it is."

"Great, a burglar with an iron will," Nathan scoffed, then grew a little frantic again. "How did they avoid setting off the alarms?" He rose to his feet, ready now to run into Danny's room and raise havoc, but he stopped when Luke rose as quickly, grabbing hold of his arm. He spoke in a low and ominous whisper, face growing whiter with each passing moment.

"He's reading me," he said through taut lips.

"Who, Danny?" Nathan asked, incredulous. Luke shook his head slowly.

"Shit!" Nathan spat. "C'mon, we'll wake Joanie!" Luke, unwillingly drawn short of his introspection, threw up his defenses against the intrusive reading of his mind and bound free of the sheets, after his brother.

The three of them waited outside Danny's door five minutes later, breath bated, ready to crash in. Joanie, still muzzy, mentally tuned in to the low-down from Luke. Nathan, becoming impatient again, glared at them, again wishing he could at least receive mental communiqués. In spite of having nearly nonexistent powers on a mental basis, he did think it logical that a lid be kept on telepathic traffic, considering there was an unidentified presence of unknown telepathic potential inside Danny's room. He made sure his brother and Joanie were looking at him before cuing them, holding up one hand and raising three fingers, which he began lowering. On the last count, he grabbed the handle and threw the door open.

Luke and Joanie darted past, eyes flaring, and Nathan sped past them in turn, flicking the switch beside the door, eyes scanning in the new light whatever could be different in the room. He gasped, eyes falling on the dark-clad figure standing next to Danny's bed. The man – the shoulders and features were too masculine to belong to a woman – straightened suddenly and the overhead bulbs of the lights exploded, scattering glass fragments across the floor in the returned dark. His eyes smarting from the sudden change back into darkness, Nathan heard Joanie scream, and then something unseen lifted him off his feet and hurled him against the wall, hard enough to expel the breath from his body and to leave him gasping. From the strained sounds and muffled struggles he knew his brother and Joanie shared his predicament. He attempted yelling, but his mouth too felt stopped. Rendered enraged and impotent at one go, Nathan widened his eyes, trying to let more light into his sight, hoping to discern anything in the darkness. He began to hear something, coupled with the sound of his brother being slammed again and again to the wall – Luke was trying to break free – but the sound he had started to hear was suddenly deafened by the shrill screech of a tripped alarm. In between though, he could hear the intruder speaking.

"We've got trouble. Yeah go figure, alarm's tripped. Hurry in here and give me a hand, will you? And keep your head straight, we have Changed in here, two of them psychics." Nathan heard a sound like a guitar string sounding in an echo chamber, which was followed by a rush of displaced air. Teleporter! He strained against the invisible bands holding him and yelled soundlessly against the unseen gag.

A fitful blue light flooded the room, suddenly, manifesting as a small sphere where the ruined bulbs had been. Nathan realized it was Joanie, and by turning his head he confirmed it: she was bunched against the wall, her eyes shut, but from the way her face worked and her expressions altered, Nathan knew it was her. The electric current that was open in the gaping ruin of the overhead lights screamed alive, vividly rattling into existence as Joanie coaxed more and more power from and into the current. Beside her, Luke was glaring venomously at their captors, and he managed to break his head free of the grip before it was forcefully slammed back again. Nathan looked at their assailants, and noted for the first time the new addition. It was a woman, dainty and not very tall, but with a face like a porcelain doll and girlish features. Her hand was on the man's shoulder, staying there as he leaned down and almost effortlessly lifted Danny from his bed, cradling Danny in his arms. The woman's eyes blazed aquamarine blue, and the echoic string sounded. The two of them, with Danny in check, seemed to distort backwards into nothingness, finally vanishing altogether.

Overhead, a sound rose, like a jet or some craft gathering power to leave. The bands vanished as the sound began to recede, and as Nathan fell to the ground, he howled his anguish and rage at the retreating sound of engines.

As the jet gained altitude, Charlie sighed in relief.

"You think they saw us?" Alex, the woman with the porcelain doll face asked, frowning. Charlie rolled his eyes, peeved.

"Yeah," he said sneeringly, and Alex's eyes narrowed.

"Not us you idiot, the jet!" she snarled angrily.

"You two play nice," another man named Jamie said, stepping in from the front of the vessel. He looked down at the inert form lying on the padded bench at the side of the walkway. "This him?"

"I can't read him, 'cause there's nothing there," Alex replied, shrugging.

"He's catatonic, not brain-dead," Charlie countered, eyes narrow and focused. "Alice will know what to do with him."

"Bet she will," Jamie nodded, turning back to the cockpit. Alex spared one last withering glance at Charlie, then another at the seemingly lifeless body on the bench. She followed Jamie, leaving Charlie to muse alone. He looked down at the boy and placed a single finger on his forehead, concentrating. Then he sighed, closing his eyes, suddenly weary.

"Let's hope Alice knows," he whispered.

Ancillary Documents

GOA I: Rules Of Engagement and Reach

The Gifted Observation Agency, otherwise simply known as 'GOA', spans the northern Atlantic, although it maintains primary headquarters in North America alone. There are numerous safe houses scattered throughout the northern hemisphere, in Europe and Asia as well. These masquerade under the pretense of belonging to shared, need-to-know basis pretenses of fitting into precaution-related areas of behind-the-scenes government agencies affiliated with the United States. Such places are protected by GOA's brand of technology, which is superior to that of the global generality. Born of necessity, such technologies serve to keep the tenets and actual work of GOA from the world, and safe houses rarely contain any data that could betray the organization to those who manage to breach its safety. Securely ensconced in societies that under normal circumstances adhere to the ulterior disguises of conspiracy theories and the consequent beliefs that even the most accurate allegations leveled against GOA would be construed as hysterical reactivity, GOA operates as easily and faultlessly safe as any internal security association, similar to the FBI, CIA, Gestapo or MI6.

This integration into societies under the pretexts of being affiliated with any of the above organizations allows GOA to expend more time and resources on their actual goals, which are relatively simple despite the security precautions taken to ensure their non-disclosure. GOA seeks to find and catalogue any of the Changed, the remarkable individuals who have become altered at some point in their lives to accommodate gifts, or talents, which can be scientifically classified as genetic mutations. Due to the explosive nature of such a subset within the human race, and how the world in general would react to them, this was seen as a priority security issue, and so the Agency came into being in order to:

1)   seek out the Changed and define their skills and abilities,

2)   make contact with these individuals at times to inform them of their status – where such knowledge is not substantiated and left to germinate into a destructive relationship with others – and to possibly integrate them into the GOA network, and

3)   intervene if absolutely validated as necessary that GOA restrict or restrain certain of the Changed.

These three points are the primary objectives of the Agency, underlying the obvious clause that the gifted maintain levels of security and protocol that disallows them from divulging their secret alternate human abilities from those who are not Changed. Remarkably, the gifted throughout the world maintain low levels of conspicuousness of their own accord, in keeping with the general assumption that the world and its unaltered human occupants will not take kindly to the presence of mutated beings in their midst, and that strength of force would not serve any cause other than the swift reaction of the hysterically enraged world, not to mention the general stigma that would become associated with the Changed. Subsequent dealings with the newly informed world would cause prejudiced reactions against them in the ensuing chaos of adjustment, which although considered an eventuality in the long run, has been held at bay by the astute workings of the Agency, which also acts as liaison where necessary, providing numerous governments and power brokers across the globe with very restricted information and leakage, to facilitate a very slow but certain introduction to the possibility of altered humans and their existence amongst the uninformed. Seeing as the protection of identities is a key use of GOA's active charter, it is by no means its driving force, having to deal more widely not just with the altered individuals across the globe but also with their safety. For this end, GOA maintains a military presence as well, coupled with its chartered and sanctioned agents of Changed nature that willingly participate in the Agency's ideology and procedures. This being the backbone of GOA's intentions, they are fully able to protect the people they observe, and also have the freedom to spend time in a more psychological aspect of protection as well: dealing with being Changed. As a policy GOA prepares those gifted individuals under their auspices to handle their altered states, and once this is done, to incorporate them into the world of the still-ungifted without noticeable disruption of normal everyday life.

As GOA evolved through the years of its existence, its charter expanded and went from simply an observational aid to those keenly interested in the Changed to one of service and protection, international security preventative measures engendered to shield the Changed from inevitable prejudice and finally the active research into the Changed themselves, their genetic predilection to altered DNA and the psychological aspects of awareness that these gifts set the Changed apart from the rest of humanity.

As GOA's methods became more focused and accurate, its adeptness at finding and tracing the fledgling Changed at the onset of puberty and their altered states became more precise. It became a marathon effort to place the teenagers undergoing or experiencing the Change, making contact with them and their families and preparing the newly Changed for their future prospects. This insistent surveillance forced GOA to diverge, within its collective whole, into four distinct sections: GOA Primary, which oversaw all the workings of the Agency in full; GOA Research, which while also actively overseeing the genetic stock of all noted Changed, prepared the world for worst case scenarios and adapted relevant technologies to that end; GOA Outreach, which dealt with propagandist tactics in preparing the Changed, both affiliated and non-affiliated, for the eventual future of full disclosure with the world – and also the search and identification of new Changed, and GOA Military, the defensive arm of the Agency, that also dealt with matters of a more heated nature, like failed precautions to keep GOA completely obscure in the eyes of the general global populace, renegade Changed and sensitive security matters pertinent to the safe operation of any secretive organization.

In all of this, GOA has been cleared with the United States government, in fact its creator, and certain allowances have been made to ensure the organization worked at optimum efficiency in fulfilling its intended purpose. Such matters as national security involving Changed individuals, the breaches of homeland safety which occur every now and then (where pertinent to the Changed and GOA's jurisdiction regarding them) and the overall discretion in contacting people who have come in direct contact with the Changed, are left entirely to GOA itself. For reasons of general security that encompasses not just the Changed but every single human being living side by side with them, GOA is comprised not just of Changed individuals but also of a legislative body of oversight comprised of key Changed individuals and fully aware non-Changed counterparts that regulate the Agency's workings on a level that prevents power mongering and corruption between the Changed working for the government.

Largely through the input of one Alice McNamara, who has been GOA's Changed Director for fifty years (since 2012), the diverse bodies throughout the majority of the northern hemisphere have operated independent and untouched by the deeper undercurrents of GOA. An arduous task, and definitely not a small one, which took incredible acumen. Even the successive US Presidents, fully aware of the organization they had instituted in the early 1980s, were amazed and not a little daunted – if relieved – by Alice's deft handling of a body that touched on every facet of everyday life and people, without making the un-Changed masses aware of their coexistence with the Changed. This was largely due to Alice's management of government funding within the Agency – limited in earlier years but successively increased after every averted potential disaster situation involving knowledge of the Changed going public – and her monitoring of high-level Changed in positions of wealth and power. These individuals invariably contributed to the financial needs of GOA, once they accounted for the apparent usefulness of having their oft-unwanted abilities and identities carefully guarded through Alice's machinations. The Changed were still human, prone to all the pitfalls and desires of identifying on levels of social, economic and political fields within the general human populace, and having one's secret abilities exposed to an unknowing, volatile public was a sure way of committing suicide. It must be noted that Alice never forced or coerced any of the power – and money-brokers to divert of their capital and influence. Rather their fear of discovery drove them to contribute willingly to a cause they considered most useful.

Under Alice's guidance, the Agency has achieved a stable, far reach into all matters pertinent to the Changed and their presence in the world.

CHAPTER THREE

Adjustment

They were in the chopper.

It was more than a chopper, really. Luke had never seen any craft like it, and it fascinated him. It should have intrigued Nathan as well – he liked technological gadgetry as much as Luke did – but his brother was tight-lipped and morose. Since Danny's kidnapping a year ago, he had lapsed into dark fits of rage, and his anger often led to tears of anguish. It had surprised Luke, Nathan's response to Danny's absence. It wasn't that Nathan had disliked Danny, or that he had resented him somehow. Luke, always a widely read person, knew that the youngest kids of families who adopted children often lapsed into brooding people, feeling left out when the attention was shifted away from their usual place of affection as youngest. Danny was younger than Nathan by two years, and remarkably, Nathan had never taken offense at the affection their parents had lavished on Danny, and had instead become an extremely outgoing and charming, likeable guy.

Danny, on the other hand, had never quite taken to the family setting, had never fitted in seamlessly with Luke and Nathan, in spite of every privilege granted him by the Hirsch couple and their biological sons. He had only recently become very close to Luke, a remarkable friendship between the two that had weaned Danny from his withdrawn status and had revealed him to be a clever, highly intelligent and witty individual, with a penchant for determination, stubbornness and self-confidence. He had shown himself to be an avid scholar, and had chosen to become a Classics major at the university back home, performing excellently, earning him an unspoken vote of pride and confidence from Luke, Nathan and their parents.

And then the kidnapping had happened.

Luke had been devastated as much as anyone else, but wasn't prone to overt emotional outbursts, rather keeping to himself most of his life, despite the closeness between him and Danny. To say he had simply gone on with life would have been an insult; he lamented Danny's kidnapping every day, just handled it differently. Their parents had seemingly aged overnight, and were more haggard-looking and strained as a result. Their mother still cried frequently, and their father had turned into a driven man, concerning the ongoing search for Danny's whereabouts. A year had yielded no results.

And then on one morning, just two days previous, Nathan had taken a call at their home, and a woman had answered. In sultry, almost charming tones she had told them, quite simply and to the point, that Luke and Nathan were cordially invited to Seattle, to a place named 'GOA', and had been told, even more unceremoniously, that Daniel Hirsch, or Mercer – no way Luke recognized that last name, but his parents had confirmed it as Danny's original last name – was there, safe and sound, and had been for the last year.

Nathan had nearly exploded, but by that time Luke had joined him at the phone terminal in the kitchen and had listened to the broadcasted call, and the woman speaking to Nathan. Nathan had somehow kept his composure, though Luke – himself suddenly boiling over with anger – had noticed the visible effort it had taken to do so.

Their parents had been devastated. Luke's mother had burst into tears, and after a while she actually started laughing, which she had said were tears of joy at knowing that at least Danny-boy was safe. Their dad had become frantically furious, and it took several hours for him to calm down, after which he had asked if the woman who had called had specified why only Nathan and Luke were to go.

"She said because we are Changed," Nathan had said simply, but had frowned, puzzled himself by the revelation that somehow the woman had known he and Luke were special.

"How did she know?" their dad had asked, and Nathan shrugged dejectedly.

"Maybe she's an empath," Luke had said, venturing a guess, but no one had known how plausible such a thing was.

Two days later, they had received another call, this time from a man, filling them in with transportation details. They had gone to the metroport downtown, had met with an unassuming man clad in a military uniform – Luke had confirmed to Nathan that the man wasn't Changed like they were – and were then led to one of the private ports, where the strange-looking craft, half-plane half-chopper, awaited them. Without any ceremony, they were led inside, assured they would be safe and that their parents would be notified once they arrived in Seattle. When the craft lifted off they were treated to an impressively speedy departure.

The interior looked like a limousine or a private jet's; small, luxurious and comfortable, with large plush seats and elegant wooden tables bolted to the floor and walls. Their uniformed escort gave them a wordless nod of his head and moved into the front section, closing the door behind him. Nathan and Luke, still appraising the inside of the craft, didn't notice another man walking in from another part of the craft.

"It's called a boomer, in case you wanted to know," he said. The two brothers spun about to face the new presence. "It moves real fast, you might want to sit down for lift off." Luke and Nathan complied, both of them regarding the new arrival. He was a short man of stocky build, appearing to be no more than a disproportionately muscled boy, with smooth, angular, almost blocky features, a square jaw and a snub nose. He had a winsome smile to highlight the blue of his eyes.

Nathan and Luke strapped themselves in and endured the boomer's vertical lift, followed by a swift jarring jerk forward, which pressed them into their seats. After the initial burst of speed, the craft levelled out and achieved a fast but almost motionless flight pattern, with the terrain visible through the rounded windows speeding by at a relatively impressive speed. The man unclipped himself from his harness and rose, approaching the two brothers.

"So, Nathan and Lucas Hirsch, welcome. We'll be landing in about half an hour at Seattle, after which we'll take a groundcar to the Headquarters. Oh, yeah, my name's James Arden, but you can call me Jamie."

"Where's Danny?" Nathan asked, startling Luke. In spite of the insistency of the tone, it was laced with barely controlled belligerence. Luke, slightly appalled by his brother's rudeness, cleared his throat. That kind of approach by Nathan often promised violence of some sort later.

"Ah, I'm sure they'll tell us where Danny is later, Nate," he said, and whispered Nathan's shortened name with some fury. Nathan looked at his brother as though he was being insane and stupid not to ask the same question, but he remained quiet.

Luke turned to Jamie. "We're really concerned about Danny's whereabouts. Why wouldn't we be?"

"Understandable," Jamie replied. He even sported a boyish voice, matured by age but still coming over as barely legal. "But you needn't worry overmuch, if worry you must. Daniel has never been safer than where he is now."

"I beg to differ," Nathan whispered, almost inaudibly, so that only Luke could hear it. Luke ignored him.

"Guess you guys are wondering what's going on, and who I am." Luke nodded. "I'm one of the Changed, just like you two."

"Changed?"

"The name we give to people who have undergone mutation at a predetermined age, and maintain those mutations, or gifts, as we'd like to call them, throughout the rest of their natural lives. By predetermined I mean at the age of sixteen, mostly, when some teenagers experience powers, shifts in the normal balance of things.

Some of us undergo only mild adaptations: small strokes of prescience, emotional reading, slightly increased strength or reflexes belying physical body size, stuff like that. The more gifted of us have these kind of things in greater measure. I know that you, Lucas –"

"Call me Luke."

"– are a skilled long-range empath, and you, Nathan, have a high range of physical gifts." Luke listened attentively, fascinated even as he kept looking at his brother's reactions. Nathan absorbed it all in silence, but the hostility never left his eyes. He felt it would be impolite to inquire after Jamie's proficiencies, or gifts. He ran the new info through his head, sampling the idea. The Changed. So that was what they were.

For some reason he didn't feel at all distanced or isolated from the rest of the human race. Just mildly different. Jamie grinned. "Hope you don't try and read my mind, though," he said, tapping the side of his head.

"I wouldn't do that," Luke replied, sounding a little offended.

"Sorry, just had to advise caution. You see, a lot of the more powerful Changed don't have a lot of self-control, even with some training, and their gifts, especially empathic ones, can temporarily go a little haywire, even out of control."

"So you were the guys who broke into our house and kidnapped Danny," Nathan said. His eyes were far-off, and he deliberately ignored the venomous glare Luke gave him. Jamie's smile never faltered remaining, dangerously in place.

"You have to understand, Nathan, that you weren't safe when Danny changed. He is an exception to the general rule of the alterations occurring at sixteen in most of us. A dangerous exception: when GOA ever detects an alteration occurring right after the normal window of change has technically closed, something's usually up. Past policy – this'll all be explained by people who know more about it than I do – has indicated that such individuals are often highly powerful, far more so than us garden-variety better-than-your-averages. They also lack any control, so they pose a significant threat to those people around them."

Nathan listened, and then lapsed into silence again, for which Luke was thankful. He mentally congratulated Jamie for tactfully diffusing the potentially explosive situation. "If you stick around, you might meet the exception to the exception, that we know of."

"Exception to the exception?" Luke queried, puzzled. Jamie's eyes seemed to twinkle, as though he was reliving some sort of running private joke.

"An old woman, changing when she was about sixty. GOA was up in arms – in eighty years of history and close observation, nothing like it had ever been documented. And trust me, we're extremely capable at monitoring any burgeoning and existent Changed, even the ones who have no affiliations with us whatsoever. False alarm though, but the old woman is pretty strong, regarding her gifts."

The boomer banked slowly to one side, then resettled in a straight flight path.

"Can I offer you anything to drink, to eat?" Jamie asked. Luke shook his head, and a moment later Nathan followed suit. "Is there anything else you'd like to ask that I can answer?" Again, Nathan remained silent, but Luke went on.

"What do the initials stand for?"

"GOA? Gifted Observation Agency. The acronym is easier to employ than the full name. When we arrive at Headquarters, the chief lady will tell you more."

"Lady?"

"Yup, her name's Alice. Tough woman, I'd advise you to be courteous, and to keep a rein on tempers." The last part was directly aimed at Nathan, who didn't respond save for a small shrug. Satisfied, Jamie leaned back in his seat. "For now, just sit back, relax and enjoy the ride. Not a lot of people get to ride in these things, and riding in a commercial equivalent will cost you an arm and a leg."

"Just one more question," Luke asked quickly, and Jamie nodded. "You said 'if we stick around.' What did you mean by that?" Jamie smiled.

"GOA is always on the lookout for new recruits, people with specialized gifts, like empaths, especially. We never force anyone against their will, but we never pass up the opportunity to invite more Changed to join us, either."

"Never force anyone against their will, huh? What about Danny?" Nathan asked, treating Jamie to careful scrutiny. This time Jamie shrugged, but the smile went from amiable to veiled triumph.

"Daniel isn't a GOA employee." For a moment there was an instant of suspended silence, as Jamie and Nathan faced off across the short distance between the facing seats. Luke, with an indrawn breath, prepared to intervene in case something unnecessary happened, but Nathan looked away first, subsiding into final silence for the rest of the trip. Luke looked over to Jamie's side, but the man seemed unperturbed, and betrayed no hint that he was upset by the silent challenge Nathan had offered, or his subsequent retreat.

"Alice will tell you more," he repeated. Luke nodded, then also lapsed into silence. He had the seat next to the window, so he let his mind race through the new information and impressions, as he watched the scenery flit by at astonishing speed. The pilot announced that they would land in twenty minutes, and then there was only the quiet hum of the boomer, cutting a swathe through the air currents.

The room they entered was larger than it looked at first. It was spacious and filled with light, the effect gained from the large floor-to-ceiling windows that comprised the western and northern walls. There were few pieces of furniture to complement the wide and uncluttered desk that dominated the north section of the room. Alice walked to stand behind the desk, leaving the rest of them waiting on her orders. She remained staring out the window at the spread of greenery and square constructions of the buildings outside.

"So where is this?" Luke asked after a while, becoming uncomfortable with the silence. Alice didn't turn around, but she did answer.

"This is the North American Gifted Observation Alliance Center," she stated. "This particular building is dedicated to the Changed that work with the GOA, which makes it mine, so to speak." He thought she was an incredibly strong woman, charismatic even, but iron-willed, and he noted quite quickly that she also wouldn't brook any nonsense. As if she read his thoughts – quite possible, since he had experienced that strange mental twinge of one empath encountering another, on entering the office – her eyes narrowed, but they remained warm.

"But where are we?" Nathan interjected, irritated. Alice pivoted on her feet, fixing him with a critical expression. She wasn't a very tall presence, but made up for it with her strikingly handsome features, and that commanding aura to boot.

"We are about fifty miles east of Seattle, if that is the answer you're looking for."

"What exactly does GOA do?" Luke queried, casting an uneasy glance at his brother, who maintained his frown.

"I suppose this is the time to answer as many of your questions as possible," Alice said, and held out a hand to the seats arranged before her desk. "Please." She took a seat herself, and waited for Luke and Nathan to follow suit. Jamie remained standing, but his attention was riveted to Alice. "Now, which question would you like answered first?"

"Where's Daniel?" Nathan snapped, before Luke could prevent him. He mentally calculated Alice's possible responses, coming up with more in favour of negative than positive. He hoped she didn't read too personally into Nathan's cheekiness.

"Daniel Mercer is not really a topic I can discuss with you. That is Charlie's province," she replied neutrally.

"Yeah, and Charlie has been very forthcoming," Nathan sneered. "Where is he anyway? I'd love to meet him."

"Nathan!" Luke snapped, mortified by his brother's lapse in courtesy.

"It's alright," Alice amended with a small smile. "I take it you are still very angry at what happened about a year ago. It had been a delicate situation, no doubt, but a necessary one."

"Necessary how?" Nathan asked.

"In order for me to make this understandable for you, or acceptable, there are other things that need explanation first. Such as the methods of the GOA, its organisational system and its way of classifying the Changed. I'm sure the two of you would also like to know where you stand with the GOA."

"Where we stand with them?" Luke asked, puzzled.

"Yes. You see, GOA came into being about eighty years ago, when the Changed first became a noticeable, or at least detectable presence within human society. Don't get me wrong, we're still human, but the Changed are no longer simply classifiable as random mutations. Yes, we are discovering new strains and genetic variations every day, but there is a set pattern to these changes, and GOA has perfected a system that categorises these gifts in the Changed. That is one of the main reasons why we apprehended Daniel Mercer."

"Kidnapped, you mean," Nathan scoffed, refusing to back down.

"Kidnap is such a strong word," Jamie said, sparing Nathan a smile, but Luke read the veiled demand for respect in the shorter man's tone of voice.

"Daniel's retrieval was paramount," Alice continued. "There was no way you and your family could have protected him where he was, at least not indefinitely. Daniel is far too important and powerful for that."

"Important?" Nathan asked, this time frowning in puzzlement.

"Powerful?" Luke asked simultaneously, intrigued.

"According to the GOA classification system, Daniel Mercer is what we call an Nth Prime, a GenneY Gifted: a rare individual with the potential to have more than five changes, or mutations, whichever way you look at it."

"Considering how the rest of us mortals match up, that's pretty damn scary," Jamie said. Alice spared him a thankful smile, then continued.

"Jamie, for example, ranks as a Quaternary Prime – Q-Prime, because he has three major-class gifts. You, Nathan, would also fall under the Quaternary Prime level, physical powers as well as some other interesting additions. Luke would also fall under such a distinction, having great empathic potential."

"How do you know all of this?" Luke asked, feeling the first real tremors of apprehension.

"GOA knows of nearly eighty percent of all Changed within the northern hemisphere. Though there is little by way of electronic data other than you and your brother's classification, we do know of you. We also know of your girlfriend's abilities." The last statement was directed at Nathan, who swallowed. "And I am also quite skilled at reading and detecting the mutations within other Changed." Her eyes narrowed again, this time with an almost merry shrewdness. Nathan was adamant though, much to Luke's growing frustration.

"If you guys knew about us, why didn't you ever make contact? Luke asked.

"We observe every change in some way, and make judgement calls only on some. If we feel it necessary to intervene, to guide or inform, we do so. But your parents seemed capable and willing to raise you both, and there have been no mishaps, so we did nothing. Neither you nor Nathan showed inclination to make use of your abilities - you seemed to prefer acting 'normal' - so we never approached you." Alice explained and Luke nodded acceptance.

"But you have Daniel here?" Nathan asked.

"Daniel is an Nth Prime, a distinction which sets him above the rest of us all," Alice replied, as though she was deliberately ignoring the tactlessly rude assault Nathan was hammering at. "Nth Primes have more than five gifts, or powers, whichever way you look at it. They are extremely rare – Daniel is the first Nth-er we've found in seventy years – and from the limited past experience we've had with Nth-ers, they are high-priority interests to GOA."

"So what do you intend to do with him?" Nathan asked, after a silence of several seconds. He seemed calmer now, strangely enough.

"For the moment, what we've been doing with him for the last year: training. GOA is a Changed agency; they observe and intervene at correct and premeditated intervals, usually never without consent. Daniel is only the second incident where GOA interceded without prior admission." Alice leaned back in her seat. "I am the primary spokesperson and director of the Changed that are affiliated with the GOA, and aid its work. In short, we're Changed who work for GOA, helping it with its tasks, overseeing the manageable Changed, monitoring the ones we know of and training those who are inducted into the organization."

"Inducted?" Luke asked. Alice nodded.

"Of their own free will. GOA has no agenda other than this, and there are more than five hundred Changed working for us at present, throughout the northern hemisphere."

"Did Daniel actually agree to work for you?" Nathan asked, incredulous. Alice shook her head.

"Daniel does not work for us, yet, though he has expressed a marked desire to do so. He is a unique case: at the onset of his Change, which was a recent thing, and quite astonishing, he already had command, to a certain degree, of four major skills, but no experience with controlling it. From what we've discovered, and which we hope you will see fit to share with us, there was no slow progress, but rather a very rapid and uncontrollable fit of power. He had no control whatsoever, and needed guidance. GOA to the rest of the world is an unknown organization, a best-kept secret of many countries in the world, so there wouldn't have been any way for you to contact us."

"Don't call us, we'll call you," Luke breathed, astonished at the range of the people they found themselves amongst. Alice nodded.

"You could have been decent and arranged a meeting with us," Nathan remarked. Again that iron-clad grey gaze swivelled to Nathan, and Luke all but gulped in apprehension for his brother's sake. Jamie came to Alice's rescue again, though Luke thought it hardly necessary. From the looks of it, Alice would eat Nathan alive. The magnitude of his brother's stubbornness still amazed Luke.

"And how would we have convinced you, in time, that Daniel would be better off with us, with complete strangers?" Jamie challenged. "You had him for about two weeks after the Change. Had you kept him like that for another day, possibly, you wouldn't have woken up."

"What?" Nathan asked, and Luke frowned, also intent now on Jamie's words.

"His power was growing at an exponential rate, without any form of control, as Alice had said. When you speak to Charlie, he'll tell you more, but the bottom line is that your young sibling was at critical mass, mentally speaking; he has a telekinetic range that can crush houses and demolish industrial material."

"Shit," Luke breathed, and the shocked expression on Nathan's face echoed the spoken sentiment.

"So you see, we had to act fast, not only to save you, but to avoid a media fracas," Alice interjected.

"So who's training him, if he's so strong?" Nathan asked.

"Many of us are. You see, apart from Daniel's telepathic and still-burgeoning telekinetic power, he also has other divergent strains of mutation within him. The problem is that we don't fully know yet what else he is capable of." Alice rose, and the door to the office opened. In came the man Luke and Nathan remembered from that evening when Danny had been taken. He was tall, as tall as Nathan was, with an angular but symmetrically appealing face, searching brown eyes and short-cropped blonde hair. Luke immediately assumed this to be Charlie, and by default took hold of Nathan's upper arm, though he himself wanted to lash out somehow at the man, to retaliate for the strong sense of anger and frustration he felt within him.

Nathan's upper arm tensed dramatically beneath Luke's hand.

Behind Charlie, the eerily beautiful woman that had accompanied him that night entered. She was astonishingly beautiful, like a living, breathing porcelain doll with exquisite petit features and smouldering blue eyes, and where Charlie looked upset, she was all smiles and radiant exuberance. Nathan frowned immediately, his mouth pulling into an expression of barely contained anger. His arm began to shake.

"I am unfortunately a very busy woman," Alice said with an endearing smile. "Charlie, Alexis and Jamie will take you further, give you a tour of the complex and fill you in further." She waited for the lot of them to leave before taking her seat, face down, already seemingly lost in her duties as GOA Director.

Luke and his brother followed Jamie out of the office. Charlie trailed behind somewhat, not showing anything beyond a scowl and veiled distaste. The woman, Alexis, smiled warmly as she fell in beside Nathan.

"Hiya there, I'm Alexis, but you can call me Alex, or Allie, whatever. You must be Nathan Hirsch."

"Yeah," Nathan said, managing a weak smile for Alex's candid friendliness. Luke did better and extended his hand, taking Alex's in his own.

"Lucas Hirsch, I'm his brother."

"Yeah, I know," Alex answered brightly, and gave Luke's hand a shake. "You know Charlie." The last sentence carried a massive hint of amusement, and Charlie's scowl deepened. "Charlie's scared of you."

"Alex!" Charlie snapped angrily, and marched ahead, taking up stride beside Jamie, who snickered.

"Don't mind him, he's mostly as annoyed as you are," Alex said, drawing closer to Luke and lowering her head in a conspiratorial manner. Luke nodded, falling in with the joke. "So Alice and the 'limited' database we have here at the GOA facility tells me you're a high-range empath."

"Yup," Luke answered, not quite sure how to field the obvious warmness of her statement.

"Neat. I'm an SP, which basically means –"

"They know what an SP is, Alex," Jamie interrupted. Alex smirked at him, then continued.

"Anyway, as I was saying, I'm an SP, with high potential in telekinesis, external mental overrides and teleportation."

"External mental overrides?" Luke asked.

"I can take control of people's minds," Alex said, sounding ungodly happy, and smiling to boot. Luke nodded, intrigued but also a little wary. Seeing his expression, Alex squinted and aimed a soft punch at his shoulder. "Oh relax, I'm still at the early stages of that particular gift of mine. Weak-willed individuals have trouble coping when I'm around – it makes it so easy to get what I want!"

"Didn't Alice warn you about that?" Jamie quipped.

"Didn't she threaten to halter you?" Charlie remarked softly. Alex's mouth opened in affront, her cheeriness gone in an instant.

"You bastard! You can't say that in front of the guests!" she snarled.

"Alice said she'd halter both of you if you didn't play nice," Jamie cut in. "Alex is right. We have guests, potential allies and friends, and it won't do to have them see you bickering. Not on the first day, at least."

The jibe was meant to lighten the sudden dip in the atmosphere, but it fell flat, and Jamie didn't seem to care either way, except that it shut Alex and Charlie up for a while. The five of them walked in silence down the long corridor that led from Alice's office. There were windows along the left side of the wall, so at least the scenery allowed for more than immensely awkward silence. They then took a large elevator down four levels, and were then disgorged from the silent chute into a wide, open-plan area that was tiled and decked in large arrays of plants and trees.

"It's like a mall," Nathan said moodily, not really in the mood to be impressed despite the opulence of the setting.

"This is the Mess Level, where all the GOA people can get themselves something to eat and drink. Here everyone hangs out in between work hours and shifts. I thought it would be nice for us all to have a sit-down and something to drink while we sort this situation out." Jamie led them ahead through an archway and into a massive promenade filled with people who paid them little attention beyond perfunctory nods of acknowledgement. They walked straight down beneath a massive ribbed ceiling that let in an abundance of wintry white light, finally stepping left into a luxurious restaurant-like area filled with warm wooden tones and exotic wall motifs. Luke's eyes widened with interest and awe, and even Nathan was temporarily relieved of his distrust for everything around him. Jamie led them to a large booth overlooking the immense take-off decks outside, where they themselves had landed earlier. Planes, choppers and other stranger forms of aerial transports landed and took off at regular intervals, leaving the scene filled with activity enough to merit interest.

"Okay then, I'll order for us. Any particular preferences, anyone?" Jamie asked, flagging a waiter.

"Ummm, we don't have any money on us right now," Luke admitted sheepishly. Jamie shook his head.

"This isn't a restaurant, it's a private dining saloon for Gifted agents and guests. Alice's idea, supported avidly by the rest of GOA. Supposed to create an impression of comfort for the uncomfortable." Jamie spared an almost obvious glance at Nathan, who was idly staring out the window at the jets taking off outside. "Anyhow, it's free, you can order what you want and as much as you want."

After the food had been brought in, and everyone was biding their time with eating, Luke turned to Jamie.

"So Jamie, I hope you don't mind me asking," Luke began, after swallowing a mouthful, "what gifts do you have?"

"Oh, I'm a flyer. That, and I'm a phaser, as well as an elementalist. Phasing means I can move through solid matter, and elementalists have innate energy gifts, like optic beams and organic rays."

"Like Joanie," Nathan said absently, taking a sip from his drink.

"I hear you also can fly, Nathan," Jamie said, turning his attention to Nathan. "That and lots of other physically-driven gifts. Guess you're a combat kind of guy then." Nathan merely nodded.

"Who is Joanie?" Alex asked, interested.

"My brother's girlfriend," Luke said.

"Ooh," Alex said, all smiles. Her face lit up. "Oh yeah, I remember, the girl in your house the evening we came for your friend. I scanned her quickly in passing, you should really bring her here, we could teach her a lot of things about controlling her gifts."

"Dammit Alex you really love shooting your mouth off, don't you?" Charlie grated suddenly, nearly throwing down his cutlery. His face was thunderous. "What part of courtesy don't you understand?"

"Lighten up boresville, jeez! Talk about courtesy, you don't even make polite conversation around the table!" Alex countered.

"Yeah Charlie, how about that?" Nathan asked with a devious smile, seeing an opportunity. Alex, flustered, saw only support and leaned forward eagerly, daring Charlie to react. In turn, the heretofore silent Changed put down his knife and fork, not taking his eyes off Alex, and rose, turning swiftly on his heel and marching resolutely from the saloon. Jamie looked at Alex, and his boyish features seemed carved from angry stone, sporting belligerent blue eyes.

"You really should learn to be more tactful, you know that?" he directed at Alex.

"What'd I do?" Alex protested, confused.

"And you," Jamie said, looking at Nathan. "You are our guest here. I don't care how angry you are at Charlie, or us, but a level of decency is required in return for our hospitality."

"I only came because you told me my brother was here," Nathan growled, not backing down. "Instead I find a top-secret agency that kidnaps people based on choices they make without consulting those people first. I find the people who kidnapped Danny and they try to buy me off with offers of joining their little party, and then expect me to just bend over backwards!" He practically snarled the last, nearly rising from his seat, but Luke pulled him down forcefully, making him grunt. Nathan had always had a flighty and aggressive streak to him, but this was worse than usual, even if it was Danny they were talking about.

"You're overreacting!" Luke hissed. "And your behavior is disgusting!"

"Like I care!" Nathan snapped. He threw his brother's hand off and rose from the table, storming from the saloon. Luke looked down, embarrassed. When he looked up again, Jamie was seated, eyes focused on his plate before him. He seemed remarkably unperturbed, taking knife and fork in hand and digging in again.

Alex merely sat there, staring at her food.

"Look, I'm really sorry about this," Luke started.

"I know you are, which is why I'm not sending your brother packing right away. I can also understand that you'd be upset about Daniel's taking, but you seem to handle the story pretty well."

"I'm just glad he's safe," Luke breathed, relieved by Jamie's amicability.

"He is safe."

"Where are you keeping him? Is it a sanatorium, or an... asylum?" Jamie looked up, puzzled by Luke's halting query.

"Your brother is not insane, Luke. He had a hectic time adapting, but we don't keep him in an asylum or any other form of loony bin, if that's what you're wondering. He lives with Charlie in a large estate to the northwest, by the sea."

"He lives with Charlie?" Luke asked, really mystified.

"Charlie is his keeper, so to speak, his number one teacher and mentor." Luke's mouth opened in a silent 'o' of understanding. Jamie continued, in between bites. "When we brought him in, Daniel, I mean, he was catatonic, showing no reaction whatsoever. The only way we knew he was still in there at all was because the rooms started shaking, and sometimes when it became bad, the windows exploded or any wooden objects close by splintered. A month after we retrieved him, he suddenly began getting aggressive. Anyone who came near him was thrown away from him forcefully, or they simply blacked out." Jamie took another bite. Once done, he went on. "Alice, despite the importance of finding a potential Nth Primer, had no time to dedicate exclusively to breaking him in and calming him down, so Charlie was brought in on a regular basis to work with Daniel."

"Why Charlie?"

"Because Charlie is an empath strong enough to warrant him Prime status irrespective of the fact that his gifts are specialized in only one major class. On a scale of one to ten, with one being sporadic and ten being terrifyingly powerful, Charlie rates at least a seven on telekinetic and telepathic scopes. That, and as a chartered GOA affiliate and employee, Alice basically managed to order him to do the job."

"He really liked that," Alex ventured softly. She had resumed eating at some point, but had made no attempt to rejoin the conversation, still a bit upset by Charlie and Nathan's animosity, and her part in fuelling it.. Jamie didn't seem to mind that she joined in again now, and simply went on.

"Yeah, Charlie was really upset at his assignment. He liked field work, not babysitting, as he called it. I can't say the same is true nowadays."

"How so?" Luke asked. He pushed his empty plate away from himself and leaned back, satisfied, holding his drink in one hand as he prepared to listen further.

"The two of them are nearly inseparable, these days," Jamie said, polishing the last of his own meal. "The reason why Charlie is in such a foul mood is because he's been away too long from Daniel, not because he dislikes you guys. All that much, I might add." Jamie ordered a bottle of white wine to complement dessert, which he allowed Alex and Luke to choose. Once the table had been cleared of dishes and the wine and dessert was on its way, Alex took over.

"No one really knows much about why Charlie's attitude changed so much. I bet Alice knows, but she won't say, and Charlie is impossible to crack open under any circumstances. His head's too thick."

"Alex," Jamie warned, but just barely managed to hide a smile. Alex also wanted to smile, but Jamie's reprimand was still in force, so she backed down somewhat.

"Anyway, Daniel's a nice guy, I guess. A little creepy, the times I met him. Besides, compared to Charlie's head, Daniel's about as accessible as the inside of a mountain; you could only get in there if he let you."

"Were Nathan and Daniel close?" Jamie interrupted, leaning forward. Luke, startled by the question, mulled a little over it before answering.

"Danny's been living with us for nine years – we adopted him," Luke replied, making sure the insinuation of Danny's adoption stressed how close he had been to Nathan, and to Luke. "Me and my brother both are quite close to him, yeah. Why'd you ask?" The wine and desserts arrived. Alex smiled, girlishly clapped her hands together and grabbed a spoon. For all her excitement she took delicate bites and behaved as though she were enjoying the etiquette standards of a first-class restaurant. Which the saloon practically was, Luke thought.

"It's up to Charlie when you'll see Daniel," Jamie said. "Even Alice has to ask him if she can see him, politely, mind, and Charlie never refuses Alice, but the lines are there. I'm just telling you that you have to be prepared for the eventuality that you might no longer really recognize your brother."

"In what way?"

"We never knew Daniel before the Change. He might not have changed at all, with regards to his personality, but he doesn't entirely look the same anymore."

"He was really cute, in a weird way, before," Alex said matter-of-factly, "but now he's kinda gorgeous, still in a weird way." She nearly laughed at Luke's cocked eyebrow. "Relax honey, he's not changed drastically. Alice says it was merely a perfecting of what was already there in the first place."

"I still don't understand," Luke said, bewildered.

"He looks different," Jamie qualified. "Physically, that is. He's stronger, in shape and physically toned. Charlie and the others keep him on a rather rigid regimen of dieting and exercise. Preparing him."

"For what?"

"Daniel is going to join Alice in the GOA team, once Charlie thinks he's ready," Alex said, toying with her spoon before opting for an extra helping. "Daniel's choice, not anyone else's."

Luke resorted to silence, slowly demolishing his dessert. His mind was lost amid the welter of new information. Mostly he felt eager to see Daniel again, if not as angry and possessive as Nathan was in the process. But he felt an inexplicable sense of unquiet creep over him, as though the lavishness of their surroundings was a cover for something dark. Not evil, but a tawdry sham that covered something potentially dangerous. He kept his feelings to himself though, deciding that he would look for Nathan later, and enjoy the company of the two people in front of him for now.

Nathan chased after Charlie.

He could see the man moving resolutely along the corridors. He followed at a safe distance behind, not wanting to let the Changed know he was following. The pursuit continued until Charlie ducked in at a sliding door, passing through into the harsh white winter glare. Nathan waited for a few moments before following suit.

Outside, they were on the rooftop, an unrelieved, coarse surface stretching towards a low rail to the sides. He was surprised to see Charlie facing him, standing with his back to the concrete rail. The Changed had a frown in place. Nathan swallowed, then gave a few steps forward.

"I knew you'd follow," Charlie said. Before Nathan could ask how, Charlie titled his head askance and tapped his temple with one finger. "Your brother is enjoying himself. I don't see why you can't either."

"Because I need answers," Nathan grated. "I don't need other things from you people. I just want to know where Danny is."

"So you believe what Alice told you?"

"About what?"

"About why we took Daniel from your house?"

"Is it true?" Nathan challenged, allowing venom into his voice. "Or do you have a different story?" Charlie shook his head, a mirthless smile in place on his lips. His eyes remained purposely untouched by the expression.

"Every word of it is true. There were never any ulterior intentions, or sugar-coating. But you're not the kind of guy to back off. At least, not until Daniel himself tells you so."

"So where is he?" Nathan reiterated. Adrenaline surged through him, he just needed an excuse to loose whatever gift he could at Charlie.

"He's safe," Charlie repeated. "But you can't see him yet."

"Why not?" Nathan snarled. He had taken slow steps towards Charlie, and was now within arm's reach.

This didn't seem to perturb Charlie at all. He remained casually staring as Nathan drew closer.

"Because he's not ready to see you yet. He doesn't even know you're here." This news had a dramatic impact on Nathan. His face scrunched up in anger. Even as he lifted his arm to strike, Charlie's voice cut across his intentions. "Remember what happened the last time you tried?" Charlie watched as Nathan halted, arm shaking with rage. He was breathing heavily as if from some strain, but Charlie hadn't stopped him, save for his words.

"What game are you playing?" Nathan grated.

"I don't play games with other people's lives. Certainly not with Daniel's."

"Why didn't you let him contact us?" Nathan asked, dropping his arm and resorting to angered querying.

"Because he didn't want to. He knew you'd come looking for him, and do something stupid, once you found out where he was."

"Danny wouldn't do that," Nathan snapped, shaking his head in denial.

"Daniel knew what was happening to him. He knew no one else could help him save for us, so he stayed of his own free will."

"We're his family!" Nathan snapped. Infuriatingly, Charlie shrugged.

"Now you know," Charlie said, nodding. He stood staring at Nathan, who was still breathing heavily. But his face was now a picture of empty anger, and of slowly dawning misery. "Any more questions?"

"Why wouldn't he trust us?"

"Because of that, he knew exactly how you'd react," Charlie said. He was still wary, unwilling to let his guard down as yet, but he could barely keep the concern and sympathy from his voice. "The only reason Alice finally caved and let you and your brother come here was because Daniel had begun withdrawing."

"Withdrawing?" Nathan asked.

"He missed his family." At that statement, Nathan looked away, and Charlie could see the tears pooling in Nathan's eyes. Charlie waited, leaning back against the rail behind him, allowing Nathan a moment to recover himself. "It helps that both you and your brother are also Changed, else you would have died some day, never knowing what had happened to him."

"You say that as if you're enjoying this!" Nathan snapped angrily, wiping the back of his hand across his eyes. Charlie shook his head, and his expression finally softened. He turned his back on Nathan and stared out over the complex grounds below.

"You don't have a clue just how important Daniel is."

"I don't care how important he is to you!" Nathan challenged.

"If you knew his worth you wouldn't say that," Charlie amended. He was surprised when Nathan joined him at the rail. He expected some or other blow to land soon, preparing his defences, but Nathan merely stared out beside him. "I didn't like it when Alice told me I had to coddle a new Changed. I hated assignments like that – I didn't have the training for it. Usually Alex, Chris or Jamie handles stuff like that. But I did it, and I didn't regret it. Daniel is an extraordinary person." Nathan remained silent for a long interval, gathering himself, regaining control of his emotions. He sighed.

"You say he didn't want to contact us?" Nathan asked, voice still sounding hoarse and emotional.

"He often said that the one thing his family could always rely on from him was consistency, and level-headedness," Charlie said, glancing sideways at Nathan. He was surprised to see Nathan smile through his almost-tears.

"Yeah, that's Danny-boy," Nathan whispered, with touching fondness. Charlie, realizing the worst was over, leaned on one elbow, so that he could face Nathan.

"We've always wondered what kind of person he was before the Change. We didn't know him before then, he wasn't in our scopes. It should be interesting to see what happens when the three of you meet again."

"And when is that?" Nathan asked, voice assuming a dangerous hint of impatience again.

"Soon. Daniel isn't ready for something that emotional just yet. His emotions intrude often on his progress."

"What happens until then? With me and Luke, I mean?"

"You can stay here, or we can take you back to your home. I think Alice would prefer it if you stayed. She's dead-set on recruiting you and Luke, and maybe even your girlfriend, if she's willing."

There remained an awkward silence between them for several minutes. Charlie glanced at Nathan often, knowing he could read the surface thoughts without much effort, but also knowing that such a violation was uncalled for. At length, Nathan spoke again.

"Would you just tell me how he's doing? What's changed? How has he been?"

"He's doing great. He's lonely, and I'm the only real company he keeps. Alex bores him after a while, and Jamie and Chris – you'll meet Chris at some point – can't stay with him for too long because he unwittingly scans their minds and tells them what they're thinking. He gets mischievous out of sheer boredom." Charlie found himself smiling at the recollection. He turned to Nathan. "You have to know that by now he's becoming enormously powerful. Off the scale powerful."

"We always joked, my brother and me, about what kind of powers Danny-boy would have, if he somehow became like us. A Changed. We didn't think he would, though," Nathan said softly. "How powerful is off the scale?"

"He can read the thoughts of people a hundred miles from him; he can telekinetically lift an eighteen-wheel truck and flatten a two-storey house. His phasing has improved up to the point where he can walk through most of our shielded safe rooms, and he can teleport to any place he can see, no matter how far away it is. He doesn't like it a lot, teleporting, so he keeps it to a minimum. Above and beyond that, we expect him to exhibit a new strain of gift every day, maybe even a new gift every now and then."

"How'd you figure that?" Nathan queried, his sour mood of before seeming forgotten in light of Charlie's forthcoming sharing of information. But there was also the incipient look of awe growing in Nathan's eyes.

Charlie smiled, wondering if the Changed before him could have conceived of finding his brother so altered.

"We've never in seventy years found any Changed that hasn't told us of their tale of Changing. All of them speak of gradual changes, small things that feel out of place, minor things pertinent to their unique gifts showing themselves before the actual gift, in very weak and erratic form, becomes apparent. We have only the reports of the last Nth Primer to go by when judging Daniel's progress, but he matches that profile: a monumental and sudden shift from normal non-gifted human to full-blown Changed, often in a matter of days. Little or no control, and gifts almost beyond compare. Alice is an FP, at the height of her potential, and she can hardly keep track of Daniel's skill. And as far as we know, Alice is one of the strongest Changed ever. That says a lot about Daniel."

"I can't wait to see him again." Nathan actually smiled, staring at some space far away.

"Just so you know, we are keeping him safe," Charlie said. "As long as you know we'd never hurt him, and we only did what we thought was best for him." Nathan lowered his head and sighed.

"I'm still getting used to the idea of a sanctioned kidnap, but I guess I'll get over it. Once I see Daniel, that is."

"Then until then," Charlie said, and drew away from the rail.

Luke looked up when Nathan entered.

"Did you find what you're looking for?" he asked critically. Nathan frowned, eyes taking in his brother's expression, as well as scanning the room they were in. Luke was lying on one of two beds,

84

both of them large and comfortable-looking, set amid a chamber filled with opulent but relatively simplistic furnishings. Luke stared at his brother from beneath elevated brows, glaring from below.

"I don't know what you mean," Nathan returned, and moved to the empty bed. He sat down on the side, body half turned away from Luke.

"Are you happy with yourself, being that rude?" Luke asked, heat rising in his voice even as he rose from his languid pose on the bed. "Don't you have any respect for these people?"

"I'm sorry, alright?" Nathan snapped, facing Luke. "And yeah, for your information, I found out some stuff."

"Like what?" Luke asked.

"Oh, so now you want to know? Fancy shitting on my head some more?"

"I'm interested in what you found out, but I want you to go and apologize to Jamie and Alexis at some point," Luke said, in a tone of voice which brooked no nonsense. Nathan pointedly looked at his brother. It was rare that Luke pulled rank, even though as the eldest he was fully entitled to it. Yet when he did do it, it was best to listen, Nathan had found. He nodded tightly, a simple gesture which mollified his brother's expression. "So, what'd you find? Did you and Charlie come to blows?"

"Nearly," Nathan admitted. "In the end he simply told me where Danny is."

"He did?" Luke asked, surprised enough to sit up straighter. "Where?"

"Not exactly where," Nathan amended. "But he told me that Danny's safe, and that we'll probably get to see him soon." Luke regarded his younger brother with some trepidation when he didn't continue.

"That's it?" he asked softly. Nathan nodded. "So at least you and Charlie won't hit each other when you come face to face again."

"Afraid not," Nathan quipped without smiling, but the sarcasm was there.

"Jamie told me that Danny lives in a big house northwest of here." Now it was Nathan's turn to rise, face painted in incredulity. "Yeah," Luke continued, amused. "But he also told me that Charlie is the only one with access to Daniel. Even Alice asks nicely before seeing him."

"Why Charlie?" Nathan asked, puzzled, asking the question which bugged him.

"Charlie is a high-level empath. A very high level one, actually. He was the one put in charge of training Daniel."

"Guess that explains a lot," Nathan breathed.

"So what do we do now?" Luke asked. "We know Daniel is safe, and we know he'll stay safe here, with people like us. So I guess we did what we came for."

"No, we didn't. We haven't seen him yet, talked to him or found out what he thinks," Nathan countered. "And he's still family, there's no way we're leaving him just like that. We have to see if these people lied to us or not."

"Alright," Luke breathed, relieved. He too was unwilling to leave before having seen the truth behind Jamie and Charlie's words, and he had entertained remaining behind alone here at the GOA station. He could hardly contain his relief that Nathan was also staying. "But what about Joanie?"

"I don't know. We've been gone for three days. I wonder if they let you call relatives," Nathan said.

"Ask Jamie, he's a nice guy. I'm sure he'll set you up." Luke placed a hand on the pillow beside him, then leaned down and began untying his shoelaces. "But I'm gonna sleep now. Jamie said he'll take me to see the hangars and the manufactory facilities tomorrow."

"Why?" Nathan asked, a little puzzled.

"We'll talk in the morning," Luke finished, then heaved both legs onto the bed and stretched full length, breathing deeply and closing his eyes. Nathan stared at his brother, but decided against pressing the matter. He undressed and climbed in underneath the covers of his own bed, and once he felt composed enough for sleep, he pressed the dial that dimmed the lights.

CHAPTER FOUR

Adjustment

Alice was standing at the window when he entered.

It was already past midnight, and the base was quieting down, with only the running lights of the runways and the small glitters of the distantly lit windows of outlying buildings still testimony to the constant wakefulness of the GOA Headquarters and its sprawling mass of structures. Charlie took up position before Alice's desk, but he didn't sit down.

"You spoke to the two brothers," Alice said, making it sound more like a statement than a question.

"Just to the younger, Nathan," Charlie said. Alice turned from her vantage at the window, her face blank. "I was actually hoping I could ask when I can go home."

"What did you tell Nathan, exactly?" Alice queried. Charlie shrugged.

"What he wanted to hear: that Daniel's safe and okay, and that they'll see him in a couple of weeks."

"You neglected something critical, then," Alice said. "Something which might anger Nathan and his brother all over again."

"Alice, I can't tell them that just yet," Charlie interjected, apologetic. "Like you said, they might just blow their tops again."

"So instead you decided to placate them with limited information, when you could have told them everything and had them work through it eventually."

"If I didn't you would have denied me leave," Charlie snapped. "This way, they can deal with the issue without me being present, constantly aggravating them."

"I am considering denying you leave anyway, so you can explain the exact truth to them," Alice countered, face assuming a critical expression. "This is unlike you, Charlie. You've been away from Daniel for a month, and yet you go about your duties as if you can't wait to see him again. What has happened?"

"You know what I had to do in order for him to accept me," Charlie explained. "You all but ordered it!"

"I know I did, so cease the accusations," Alice fired back. "But what has happened after that? A bond like that is professional, a teacher to a student. A friendship may occur, but why have I got the feeling that this is now beyond that?" Charlie looked down, avoiding the inquiry in Alice's face. When Alice remained pointedly staring, Charlie placed his hands together and walked from the desk, agitated. When he looked up again, defiance was clear in his face.

"Did you know what you were asking me when you commanded me to take Daniel's training in hand? Did you know what would happen when you ventured the plausibility of a mental bond with him?"

"I would not have brought such a possibility to your mind otherwise," Alice replied carefully.

"Then you knew what could happen?" Charlie challenged angrily.

"I expected you to maintain a distance born of professional duty. Even business has its friendship values."

"Daniel was a wreck!" Charlie retorted, voice growing heated. "He responded to nothing, not even the bond at first! I was about to give up hope then but I realized what he required of me, and in order to support him and to bring about his withdrawal from the catatonic state I gave it to him!"

"Which was?" Alice asked softly. Charlie swallowed, eyes downcast, as though he were contemplating something.

"Love. Understanding. Companionship. A mutual respect that requires more than a mere platonic friendship can give," he answered, eyes alight.

"Are you lovers?"

"No!" Charlie rejoined, angry. "Daniel didn't ask for such a level of contact. He never did. He needed understanding and guidance, but never that. He needed... he needed a brother." Alice nodded.

"I see. So this constant demand that you be by his side, it is not the reaction of a lover?"

"Why are you doing this?" Charlie demanded, growing frustrated. "Let me ask you something: have you ever been bonded, mentally, to another telepath?"

"Yes," Alice said, and her voice sounded calm. "But my husband was killed in the Gulf War, a long time ago. And such a bond was brought about by the utmost of trusts, which could only be consummated by total immersion of everything: physical, emotional, mental and spiritual. These things I gave to him freely, even as he did to me. So yes, Charlie, I once had such a bond."

"But you look down on me, because you think I'm misusing my bond with Daniel? Is that it? Am I a rapist or a pervert?" Charlie hacked.

"I am merely questioning the depths you have let yourself slip into with Daniel. I am questioning whether you aren't in too deep, because of what you may have wanted from your own brother, and could not get."

Charlie's face grew thunderous with rage, draining of all colour, as his mouth worked soundlessly and his jaw grew taut with suppressed feelings. When he spoke, his voice was low and filled with fury.

"You have no right to bring that up! None!"

"Really?" Alice asked, and her voice, by contrast, was filled with sadness. She moved to her desk, took her seat and leaned forward, both hands on the table. "Don't I? Charlie, you lost your brother when you were a teenager, and your father right before that. I do not question your motives, but your involvement."

"And why not?" Charlie rejoined, and his voice cracked under the emotional strain. "Why can't I have a brother, why can't I take care of someone who needs me? Isn't that part of your plan? Heal the wounds of one and heal the other in the process?" In the deafening silence that followed, Alice noted the twin trail of tears running from Charlie's eyes. She leaned back, allowing her own face to show remorse.

"I am sorry," she said softly. "Forgive me. I had assumed you were"

"Abusing Daniel? Using him for my own ends?" Charlie demanded, still furious and on the brink of further tears.

"If that is how you wish to see this, then yes," Alice replied, sounding weary. "I didn't mean for this to sound so harsh, or so judgmental. I am merely concerned."

"Well, like you said," Charlie replied, taking a breath and calming himself. "This was your idea. I only signed on because you commanded it, and now that everything is going smoothly, you wish to rein me in."

"I had not thought of this as therapeutic for you," Alice managed. "I apologize for the misunderstanding. I had only wanted assurances that you knew what you were doing." Charlie backed off, letting the relative gloom of the darkened office hide his angry tears. His voice had steadied somewhat.

"Alice you have no idea what Daniel means to me. Yeah, I miss him, because he fills the space my brother and my dad left empty. And he lets me, because he's used to having brothers. And I guess you can, in fact, understand the depths of a mental bond that is willing from both ends." Alice nodded. "So, apology accepted."

"But we have not yet discussed how we will handle the two Hirsch brothers," Alice said after a moment of almost reverential silence. Charlie, almost completely recovered from his outburst, sighed and sat down.

"That's why I wanted to go back to Daniel. Because of the other thing that neither Nathan nor Luke knows."

"And what is that?" Alice asked, again critical. Charlie, knowing he would find no mercy, bit down and continued.

"Alice, Daniel doesn't recall them at all. Not the people they are, or the things they had done together as friends, as brothers, as family. Yeah, he knows he had friends, and he remembers his family. But he can't remember anything else."

"Then why are the two brothers here?" Alice asked, shocked. "More to the point, why all of this then? Why did you bring them here?"

"Because for the last four months, I've had to listen to Daniel as he talks in his sleep. He," Charlie paused, then continued. "He says strange things that make no sense. Then he mentions his brothers and stops dead, as is surprised that he did. When I ask him the next morning what he said, he never remembers, and he has this look of... hurt, all over his face. Can you blame me for wanting to help? Daniel knows he has family, somewhere, he knows that they know about him and his situation, but he doesn't recall the familial link, the concept of being unbreakably close to the people who raised him," Charlie explained.

Alice seemed to stare at some point beyond Charlie, but then her eyes regained focus, and she looked him squarely in his eyes.

"I see now," she almost breathed. "I was indeed wrong to doubt you. You would do anything for him," she said, meaning Daniel.

"I would die for him," Charlie replied, voice and face resolute.

"You have my leave," Alice said. "But I want this resolved as quickly as possible. Don't drag this out too long. I have no doubts about your concern for Daniel's wellbeing, but the two brothers are obviously key to finally healing Daniel of many of his demons."

"Do I tell them the truth or do they find out later?" Charlie asked.

"As I said, I leave it up to you. Personally I would have wanted you to tell them everything. The youngest brother, Nathan, will not take kindly to this. He'll see it as a betrayal."

"Then I will just have to make sure that when they do find out, Daniel is nearby," Charlie said. He rose, gave a small bow to Alice and turned to go. Alice's voice halted him.

"Be careful, Charlie. The road to hell is paved with good intentions, and you may mean no harm and only well. But others might not see it that way."

"Then I hope that you won't hesitate to validate my motives, when the chopping block comes" Charlie replied, and departed.

Morning dawned.

Luke was hardly surprised when he saw Nathan's empty bed. His brother was by nature a more robust sleeper, requiring less than he himself did, but what gave him pause was that he didn't detect Nathan at all within the limits of their shared chambers. He jumped from the bed and sent his mind running ahead. He had long ago decided that it was a breach of privacy to intrude on his brother's thoughts, but it required no effort at reading minds to find someone, especially someone close and familiar.

"He's on the Mess Level having breakfast with Jamie and Chris," he heard clearly in his head. Luke frowned, not used to such a manner of sharing thoughts.

"Uh, thank you?" he sent, and received a snicker which conveyed the exact identity of the person who had alerted him of Nathan's whereabouts.

"Yeah, I know, it gets lonely when you can do this and there's no one around to have fun with," Alex returned, sounding bored and nonchalant in Luke's head. *"Or when the only other people who can actually do this well refuse to join in. Like Charlie and Alice. Oh, and your friend Daniel too. Like I said, as easy as cracking open a mountain."*

"Where are you?" Luke queried.

"I'm on my way to join your brother and the rest. I heard he's apologizing this morning, and I got the feeling when I spied in there that Jamie expected me to show. You know, to take my share of the

93

blame and take my lumps, whatever. If you want, I'll meet you halfway. Take your time, get clean, see you there soon." There was a moment of silence, and then Alex's terminally cheerful tones relayed again. *"And you might wanna get dressed too, at least by way of pants. Although about the view, I'm not complaining!"*

Luke gasped and started, realizing that he was still in his underwear and shirt, and shy of his pants. Hastily he spied about for them, and once he found them commenced pulling them on, eyes roving as though he expected Alex to be close by, or spying on him. He knew she was remote viewing him, probably, usually a gross breach of privacy, but the way her laughter receded in his head, he knew she had done so fleetingly and mischievously. He could hardly contain a rueful smile, and aborted the dressing session. Instead, he went for a shower and made certain this time that no remote viewers were in range.

He found Alex halfway to the Mess Hall.

She smiled brightly in that girlish way of hers, crisp blue eyes glittering with amusement. Luke, never one to belabour something, pursed his lips, rolled his eyes and spread his hands in a gesture of acquiescence, striding closer. Alex grinned and hooked her arm into his, and they set off for the dining area where the others were having breakfast.

"You kinda surprised me, Luke Hirsch," Alex said, raising her eyebrows by way of greeting someone who walked past. "I thought only me and the other empaths on base were capable of a telepathic range for communication further than a couple of hundred yards. Not to mention blocking a remote view."

"You tried again?" Luke asked, nearly stopping their progress, mouth and eyes widening in the beginnings of affront. Alex smiled sheepishly.

"Hey, I said I liked the view."

"So you tried invading the privacy of my shower?" He didn't know whether to be outraged or amused. And secretly flattered. At least Alex had the good grace to blush deeply.

"Okay, so I'm bored a lot, and besides, Chris and Jamie have natural blocks even though neither of them can remote communicate worth a damn. And you can never pull one over Charlie. So all the cute guys but you and your brother are off limits."

"You spied on Nathan in the shower?" Luke asked, flabbergasted. Alex's sly smile gave him his answer.

"If Joanie ever finds out she'll claw your eyes out."

"Then let's hope she never finds out," Alex said, one manicured fingernail tracing the bottom of Luke's chin and forcing it up slightly as she disengaged from his arm and strode ahead, swinging her hips and walking as saucily as she could. Luke, flustered by her frankness, followed slowly behind.

Inside the saloon, everyone was already finished with breakfast, and engaged in conversation. Luke's eyes fell on an unknown face beside Jamie, and the man rose to greet him.

"Christopher Bellman," the man said, face casual despite the sense of warmth and friendliness Luke received from the handshake. He sat down next to Nathan, who spared him a quick smile before looking back at Jamie.

"What's up?" he asked his brother.

"I asked Jamie if I could call home and talk to Joanie," Nathan replied. "He said yes, and he even said we could go get her if she was up to it."

"So did you call?"

"Not yet. Jamie's telling me about the stuff GOA does to get money other than government funding. Really interesting stuff." Luke nodded.

Nathan had always had a penchant for business schemes and economics. He was remarkably apt with anything connected to such ventures and matters, so it would of course intrigue him to know how GOA supported itself beyond the provision of the US government. But it worried him a little that his brother wasn't out of his seat like a gunshot, making for the nearest comm-booth to call

Joanie. Neither their mobile uplinks worked, something Luke chalked up to GOA's security protocols and whatever civilian transmission restrictions a top-secret facility like Headquaters probably had. But he put the thought from his head and honed in on the conversation.

"Sleep well Luke?" Jamie asked him, and Luke nodded. "When we're done here I'll take you to the bays to check out the gear we use. Your brother will probably be joining Chris on some wild goose chase, so we have the whole day to introduce you to the stuff and the people working it."

"Goose chase?" Chris interjected, quirking one eyebrow. Luke grinned, amused at how the man's eyes and face seemed to remain absolutely deadpan in spite of the gesture. "Test driving new toys is not a goose chase."

"Because of your approach to toys, the techs have had to introduce an entire new set of safety regulations and precautions," Jamie challenged.

"And you blame me for that?" Chris rejoined. Alex snickered, so Luke realized this was commonplace banter between the two men. "How could more safety measures do harm?"

"If you crash another glider pod Alice will start billing your ass for damages."

"She's been threatening to do that for years," Chris snorted derisively and took a sip of orange juice. He grinned and looked over to Nathan. "Besides, my new buddy here looks like a guy who can handle himself at high speeds and dangerous situations." Nathan merely grinned, and Chris rolled on. "See? Told ya!"

"Just be careful alright?" Jamie concluded on a serious note. "I don't want to hear about accidents and broken bones."

"Then we'll make sure none of the bad news reaches you," Chris quipped, effecting a wide smile. He all but sprang from his chair. "C'mon Nate, let's get you to a comm-booth." Nathan clapped Luke on the shoulder in passing and followed Chris. Luke shook his head at his brother. Nathan always had a habit of trying to smooth things over after heated conversations, actually downright ignoring them sometimes, as if that made them go away. Luke barely heard the rest of the conversation as Nathan and Chris moved off. "Her name's Joanie, right? She's gotta be hot, right? How long you been together?" Luke turned to Jamie and Alex, the latter engrossed in ordering breakfast, and Jamie slowly shaking his head.

"Chris means well," Jamie said toothily. "You can always go with them if you want."

"Nah," Luke shook his head. "I'm not into the whole adrenaline thing. But I am interested in what they're gonna do."

"Chris tests all the stuff the techs come up with, and he actually has a Lab job in one of the research facilities nearby. We'll probably run into them again today, round and about the place." Jamie looked at Alex. "What are you going to do?"

"You don't need to know," Alex replied with a knowing smile. For a moment, Jamie simply stared at her, then nodded.

"Fair enough," he said, and rose. He and Luke left the saloon, but Luke looked back for one second, and Alex waved almost conspiratorially at him, before she thanked the server for bringing her breakfast.

She turned left instead of right.

She wasn't supposed to be here, she knew, but then, she loved breaking rules and upsetting people. It was second nature to her, the conditioning of a lifetime of having money thrown at her instead of attention, and neglectful parents. At least she had found a niche to exist in, and here at GOA she could ply her charms. Heavens knows there were enough men, but they only served as diversions and occasionally, bed sport. Except for Luke Hirsch.

She would never admit to anything at first, and true to her personality, she grew to love people very quickly, especially the ones she knew she would manage to get closer to. And she had a good feeling about Luke and his brother. She liked the brother already – he was handsome in a lean, raw-boned way, but she preferred Luke, who appeared stronger and more in control in a withdrawn kind of way. And if there was one thing she loved it was a passive challenge, which Luke Hirsch embodied in full: a big old softie with a heart of gold but a soul of steel. And she felt an uncontrollable surge of desire when she saw him. She had even been pleasantly amused when he had unwittingly blocked her remote view. In spite of spoiling her morning sports, she had felt elated. It wasn't like Jamie or Chris. With those two it was merely a matter of them blocking her without knowing it, so it ruined the fun of possible discovery and the reprimands. And with Charlie there was just no point. She would never admit, not even to herself really, that Charlie, for all his classification according to the GOA standards, was a far more adept empath than she was, and he was hardly more than three years older than herself. It rankled, but she ignored the matter like she did most other things: focused on something, or someone else.

She paused in front of a small, ordinary-looking door, her thoughts immobilizing her. She remembered the time she had come close enough to Daniel to try the view. She shuddered involuntarily, recalling his reaction. Needless to say, only Alice knew what had really happened, but the fact of the matter was that Daniel had given Alex a nasty shock, literally and figuratively. She would go as far as saying that Charlie could give her a lot of grief, were they ever matched head to head in a struggle of wills, but facing Daniel, even for just a moment of intended mischief, had been as exhausting as running full speed up a vertical slope. And what he'd shown her… she shuddered just thinking about it.

She placed a hand against the electronic lock, let her mind soar down a path slightly different than mere telepathy and blanked the sensor detection grid, masking her presence before unlocking the door and slipping in. She couldn't dally overlong – Alice would invariably track her down – and she had a reason for being here today.

The room was far larger than anyone would give it credit for. Right behind the door one was faced with a narrow stairwell that led several levels down. Alex flipped the light and basked in the physical archives, the old systems of paperwork that had been a strange addition to the actual electronic versions. Heaven knows a data crash on the archive servers was damn near impossible, but Alice had insisted on keeping hardcopy updates and addendums in case of emergencies. It suited Alex fine, because even her skill at cybernetic contact immersion was too hard-pressed in trying to engage the electronic archives. She'd tried once, and had suffered a migraine of monumental proportions for her efforts – she still suspected Jamie had something to do with that – and had instead switched to raiding the hardcopy rooms every now and then.

It wasn't very hard to find the 'H' section of the archive, seeing as she was practically a regular. So she tiptoed down to the cabinets reserved for 'H' and began snooping. Finding the Hirsch files weren't very hard, and she made herself relatively cosy as she began paging through.

"Lucas and Nathan Hirsch," she said to herself. "Lucas Hirsch, born April 3rd 2037, Nathan Hirsch, born September 10th 2040. Hmmm, no former history of Changed within the family, from both sides. Oh well, pioneers are always strong. Lucas, Lucas, Lucas, ah! 'Lucas Hirsch, GQP classification with signs of burgeoning telepathic and telekinetic skill. Possible penchant for foresight noted.' Ooh, a precog in the making! Wonder what'll happen when Jamie hears that." Alex squinted, then frowned. "No more on Lucas Hirsch. What about Nathan? 'Nathan Hirsch. GQP classification with high-range physical gifts, including flight.' Great, another fly-boy, just what Chris and Jamie need to cheer them up. What else?" Alex squinted again, this time to make out a small line of red type at the bottom of the page. " 'See file on Joanie Stratford, yada, yada, yada. See file 307 on GenneY affiliates and cross links.' What the hell is a GenneY?" She looked up, momentarily perplexed. She was no precog, but somehow she knew that were she to access the hardcopy of the cross links stipulated in the Hirsch file, she would no doubt be caught, somehow. It was never wise to underestimate Alice's resources.

She replaced the Hirsch file, powerfully intrigued by an even greater mystery. She calmly glided between cabinets, searching eagerly for the section where she knew some of the more suspect of files were kept: a nook close to the lowest level of the vaulted hardcopy chamber. She suppressed a yelp of triumph when she got there, and began rifling through the cabinets, on the alert for anything eye-catching.

After half an hour, she came up with nothing.

"You are such an idiot," she berated herself. "Of course there's no hardcopy backup of the GenneY thingy. Too classified." She swore loudly, banged shut the door of the last cabinet she had gone through and marched pouting back the way she came. Either it was a standard thing, or someone had purposefully set out to trick her, knowing she loved to snoop around in the hardcopies. No matter. For something this tantalizing, she would risk another monster migraine, and a trip into the cyberspace trammels of the electronic archives.

Ancillary Documents

GOA II: Classification of the Changed

Due to the great interest that GOA has invested into observing, documenting and influencing the Changed that are either on their systems – monitored even if left uninitiated into the Agency – and because of those individuals who on hearing of GOA's ideology and agreeing to join the Agency in a career level, GOA Research eventually came up with a classification system that, for all that the Agency has been in existence for only eighty years, has managed to considerably expand the level of scientific scrutiny regarding the various gifts and talents of the Changed. This classification system, sometimes averred to as the 'CC' (short for Changed Classification) is responsible for GOA's acute skill to identify the abilities in the Changed and to act accordingly. It has facilitated the ease with which GOA personnel can identify new Changed, discover the level of aptitude these abilities engender within the character and at times allow the system to expand by documenting new abilities and classing them according to predetermined behaviours, or major classes, as the system provides.

The first subdivisions in the CC are definitive with regards to the level of expertise and strength of a particular gift. A Changed is either an Initiate-level, Masterclass or Paradigm-level in any gift, and where such determinants fail to adequately describe the individual – either the ability is too weak to classify within the three subdivisions, or too strong – the individual is relegated to either Sub-Prime (beneath notice that might cause upsets) or Unknown (the general term for a gift that defies even the system's delineations

– a very rare occurrence). The reason for these expertise planes is to acquire a numeric value according to theoretical expostulation and practical proof, thus leading to an end-result categorisation in terms of 'Prime': the cataloguing starts at the fifth level, known as the Quaternary Prime, and progresses up to the extremely rare Nth Prime level.

At Quad Level, or Prime (CCQP), the Changed individual is in control of an amount or level of gifts equal to a numeric value of 10. At Tertiary Level/Prime (CCTP) the value is raised to 15; at Secondary Level/Prime (CCSP) the value is equal to or greater than 20; at First Level/Prime (CCFP) the value becomes greater than or equal to 25 and thus by way of logical assessment, the rare Nth Level/Prime Changed has a numeric value accorded to his/her abilities greater than or equal to 30. (These individuals are also called GenneY Primes, a lexical aberrant form that describes the mutational genes as beyond the normative association of 'X', instead fixing on 'Y' which is the next step on the road to unknown variables.)

Parallel to these subdivisions are the four major aptitude divisions, acting in concert with the expertise levels. The four aptitude divisions are Physical, Mental, Phasic and Elemental. Here follows a breakdown of each division, coupled with the expertise level that leads to a final classification of the individual in terms of Prime:

I: PHYSICAL APTITUDES ('Q' here means qualification, and is accompanied by a number that comprises the value to be added to the collective in order to achieve a primary classification. Note: Q6=1; Q5=2; Q4=3; Q3=4; Q2=5; Q1=6

– Strength: Initiate(I) – Q6; Masterclass(M) – Q5; Paradigm(P) – Q4

– <u>Speed</u>:   I – 0; M (great speed) – Q6; P
(incredible speed) – Q5

– <u>Agility</u>:   I – 0; M (high agility) – Q6; P(inhuman
agility) – Q5

– <u>Levitation</u>: I   – Q6; M (gravity defiance) – Q5;
P (gravitic immunity) – Q4

– <u>Polymorphic</u>:   I – Q6; M (feature-shifting) – Q4; P
(shape-shifting) – Q2

– <u>Regeneration</u>:   I – Q6; M (fast, resilient) – Q4; P
(superior, immunities, rejuvenating) – Q3

II: MENTAL APTITUDES

– <u>Empathy</u>:   I (Intuitive) – Q6; M (accurate
scanning) – Q5; P (mass and distanced reading capacity) – Q4

– <u>Telepathy</u>:   I (tactile) – Q6; M (complexity
differentiation) – Q4; P (high strength, distance-oriented) – Q2

– <u>Telekinesis</u>:   I (lifting and moving objects) – Q5; M
(destructive bent) – Q3; P (high-strength, distance-oriented) – Q2

– <u>Pyrokinesis</u>:   I (minor) – Q5; M (major) – Q4; P
(nuclear) – Q3

– <u>Dominance</u>:   I (singular coercion) – Q3; M (absolute
coercion) – Q2; P (en masse coercion) – Q1

–<u>Imprinting</u>:   I (low-level) – Q6; M (indefinite
duration) – Q3; P (destructive, terminal) – Q1

–<u>Precognition</u>: I (impulsive, erratic) – Q4; M (controlled, accurate) – Q2; P (prescient far-sight) – Q1

– <u>Cyber-Immersion</u>: I (scanning) – Q6; M (manipulative) – Q5; P (integration and control) – Q3

– <u>Profiling</u>: I (impulsive, vague) – Q5; M (accurate) – Q4; P (temporally acute) – Q2

III: PHASIC APTITUDES

– <u>Phasing</u>: I (fast) – Q5; M (sustainable) – Q4; P (manipulative) – Q3

– <u>Molecular Fusion</u>: I (slight) – Q6; M (marked) – Q4; P (total) – Q2

– <u>Transmutation</u>: I (minor) – Q5; M (major) – Q3; P (colossal) – Q1

– <u>Teleportation</u>: I (short-distance) – Q6; M (long-distance) – Q4; P (unsighted) – Q2

IV: ELEMENTAL APTITUDES

– <u>Biokinetic</u>: I (friction, tactile) – Q6; M (friction, distant) – Q5; P (strength, sustainability) – Q4

– <u>Light Manipulation</u>: I (blasts) – 0; M (webs) – Q6; P (arrays) – Q5

– <u>Shadow Manipulation</u>:   I (blasts) – 0; M (webs) – Q6; P (arrays) – Q5

– <u>Electrical</u>:   I (manipulation) – Q5; M (counter-manipulation) – Q4; P (meteoric) – Q2

– <u>Hydro-Related</u>:   I (minor) – Q6; M (major) – Q5; P (skilled) – Q3

– <u>Bioplasmic</u>:   I (minor) – 0; M (major) – Q6; P (skilled) – Q5

The CC is not set in stone and is in fact adaptable, with the eye on maintaining a constant vigil and awareness of the gifted traits of the Changed. Using it is fairly easy. For example, tracing the aptitude levels and eventual final classification of the GOA Changed field agent Jainsa Narayanan would be done numerically and logically according to her gifts: M-class regenerative, M-class telepathy, M-class telekinesis, P-class dominance and P-class profiling amounts to the numeric value of 3+3+4+6+5. Added up, this yields the number 21, which is greater than the value of 20 minimum required for the Secondary Prime (CCSP) category.

CHAPTER FIVE

Converging Risks

Tea-time.

Such visits were often enjoyable and far in-between, but Alice relished them, because it allowed her to visit an old friend. Margaret de Witt-Emerson was someone with whom Alice had shared a lifetime, and the one person outside of the GOA Headquarters who knew exactly what was going on inside it. Alice's initiative, yes, but she felt she could deny Margaret nothing. She always justified her info leakage to the fact that Margaret too was a Changed individual, and though by no means classifiable on the GOA scales, she was nevertheless one of those few elder Changed who had such finesse with their gifts that it didn't matter in any case. It always puzzled Alice, how Margaret's Change had eluded her until in her late fifties, when Alice had already passed that age. Margaret was now about a hundred and twenty, and looked not a day older than a well-weathered sixty. Despite her aged appearance, no one could last long under the critical scrutiny of those winter-grey English eyes and the pursed lips that only British condescension could muster. With Alice, Margaret smiled more, because there were no secrets between them. Margaret, though by no means a scarce individual – she had the kind of quiet wealth that spawned mega-conglomerate business empires – kept to herself mostly, save for the occasional forays into social circles. Such instances would never have worked in the past, but with gene-driven rejuvenation a standard, everyday perk of the wealthy these days, Margaret could risk herself in the social circles of New York and Washington for longer these days, without attracting attention based on how little her physical appearance changed over the years. So to the world, Margaret de Witt-Emerson was a chic, aging dowager of a woman with massively far-reaching contacts in every avenue of life, and a marvellous organiser of the most elegant parties where the rich and mostly non-famous hobnobbed until the early hours of dawn. To the few who knew, and GOA did know of her, she was in fact a Changed individual with regenerative and rejuvenative properties in her repertoire.

"I see you've redecorated the place, it looks nice," Alice said, taking a delicate sip of her tea. She savoured the brew – Darjeeling – and closed her eyes. She opened them again when Margaret snorted.

"You visit me far too little for my liking, Alice. I've redone the entire house twice since the last time you came!"

"You know how busy I am, what with the new addition to GOA's observations," Alice remarked, maintaining pointed eye contact to alert Margaret of what she spoke of. The older-looking woman placed her own tea cup and saucer on the table before her, edging forward on her seat, rapt.

"And how is it going with your young prodigy? The last time you were here, you were haggard with the strain of taming his wayward gifts. But I must admit, you look much better now. And it's not the weather, I can assure you," she finished, sniffing. Alice smiled.

"He has been tamed, so to speak. But with every day that goes by there is something new. Different. He is inconstant yet."

"Then you were right to suspect," Margaret replied, gasping. She placed a frail-seeming hand on her bosom and breathed deeply. "I cannot believe it! So soon, within seventy years of the last!"

"There is no precedent for such individuals," Alice amended. "He is only the second to come close to the power of the one we lost seventy years ago."

"But you've said it yourself," Margaret interjected. "There is as yet no constancy. Granted, that is always the case with any Changed growing into his or her powers, but for the fact that you also mentioned a daily alteration. I have very little doubt about what

GOA is going to place on his classification table." Margaret leaned back, eyes glinting. She took a genteel sip from her own cup and stared out over the Delaware Bay, which appeared grey and drab despite the crisp morning blue sky and the green of the lawn of her estate which stretched to the water's edge.

"I'm afraid of what will happen when that occurs," Alice confided. "He has expressed, on numerous occasions, his wish to join our ranks as an operative, but what job do you give such a gifted young man?"

"He need not become a field worker," Margaret mused, "but a desk job would also be tedious. You could always give him free rein."

"I'm sorry?"

"Let him pursue a life of normalcy. As whatever he likes. But by his own allowance, keep watch over him, monitor his movements. Allow him a normal existence, within limitations set by himself."

"That is all very well and good, but not entirely the matter that bothers me right now," Alice said, finishing her tea. Margaret's eyes narrowed.

"Then what is it? Come now my dear, I am no mind reader, thank goodness, but I am a curious old woman."

"Hardly," Alice said, chuckling. She was older than Margaret, but looked in her mid-forties. A perk of having her Change come over her far earlier than Margaret's had. Her merriment lasted no longer than the chuckle, though, and was replaced with a sigh. "In the last decade or so, there have been several casualties in the GOA Changed ranks. Heaven knows we are so few, but we've had losses on our side."

"Side?" Margaret queried critically.

"I say side because it would appear there are several places where the Changed, whether GOA affiliated or simply monitored, cannot stray into, or else suffer death."

"How do you know they died?" Margaret demanded. A young doe-eyed maid arrived to take away the tea cups and confectionaries, and Alice waited for her to leave before she continued.

"A hunch, confirmed by our auric profilers. We risked a lot in taking them to the places where these Changed individuals were last seen, but the prognosis is usually the same: violence, death."

"Faugh! Profilers. An inexact gift at best," Margaret scoffed.

"Like precognition, yes, but then there they are, and at least seventy-five percent of all such assumptions and predictions made turn out to happen, or have happened, as they were said to. I myself have not enough trust in such things, but they are evidential, and the only proof we can garner. And if they are right, then GOA faces a serious threat."

"How so?" Margaret asked, thoroughly entertained even as she was intrigued.

"We fear there are some Changed who hunt others. They are like vampires, cannibals, feeding off their own kind or simply destroying them outright," Alice all but whispered.

"What hot spots?"

"In the northern hemisphere: New York, Chicago, Boston, London, Paris, Barcelona, Berlin, Cairo and Beijing. In all of those cities we have sketchy reports only of Changed activity, even though in the smaller communities just outside these cities we have reports of many Changed. I suppose 'dead zones' would be a better description of these cities."

"And you suspect other Changed are responsible for this?"

"It is a suspicion, nothing more. But it opens up so many possibilities: how many Changed that kill their own kind in these cities? Is it a cult of sorts? Why these cities? Is there any significance to the fact that there are nine such zones, one for each city? All of these questions cannot be answered. Unless things get desperate."

"And when do you suppose that is?" Margaret asked. "You sound desperate enough already."

"I don't wish to send any of my people to their deaths," Alice breathed, eyes focused on some unknown point in the distance.

"Then train your young prodigy into the best damned powerhouse there is and launch him at those places," Margaret shrugged, leaning back in her sofa. She regarded Alice beadily, like a bird eyeing food. And then, after a few more moments of scrutiny, her eyes widened. "You think he's not just the second potential GenneY, do you?" Alice shook her head, and a faint tugging of the corners of her mouth alerted Margaret to how accurately she had scored. "You think there are more, and they're in these cities. Monstrous!"

"But what if I'm right? If there are nine other Nth Primers in these cities, what manner of chaos could occur if GOA cannot restrain them? These people are dangerously powerful, and there is little anyone can do to stop them if they get it into their heads that hiding from the eyes of the unsuspecting world is no longer necessary!"

"You're clutching at straws, dear," Margaret said, firmly but kindly. "This is an elegant little theory you've concocted, but a theory nonetheless. Leave it at that until you can fling enough resources at whatever is bothering you."

"And if by then it's too late?" Alice asked.

"Then perhaps your task is to make sure you and your people are prepared before it is too late," Margaret replied, eyes glittering.

"You ever wonder what it is they're talking about?"

The girl ducked in fully behind the door, which she had painstakingly pushed ajar in order to hear. But she had known exactly what would happen; the same thing that happened every time: nothing. She could never hear anything, and she blamed it largely on the presence of the strong-boned, handsome woman who often came for tea with Maggie.

110

"This is the reason you demanded I be here?" the girl's companion asked sharply, raising a peremptory brow.

"Oh shush, your library can wait," the girl snapped, flapping her hands. "The acoustics in that room are superb, so why the hell can't we hear anything?"

"You say that as if you're about to launch into a train of thought," the boy said condescendingly. He received a punch on the shoulder from the girl, and proceeded to rubbing the spot vigorously. "Ow! Jeez, what was that for?"

"Be quiet, I'm trying to figure this out," the girl said, forehead furrowing. The boy rolled his eyes.

"Oh for God's sake, you really don't need to be a neurologist to figure this one out!" he snorted. The girl's eyes narrowed, and she moved closer to him. She lifted one hand, finger pointing. She was barely tall enough to reach his chin, but she made up for it in sheer belligerence. "Shall I continue?"

"You better," the girl demanded. The boy shook his head, indicating his clear disdain for the situation.

"Maggie is like us, right?" he asked.

"More or less," the girl replied.

"She's a Changed. That's why we're here. No other real reason. We're her protégés."

"Get to the point."

"Patience is a virtue."

"Long-windedness isn't so hurry up!" she threatened, raising a balled hand.

"That woman in there with her is a Changed too, why else do you think we can't hear anything?"

"I would have chalked it up to Maggie doing something we've never seen her do. Like a gift she's been hiding from us."

"Yeah, that's it," the boy replied sarcastically. "Maggie told us all about her high-level gifts like regeneration, rejuvenation and the scary thing she does with trespassers –"

"You mean the part where she places her hands on their heads and drains them dry of info?"

"– yeah, hint, hint, and you think she wouldn't tell us about a sound blanket gift she has? Please!"

"I don't like that tone, mister!" the girl snarled, but hardly angrily.

"Like I care, I'm going back to the library," her companion said, and turned to go. She grabbed him by the arm, face suddenly beseeching.

"Oh come on Ryan, help me out here! Aren't you the least bit interested to find out what's going on in there? I bet it's a secret government plot, or a cover-up, or someone trying to blackmail Maggie into giving them money!"

"And so she invites them in for tea," the boy, Ryan, replied. "Alyssa, grow up! That woman in there is either a Changed, or Maggie has devices that dampen sound when she needs it."

"Ah hah!" Alyssa yelled, jumping up and down. Ryan frowned.

"No way," he breathed, then frowned again. "Now look what you've done."

"Got you interested there, didn't I?" Alyssa queried, grinning.

"Sometimes I think I hate you," Ryan remarked.

"But it never lasts, does it?" she replied.

"How is Alexis doing?" Margaret asked.

"She's wayward and rarely applies herself. I'm told its common among highly gifted people sometimes. A reverse reaction to the expectancies placed on them," Alice said. "She baits me sometimes, and though I dislike it to. instruct her, it seems to be the only way to get anything through to her. Fortunately she enjoys field work, which keeps her in check most of the time."

"You should send her to me. I know how to handle girls like her," Margaret replied acerbically.

"Though I have no doubt you can, Margaret, I feel Alexis needs to be shaped by the people she will one day work intimately with. And I don't want her broken, I want her to find her own way and realize the importance of matters by herself, not have it forced onto her."

"You were always too lenient. I keep a firmer hand on my two."

"The two listening at the door," Alice asked, mouth hinting at a grin. Margaret's eyes widened with affront, and she was about to rise when Alice shook her head. "Wait. Sometimes a shock can be more formative, than a direct outburst."

"But you were always so much better at scheming!" Margaret replied, smiling widely, conspiratorially.

"Misdirection," Alice said, and smiled fully.

"Why is Maggie smiling? I've never seen her smile like that before!" Alyssa said, whispering furiously.

"What exactly do you want me to do?" Ryan demanded, reluctance evident in his voice.

"Moral support, in case we get caught," Alyssa rejoined.

"Oh, right. In case we get caught."

"Shhh! Keep it down, they're talking again. Hey, I think I can hear something."

"It gets quite hard to maintain more than three illusions at one time, I can assure you," a voice said, and both Ryan and Alyssa yelled as they jumped with fright. They spun about defensively, locating the origin of the voice from behind them. Maggie was standing beside the red-haired woman, both of them smiling, though Maggie's smile was almost predatory. "Alyssa and Ryan, right?"

"Maggie we didn't mean to eavesdrop, we swear –" Alyssa began, and Margaret's smile slipped away completely, replaced by a strict posture and expression.

"Of course you did!" she snapped sternly. "I thought I've told you how rude such a thing is, Alyssa!"

"Curiosity is not uncommon with the Changed," the woman said. She walked forward a step – she was only slightly taller than Alyssa, but also seemed to be buoyed up by a sense of inner confidence and self-assurance, which lent her more than physical height. "My name is Alice."

"Alyssa," Alyssa replied shakily, taking Alice's proffered hand. Ryan remained behind her, and waved weakly.

"Ryan!" Margaret snapped, and he jumped, hastily extending his own hand as well. Alice stared deeply into their eyes, marking their faces for anything. Her almost-smile remained in full force.

"They seem wonderful," she said after a moment.

"How did you do that?" Alyssa interrupted, ignoring the thunderous look of affront on Margaret's face. "The illusions, I mean."

"I am what you call an empath. A high-level one. Such things are not hard to do, and the curious and snooping mind is open to almost anything, so it wasn't hard for me to place the false images in your heads."

"You can read minds?" Ryan asked, still timid, but intrigued as well. Alice nodded. "I've read about telepathy, and Maggie's told us about empaths, but I thought they were really rare."

"Geek," Alyssa whispered under her breath.

"Oh they are remarkably rare if you don't know where to look. And unless you are one yourself, it is even harder to find one," Alice replied conversationally. She turned to Margaret. "I've never spoken to them before. Surely they can join us outside for a refreshing walk?"

"Ryan may, since it is clear he has run afoul of another of Alyssa's schemes," Margaret replied airily. Her eyes silenced the explosive protest from Alyssa, whose face became gloomy and dejected, as she turned around, attempting to stride holes in the wooden floorboards of the hallway, making off for her room. Seemingly satisfied with her rebuke, Margaret once more affected a smile, and indicated that Ryan fall in line with her and Alice, as they walked outside.

"I've seen you here before, but I've never plucked up the courage to ask Maggie who you are," Ryan said awkwardly. He towered over both Margaret and Alice, but seemed by far the less confident one.

"Keeping to oneself is not a bad thing, Ryan," Margaret replied. "And Alyssa is far too curious for her own good."

"Margaret tells me you're a low-spatial Changed," Alice said.

"I beg your pardon?" Ryan queried owlishly.

"A visual adept," Alice amended, none too hastily. "Someone capable of fooling the eyes of onlookers, as well as a gifted teleporter."

"Only to places I can see," Ryan replied, blushing as though he had received a compliment.

"My illusions are placed in the mind, whereas yours can fool even the most gifted," Alice added. "A unique skill, I might add. I know of two other teleporters, you might be interested in meeting them."

"Uh, I'd like that if Miss Margaret will allow it," Ryan stammered.

"Ryan dear, please wait here a moment while I ask Alice something," Margaret said cheerily, then took Alice aside. "You're not doing what I think you're doing," she grated under her breath, sounding furious.

"I understand they are you protégés, but someone like Ryan can hardly learn confidence from boarding school tactics lacking the input of a man," Alice replied amiably.

"Recruiting for GOA is not something I expected you to peddle right here!" Margaret snarled.

"I simply think he needs to know what his options are. Will you keep him locked up here forever?"

"That is his decision!"

"Then allow me to broaden his horizons, and we'll see what he decides," Alice replied. Margaret, not really mollified but also incapable of denying Alice's reasoning, sighed and gave a curt nod. When they turned around to face Ryan again both wore smiles. Alice took the lead by a pace. "Ryan, I'd like to tell you about something important. Something I'm sure you'd like."

There were days she hated New York. She often felt as if something was lurking just beyond her senses. She was hardly as powerful an empath as some, but the centuries of being what she was had honed her mind to be receptive of many things, and she had also learnt to augment her deficient powers with her sufficient ones, a nifty skill. And she knew enough to trust her instincts when something began gnawing at her perceptions. And it was definitely not *him*; there was never any warning when he did something impulsive, or decided to drop in. Which happened rarely these days, mercifully.

Persephone toyed with the champagne flute in her hand, letting it loll about in her grasp. She stared at the never-sleeping city below, the view that was normally breathtaking now without any charm at all. Whatever was out there had to be found, and fast. If it was another Changed, she wanted to know, and if this Changed was powerful, he or she had to be eliminated. She might not like the city all that much any more, but it was hers, and she brooked no interference. She had been very persuasive in the past, and those who refused to leave were simply killed out of hand.

She knew there were other Changed in New York. You could not have a city that big without any gifted individuals, but most of them never warranted her attention. They would never amount to much, at least not enough to threaten her. But that was beside the point, beyond the fact that it gave her an amusing way to pass the time, rooting out and obliterating the ones that could threaten her. It gave her supreme joy when she killed off another potential danger. But that was all, really. Other than the thrill of hunting and killing, there really was nothing else for her here. She didn't know what else there was, apart from the occasional lover. Anything that caught her eyes: strong body, strong facial features, the eyes, anything. Sometimes she would even entertain a low-level Changed, enjoy the pleasures such bed sports could allow, and then execute him with brutal force. Doing that often required her to change the sheets, because blood hardly washed out of satin, but then, the ecstasy of the kill made up for it. And her power was such that no one questioned her actions. Not even her most trusted aides.

She vacated the privacy of her bedroom and made down the elevator for the work hub. She had nothing else to do, and sleeplessness robbed her of rest. Perhaps doing something distasteful would alert her once more to something interesting to do, and then she would eventually fall asleep. And she had just the right kind of distasteful thing in mind.

Inside the hub, there was only one solitary light burning. Persephone didn't even know why, it wasn't as though the Circuit needed light to see. Maybe he... it... needed the comfort of the glow, or some such nonsense. Persephone walked closer, as close as she dared come to the scruffy excuse for a Changed being, and tapped her foot, waiting for him to appear from underneath the desk, where he had purportedly made a nest of sorts. At least it wasn't like an animal's nest, Persephone thought, or she would have crushed the life from the onerous little beast before he could even start working. No, it was a nest of cables and wires, like a self-rigged hole that seemed to charge him up. Like a battery. Even the thought of such a thing curled her lips with disgust.

"Any progress?" she asked, not bending down or deigning to look at him. She had seen enough the first time: the Circuit looked like a rat in dishevelled clothes, a rotund and smelly individual who had made several passes already at the other women working in the hub. Persephone had given them enough leeway to repel the odious creature's attentions, but not to disrupt his work. "Well?"

It took a few more moments for the Circuit to emerge, his hair standing in tufts from his otherwise bald pate. He looked up at Persephone, who stared down through slit eyes, radiating contempt.

"Not much, but I think there are some of your people who are working against you, from the inside."

"And this is not news?" Persephone barked angrily, throwing the flute explosively to the floor. "I said any information, you little worm!" The Circuit knew not to mess with his current employer. He ducked out of what he hoped was harm's way, head bowed, hands held up pleadingly.

"You did not specify what you were looking for my lady!" he whined. "I am merely doing routine checks through the systems to see where data streams don't match and where the information relays have been –"

"Enough!" she snarled. "Spare me the techno-drivel and get to the point!"

"Someone has been erasing the day-to-day rosters concerning data storage."

"Meaning?" Persephone asked, immediately sounding bored. It was merely to hide the fact that she disdained the fact that she knew nothing really of what the Circuit was jabbering about. She wanted a straight answer, not tortuous explanations.

"One of your people is siphoning information to an unknown location and erasing their tracks," the Circuit replied. He still kept his head down, because if there was one thing he had discovered recently, it was that Persephone was mercurial and killed on a whim. He had seen it happen twice now, once with one of her supposedly most trusted aides, and he knew that any lapse on his behalf would be his head. He waited for an unseen blow to land, but none did. He looked up very slowly and warily, and was mildly surprised to see Persephone staring off into the distance, her exquisite mouth working soundlessly, eyes first narrowing and then widening. If he hadn't known better he would have thought she was insane and ready to foam at the mouth. "My lady?"

"A leak?" she queried, half to herself. The Circuit nodded vigorously.

"A spy, perhaps?" he ventured.

"Don't be a fool!" Persephone snapped, focusing on him again with all the aggression and insistency of her darkly glittering eyes. "In twenty years that I've been here there has only been one spy found amongst my people, and I took care of that. No, my people are loyal, but obviously they can still be bought. Or threatened by someone stronger." The words twisted her mouth – admissions that she was not the strongest of the Changed galled her greatly, but the truth was rarely kind. "Continue with what you're doing. Find the leak, and I will reward you handsomely." She spun on her heel and strode from the hub, remembering what she had just done, and shivered. But then she smiled: it was distasteful, speaking to the Circuit. He made her feel dirty. Still, she had achieved the desired effect. She was beginning to grow tired, but just enough so to ration herself. She would have some fun. Once back inside her bedroom, she spoke to the vo-comm, "Karen, send someone to run my bath. And send for someone to join me. Tall, tanned and blonde." She smiled after relaying the orders, knowing that the small things in life that still amused her, were at the very least still also engrossing enough to banish the boredom.

CHAPTER SIX

Trade-Offs

He was having trouble concentrating.

The bottom line was that he had never quite considered having himself trained. The thought had never crossed his mind, if only because entertaining such a notion had seemed absurd; who could train him? There had never been the possibility of training because there had never before existed such a place as this, with people like this. And Alex had been quick to offer to teach him things. Still, after assuring their parents they were fine, and would see Daniel soon - they hoped – it had only been a week since they'd arrived at GOA HQ. They'd taken the tour, seeing everything except highest classification locations, and then, Alex had stepped in, offering to start him on some training.

"Concentrate!" Alex snapped moodily. His eyes snapped open as he started, regarding her thunderous expression. "You won't get anywhere without concentrating!"

"I *am* concentrating," Luke replied apologetically, but he raised an eyebrow. "Something wrong?" It was exactly the question she had wanted to hear. Like a tsunami she broke down moaning, tears threatening, her exquisite doll features puckering as though she wanted to screech.

"Alice is sending me away!"

"What?" Luke gasped, stunned. In his head the small world that had begun forming around Alex and the people at GOA the last two weeks took a knock as he ran through the possibilities of what would happen, should Alex leave. "Why?"

"Discipline!" Alex snarled, and then her face scrunched up in a fit of squealing rage. "Why do I need discipline?" Luke remained silent, feeling ill-equipped to answer such a question. "I mean, I know I'm a little wayward, and I like breaking rules, but why do I get booted? Why not Chris, he's the fucking 'break-everything-expensive-with-glee' boy!" Alex rose and began pacing about, leaving Luke to stare after her. "And I bet I know where she's sending me."

"Where?" Alex turned to face Luke, her face etched with excessive revulsion and horror.

"Margaret!" she said, voice breaking.

"Margaret?" Luke queried. He also rose, and took an experimental step forward, not quite knowing what would happen if he did. Alex nodded, as if Luke simply saying the name as well made it more horrific.

"She's a crazy old bat from ancient England, and she breaks little girls' spirits and turns them into small-minded fifties wives who have dinner ready at eight!" Alex charged ahead, her words made all the more amusing by the fact that she pronounced them with all the conviction of an atomic bomb. She was shaking her hands with agitation, her eyes growing larger and larger. Luke held up his hands, feeling as though he was approaching a rabid animal. He was both shocked and amused, but he didn't want Alex to see he wanted to grin at her exaggerated predicament. He had no idea what this Margaret woman did, or what she was capable of, but he warranted that since Alex was having such a reaction, the woman was a Changed, and an intimidating one. "Why would Alice do this to me?"

"I don't know," Luke ventured, taking another step closer. "She's coming back soon, isn't she?"

"She's gonna make me pack everything I own while she watches!" Alex wailed, eyes now wide and frantic, on the verge of a breakdown. "She'll be smiling happily!"

"I don't think it's that bad," Luke added, and Alex whirled, her furious eyes fixing on him.

"Not that bad? Not that bad? A finishing school for the Changed, that's what Margaret de Witt-Emerson is good for! She's a flashback out of the nineteenth century! I bet she even comes from there! A special case of vicious mutation, someone who's been old for so long she exists by crushing the youthful until they look just like her!"

Luke couldn't help it. He suddenly doubled over and burst out laughing, preparing himself for a vicious mental lash of some sort in spite of his amusement. But nothing happened, except that when he lifted his head, Alex was glaring at him in utter shock, her mouth open and working soundlessly. He continued laughing, leaning against the nearest wall as he shook with merriment. Finally, after composing himself a little more and wiping the tears from his eyes, he looked at her.

"I'm sorry," he managed in between gulps for fresh air. "But that was the most paranoid collection of descriptions I've ever heard!"

"You wouldn't say that if you knew what Margaret did," Alex countered moodily, her anger subsiding but nowhere near gone yet.

"And what does Margaret do?"

"She'll put me in the same class of handling as her other two flunkies," Alex said, looking straight ahead into space at no discernible point. "Two low-level Changed who do her bidding."

"How do you know all this?" Luke asked, puzzled. He took Alex by the arm and manoeuvred her to one of the seats. Alex allowed herself to be seated, appearing as if in a daze.

"Archives," Alex mouthed. "Hardcopy records of most of the Changed GOA keeps track of. I go there a lot, when I'm bored. Margaret, or 'Maggie' as Alice calls her, is a powerful Changed with physical and spatial-immersive skills. Also quite hard to crack – she has a very dense and natural mental barrier. That's why she's so damn scary."

"So you're afraid of her," Luke said.

"Honey you don't understand how that woman upsets me," Alex said, placing a hand on Luke's shoulder, a small show of thanks for his support. Even if he was only really talking and not much else. "She and Alice go way back. They're like school friends or something, I don't know, the history's vague. Needless to say, Margaret is terribly rich, partly funds some of Alice's GOA ventures and always keeps an eye out for anything useful or interesting regarding other Changed. She's like a vulture with observational tendencies and no appetite for the kill."

Luke merely listened attentively, amazed at how the information just streamed from Alex's mouth. He had never quite realized what she did with her spare time, but apparently, snooping was one of her favourites. And then his former thoughts returned, and he frowned. He remained silent until Alex asked after his hush.

"So I guess Charlie will take over training me, unless you guys have another major empath stashed here somewhere."

"Charlie won't be able to do that, he's cleared of such things while he takes care of –" Alex's eyes widened, and she stared pointedly at Luke. "Oh my word, you. Luke, baby, are you going to miss me?" She sidled closer, smiling widely, her features transformed by a pleased look. "I didn't know that." Luke, not quite sure where this would lead, and holding back bashfully, remained silent. "That is probably the sweetest thing anyone's ever insinuated!"

"I want to stay with the GOA," Luke amended. "I think maybe for the first time I feel welcome somewhere. So I will need training."

"Ooh, maybe Alice will let me stay if she grants me full control of your training!" Alex gushed, her elation now cresting sharply in contrast with her former disconcerted outburst. "Or maybe you could come with me!"

"What?" Luke asked sharply, shocked for the second time.

"Yeah, then at least I won't be alone with the bloodsucking scow from the seventeenth century!"

"But I can't leave my brother," Luke challenged. Alex halted, then stood and grabbed Luke's hand, tugging at his arm.

"He's a big boy, he can take care of himself. Plus I heard he was going back home for a week or so to get Joanie, so he won't be alone! C'mon, Luke!" she whined imploringly. "Please? For me?"

Luke didn't know how to say no, so he merely trampled after Alex as she made for wherever. But something told him the next week would be a very interesting one.

On Alice's return, Alex and Luke were waiting.

They met her at the landing platform, Luke barely containing Alex as she stormed down on Alice, who regarded her with a nonchalant air.

"You're not sending me to that woman, are you?" she demanded immediately, face a mask of anger and petulance.

"Hey!" a tall man behind Alice fired, frowning. Alex fixed him with a baleful stare, but then decided to ignore him.

"Alex, meet Ryan Alford, he will be staying here for a while."

"Oh, I see," Alex replied, slowly nodding. "An exchange. I get it. When do I leave?"

"Not immediately," Alice countered, and then she did smile. The desired effect happened, for Alex practically exploded.

"How can you do this to me? I belong here, I live here! You can't just evict me!"

"Can we take this to my office?" Alice asked, and instead of waiting for an affirmative she strode past the outraged Alex. She smiled warmly at Luke, who nodded and held out his hand to Ryan. Ryan, still a little upset and flustered by his situation, took it gingerly and with a wan smile. He looked askance at Alex, then followed after Alice.

"Is this punishment?" Alex asked, when they had entered Alice's office. "Is it really that bad?"

"Do you want me to spell it out for you?" Alice asked, seating herself and organizing folders on her desk. She didn't look up at Alex.

"Yeah, maybe!"

"Then let's put things in perspective. You will be sent to New York, on assignment from GOA, to monitor activity on a peculiar Changed situation there. While you are there you will keep a low profile and you will be the guest of Lady Margaret de Witt-Emerson, a close friend –"

"I know who she is!" Alex snapped. "The breaker of spirits, the changer of personalities!"

"I resent that!" Ryan rejoined, rising. He didn't back down from Alex's glare. "Margaret is the soul of generosity and kindness, and she –"

"She takes pride in beating the spirit out of young people!" Alex overrode him.

"Enough!" Alice said, not loudly, but very finally. "Alex, you are a chartered GOA affiliate and subject to the orders of the command section, which I am part of. The decision is final."

"So you think I screwed up, is that it? How exactly did I do that?"

"You are a wayward girl too enamoured of her own power, and you need discipline," Alice replied. "Margaret will give you a little perspective on that."

"So why didn't you just come out and say that in the first place? Afraid of flaunting your own procedures?"

"There is actually a Changed situation going on in New York," Alice said with a knowing smile. "You will be the eyes and ears. Staying at Margaret's estate will provide you with perfect place to lie low when you scout out the situation."

"Oh, how convenient!" Alex hacked. "So I get sent on assignment and boot camp at the same time. But this guy," she pointed at Ryan, "fills in for me while I'm gone, which I bet is indefinitely. Nice, oh, very rich too! A chartered GOA affiliate, and because I show some guts and spirit you think you can handle me like a little robot. Switch on, switch off! There are rules against you abusing your power!"

"There is no real time window for this operation," Alice said, eerily calm. "So you will be gone for some time. If you settle down and handle this like the twenty-four-year-old you appear to be, perhaps then you will see the change of surroundings as a welcome thing."

"You're sending me away from the people I care about so you can gratify your own sense of security. Admit it, you're afraid you can't control me," Alex said, her voice lowering to a dangerous level. Alice merely stared at her, her face a featureless mask that betrayed nothing at all. At length, when Alex became uncomfortable with no show of emotion, Alice's eyes narrowed slightly.

"Without ego or arrogance I can tell you, Alexis Neiman, that there is not a thing you can do that would upset me for long. There is not a gift in your body or your mind that can threaten me, and there is not a place you can go where I cannot find you. Do you want to know the absolute truth?" Alice rose, and Alex backed away, terror at the calm simplicity of Alice's convictions plain on her face. "I am sending you away because you are a menace, an annoyance that I cannot write off. And so I am sending you to Margaret, because there you will be under her jurisdiction, under her eyes and her tutelage. Here, you only serve to annoy me, and you hardly ever do as you are told. So do not, *do not*, throw about your paltry excuse of being a GOA affiliate, and me abusing my power. You snoop and you ferret out information and you think I don't know, but my dear Alexis, you failed to read up on me. You missed some key pieces, if you did."

"Really?" Alex asked, mortified but forced in spite of her rising terror to continue. Luke watched first her and then Alice, and he didn't know what to do. He didn't know Alice well save for the individual reports from the other Changed she had contact with, but this quiet horror and irrefutable power was definitely not part of any story he'd heard. He looked quickly at Ryan, but the young man seemed lost in his own world, or else petrified of the woman that had brought him here.

"You do not cross me, Alexis," Alice continued, and judging by the slight rise in the cadence of her words, she was building to a finish. "You do not flaunt your spirit before me when you are sworn by oath and contract to obey my words. And when you exaggerate something, have the courage to admit its falsehoods. To Margaret you will go, and until I have heard favourable reports of your progress, both personal and regarding the assignment, you will not set foot here. Your clearance is revoked." Silence, utter and absolute, followed the chilling commands. Luke swallowed, and cringed, hoping even that sound didn't make any impact on the silence surrounding them. Alice was staring pointedly at Alex, who was stifling tears that pooled in her eyes. Ryan showed nothing beyond a very pale expression that hovered between indecision and fear. After what seemed the most excruciatingly awkward of times, Alex sniffed, wiped the palm of her hand vigorously across her eyes and tilted her chin upwards, gathering some dignity. The gesture was lost on Alice.

"So that's it, huh?" Alex asked, smiling weakly though the tears still threatened. "I sign a contract and my life gets balanced without my consent."

"Then maybe you should have read the finer details, instead of signing out of sheer curiosity," Alice remarked. There was no sarcasm in the words, but the sheer lack of emotive force indicated the disregard for Alex's plight. If Alice felt remorse over her words there was no power in the entire GOA Headquarters that could persuade her to show any of it. "Perhaps when you've learnt that life is not what you want of it but what you make of it, you will appreciate the decision that I've made in sending you away. And if you truly want to return, then you will know what to do. Now, you are dismissed. Your flight leaves within the hour." Alice looked away, and an even clearer sign of dismissal Alex would not get. And yet Alex was not cowed that easily, at the least not for too long.

Scraping up one final iota of defiance, she remained and voiced her demand.

"I want Luke to come with me," she said simply, sniffing back the last of her tears. She remained where she was, by her posture if not by her facial expression demanding that Alice take notice. The GOA Changed Director looked up, her face betraying nonchalance and no-nonsense business intrigue, but nothing more.

"And why is that?"

"Because he needs training. And because Charlie doesn't handle training now that he has Daniel. And because Luke wants to join GOA eventually, and he will need training."

"And what makes you think that you are the only higher-level empath that GOA has that is capable of training Luke?" Alice queried. Luke took a quick breath, almost unnerved beyond his ability to hide just how much Alice's deadpan, interrogative methods of dissecting a simple conversation upset him. His reaction forced Alice and Alex both to regard him, and though he felt trapped like a worm between the intense scrutiny of two birds, he stood his ground, and opened his mouth before he could even think carefully over what he wanted to say.

"I wouldn't mind going with Alex," he said in a rush. "But there is something else I need to know before I agree!"

"What?" Alex demanded, the desperation clear in her voice. Alice, by contrast, sighed and looked away as if perplexed, the first real show of emotion she had given since entering her office.

"Why is it that everyone feels the need to voice conditions when an executive decision has been made?" Alice queried. But she didn't seem eager to try the same tactic on Luke that she had just used to derail Alex, so she pursed her lips and looked at him in silence. After a tense moment, Luke realized she was waiting for him to speak his piece.

"I don't know how long it will take, but if I go with Alex now, I want to come back the moment Charlie agrees that we may see

Danny. That's the main reason I came here, and it hasn't changed despite my other choices."

"Is that it? No tax-free existence for life, no erasure of family records for safety reasons?" Alice challenged snidely, and Luke drew a sharp breath. Alice was irritated, and she didn't mind showing it to him. Alex seemed beyond her usual self and didn't seem to register Alice's changed approach. Luke merely shook his head slowly, unsure what a faster reaction would get him, or reveal to Alice. She nodded curtly, and he turned to Alex. "Done. And now, Alex, before you leave us for the nonce, take Ryan outside with you and take him to the Mess level." Alex pressed her lips together, not making eye contact with Alice. Ryan, quiet and unresponsive the whole time, came alive and very nearly ran for the door, and was only too eager to follow Alex outside. Alice crossed from behind her desk slowly, in measured steps, and halted a few feet from Luke. He towered over her, but even untrained eyes would see who was by far the superior. Luke stared at her as much as he dared, trying to gauge her intentions. The coldly glittering grey eyes remained placid pools of immutable inspection, and her mouth was parted slightly; it could go anywhere, from a smile to anger. "Did you really think this decision through?" she asked, causing Luke to start. She noted it, and a very vague curvature of the corners of her mouth seemed to melt the sensation of danger he felt coming from her.

"I didn't really," he admitted, and Alice did smile, though if the smile touched her eyes Luke was unwilling to guess.

"I thought as much. One can get caught up so easily in Alex's wake. The lack of attention given to the right kind of personality can lead to methods of monopolizing the deficit in a completely demanding way from other people."

"I'm sorry, I don't quite follow," Luke said, swallowing.

"Alexis craves attention, and she will force that demand on anyone remotely willing. I doubt she would resort to coercion – even a very weak empath can resist the most focused attempts at coercion, and you are by all accounts above average, Lucas Hirsch. So I guess we can rule such a thing from the picture. But then you must have fallen for her charms, one way or another. Which is it?"

"Alex offered to train me," Luke said, feeling like a prisoner being interrogated despite Alice's amiable tone of voice. "She said Charlie wouldn't agree to something like it."

"And did you think perhaps that I myself could handle such a matter?" Alice asked.

"No, I...I didn't think you would have time. Nor would I presume." Luke replied, unbalanced. Alice laughed then, a very disarming show of emotion.

"The truth is that I don't have time. I rarely have time for anything beyond work these days. And Alexis does seem to be more than willing to train you. Very well, it is settled." Alice turned back again, ready to retake her seat behind the desk. When Luke remained, she halted before sitting down. "Something else?"

"Are there any others in GOA? Other empaths, I mean, who can train me?"

"No," Alice said, shaking her head. "I am sorry to say that GOA has a limited amount of Changed personnel beyond the ones on the base, and some in the field. We have empaths, but none capable of training someone of above average capacity such as yourself. I'm afraid Alexis will train you."

"May I see my brother before I go?" Luke asked finally. Alice had already seated herself, and did not deign to look up again as she answered.

"If you can find him fast enough. Otherwise I will have someone give him the news, and if you want, a missive sent to your parents via your brother." Luke nodded, hoping she caught his compliance, and left the office. He hoped Alex was in her rooms, because he didn't feel like making detours with so little time before departure. He waited until he was several doors from Alice's office, then leaned against the wall, closed his eyes and sent his mind outward.

"Alex?"

"In my bedroom," the despondent reply came. Luke, relieved that he could cut back on unnecessary time consumption, began walking again.

"I'll see you in the Mess saloon in twenty minutes. I have to find Nathan."

"You're going with me?" Alex sent hopefully, and Luke nodded, flooding the link with affirmation, hoping it would soothe her.

"I have to tell him, and I don't think he'll like it, but I will be leaving with you, okay?" he sent.

"Okay. He's in the fourth hangar bay, near the testing facilities." Luke severed the connection and hurried towards the nearest lift, hoping he could secure a fast hovepad to the testing facilities.

Nathan watched the scene with rapt interest. He stood with Chris in the in-hangar laboratory where a multitude of devices and small vehicles rested on platforms or hung suspended from razor-fine wires, or else floated in the soft but powerful currents of zerograv energy fields. The particular thing that held his attention now was a suit that felt like liquid fiber beneath his touch. It felt almost too soft to be of any use, almost like an expensive silk shirt that could be worn only once. He withdrew his hand as Chris grinned next to him.

"I know, isn't it the weirdest thing?" the man asked, as if he had read Nathan's thoughts. "Techs came up with this baby because you can't always be wearing a field ops suit when you're on assignment. This baby fits nicely under any other clothes you can wear, and its actually stronger than a field suit. Bad news is you can't survive too long in cold weather with only this on. They're still working on a bio-adaptive addition that will monitor body heat and adjust to compensate for outside forces."

"So this is actual government standard stuff?" Nathan asked, thrilled. Chris, noting his interest, chuckled.

"Betcha you didn't think you'd ever get to see some of this stuff, right?" Nathan shook his head. "Well, there's actually a reason you're allowed to see all of this."

"Yeah?"

"Alice thinks you're gonna join GOA if you get a taste of the things we handle, do and create," Chris continued. "Shrewd woman, Alice. I think she knew exactly what would catch your fancy."

"But I didn't say I would stay," Nathan said, not so thrilled anymore. Chris shrugged.

"Working for GOA ain't that bad, I can guarantee it. And the last two weeks have shown me just how much you enjoyed all the high-tech gadgetry here, so Alice couldn't have been far wrong, could she?"

Chris nodded at the tech standing close by, and the man removed the suit. Nathan watched the procedure without really focusing. He mulled over Chris's words, thinking what to say.

"Do I have to work for GOA? What if I decided I want to go home, marry Joanie and live like a normal human being?"

"Hey, its no sweat off our backs. I think that Alice merely wants all the people she can get. And let me tell you Nate, you ain't never gonna fit in anywhere but here. Besides, I think your bro wants to talk to you."

"What?" Nathan asked. "How do you know?"

"Well, he looks pretty determined and in a hurry, and like that hovepad isn't moving fast enough for his liking," Chris answered, looking past Nathan and at the exit of the hangar doors. Nathan, following Chris's line of sight, made out his brother coming in fast. Luke jumped off the hovepad before it came to a halt and jogged the rest of the way towards them, sparing no glances at the presence of the machinery and devices around him. Nathan, wondering at his brother's lack of interest in things that would normally send him into fits of fascination, began trotting to meet him halfway.

"What's wrong?" he asked, as Luke slowed down and leaned forward, hands on knees, catching his breath.

"I can't stay long, I'm leaving on the next flight from here to New York, GOA-controlled."

"What?" Nathan asked, perplexed. "When did this get decided?"

"Just now."

"Who decided?" Nathan asked critically.

"I did. I'm going with Alex, she's being sent to New York on assignment. I'm going with her."

"No way," Nathan said, shaking his head. "Mom and dad will be furious if they find out you're not coming back with me in two days time. They're already pissed that it took us a week before we contacted them, and now you want me to tell them this? Forget it!"

"Alice approved it."

"Screw what Alice approved, why are you even considering this?" Nathan demanded. "What, did you sign a contract when I wasn't looking?"

"You know I've made up my mind on staying to work with GOA anyway," Luke said, regaining his breath. "Look, my flight leaves in about thirty minutes and I haven't packed anything. Tell mom and dad I'll see them in a while. I have to go."

"Why? Why are you going?" Nathan snapped, getting angry.

"I need someone to teach me how to use my gifts," Luke said. "Alex is the only one who can do that right now."

"What about Charlie?"

"Charlie teaches no one while he has Danny." At the mention of Danny, Nathan frowned.

"So you're going away before we even get the chance to see him again? Isn't that why we came here in the first place?" Luke nodded as though he had heard the argument before.

"When Charlie finally agrees to let us see Danny, Alice will have me on the first flight back here. Until then, tell mom and dad I love them, and I'll see them soon." Before Nathan could protest further, Luke embraced him and then ran off, back to the now-stationary hovepad. Nathan watched his brother go, not sure what had happened.

"Guess you'll be staying too, then," Chris said from behind Nathan.

"Don't be so sure," Nathan returned. He made to walk off but Chris called him back.

"Whatever you do Nate, don't tangle with Alice. She's a friendly woman but she doesn't like being crossed or yelled at. And I know one thing."

"And what's that?" Nathan asked, in no mood for pleasantries.

"Alice wouldn't send your brother off unless she knew it was safe. He's not GOA chartered yet, so he's a bigger responsibility than us Changed fools who are chartered. Alice doesn't play around with people's lives." Nathan waited, unsure of what to do, and then he moved off, deep in thought, brows thunderous.

"See ya at the saloon tonight, buddy!" Chris called after him.

Sirtis watched the Circuit at work. He was an odious little creature, and when she thought of him in comparison to Persephone, the very thought of the two matching out as the same, Changed beings caused her skin to crawl. No matter how deep her distaste and loathing for Persephone and what the woman had done, Sirtis would choose someone like her any day before selling her services to something like the Circuit.

She remained attentive on her own work, rapidly completing the schedules she had set out to do. It would give her more time to focus on how to evade the obvious trap the rat-like fool was attempting to snare her with. It irked her greatly that she hadn't foreseen something like this happening, but then, who knew there were Changed that could immerse their consciousness inside a cybernetic environment? Had she known she would have planted a myriad of traps inside the system. After all, one did not rise as high as she had by remaining ignorant of the finer details concerning such a vast database. And the very fact that the Circuit was taking so long – it was almost a month now – working out the delicate strands of the high-end system that Sirtis made use of every day.

"Not a very challenging system, is it?" the Circuit asked her suddenly, squinty eyes filled with lascivious intent. He grinned shamelessly at her, and she let her mouth curl into a sneer.

"If it isn't, then why are you still here?" she asked coldly. The Circuit, undeterred, rose from where he had been inspecting the lower lengths of the relay canisters, and made his slow, ambling way towards her.

"Such an icy reply. You must not have many friends," the Circuit said.

"I reserve all warmth for people and things that matter to me," Sirtis replied, looking back at her screens. She traced fast fingers across the lower ends, wiping all her current gathered information and deleting all traces. The work had been transferred to a secure location far outside the city the moment she did – she had merely waited for the Circuit to be distracted from his work, and his immersion. "You fall in neither category."

"I'm hurt. And I have feelings too. I am, for all intents and purposes, human."

"You are one of the Changed," Sirtis said, rotating her chair to face the oncoming creature. She smoothed her face and schooled her voice in indifference. "And yet you lend no credibility to that exalted caste of people. In fact, even were you completely human I would have considered you the lowest imaginable thing."

"Now don't go saying things like that," the Circuit said, casting his face in a mock hurt expression. "You wouldn't want your mistress to hear how you've mistreated me, would you?"

"What do you want, rodent?" Sirtis challenged, knowing where this was going. She stood, and in doing so managed to tower over him. This did not seem to deter him, since he was still shuffling towards her.

"Oh, now something from you is like a gift from the heavens! For someone like me of an exalted breed fallen on hard times, anything you can give me would be greatly appreciated." From the way his eyes darted down and back up again as he seemed to take in her entire frame, Sirtis knew what he wanted. She suppressed a smile. The Circuit had no idea how Persephone felt about him, or that Sirtis' mistress had commanded her and the other female aide of the four to repel the little beast by any means necessary, if he became testy and amorous.

"I advise you to back off, worm, or you will see just how much my mistress cares about your sanctity and your whims!" This seemed to startle him somewhat, but he remained stubbornly on the approach, as if his slow manner would endear him or allow him to come in close enough for it to make no difference anyway.

"Now go back to whatever it is you're doing." Sirtis turned about, prepared for the inevitable. She took two paces from her desk before she felt the cold, clammy grasp of the Circuit's pudgy hands. They were strong, and she knew she would have a hard time breaking free. But she also knew that relying on inherent physical strength alone was not the only way to deter a foe. She swung about, not allowing him to get another word in edgewise, and brandished the stun baton she had secured in a strap on the inside of her leg. She pulled the baton free, let it sing one short burst of angry energy and pressed the flaring points up front against the Circuit's hand, thrusting hard to cause a little bleeding.

She hardly expected the creature to put up such a racket. He screamed and screeched like a mortally wounded animal that saw no way out. Almost too late Sirtis realized what an energy current of such strength would do to someone uniquely capable of tapping into such sources, and to be caught unawares with their defences down. Hastily she withdrew the baton and let the Circuit fall to the ground. He whined and mewed piteously, and she ventured to prod him with one foot. Though she felt a twinge of remorse, it was only because she had realized how close she had come to killing the thing. Leaning forward slightly, she made sure he could hear and see her.

"If you try to overstep your limits with me again, I will make sure you feel this much pain for a long time, before you die. Do you hear me?" The Circuit nodded, as vehemently as he could. Satisfied, Sirtis pushed hard with her foot and rolled the tubby mass off the dais where her console was, then recalibrated the relays on the canisters where he had been working and waited for them to register an 'overload', which she patiently engineered, all the while making certain that the Circuit was still out for the count, his unique physiology damaged by the current she had sent charging through his hand. It would take a few days before he could speak, and by then his hand would have healed sufficiently from her sharp jab so that he couldn't cite her actions as the cause. Sirtis knew she was always on dangerous ground with Persephone, but she also knew how much her mistress loathed the Circuit as a necessity, and would hardly take its side over that of one of her most trusted aides.

Assured of her success, she began wondering just how far she could manipulate matters, before the Circuit was expelled for some or other inane reason. With these thoughts going through her head, she powered down her console and left the building.

CHAPTER SEVEN

Lessons Learned

When Joanie first set foot on GOA Headquarters grounds, she was as stunned as Nathan had been. She listened attentively to everything Jamie told her, but she held on tight to Nathan's hand and arm nevertheless, fearful despite her curiosity. The landing platform was empty of any traffic, so she was entitled to the full, uncluttered view of the main touch-down site where the majority of the GOA aircraft brought visitors, dignitaries and the occasional Changed individual bent on joining GOA itself. Nathan had briefed Joanie on everything that was needed, and it had been with much reluctance that she had vacated her safe space and joined her boyfriend on the other side of the country.

She remembered the evening they had gone to the nearest metroport and picked Nathan up. Three weeks since she had last seen him, and she could hardly contain herself from hogging his attention and holding on to him as though she hadn't seen him for years, never mind weeks. But he was as happy to see her, if less happy to be talking to his parents, explaining himself. He'd always been like that: he would gloss things over, put a brave face on everything that was good, inquire after everything and anything that had happened while he was gone and avoid the real issue, especially if it meant a browbeating. Joanie had done her best not to filch his mind for any stray bits, but then, having been with her for the last two years had made him a little more skilled, somehow, at hiding his thoughts. He did it unconsciously, without trying very hard, as if by sheer strength of will his being in her presence most of the time had granted him some form of immunity from all but her gentlest probing. That, or she was simply less inclined by unconscious will to breach his privacy.

After a day – his parents had kindly allowed him to rest first, and become more at ease before they demanded he talk – they had repaired to the back yard of the expansive house. They had gone to sit by the poolside of the Hirsch residence, the night air brisk but refreshing, glasses of wine at hand, Nathan chattering on about GOA, other people like him, Joanie and Luke, and also about what was going to happen and what their options were. It was only after he had seemingly exhausted himself and began repeating things that his father had finally interrupted, after carefully listening to everything his son had said.

"So you say Luke is in New York," his father had begun. Nathan had replied with his apologetic smile, not sure of how to field the statement and what his dad wanted to hear.

"He wants to join GOA as an active member. He thinks he'll fit in well there, but the only person who could teach him to control and fine-tune his gifts had to be sent to New York on assignment."

"Assignment?" Mrs. Hirsch interrupted, taking a delicate sip of her wine. Joanie had noted that her face, though neutral throughout Nathan's discussions, had a strained appearance to it. Joanie knew she had been worrying, despite the missives from her sons. It was only natural.

"I don't know what the assignment is, but Luke is safe. He even sent a letter with me." Nathan, having just remembered the letter from his brother, gingerly took it from his jacket, realizing his parents would have liked to have the letter up front before he had launched into the situation with GOA. His father took the letter and began reading through it, face indifferent. Nathan waited in awkward silence, mind darting about in search of other topics worth discussing, as far as Joanie could tell by reading his feelings.

"So you allowed your brother to leave without contacting us," his father said after a while, folding the letter and handing it to Mrs. Hirsch. Joanie watched, knowing the usual disapproving signals from Nathan's dad when she saw them.

"It wasn't as if I could make him stay," Nathan managed by way of apology. "He's the eldest; he can do what he wants, right?"

"It's still polite to let us know about these things," Mrs. Hirsch said, eyes still avidly scanning her oldest son's letter. Mr. Hirsch nodded.

"I want you to go to wherever your brother is and bring him back here. Then I want the both of you to stay and let me and your mother discuss whether we'd let you join this organization. I know both of you are old enough to make your own decisions, but not alone with something as big as this."

"Dad!" Nathan protested, but his father merely looked at him, silence a demand in the iron grey eyes.

"That's final."

"Alice won't disclose the exact location to anyone," Nathan added defiantly. "Luke didn't even tell me the name of the woman he's staying at."

"There's nothing in the letter either," Mrs. Hirsch said, placing the letter on a small table by her side. "How could you let this happen?"

"Why am I being blamed for this? Mom, you knew we were going away, and when we first contacted you and didn't come back immediately you must have known something was going on. Don't you see? These people are like us! They're different! They have gifts like or better than ours, and they're offering to help us!"

"Just like that, no strings attached?" Mr. Hirsch asked critically.

"We sign contracts but we don't necessarily have to become field workers. Dad, they train anyone who is Changed and willing to accept their help, and if these people don't wish to join GOA itself they get sent away again, allowed to live their lives as normally as possible. They get watched, to make sure they're alright, but nothing beyond that."

"And this woman, this Alice, she told you all of this?" Mrs. Hirsch queried.

140

"A bit unprofessional, if you ask me, letting people with no ties and obligations into their Headquarters," Mr. Hirsch added. "Or is this woman a mind-reader like your brother? Was she the one who called you about Daniel?" Nathan nodded, ignoring the obvious discomfort his father still conveyed when speaking about Nathan and Luke's differences. But he also knew that his father was a shrewd man, and caught on quickly. He was proven right when his father leaned forward, concern clear now in his eyes. "You truly want to join this organization? You and Luke?"

Nathan nodded, a small smile on his lips. His parents exchanged glances, and he waited in bated breath for their reaction. Inevitably his father would make the final decision. In the meantime he looked again at Joanie and gave her hand a squeeze, which she returned. Her eyes held only agitation and exultation, the former because this was a family matter, of a family she was part of in all but name and still excluded, but exultant because Nathan was back.

"What of Joanie?" Nathan's father asked suddenly. "What happens to her if you leave?"

"She can come with me. GOA has records on almost every Changed in the northern hemisphere, and they know about Joanie. In fact I think they'd like it if she could come with me."

"What?" Joanie asked, stunned. Nathan smiled reassurances.

"No, they haven't been monitoring us, simply making sure they keep tabs on all the Changed people. I would, if I could and I had government funding."

"So this GOA organization is a government scheme," Mrs. Hirsch stated.

"Mom, there are a lot of people out there like us," Nathan explained. "I mean, sure, we could have gone on with our lives as normal despite the gifts, but now we know a little more about others like us. Don't you see what this means?" Nathan was overjoyed, but Joanie watched his parents closely. Despite having long ago accepted the differences in their sons and Nathan's girlfriend, they would probably never get used to seeing their children in a different light than they already did. Mrs. Hirsch looked down, resigned. Nathan's father remained carefully scrutinizing his son. "Wouldn't you want something like this for us?"

"We don't want to keep you from something like this," Nathan's mother said. "But we are concerned."

"Why? Look, I only said I wanted to join GOA for the training. I still want a normal life with Joanie someday." He looked meaningfully at Joanie, and she smiled back, "and Luke is the one who wants to play an active part. And I bet there's nothing against family visits and stuff like that. It's not like we're leaving the country, mom, we're just exploring new options." Nathan waited now, having given his pitch. Now it was up to his dad, who did everything more slowly, but more assuredly.

"Then I suppose there's little we can do to change your mind," Mr. Hirsch had said finally. Nathan had been exultant, sweeping Joanie off her feet and spinning her around as he nuzzled her neck, and then had bent forward to give his mother a kiss. There he stopped, not quite sure what to do for his dad, but Mr. Hirsch had merely smiled.

Joanie left the musing behind as she stepped onto the platform. She smiled shyly as Jamie passed her, grinning and leading the way. She found Chris a strange character, a bit too wild for her taste, but he was pleasant enough, and Nathan enjoyed his company. She hadn't met any of the other people Nathan had spoken of, and she suspected she would meet the woman, Alexis, or Charlie, real soon. And she admittedly missed Luke, and knowing that he was with Alexis, who had played a major part that night when they had broken in at the Hirsch house, didn't make her feel any better. Luke always followed his own heart and head, often blindly and with bad consequences to himself, but Joanie still wished he had stayed until she had arrived. Maybe her own insight, when she had met Alexis, would have provided more reassurances the next time they spoke to Luke and Nathan's parents.

"Okay, onto the hovepad, we'll go for lunch and then we'll give Joanie the grand tour, alright?" Jamie interjected. Joanie nodded despite not paying much attention, her mind driven inward. She climbed almost mechanically, allowing Nathan to support her. She paid half a mind to what was happening around her, mildly interested and also worried about what would happen. Nathan sounded immensely pleased with GOA, and from all accounts Luke, who rarely committed to anything unless it was worth committing to, was already on his way to being accepted into GOA. But what bothered her most was Danny.

Before she had become Nathan and Luke's friend, Daniel had been one of her friends. They had come a long way, since high school, and when they had gone off to study together, she had been thrilled, never quite having been a social adept. Neither was Danny, but just knowing someone familiar was along for the ride had been an immense relief. With frequent study sessions, most of them at the Hirsh home, she'd met Nathan, and by default Luke, and after a while the four of them had become fast friends, and more than that, with Nathan. And though Joanie had missed her old friend, the fact that Nathan had returned with news of Danny's whereabouts and predicament had opened up old wounds, ones she had decided, after a year had gone by with no word, served no purpose but to upset her. And now that Danny had been found, she would not let up until she had seen him, heard from his mouth that he was alright, and then appraised the situation more positively if he was.

"So where is Charlie?" she asked suddenly, interrupting whatever Chris had been saying to Jamie. The two of them looked at her, and she was also aware of Nathan's eyes on her. "Nathan told me he's Danny's mentor and he takes care of him, but I would have thought he would be here too."

"He doesn't like to be far from Danny-boy for too long," Chris said matter-of-factly, and grinned. Joanie frowned.

"Meaning?"

"Whoa, no offense," Chris said, holding up his hands. "Charlie's grown real attached to your young friend. Kinda jealous of his attention, me and Jamie think." Chris tilted his head in Jamie's direction, and the shorter, stockier man rolled his eyes.

"You're as bad as Alex sometimes, you know that?" he said softly.

"Anyway," Chris said, rolling over Jamie's protest. "No one knows exactly why Danny is held under such close observation. Charlie isn't exactly an easy character, but we suppose he has his reasons." The way he said it sounded as though he really didn't believe it. Joanie, flustered by what Nathan hadn't told her about Charlie, turned away and stared off into the distance. She vaguely heard Chris say something, and a mild thump followed by a cry of outrage; she smiled, having seen Jamie punch Chris on the shoulder.

The hovepad took them to the drop-off point just outside the main entrance of the main GOA building. Once there, Chris took off, winking at Nathan and saying something about getting a drink sometime and going over some more things at the GOA Tech Development Labs. Jamie led Nathan and Joanie to meet Alice, after which they would take the tour of the facilities. Joanie watched everything with some trepidation. For all Nathan's assurances, the GOA facilities were daunting, and she felt lost amidst the bustle of personnel, many of whom she realized knew exactly what and who she was, or so she thought. After a while she sighed and realized that her empathy was working in paranoid overdrive, so she calmed herself in spite of it, biting down and following the others, still holding on to Nathan and hoping that, in time she would feel the same as he did about the place.

The trip had been uneventful.

Luke climbed out of the cab right after Alex did, and though he saw her reluctance at having arrived at their destination, he was far from distraught himself. The massive front door that served as the entrance to Lady Margaret de Witt-Emerson's massive mansion was more an inviting, exciting change of scenery. Maybe, he reasoned, it was because he wasn't the one who was here for assignment purposes and, on a more ulterior note, training and discipline. The doors swung open and a frail old man with thinning grey hair and a no-nonsense air about him greeted them. The man, obviously a butler of sorts, commanded the cab porter to take the bags inside, then clapped his hands to summon someone from inside the house to take the bags to the designated rooms. The butler sized up the two new people that stared about them, one with an air of dejection and disinterest, the other with barely contained awe and excitement.

"My name is Raymond," the butler said dryly. "Please follow me, Mrs. Emerson is awaiting your arrival. This way." He led them from the entrance foyer and through a sitting room with lavishly old antique furniture and sumptuous carpets. From there it was outside through some large glass doors and onto a very expansive paved walkway that led in terraces towards the expanse of the massive lawn below. Luke marvelled at the extent of the gardens and the opulent state of the greenery all around. His eyes alighted on a cast-iron awning that appeared as though it had jumped, fully-formed and terribly Rococo in style, from the ground. He could just make out two people seated beneath the shade. Raymond led them towards the two, and once there he took his leave.

"Well, come closer. I'm not as far-sighted as I used to be," a thin voice called from the awning. Luke stepped forward, noted Alex lagging behind and fell back, taking her by the arm and forcing her forward.

He was surprised by the appearance of the woman who had spoken. Margaret de Witt-Emerson appeared in her mid-sixties, with grey hair coiffed into a very antiquated bundle atop her head. She was clothed in a very chic business suit which revealed her physique to be quite youthful, even underneath the enormous sunglasses. And then Luke's eyes fell on the other occupant beneath the shade. It was a girl, or so it seemed, not very tall but undeniably luscious and attractive, with her skimpy shirt contrasting with the knee-height leather boots and the tight-fit skirt. She looked at the new arrivals with a faint smile on her face, and only when she noticed Luke – he thought – did she smile winningly, her dark brown eyes warm and appealing. Luke affected a smile himself, and drew closer.

"Hi, my name is Alyssa, I'm Maggie's assistant," she said, standing up. She didn't even quite reach his shoulders, in spite of the boots. "You must be Luke, and this is Alexis." Her eyes darted towards Alex, who remained completely immune to any attempts at courtesy.

"Alex will do," Alex murmured from the side, not making any effort to appear more convivial. Alyssa gave her a cool stare, returned her attention to Luke and took him by the arm.

"Well, there's not much more to say really, except welcome. Please, join us for lunch."

"Ah, so this is the headstrong young woman Alice promised me," Margaret said as Alex and Luke joined them. Soon, a cavalcade of servants began arriving, carrying tables, cutlery, glasses and finally, food.

Margaret regarded Alex with unveiled interest. "Alice neglected to tell me of your remarkable beauty, I must admit." Alex merely smiled weakly, but broke eye contact after that. "And this young man? I was surprised when GOA reported two people inbound, but then, the house is always empty with only two people around now, and the servants hardly contribute to the conversations. You're Lucas, correct?"

"Yes." Luke began, then hastily added "ma'am."

"A pleasure, I'm sure. So, here we are," Margaret said, spreading her arms to encompass the setting.

"Please, help yourselves to everything. It would not do to have guests going about the mansion with hunger pangs. And don't skimp on anything, there's never a lack." Luke, all too willing, began to load his plate with food, after politely inquiring whether Alyssa and Margaret would like to go first. When they told him to go ahead, and when Alex didn't show any sign of helping herself, Luke went ahead, but then took another plate and added some of the choicer morsels onto it. He placed the plate in front of Alex, who gave him a sideways grimace, and the old Changed woman and her young protégé shared a quick glance in each other's direction. Only after Luke had provided food for himself and Alex did Margaret and Alyssa help themselves.

"Now Luke, Alice's missive tells me you're an empath of no mean skills. I've never had an empath of any description above 'moderate' in my care before. And of course, Alexis, you yourself are far from inadequate. That is why Luke came along, is it not?"

"I have to train him," Alex said simply.

"Well then, when you have spare time, feel free to do so," Margaret added. "Of course, since you have other matters to attend to, you may come and go as you please, but do be so kind as to let me know when you go out. Sneaking about is so uncouth and ill-mannered." Luke managed a sideways glance at Alex, and noted how her face went white. He could almost commiserate: Margaret seemed the soul of equanimity and kindness, but there was something deliberate about the words that not only clearly outlined the level of intolerance but also stated quite pointedly that Alex would by no means be allowed her usual leeway. And Alex knew it. "Luke, since your sole purpose it seems is to keep Alex occupied when she has no duties to perform, I daresay you may do as you wish. And if you will be so kind, I would appreciate it if you could every now and then entertain Alyssa. She grows bored quickly now that Ryan isn't around for her to badger." Alyssa smiled slightly, and Luke mused that he had noticed the first sign of possible truth behind Alex's misgivings. Obviously Alyssa wasn't all too happy with this arrangement, but acquiesced to Margaret's demands.

Lunch was concluded with little other conversational topics, beyond Margaret's piercing queries about room preferences and any schedules that were already in place. When they rose, and the

147

servants returned to clear the tables and the awning, Margaret hooked her arm into Alex's, startling her.

"Really my dear, I know how you must feel. But please, consider this a break from normalcy rather than a task. I daresay Alice has been shooting her mouth off again about what kind of woman I am, but really, there's no real need to be so dour."

"Yeah, probably," Alex replied neutrally, uncertain really of how to respond.

"Of course! I suspect Alice had her reasons for sending you here, but you are a grown woman. I will hardly check up on everything you do. And I have been told in no uncertain terms that you are remiss in your social skills. Now the only way to remedy that here is to make sure there are many trips into town to secure suitable wardrobes, and not to mention the parties. Alyssa grows tired of those, but I doubt you will."

"I grow tired of them because the people are all the same," Alyssa interjected amicably from her side.

Margaret didn't spare her a single glance, and Luke noted a sullen edge creeping into Alyssa's face. Alex, on the other hand, had a strange expression on her face: he couldn't decide whether it was shock, elation or disbelief, but decided a mix between the three was as close as he would get.

"Tomorrow we will take the car into town and spare no expenses. I haven't felt the need for a party for a long time, but I would be remiss in my repertoire as an entertainer and woman of standing if I did not introduce you to some of the people I know. So, off you go. There is nothing planned for the afternoon, so feel free to move about. Supper will be served at eight, so please try not to be late." Seemingly pleased with her announcements, Margaret walked off, a picture of aged elegance. Alyssa followed close behind, not looking back at Luke or Alex. Which left the two of them alone and halfway back to the glass doors of the estate. Alex sighed and sat down on an ornate granite bench, and Luke followed suit.

"You see?"

"She seemed nice," Luke countered. "A character, no doubt, but eccentric rather than domineering."

"You mean you didn't see the looks on Alyssa's face, every time 'Maggie' goes on about parties, preferences and social skills? The woman was practically dying to wring someone's neck. If that's the case, she and I might get along better than I'd have thought."

"Maybe you shouldn't look at this as a bad thing. And don't think I didn't see that nearly hopeful look on your face when Margaret spoke of tomorrow's excursion." Alex frowned, staring at Luke.

"I'm beginning to wonder if I should have brought you along after all," she mused, not unkindly.

"I could always return to GOA Headquarters and leave you here alone," Luke said teasingly. Alex's gasp told him he had scored, and he nimbly ducked out of the way of her fist. "Whoa!"

"I'm in no mood to go snooping about this place. Not yet, anyway," Alex qualified. "You?"

"It's up to you," he replied.

"What, now I'm your chaperone as well? You can do whatever you want!" Alex said.

"What I really want is to take advantage of the real reason I'm here," Luke replied. "I was thinking we could ask Margaret for a safe place where we can practise."

"Practise what, exactly? Luke honey, I did bring you along for your training, but I also needed someone I could rely on when times got bad here," Alex admitted, biting her lower lip. She was surprised when Luke simply shrugged.

"I knew that. But don't think it's gonna get you off the hook. You owe me, and big-time, I might add."

"Fine," Alex sighed. "Since we know you're not bad at all with telepathy and remote transmission and reception, I suppose telekinesis is the next big step."

"Yup," Luke grinned, and got to his feet.

"Why are you so smug?" Alex joked, rising and finally managing a genuine if tired smile. "I'm not exactly the best telekinetic expert there is."

"Whatever you think you know is probably more than I do," Luke added. He held his hand for Alex to take, and they returned to the estate. Almost as if on cue, Alyssa appeared, when they approached the double glass doors.

"You probably want to know where your rooms are, right?" she queried.

"Actually, we're looking for a safe spot to do some training," Luke said. Alex appeared unready to talk freely with Alyssa just yet. He was pleased when the shorter woman grinned, a very mischievous look that complemented her face even further.

"Ah. Sparring. I like it. Mind if I watch? Ryan and I hardly coincided with anything, since I usually beat the crap out of him." Looking to Alex for affirmation, Luke waited. When Alex gave a curt nod, he then nodded at Alyssa, who appeared only too pleased to be in the company of someone other than Margaret. As she led the way down one of the corridors, she looked over her shoulder. "So, what are you guys good at? I mean, what gifts do you have?"

"Mentalist," Luke said, nodding. "Alex is that and more."

"Really? In what way?" she asked. Alex gave Luke a murderous glare, then sighed and stepped between the two of them.

"Which way and how far?" she asked in resigned tones. Alyssa, puzzled, took a moment to figure out what Alex was going on about, but then pointed forward.

"About two hundred feet, roundabout," she said. She barely had time to register before the draft caught her, and when she stepped free she suppressed a minor scream, noting how drastically the surroundings had changed.

"This is a nice room," Alex said, and Luke noted a saucy grin on her face. She wasn't looking at Alyssa, which meant she was enjoying the discomfort she had caused the woman, if only for mischief's sake.

Alyssa regarded Alex as if she had sprouted wings and grown horns.

"Teleporter," she breathed. "Wow."

"You might wanna keep your computer systems out of harm's way too," Luke whispered conspiratorially close to Alyssa's ear.

"I heard that," Alex said from her side, sounding relatively unconcerned. Alyssa's eyes merely grew wider and wider with every mention of Alex's extensive gifts, until she seemed ready to leave them alone. But after a while Luke gave up needling the situation, if only because he didn't want to cause any real upsets.

"So where do we start?" Luke inquired after Alyssa had taken a safe seat to the side of the large room, happy not to interfere, now that she knew what Luke and Alex both were capable of. The room was round and devoid of furnishings save for a cast-iron table and chairs, and a set of deck chairs that stood strategically placed to catch the sun from the one side of the room that consisted solely of windows.

"Let's play catch," Alex said, and the table lifted from the ground as though someone was pulling it up with rope. Not to mention easily: the table spun and rotated experimentally for a few moments, and Luke's eyes widened. He looked at Alex, who grinned. "Or maybe it's 'revenge!' she crowed, and the table flew towards him.

There was no way out now.

Or was there? Sirtis sat quivering in front of her console. It had been a week since she had caused the Circuit's little accident, and now, a week later, the beast had challenged her. Instead of backing off when she had made her warning plain, he had gone straight to Persephone, supposedly with some very incriminating evidence. When he had returned to the primary consoles where Sirtis worked, he had given her a vengeful leer, a sure sign of something amiss.

And now she was primed for a meeting with Persephone, and from her sources, she knew she would be alone. None of the other aides would be present. And from the frown she had seen marring Persephone's forehead earlier in the day, she knew the Circuit was playing fully along with the dangerous dance she had initiated. Inwardly she cursed the day that creature had been allowed access to the systems, and vowed bloody vengeance. But first she had to extricate herself. Thinking fast – she had another hour before the meeting – she realized this was it. All or nothing now. She would have to play all her cards this time and hope the hand she received in return was a favourable one. Sighing, deploring the lack of finesse her forced hand would achieve, she began accessing her data.

When Linda Randall had begun her bloodhound tracing based on the hints Sirtis had dropped, she had thought nothing could go wrong. Persephone, though not a very strong telepath, when held against some of the Changed Sirtis had read about in the encrypted folders she had found in the databases, could nevertheless do the unexpected. Linda had been proof of that; Sirtis would never have guessed that Persephone was what the database had termed a 'fluidic displacement empath', an empath with the ability to boost her other mental powers using her strongest ones. So Persephone had no problem blasting ahead into the minds of others, without remorse, using her telekinetic strength to enhance her mind-reading skills. A fact that had nearly cost Sirtis her designs, but one she had managed to work into her scheme right after Linda had been killed. Now, drawing on the sources she had painstakingly assembled outside the city and across the globe, she assembled a carrot to distract Persephone from whatever the Circuit had told her.

That, and she gave orders for her own team of experts – hundreds of miles away, hidden in an abandoned bunker – to initiate the protocols for her swift retreat from Persephone's service.

She waited until half an hour before her meeting, made sure no one was looking her way and that she was standing in a small but effective blind spot within the camera sensor networks emplaced throughout the chambers and swallowed the Neuronull capsule she carried on her in case of emergencies. The capsule was at its most potent after half an hour, and Sirtis relied heavily on that fact. After all, Persephone could kill her, but she could also settle for the other alternative: demotion and restricted access, as well as a severe mind probe to reveal any secrets. If she found no secrets then Sirtis would at least be spared one of the alternatives. But if the Circuit had somehow managed to gain access to Sirtis' private core bubble within the databases, the chances were she would die here today, right when she was ready to free herself from Persephone's grasp.

She returned to her console and began compiling the information she would feed Persephone. The one flaw her mistress had was a tendency to act impulsively. It was her most awe-inspiring and terrifying trait, as well as the one weakness Sirtis knew she could exploit without fear of retribution. After all, would Persephone hold her accountable for giving her information she desperately wanted? So Sirtis included all her most precious pieces of info, some of them which she had withheld from her mistress for just such an occasion. If the Circuit had been bluffing, then Sirtis could delete necessary info from the pad in her hand easily before she had to give it to Persephone.

The digital clock beside her console went off, and Sirtis rose, composing herself and holding her head high. She passed an eviscerated data router where the Circuit was working, and he glared menacingly at her before grinning at her discomfort. She spared him a neutral glance in return and moved confidently towards Persephone's office.

She entered unbidden – supposedly a distinct honour reserved only for Persephone's highest-ranking aides – and went towards the massive domed side-chamber where Persephone usually lazed away the daytimes.

She didn't see her mistress there, so Sirtis waited patiently, knowing also how little one could rely on Persephone's sense of time. But she didn't have to wait long.

"So, my wayward aide comes of her own accord," Persephone's voice rang thinly through the chamber. She appeared from the shadows close to her personal suites, face arrogant and forceful. Sirtis bowed her head slightly, and thought fleetingly again on the terrible beauty which her mistress possessed. It had been that beauty, coupled with the power Persephone wielded, that had first attracted Sirtis to her side. Now, she dreamed only of escaping the woman's grasp. "I have heard some very disturbing rumours about you. Or at least, the Circuit gave conclusive proof of facts."

"If you will only let me explain –"

"Oh, I will. Make no mistake Sirtis, I will hear every excuse you pander before me, and when you are done I will wreak bloody havoc on your body!" Persephone snarled, a faint hint of luminous blue rising in her dark eyes.

Sirtis swallowed, then straightened her neck and stared her mistress fully in the eyes. "What am I accused of, if I may ask?" she ventured.

"Treason!" Persephone snapped. "My closest aide, my most trusted servant, turning against me!"

"How did this treason occur?"

"Do not bandy coy words with me!" Persephone all but yelled, and Sirtis actually felt her hair lift. She affected more subservience, even lowering her eyes. No need to irk Persephone further than she already had. "Or did you think you could hide your little secret research from me forever?"

"The research I have done is incomplete, mistress," Sirtis began explaining. "I did not wish to give you false hope."

"Then pray enlighten me. And I hope that pad contains this research, or I really see no point in keeping you alive for much longer." Sirtis nodded and handed over the pad, which Persephone rudely took from her and began scanning. Sirtis cleared her throat and began speaking, amazed at how steady her voice sounded.

"Three weeks ago I began assembling a background sweep of three Changed within New York. They are closely linked to someone whom you may be familiar with."

"The Circuit said he found treasonous data in your core. Data pertinent to a device you are working on," Persephone snapped again, ignoring Sirtis' commentary.

"I beg your pardon?" Sirtis queried, allowing a little resentment to colour her voice. The device existed – her people were working on it – but she had prepared for the eventuality that Persephone would discover it. So, she resorted to her memorized excuse in case of this particular emergency. Persephone shoved the pad back at her, and the face was displaying an intricate blue print.

"Mistress, why would I require such a device?"

"Who knows? Jealousy? The desire for powers of your own? Tell me, what exactly does this device do? Tap deeply into electronic systems? Telekinesis? Read minds?" Sirtis calmed her breathing. If only Persephone had known how close she had just come. But Sirtis moved ahead.

"Mistress, I am in awe of what you can do. And I have reason to think that the Circuit may have planted the data."

"Planted the data?" Persephone asked critically. "Why would he do this?"

"A week ago he made advances on me. Advances which I would not care to retell," Sirtis said, hoping she was convincing enough in her pathetic plight. "I delayed his actions until he became very insistent, after which I had no other alternative but to use force. So I used a stun baton. I had no idea then how the device would react to his unique physiology. Needless to say, I cannot conceive what he could have thought up. He strikes me as a vengeful creature."

"Enough speculation," Persephone demanded, holding up a hand. "So he may have planted the data for vengeance. Then how do you explain the hidden traces he found, sending information to your home consoles? Why would you wish to do such a thing? And do not think to use 'taking your work home' as an excuse!"

"But mistress, that is the only excuse I have!" Sirtis protested. "All data edited at home is sent back here on completion! Did the Circuit not tell you this?" She held her breath, knowing that to imply a lack of understanding in Persephone's presence was a sure way for a beating. Especially if one implied Persephone herself was the ignorant one. But in this case the gamble played off. Persephone's eyes darkened, then glowed blue, but she looked away from Sirtis, staring at the wall to her side as though she was looking through it at the Circuit. Her mouth worked soundlessly, and from the way her body heaved, she was building up a violent explosion of anger. With the pad back in her hand, Sirtis erased the data she had prepared to offer up in exchange for her life. Such information would not be necessary now. But something told her she wasn't out of the woods yet. Persephone visibly calmed herself.

"And these three Changed you spoke of? Here in New York? Why are they important? There are many weaklings in my city, none of them capable of harming me in the slightest!"

"The three Changed I have tracked down are not the threat, mistress," Sirtis said meekly. "It is the person they are in contact with." Hastily she cleared the erasure screens and called up the personal info she had managed to find. And hard it had been too! She was almost reluctant to let Persephone see it. But sacrifice and deceit was the name of the game now. Her life could still end here, now, if she faltered.

Persephone once more grabbed the pad from her, glittering eyes voraciously scanning the screens. When her face grew almost still, Sirtis wondered if she had miscalculated, but then her mistress' eyes flared vividly, enraged despite the placid expression on her features. She held out the pad.

"So, you have been telling the truth after all," Persephone remarked. Her voice held frustration – she had not been prepared to make an apology of any kind to Sirtis. A small victory amidst the potential death, but one Sirtis acknowledged by simply bowing again. "You will track down this woman, and quickly. You may resume your duties without access restrictions."

Bowing again, this time deeper, she prepared to back away.

"Stay where you are," Persephone said suddenly. Sirtis looked up, puzzlement in her eyes. Persephone was smiling, a cruel grin that did nothing at all to detract from her beauty. She stepped closer and reached out with one hand, running the long fingers through Sirtis' hair, eyes almost loving despite the coldness in them. "A final test, my dear servant. One which you will have no problem in passing if you have been telling the truth."

"Mistress?" Sirtis asked uncertainly, but knowing full well what would happen next. She had resigned herself to this anyway. And it wouldn't be very hard to fake the pain caused by such an invasive probing as Persephone preferred. So she bowed her head.

"Excellent," Persephone breathed.

The pain lanced into her head like a serrated piece of metal, one that grated on the inside of her skull. The brain had no pain receptors, she knew, but who said a mental invasion was without pain? She bit down to stop from crying out, as she felt her mistress's presence root around inside her head, a forceful entity that smashed aside barriers. The last thing she remembered before the usual temporary blackout was hoping that the Neuronull capsule was working.

When she woke up, she was propped on Persephone's personal couch. She attempted to rise, and fell back weakly. She was surprised when Persephone moved next to her. The Changed was standing beside the couch, looking down with an expression that could only be described as possessive. Even pleased!

"I am pleased that the Circuit's accusations are unfounded," Persephone said, and her voice was all velvet and cream again. "And since he has lied so profusely to cover up his own depredations, I have decided that you may remain a witness to what happens next."

"Mistress?" Sirtis queried, puzzled again.

Persephone smiled, and it was a smile Sirtis had seen her mistress give only when she was about to kill. So she rose slowly on the couch, careful not to let the blood rush overmuch to head. Persephone stepped towards the centre of the domed room, heeled feet clipping the marble floor like the tattoo of death. She raised an arm, and the ornate doors swung open. Sirtis had seen Persephone use her gifts before, but only in small ways. She watched, horribly fascinated, the full scope of her mistress' power. The Circuit came flying into the room, screaming and snivelling, a bundle of obnoxiousness lifted as easily as a child's toy. He came to halt, floating like some rotund gas sack in front of Persephone.

"You scheming, lascivious little beast!" Persephone snarled despite her smile. "Attempting to frame one of my people because you were thwarted! I warned you what would happen!"

"Mistress, I beg your forgiveness!" the Circuit whined piteously. "I am innocent! That wench!" he grated, pointing at Sirtis. "She lies! She is the one who has compromised your security!"

"I have seen what goes on in her mind, worm! Are you saying I am mistaken?" The Circuit squirmed, and Sirtis could almost not help marvelling at her own ingenuity. She had no idea that her lies would force Persephone in such a direction, or that the Circuit would now be caught between a rock – calling Persephone's information flawed – and a hard place – proving his own innocence. Because Persephone herself had let drop, weeks before, that trying to read the Circuit's mind was as easy as digging a hole in water. And now, Sirtis realized, the Circuit would die.

"She lies! She lies!" the fat Changed whined, tears dripping from his eyes.

"You found nothing to incriminate any one of my people, and so you planted some for revenge! Oh yes, I saw the incident in Sirtis' mind! A dirty, facetious reptile has more restraint than you! But fear not. I will make sure your predations do not concern anyone ever again!" Persephone drew back, her hand still aloft, keeping the Circuit afloat. Slowly he began to spin, a scruffy ball of protests climbing higher and higher as he began to spin faster and faster. Sirtis held her breath, watching as within moments the Circuit was spinning so fast he was a blur! His screams began fading, and soon the blur also contained his vomit, but none of it hit the floor, instead remaining in a tight, sickening arc close to the Circuit's body. His screams became so frenzied that Sirtis closed her ears against them, horrified despite wishing the creature dead and gone. She bit back a startled scream when the Circuit exploded, the sheer momentum of his rotation ripping his arms and legs off his body and tearing his organs to pieces. None of the blood dripped onto the floor, though, kept in check by whatever unseen force Persephone had employed to shred the Circuit.

"Send me a cleanup team," Persephone said to no one in general, her words sure to be caught by the vocal sensors in place throughout her chambers. Sirtis rose shakily from the couch, enthralled and horror-struck by the still-floating mass of human dross. She began slowly circling it, attempting to come closer to the exit. Persephone's laughter checked her progress. "Inelegant, but also very entertaining! I know you did not betray me, Sirtis, but let this be a warning."

"Mistress?"

"If you should entertain notions of treason at any time," Persephone finished, then left. Sirtis, still appalled by the show of power she had witnessed, started when the cleanup team entered. Persephone was already retreating to her personal suites, and only when the double doors thereto had closed did the sodden mass of flesh hit the floor. Sickened and feeling ready to become nauseous, Sirtis rushed from the domed room.

She waited for the day to end.

She waited patiently, but inside she felt as if a hand was twisting her innards. The repair teams had already completed the bulk of the reassembly work the Circuit had tangled up with his search. The fact that the cybernetic freak was no longer close by to

159

scan or route any discrepancies and leaks didn't soothe her much. She had spent the rest of the day erasing the final shreds of data pertinent to herself and her secret work. What she had seen today, what Persephone had done, it filled her with such horror and revulsion that she knew she had ultimately made the right decision, when she had begun extricating herself from Persephone's web of control. When she walked out of the office today, she would not come back. She had already activated the protocols of her team to begin cleanup and relocation. When she returned home she would sort out a few final matters and be on her way. She wanted nothing more to do with the Changed.

When the digital clock chimed the end of the working day, she rose hastily, ran a final check through her files to make sure everything was either in order or erased, gathered her things and made for the door.

"When you come back tomorrow, I want you to begin a sweep of the city. I want a catalogue of every Changed, no matter how insignificant, compiled," Persephone called to her. Sirtis, nearly jumping, looked at the woman who employed her. Persephone was standing at the top of the stairs leading to her domed room and suites, an unreadable expression on her face. "And I want you to track down the woman."

"Of course mistress," Sirtis said, and bowed again. Let Persephone think her cowed – she wouldn't be far from wrong. But it was with an uneasy step, and a forcefully deliberate one, that she left the office. She took a cab to the hovetram station and made for home.

When she got there, she leaned against the door and let herself slide down. She bit back tears born of frustration and remorse. She had been key in disposing of the Circuit, and her hand was almost as complicit with Linda Randall's death. But now she was free, even though the fact brought her little relief. Hastily she began calling people, preparing for her departure. She called her own teams last, alerting them to her status and demanding a pickup within the hour.

Only after that did she relax a little, take a shower and prepare for her pickup. She gathered the few bags with her most treasured possessions and some clothing, then set her personal home console to overload. When that was done, and she stared at the smoking ruin of the electronic screens, she opened the door and left. She made for the entry foyer of the apartment blocks she lived in, smiled unfeelingly at the polite older man who opened the door for her and went outside. One of her people drew her attention, and taking her bags from her escorted her to a car. She climbed in and breathed deeply, aware that it was over. She didn't look back as the car sped off soundlessly, making for outside the city. Far from the Changed.

Ancillary Documents

GOA IV: Annabel Swanson, The First Documented GenneY Prime

By the beginning of the twenty-first century, GOA had made startling amendments to the Changed Classification system, having moved within two decades from a mere observational agency that simply monitored the gifted to an organization that was required to take an active hand in shaping the future of Changed-kind and the non-gifted remainder of the human race. Gifted theorists and philosophers affiliated to or aware of GOA and the CC began hypothesizing the possibility of a super-Changed, an individual with immense powers that effectively dwarfed the relative mundane settings of the CC. It wasn't a topic beyond plausible speculation, seeing as people like Alice, who herself was the only known First Prime class Changed in recorded history, held an obvious advantage in power and ability beyond the other documented Changed. By the time GOA agents found the ruined town where one Annabel Swanson first made her latencies known, Alice McNamara was a mere GOA field agent, held in high regard for her massive potential.

In spite of radical advancements in genome mapping and genetic scrutiny, by the early twenty-first century humans were still unable to identify the full scale of DNA complexes that invariably unload the potential alteration within a non-gifted in order to facilitate the scope of mapped gifts.

In part GOA's charter went from benignity to active participation because of GOA Research's insistence that more of the gifted become genetically mapped, for the sake of security and – by default of obvious intrigue – the furtherance of understanding the next chapter in supposed human evolution. At the time of field agents becoming a definite requirement to facilitate GOA's work, more than five hundred of the Changed were actively affiliated with the Agency, on numerous occasions and in all four fields of the organization's work. The mystery of fully explored and documented proof regarding the reason for the Change occurring at puberty and at times radically altering the genetic structures of the potentially gifted remained enigmatic in spite of a widening range of subjects being tested. It came as a monstrous surprise when, in 2005, GOA field agents responded to a monstrous energy spike in their sensors. Alice McNamara, being the most experienced and skilled field agent of the organization, was sent with a team of several others to investigate.

The town of Old Canton in Virginia was decimated by a colossal explosion that wiped out its meagre population of about sixty people. All but one woman, who was found in the midst of the destruction, gibbering and raving and weeping inconsolably in turn. When Alice and her team came upon the woman, they were forced to immense efforts of control and defence, when the woman unleashed telekinetic assaults that defied logical explanation. Of the entire team, only Alice survived the initial assault, being a capable and experienced telekinetic adept herself. In spite of severe wounds – quickly adapted to by her regenerative faculties – Alice managed to contain the extraordinarily powerful woman, who in spite of her monstrous strength was inexperienced, and easily overcome once weaknesses in the attacks were taken into account.

Alice retrieved the woman unconscious and took her to GOA, where the woman's potential was mapped, genetically and according to the CC. After weeks of testing, the woman, Annabel Swanson, was classed as the supposedly legendary super-Changed the logicians had only begun to define in theory. The CC was rewritten on several accounts, and two decades of tried and tested proof on the norms of the Change were redefined: Annabel Swanson was thirty-six years old when she Changed, the onset of her mutation occurring at least eighteen years outside the accepted range. Coupled to the catastrophic exhibit of power she unloosed on her home town, her gifts were mapped as exclusively paradigm-level, most notably in the Mental and Elemental Aptitudes. Efforts were made to stabilize her alternating mood swings of deep depression and violent outbursts that often resulted in on-the-fly creation of defensive technologies to curb her wayward gifts. After three months of restraint and careful monitoring, GOA had suffered nine casualties and three building collapses, and Annabel was sedated indefinitely in order to give the scientists time to perfect a defensive null-shield that could contain her power. The field proved successful after extensive testing, and on the preliminary round of efficiency in holding Annabel's gifts in check proved immensely useful; in spite of Annabel's immense telekinetic bursts and mental forays, the field held, and it became a permanent enclosure around her quarters while GOA strove to overcome her deep-seated self-revulsion and her immense distrust of her altered state. During all this time, GOA Research furthered their genetic inquiries into not only her unique case but also the generalized domain of all Changed. Annabel Swanson was to become one of GOA's most prized scions, once her psychological limitations were overcome. In two years time, great leaps of success in that department were made, and Annabel seemed to recover from the initial trauma of her Change and the fact that she had unwittingly eradicated her own home town in what would in the future become documented as the 'classical' signs of the cataclysmic Change accompanying an Nth Prime possibility. However, Annabel's mental state never improved beyond maintaining a stable and coherent mood of indifference for more than a few hours. When early 2008 arrived, Annabel experienced her second major alteration, which expanded her genetic complexes into an exponential upsurge, driving her powers into excess and unseating the fragile balance of her hard-won stability. Safely contained and held in the null-field – despite her surging thrusts breaking uncontrollably free from her grasp – she descended into madness. In sight of the horrified onlookers who observed her twenty-four hours a day, she turned her expansive telekinetic prowess on herself and crushed herself out of existence.

Despite the tragic loss, GOA had achieved successes as well, in the form of a greatly expanded genetic database, a more plausible CC and significant advancement in neural-inhibition shielding technology.

It would be close to seventy years before GOA uncovered another GenneY Prime in Daniel Mercer, by which time Alice McNamara had become GOA's Director of Changed.

CHAPTER EIGHT

Daniel

He didn't know if he was doing the right thing.

But then, he couldn't keep Daniel from them forever. Especially not the girl, Joanie, with her fathomless grey-brown eyes that seemed to stare beyond him. He had never felt quite as unhinged as when she had calmly stated that she wanted to see Daniel, and soon. He had frowned, but it hadn't been a threat. The one thing it hadn't been was an idle command, and he had waited for another week, seeing as this girl was here with Nathan, and bound to stay. He marvelled at how singularly annoying the couple was, at how filled with righteous outrage and indignation they acted whenever they saw him, as if they blamed him for every single thing that could possibly be attributed to Daniel's situation, or how they perceived it. Nathan was more or less resigned to Charlie being Daniel's mentor and keeper, but Joanie was a whole new ballgame.

He had sensed her anger the moment he had seen her, and he knew also in that moment that she knew exactly who he was, even as he knew her. Things like names practically rolled off the mental waves of any empath, and another empath could pick it up easily. Joanie was by no means as skilled as he was, he knew, but such things rarely mattered to him, except when it came to Daniel. Everything Daniel did filled him with awe, admiration and pride, mostly because of his status as a potential Nth Primer, a GenneY adept in the making. And to think, little less than a year ago, he had bridled when Alice had commanded him to undertake Daniel's training. But the presence of Daniel's old friends and family complicated matters, and they would get even more complicated when they met Daniel again. This was a nuisance, and he hoped things drew to a close quickly so he could get on with Daniel's training, and his job.

They had taken a regular detail chopper from GOA and made northwest, towards the north-western Canadian coastline, several hundred miles above Seattle, where he had told them him and Daniel lived. The lie had been necessary, he felt, because he knew it wasn't beyond either Nathan or possibly Joanie's scope to go snooping, come across something choice and try and make contact with Daniel by themselves. So he had fabricated the story of an abode just outside Seattle – there actually was such a house, mostly used by the GOA Changed when they wanted a break from work. But the house where he and Daniel and two in-the-know servants lived was in Canada, still on Vancouver Island but almost at the very tip overlooking the Pacific. And that was where they were headed, and soon all his pretenses, lies and cover-ups would come to light.

He admitted to feeling jealous. It came with the bond he had been forced to undertake in order to prepare and recover the shattered fragments of Daniel's mind, when he had undertaken to helping him. He didn't want anyone else to monopolize Daniel's attention, like he knew Nathan and Joanie would. Strangely enough, he didn't feel threatened at all by the older brother, Luke, despite the fact that he was an empath powerful enough to figure out and even attempt bonding. It somehow didn't feature, maybe because Luke wasn't with them now, but safely away with Alex. Charlie chalked it up as a professionalism that was lacking in Nathan; Luke, though flustered and upset by Daniel's kidnapping, and the way things were now, seemed content to one day, eventually, meet his friend and brother again, knowing Daniel was safe and waiting. Luke would have come along now, if Joanie hadn't been so damn insistent that they see Daniel very soon. Charlie wondered whether Luke would be upset, at least very much so.

"Either this chopper is slow, or we aren't anywhere near Seattle," Nathan said eventually, arm against the inside of the chopper, leaning so he could stare out the window. Here we go, Charlie thought.

"There is a house near Seattle that the GOA Changed use every now and then," he began. He felt more than saw the critical glances directed at him. "We're not going there now."

"What do you mean?" Nathan asked. Charlie was about to field the question when Jamie opened the cockpit door and leaned in, taking off his headgear.

"You didn't tell them?" he asked, and Charlie shook his head. Jamie's eyebrows lifted and he sucked on his lower lip, and then shook his head and leaned back out, closing the door behind him.

"It means he's been lying," Joanie qualified from where she sat. Charlie looked at her and noted the grave expression, then looked at Nathan, who looked ready to explode once more.

"Do you ever tell the truth?" he asked.

"Whoever sees Daniel does so at my discretion. If you found out where he really was you'd have gone snooping without my say-so," Charlie recited, almost by rote, and sounding bored. "And I know you knew where the house was. You were just scraping up the courage to go behind GOA's back and go there yourselves." The furtive look Nathan shot at Joanie told him he had scored. Smiling, knowing that his lie, though blatant, would now lose credibility in the face of their complicity, he sat back down again.

"Why do you keep him from us?" Joanie asked. She sounded weary, as though she was tired of waiting to see her old friend. "I know he's important, and powerful, but why is he closeted away? Doesn't he get bored or lonely? Has he ever asked to see any of us?"

Charlie opened his mouth, and suddenly he knew he was at the brink, almost ready to tell them exactly why he hadn't allowed them to see Daniel earlier. But he was saved from doing so by the cockpit door opening again. Jamie ducked in fully this time, free of his harness.

"Okay, we're almost there. Give it two minutes and we'll land." All questions were discarded, and further looks of distrust passed between Joanie and Charlie, as well as Nathan. Jamie blithely ignored the animosity in the chamber, sitting down and belting himself in. Charlie waited for Joanie to look the other way again before he looked back at her, forcing his mind to absolute calm and inscrutability. Somehow she was managing at odd intervals to break past his defences, to see into his mind what he wanted to keep secret, if only to the emotional aspect. But feelings about something like lying and deceit were usually much better indications than the actual thoughts themselves. He was almost certain that was why she had asked that last particular question. That, and he had begun to feel that her mental skills did not stop at telepathy only. There were some pretty powerful, insidious and convincing insights she had dropped at times, and the fact that he had very nearly answered the question had screamed, almost too late, the warning sirens in his head that warded against coercion. He didn't remember anyone saying she had persuasive gifts to complement her repertoire.

The chopper landed softly on the pad designated just behind the house, close to the trees. The wind was chill and miserable here, and the sky that spanned across the ocean's expanse was forbidding and grey.

Charlie looked toward the house and sent a tightly focused search beam into it. He found Daniel easily enough: his protégé was in the practice rooms, indulging in some early morning exercises, and giving off waves of bored undercurrents through the bond. Smiling, Charlie unlatched his safety belt and was first to the exit, waiting for the attendants to lower the gang rails. He stepped onto the ground, turned around and affected a smile, hoping that it would smooth over the harshest of feelings.

"Well, welcome to my humble home. The attendants will bring the bags." Since there was no other way around it, and he knew that he couldn't simply show them Daniel for a few hours and then order them off, like at some petting zoo, he had agreed to a week's stay here. A week, Alice had told him, would be sufficient time in which to retrieve Luke as well, if Daniel's initial response to Nathan and

Joanie was favourable. And they would get to adapt to the newness of their estranged friend. Jamie took over, fortunately, as they began walking towards the entrance facing the landing pad, allowing Charlie to breathe easily. On the same tight band, he felt a familiar voice intrude on his thoughts, and he allowed his defences to let the access through.

"Visitors?" Daniel asked telepathically. From the casualness of his query, he wasn't paying too much attention to the people just entering the house, even if the boredom in his mind suddenly vanished.

"Someone you'd like to see," Charlie returned.

"Really?" A little more interest this time, and Charlie felt the swift sweep of Daniel's mind as it scanned the house. He cut off the link suddenly, aware for the first time that he was in fact responsible for keeping Daniel's old friends and family from him: he had made no effort, in the last year, up until now, to find them and bring them to Daniel. Sighing, he followed the others down the well-known hallways of the very luxurious and sophisticated house that he and Daniel occupied. He waited for the attendants to show everyone their rooms and to get comfortable, before telling everyone to join him in the downstairs lounge.

Joanie waited for the door to close. Squealing, she threw her arms around Nathan's neck and hugged him close. When he looked at her with some surprise, she chuckled.

"Sorry. But he's here! Danny's here!"

"You're sure?" Nathan asked sceptically. Joanie treated him to a mock grimace of affront, and he smiled, but it was a wan effort.

"Aren't you excited?"

"I'm more pissed off still at Charlie. The guy lies about everything concerning Danny, and something doesn't feel right." Joanie drew away a little and stared intently at Nathan's face.

"Premo?" she asked, and he nodded once, tightly. Joanie sighed, her suddenly cheerful mood dropping again. Nathan's premonitions were sporadic and unpredictable, but never wrong.

She walked towards the large window overlooking the ocean, then turned around and faced him.

"Whatever it is, try to look on the bright side. Danny is your brother, remember? You can't not be the least bit excited!"

"I am excited," Nathan admitted, trying his best to smile. "But I'm also a little uneasy. We haven't seen Danny for more than a year, and from what the others have told me, he's not the same as he used to be. That kinda scares me." Alex, Chris and Jamie's accounts, though all accurate in that they resembled each other, didn't sound too much like Daniel at all.

"It scares me too, but at least we get to see him again." When that didn't work, she reached out and took him by the arms, squeezing. "C'mon, I've been waiting for a week now – a year, actually! – and you for longer. Let's go say hi."

They left their rooms and made for the lounge. Charlie and Jamie were already there, both of them wearing sobered expressions. They both rose when Nathan and Joanie joined them, and for some reason Jamie looked to Charlie with an almost judgmental grimace. Charlie ignored it, managed a weak little smile and indicated for them to follow.

The practice room was an unassuming circle. The walls were bare and unadorned, and only the floor indicated change, comprising a depression accessible through three steps. There was nothing in the room but what appeared to be an easel. Other than that, the chamber had a view of the ocean, through a rectangular set of thick glass panes that curved with the walls, as did so many other rooms in the house.

Daniel was nowhere to be seen.

"So where is he?" Nathan asked, voice near to deadpan. Joanie rolled her eyes. On seeing Charlie and Jamie, Nathan's attempts at lightening his own mood had dropped again. Back on the warpath, then. Joanie decided she'd had enough, broke free of Nathan's arm and walked into the room. She looked about, sent her mind travelling the confines, wondering what Danny was at. A snicker from Charlie brought her back.

"He likes to play tricks when meeting people," Charlie said, a fond expression on his face.

"He never played tricks unless he was drunk," Nathan said darkly from his side. Charlie fixed him with a shrewd glare.

"Really? I wouldn't know, he dislikes drinking alcohol, or so he told me. Anyway, he's no pushover. He's either shielded and making illusions or he's somewhere else in the house, biding his time." Charlie looked up, eyes alert as he scanned the room and house, an almost-grin on his lips. Joanie watched, intrigued, as Charlie went to the easel. She noted for the first time a thin, old-looking box stuck to the back, which Charlie detached and held in his hands. She squinted to make out the writing on the box.

"A puzzle?" she asked.

"A very old one," Charlie said, nodding. "Daniel hones his skills with them."

"With puzzles?" Nathan scoffed. "What, did he turn into a child?"

"Nathan!" Joanie snapped angrily, and Nathan shrugged, unperturbed.

"Well, he's not in the room," Charlie said, then looked down, and smiled. The lid of the box opened, and was thrown aside. As they watched, the pieces floated free of the box, all rounded edges and tiny interlocking segments. In a whirlwind of motion the pieces danced free of their box, and Charlie stepped back as the pieces began swirling in a cardboard vortex. But there was method to the seeming madness, as the pieces suddenly bunched together, then expanded again, each piece seemingly floating at random to a certain point in midair. Within seconds the pieces appeared relatively spaced, then locked together. Joanie gasped as the entire puzzle fell flat onto the ground, fully assembled. She approached cautiously, bending forward to look at the pieces.

"How many segments?" she asked.

"Two thousand five hundred. It used to take him weeks to assemble a five hundred piece one in the same way, but he learns fast," Charlie explained.

"I haven't seen one of these since my mom showed me hers," Joanie said. Nathan gasped.

"They're rare and expensive these days," a familiar voice said by Joanie's side, and she straightened, gasping. Without really thinking she flung out her arms and hugged the figure beside her, then drew back to appraise him. Daniel hadn't exactly changed much since they had last seen him, but there were marked differences. For a start, his eyes were lighter, his hair longer, and his overall facial features had seemingly sharpened and matured: there was a cohesive fluidity thereto, as if everything had come together more perfectly, and the overall picture was one that was more appealing than before. That, and his body was more toned and shaped than before as well, when he had been just a rawboned kid. To Joanie's eyes he appeared far healthier. And true to Charlie's word, there was a playful twinkle in the steady green gaze that watched her. She hugged him again out of sheer joy, then drew back. Nathan approached, a wide grin on his mouth.

"How've you been, buddy?" he asked, extending a hand. He moved as if to embrace Daniel, but Daniel drew back, a puzzled look on his face. He looked at Charlie.

"So, who are these people?" he asked. "I mean, the girl is an empath, of sorts, and the guy is also Changed, though I don't quite recognize anything familiar."

"Danny, it's us!" Joanie said, taking it as a joke. She faltered when Danny fixed her with a steely stare that immediately disabused her of the thought. He spared a slight smile, but otherwise backed away from them.

"Charlie that was rude of you, telling them my name before I could. Or did she read it from me?" he admonished in tones of mockery, also slyly amused at the prospect of somehow having been read in spite of his defences. But the seriousness in his voice could not be completely hidden. "Anyway, I didn't get your names."

"Joanie," Joanie said in a numbed voice, eyes unfocused. Nathan looked once in disbelief at Danny, then venomously at Charlie, before storming from the room.

"Okay, you handle that one," Jamie said to Charlie, crossing his arms across his chest. Charlie snarled and ducked out as well, leaving Daniel smiling slightly at a very uncomfortable Joanie.

He ran into the lounge, eyes darting about for Nathan. He called a few times, then went for the kitchen area. He sent his mind scanning for Nathan's presence, wondering if perhaps he'd gone outside. Or maybe he was flying. Charlie sighed, exasperated. If Nathan was in flight it would be hard to trace his –

"I am so tired of your shit it makes me sick!" Nathan grated, suddenly close to Charlie's face.

It had happened so fast he hadn't had time to defend himself. Instead he found himself pinned to the wall, feet swaying above the ground as he grappled with Nathan. Who simply grinned cruelly and shook his head, as Charlie ineffectually tried to dislodge the steely grip holding him by the neck.

"Don't try any of your mind games or I will hit you so hard you won't wake up for days!" Charlie, reading the venom and anger in Nathan's voice, knew it to be true. His hands worked futilely at Nathan's, coiled around his neck.

"So, how many more cover-ups do you have? Who would have thought? Our best friend, *my own brother*, forgets us and you don't tell us that until now, when we meet him face to face for the first time in a year! Do you know how much that hurt? That lack of recognition? Huh?"

"I can explain," Charlie managed.

"I bet you can! But I'm not letting you go, or else you might just pull the same stunt you did when you kidnapped Danny. So, what else do we need to know, now that you've changed him into an immature brat who plays tricks out of boredom?"

"Nathan!" Joanie yelled, storming from the corridor. She took hold of Nathan's arm, but felt the rigidity there that she knew came from his gifts. His eyes, though relatively normal, still had a creepy glow to them, sufficient to indicate his usage. "Nathan, stop!"

"In a minute," Nathan replied conversationally.

"You have to stop now or –"

"Or what?" he demanded angrily of Charlie. Joanie backed off, and then looked at some point beyond him.

She ducked back suddenly, and Nathan returned his attention to Charlie. "Why didn't you tell us he didn't remember?" he insisted, shaking Charlie and banging the back of Charlie's head against the wall, hard enough for Charlie's eyes to lose focus. Nathan had a single moment to recognize an unearthly chill race down his spine before he felt as if his head was turned inside out. Unwillingly he lost his grip on Charlie's neck, looking about him with unveiled horror. He looked at Charlie as if it came from the harassed mentalist, but the man was slumped with his back to the wall, eyes fluttering. He couldn't have.

"Whoever you are, you're really rude," Daniel said, walking past. Nathan yelled in surprise as he catapulted towards the ceiling, slamming against the thick stone hard enough to lose his breath. Danny moved until he stood beneath him, looking up, no expression on his face except for the slightly narrowed eyes. "I hope you didn't hurt Charlie, or else I might just leave you there on the ceiling. Or I could tie you to the back of a truck, or the chopper outside, and throw you into the sea. Which one'd you like?"

"Danny listen to me," Nathan began, and then gasped. He tried to move his arms, but failed – he was pinioned completely, spread-eagled onto the ceiling.

"I've never choked anyone before," Danny said, voice sounding distant. "At least, not physically."

Nathan's face turned first red then purple, then a slow glistening white, sweat pouring from him, his eyes wide.

"Stop!" Joanie screamed.

"Daniel, don't!" Charlie managed, sounding strangled, massaging his throat. He pulled himself from the wall and towards a couch. Daniel, eyes dropping to Charlie, swallowed, then dropped his hand. Nathan hurtled towards the floor, and accompanied by another of Joanie's screams, nearly hit it full on, but she saved him in time, halting his progress scant inches from the ground, her own face rigid with the extension of her gifts. She held Nathan immobile for a moment, making certain his momentum was broken, before she released him, and both of them gasped for air. She helped him into a sitting position, hands crossing his face as he massaged his throat. Daniel regarded them critically, but also with bewilderment. Then, as if recalled from somewhere, he bunched down next to Charlie, placing a hand on Charlie's arm.

"Are you okay?" he asked earnestly, and Charlie nodded. Jamie emerged, striding nonchalant as though he had missed the entire escapade. He looked about him at the lounge, at Joanie beside Nathan, who remained seated on the ground, drawing breath in ragged gasps.

"So, everyone okay now, all the shit sorted?"

"Kinda weird guests you bring me nowadays," Daniel said, glaring first at Charlie and then at Jamie. "Or is there something I don't know?"

"There's a lot you don't know," Jamie said cryptically, then looked at Charlie. "So judging by Nathan's pose on the ground, the fact that Joanie is almost in tears and Charlie looks half-dead, I take it you guys have a lot of issues to work through." When he received no answer, he nodded. "Good, sorted. I'll leave you all to it. I'm turning in for a nap. See ya in a couple of hours."

"Seriously, what's going on?" Daniel queried, as Jamie retreated.

"It's a long story," Charlie rasped.

In the aftermath of the episode, everyone remained in their rooms.

176

Joanie sat beside Nathan on the bed, gently stroking his arm. She didn't feel any better than he did, but she was also concerned about him. He refused to say anything much, and his face had a blankly staring quality to it. Normally her sighs would break him from any silent reverie and force him to ask if she was alright, but now, even that failed. And he was never one to vacillate over an issue for too long, or take something so harshly. When she couldn't take it anymore, she rose.

"I'm going for a walk," she said simply. He didn't look at her, instead only nodding, When she left he leaned back, stretching himself out on the bed, staring at the ceiling. Realizing that she wouldn't get much of a response from him in any case, she left him to it.

She went outside. The house was a marvel of modern engineering, hidden amidst trees and rocky ground near the tip of the large island. On the approach side, from the road and the helipad, one saw only a single square building, looking like a simple single-storey construction, but from the other side, looking from the ocean, one saw that the house had four levels, stacked atop each other. The singular cubic shape remained the same, fitted with large thick windows that allowed for magnificent views from within. A narrow lawn spread off to one side, and a small garden with some flowers adorned the side of it, but otherwise the front yard was dominated by several coniferous trees, pine and spruce. Joanie spied a small rocky path that led from the backyard, winding its way down to a private beach area. Knowing there was nothing pressing to do, concerning what had happened, she took the path and began the descent. The Pacific here was cold, but she felt like walking barefoot in the cold, pressed sand, and maybe dipping her feet in the water itself.

The path was rocky and uneven, but fortunately not very steep, making its way down in tortuous angles to the beach. She actually enjoyed the numbing sensation of not thinking, of simply placing one foot before the other and taking a walk. In no time she was on the beach, and she took off her shoes, leaving them at the foot of the path. The sand was gravelly and almost hurtful to walk on, but she did so, enjoying the whipping wind that blew from the ocean.

The beach stretched for a few miles to the north, with a high cliff wall rising as cut-off point to the south, where the house perched amidst the rocks and the trees. Joanie began walking north, mentally reminding herself not to remain too long. She knew the beach belonged to the owner of the house, but that didn't mean she could simply take liberties without asking first. So she settled for a relatively brisk walk by the shallow lapping waves, every now and then reaching up to tuck a stray strand of hair behind an ear.

After ten minutes she noticed someone else on the beach with her. The figure was far off, about a mile away from her. Intrigued, she quickened her pace and sent her mind roving. She drew back a little in shock when another mental presence buffered her own and fielded her inquiry. Smiling in spite of herself, she slowed down again, and settled in the interim between herself and Daniel for the mind-play that only empaths could enjoy.

"I didn't mean to pry or anything. Should I leave?"

"You're our guests, so you can go wherever you want," Daniel returned amiably.

"Hope I'm not disturbing you or anything. I didn't feel like being cooped up in the house, with everyone mopey, so I came out here."

"I know how you feel," Daniel replied, and Joanie felt a surge of hope within herself. She hadn't really spoken to him when they'd met a few hours back, and it gratified her that he wasn't hostile towards her as well. She cut off the communiqué, until she had drawn level with him. He didn't look at her, but when he spoke his words were calm and friendly.

"I'm sorry for being so rude earlier," he explained. "I didn't actually mean what I said to… Nathan, is it?"

Joanie nodded, suppressing a twinge at the reminder of this lack of recognition on his behalf. She went to stand next to him.

"You're Joanie. I know Charlie told you who I am, but hey, here goes." He turned to her, a lopsided smile in place, and extended his hand. "I'm Daniel." Joanie regarded the hand, and took it without much thought. For an empath, tactile contact wasn't encouraged – too many unbound thoughts that could flit through the contact. But she took the hand, clamping down on her own raging thoughts, and was relieved when she felt nothing come through from Daniel. He disengaged, his eyes remaining on her face.

"I know this sounds weird, Danny," Joanie began with the diminutive, his full name sounding weird off her tongue, "but maybe me meeting you here can iron out some wrinkles."

"Oh there's no need to explain," Daniel replied, shaking his head. "It was a misunderstanding, nothing more. I just reacted because Charlie, well, Charlie's my best friend, and I don't really know you or Nathan, so it was given I would protect him."

"But that's just it, Danny," Joanie countered, resorting to the diminutive. "You do actually know Nathan and me. Or at least you did, before you Changed." She saw a dark look pass across his face, but pressed on.

"We used to be your best friends, me, Nathan and Nathan's brother, Luke. You're actually their brother as well, and you've been living with the family for eight years before the Change. I don't know what happened that could make you forget." She held out, scanning his face for any sign of recognition. All she got was a blank look laced with puzzlement.

"We were best friends?" he asked uncertainly, and from the sound of it, he wasn't even prepared yet to ask about what she said after that; about being their brother. Joanie nodded. "I don't recall any of it."

"What do you recall?"

"Almost nothing, really," Daniel said. "Vague images, places I've lived at, the place I grew up in. Nothing at all is really clear. Just...vague." His eyes grew distant. "There's this one house, its kinda large, had two levels. I had my own room, I think." Daniel frowned, as though it troubled him.

"Then you must remember us!" Joanie protested. "You pretty much started describing the Hirsch house, that's where you've lived in the last eight years, not counting this one, I guess," Joanie ended lamely.

Daniel shook his head slowly. Joanie snarled in frustration, balling her hands into fists. "I used to be your best friend in high school," she said quickly, hoping to catch him off guard. "You remember high school? Ever since ninth grade, you and I hung out and did everything together." Indecision and incomprehension flared across his face. "We had the same teachers, we took the same subjects. We even went to university together, though you went away first. You were cleverer than all the other kids in the grade, so they pushed you."

"I remember going to university, and I remember high school, but I can't remember anything about it, about the people I met, the teachers, anything." His face had a drawn look to it, and it was growing white.

"Joanie Stratford, that's my full name. You and I go back to high school – we never hung out with other kids and we just decided to do with each other after a while. It paid off really well, too. You were a math genius. Actually you were a genius in kinda everything, really. Everyone eventually came to you and me for help with homework," she explained, realizing she was babbling but still going on. "You used to love debates, and school field trips to other states and cities. You're actually studying for a degree in Classics."

Joanie stopped as Danny took a few steps forward. She followed, ready to continue, when she noted a look of utter horror on his face. Shocked, she ventured a hand on his shoulder, but he ducked clear, not looking at her.

"Joanie Stratford," he whispered. "It sounds almost more familiar now." He placed one hand against his forehead, and for a moment Joanie entertained the hope that he was remembering something. "Why is it blank?" he growled, and yelled at the sky, a short bark. It shocked Joanie, but she pressed on.

"There's so much more I can tell you," she ventured. "I remember everything like it was yesterday. And you just need to talk to Nathan too, he can tell you about all the good times at home, and university!"

"I can't," Daniel replied, voice barely a whisper.

"Why not?" Joanie queried.

"Because it hurts, dammit!" he yelled, whirling about and glaring at her, the well-remembered green eyes turning the well-remembered venomous color that remarked of his usual temper. Seeing it now sent her mind churning with nostalgia, even in the face of his anger. "When I try to reach for those memories, everything turns white and it's like shoving my head into a furnace!"

"I, I'm sorry, I didn't mean to –" Joanie began, then gasped as Danny became limned in a transparent outline of himself and vanished, a sound like displaced wind marking his passage. Joanie stared at the spot he had occupied; suddenly both horrified and upset by the way things had gone. She was breathing heavily, unsure of what to do next. She spun about and began jogging back towards the house, hoping Danny was there and not somewhere else, or she would have Charlie on her case. "Stupid, stupid!" she mumbled, spurring herself on to go faster.

"Why did you bring them here?"

Charlie started awake as Daniel's voice cut through his dozing mind. He lifted his head, staring about the room. Daniel was standing near the shadows of the curtains, and as he noted Charlie waking up he drew closer, anguish and tones of desperation clear on his mien.

"Nathan and Joanie?" Charlie asked, wiping sleep from his eyes.

"I mean I don't even know them, and they say they know me!" Daniel continued, pacing about. Charlie closed his eyes, dreading the moment, knowing that once again he would fall short of the trust department.

"Daniel, slow down and sit down," he cautioned.

"No!" Daniel snapped. "No, this is stupid! I want them to leave!"

"But they do know you, Daniel," Charlie said, settling for the most direct route, which was the hurtful truth. Charlie knew it the moment Daniel stopped pacing, his eyes searching Charlie's face, his mouth working soundlessly. "You used to know them," Charlie added.

"When?" The question sounded almost strangled from him.

"A year ago, or at least a little more than that. Right about when I brought you here." For a few laborious moments, silence greeted him, and he expected Daniel to fly into a fit of rage.

"Why are you telling me this only now?" Daniel asked, swallowing. Charlie sighed and pointed at the closed curtains. He made a peremptory snap with his hand and the curtains swung open in a quiet whoosh, allowing harsh light inside. He blinked and swung his legs off the bed, placing his feet on the floor. He didn't look at Daniel, although he knew Daniel was regarding him with undivided attention. Rubbing his face in both hands, he then let them drop to his side.

"Because you were too fragile before now to handle it. And you may still be, but we can't wait any longer."

"We?" Daniel asked, and there was a note of belligerence in his voice.

"Daniel, sit down and this will go faster."

"I don't want to sit down!" Daniel snapped moodily.

"I don't want to have to follow you everywhere when you start pacing!" Charlie fired back, as edgy as Daniel, who growled, then practically marched towards the chair standing in a corner of light. He threw himself onto it and glared. "Better. Look, there's a reason for everything I've done. A lot of it was selfish, but most of it was for your protection."

"I've been wondering about that one," Daniel remarked snidely. Charlie ignored it.

"Whether you like it or not, Daniel, you needed protection from the start. You aren't exactly as normal – and I use the term lightly – as the rest of us Changed." Charlie glanced in Daniel's direction, making sure he was listening. "There's a lot of evidence that says so, and none to the contrary. And when GOA comes across someone like you, they'd go through great lengths to prepare you, and possibly to recruit you."

"I said I'd join GOA eventually," Daniel said.

"I know, which makes their job easier already. But Daniel, unlike other Changed, you didn't get a period of grace in which to discover your powers. Others learn early on, mostly at the onset of puberty, and some, those who are more exceptional, learn when they're younger still. But you, you were different."

"So you've told me." Charlie would have bridled at the constant interruptions, but the fact that the angry tone in Daniel's voice was gone alerted him to Daniel's interest being piqued. He was always attentive when it came to important things, for which Charlie was thankful.

"About fourteen months ago, you were at the Hirsch's place," Charlie said, plowing along, ready for the nitty-gritty. "Nathan and Lucas Hirsch. They are your adopted brothers; you're the adopted son in the family. You lived there, as Joanie probably told you."

"How'd you know she spoke to me?"

"You're all but broadcasting it publicly," Charlie replied, tapping the side of his head. "Her intentions were good. And yeah, you guys were real close, especially you and Nathan."

"She said we went way back, to high school," Daniel whispered. The hints of despair were returning already.

"She's probably right," Charlie allowed. "Daniel, when you began the Change, you didn't go gradually. Until the moment you

Changed, you showed no signs whatsoever of exhibiting gifts. You were already nineteen, and by that time, almost ninety-nine percent of people who haven't Changed by then never do so: if you hadn't shown signs of gifts by the age of eighteen, normally you would never have them, which means you'd be human in full. Instead you altered drastically, two years after the usual cut-off period, and not only did you show remarkable gifts, you showed an incredible array of them. There's a term we use at Headquarters for someone like that: GenneY, or an Nth Prime." Charlie leaned back and broke eye contact.

Daniel was absorbing this very quietly, almost scarily so. But there was no turning back now. Charlie had to finish what he'd started. "GOA has only ever found one other GenneY in its entire history, and the woman died tragically after she couldn't learn to cope with the enormous powers she'd developed. GOA was determined that if another GenneY was found, they'd learn from their mistakes and make sure he or she was sheltered and prepared for what lay ahead."

"How long did this woman survive before she died?" Daniel asked in quavering tones. Seeing his fears, Charlie shook his head.

"She didn't die because of her gifts, Daniel," Charlie explained further, "she killed herself because she couldn't cope." Daniel seemed to deflate a little. "She committed suicide after three years with GOA, three years after the Change. And that was why I was ordered to undertake preparing you."

"But you're not a GenneY," Daniel countered. Though it wasn't meant to sound hurtful, Charlie felt a slight twinge. It never bothered him that he wasn't a GenneY, or even a GSP, but who wouldn't, when faced with the reality every day, envy the power of a GenneY, an Nth Prime? But it was of no consequence now, and Charlie went on.

"There is no way to train a GenneY per se, only ways to help them understand their power. To prepare their minds for what could possibly come. That task was assigned to me when we retrieved you from the Hirsch house, fourteen months ago."

"They gave me up? But you said you notified my parents, and I could see them soon!" Daniel protested.

Charlie held up his hands, and it was all he could do from crying out against what he was about to tell Daniel. He hovered for a moment between telling Daniel, and leaving it out. Sighing, he decided to let it lie for now. There was no use in Daniel turning the house into a flat pile of debris. Charlie would face the rest of the music later.

"And that was the truth," he replied neutrally, sliding the truth and couching it. "And the Hirsches didn't give you up, Daniel. GOA kidnapped you." Charlie started at the speed with which Daniel rose, anger clear in his eyes now.

"You kidnapped me?"

"We had no choice. Had we left you there indefinitely, you would have died. Gifts of the magnitude you have, left unchecked and untrained would have caused something to happen if we hadn't gotten to you."

"So you kidnapped me," Daniel repeated.

"Dammit, yes!" Charlie snapped, rising. "You would have died! Don't you get that? Don't you remember what I've told you about the first three months with me? You had no control! You set fire to furniture and you splintered walls in your sleep! You were a human time bomb, and the only way to save you was to forge a mental bond between us!" Daniel, looking somewhat chastened, mused on what Charlie had said.

"That way, I could force control on you when you needed it, until you could do it without my help!"

"So why bring the Hirsches here?" Daniel asked after several moments of silence.

"Because you don't recall anything of your life before your Change."

"Of course I do," Daniel answered defensively, but wavered as Charlie shook his head.

"You remember images and blurred visual, nothing more. Where were you in high school? What university? First girl you ever kissed? Anything?" Daniel shook his head, slowly, defeated. "I thought so. And that's why we brought Nathan and Joanie here. Luke might come later, but Alice and I hoped Nathan and Joanie could sort out the trauma that came when you Changed."

"So what am I supposed to do? When Joanie began telling me things, on the beach, I thought my head would explode," Daniel said. Charlie, noting the lost and faraway look in Daniel's eyes, moved closer and placed a hand on Daniel's shoulder.

"We'll figure it out with them, okay? Trust me?" Daniel nodded tightly, and Charlie embraced him. "You need to know these things about yourself, or else you'd live a fractured life." Daniel only nodded, but he glanced over Charlie's shoulder out the window, his mind on something else.

CHAPTER NINE

Cruel and Unusual

Amorphia sneered. "Why should I believe you? More to the point, what proof do you bring of him?"

"You will have to trust me," the man before her said. Or at least, he was a man as far as the appearance was concerned. But in all her many years, Amorphia had never found anyone else she would append the name 'Butcher' to, save for this particular example of Changed power. Henreik Kessler made her skin crawl, and not just out of sheer revulsion.

He looked amiable enough, sitting there, a small smile on his lips. Thin lips and a large mouth, a strange combination. Wide-set blue eyes, a tragic beauty on such a remorseless face. High cheekbones and a pinched nose, and Amorphia found herself staring antique German death in the face. Kessler seemed no older than twenty-five in spite of his merciless cast, but he was far older than a mere two decades. They all were, Amorphia thought to herself, she included. That was why they were so powerful, and outlasted all who came against them. And Amorphia knew she herself was Black Death in smoky coils, but the living embodiment of evil that could make even her shudder was seated right in front of her. In his nondescript suit and polite pose of legs together and hands folded on his knees, Kessler betrayed nothing of the thousands of deaths that could be laid at his feet. The perfect poise for incongruity, and yet, here he was, the slayer of multitudes, a lapdog for *him*. Kessler smiled.

"Still afraid to even mention him?" Kessler barked a humourless laugh. "You don't even think his name, in your head!" Amorphia's eyes narrowed. She despised being berated or castigated on her own turf, and amidst the rich sophistication of her surroundings, Kessler did indeed look out of place, and in no position to tell her anything. But that was just it, she thought. Of them all, Kessler was the one Changed that posed a threat to her. The proverbial leash of the proverbial master that none of them acknowledged but none of them dared disobey. Immune to disease, poison and a multitude of other things, his body was far harder than it seemed. A veritable powerhouse of strength, agility and resilience, and the man didn't even need to breathe! Against powers like hers, Kessler would stand with a smile and do nothing, for her powers could do nothing to him. It grated her that the equation of the unequal numbers somehow balanced out, that for every one of them, there was a counterpart Changed that could cause harm. It was how he kept them in check. And the greater ignominy was that Kessler, in addition to his array of physical aptitudes, had a mind that could break the strongest will under coercive barrages. A deadly combination, illusions and might.

Amorphia hated him, she hated his presence and she hated that he served as a reminder that, in spite of her words to Persephone months ago, there was still a way for him to reach her, to remind her that she still served him, in spite of her recalcitrance and wayward schemes.

"None of us trust, Kessler," she barked. "It is not in our nature. That is why we survive."

"Then you must obviously resort to something else then," Kessler added, sounding bored. "Take your pick: religion, faith, power, it matters not. He sent me, and there can only be one reason for it."

"He couldn't have found it yet!" Amorphia said, suddenly frightened, her voice nearly betraying her to fear.

"It? No, no, you silly bitch, who said anything about 'it'? Come now, has it been so long that you've forgotten the design?" Kessler rose, one flawless motion, and his face twisted into a smile that added a terrifying boyishness to his cruelty. "You have, haven't you?"

188

"And how will you force me to rejoin that foolish little crusade? I have enough power already, why submit to the will of schemes that lack fruition across centuries already?"

"There is beauty in patience, my sweet, if only you had the will to apply," Kessler droned, making her sound like a dunce. "All of us serve, none of us back out. Force you? I need not resort to such a thing. I merely need to tell him of your defiance, and he will no doubt break from his schedule and make it a personal thing. Would you like that?" Amorphia snarled and spun about, her thick embroidered skirts swishing as she stalked away. She began fuming when she realized he was following, nothing betraying his cat-like silent gait but the fact that he continued speaking. "The mind is a glorious thing, my sweet," Kessler continued, as though it was a conversation over tea-time. "Even yours can be read, as oily and fluid as it is sometimes. Such bold words, spoken, no doubt, when you had felt he no longer cared if he had your allegiance or not."

Amorphia stopped and turned on her heels to face him. In a fit of rage she lashed out, her arm coalescing into a black mass of thick vines, snaking out and striking Kessler across the face. He didn't even flinch, instead smiling, the gash on his cheek already closing.

"I will not be coerced!" she snapped.

"I wouldn't dream of even trying to coerce something as deviant and base as your mind," Kessler said cheerily. "Diplomacy is so much fun between us greater powers; it adds balance to the more physical appeal of torture and bodily destruction. Since you are still of use, words will do if action is not permitted."

"So bold, Kessler," Amorphia grated. "But we wouldn't want Persephone with us, would we?" She nearly cackled her glee as his face fell. Just a fraction, but it was clear to her. She hated resorting to trump cards and hidden hands, but finding out who balanced out Kessler in the Changed hierarchy beneath him had been a grand find, if only because she was spiteful and loathed the German Butcher standing before her.

Kessler was strong, and fast, but against someone like Persephone, who used telekinesis and fluid mind tactics, he was merely a heartbeat from dying like any human, preferably, Amorphia mused, under the might of a thousand mental hammers.

"Even she has her uses."

"Yes, she keeps your childish depravities in check!" Amorphia sneered, showing teeth. Kessler took a moment to calm himself, and then he was all smooth and bored smiles again. "Now please hurry up and say your piece."

"Are you in a hurry?"

"Even one such as I don't like sharing the same air with the likes of you for too long. Pollution is such a problem these days."

"Yes, I'm sure," Kessler replied, unperturbed once more. "Very well. He orders your immediate return to America. He is about to close in on one part of the design, and that means he will need your particular skill in one aspect. Go to Persephone, she will fill you in with further details. That is all," he finished condescendingly.

"Then you may go," Amorphia finished, smiling sweetly, turning the tables. He merely bowed to her, a very slight and relatively insulting gesture, then turned on his heels and marched off. Amorphia watched him leave, relieved both from fear and annoyance. So, back to the field then. She sighed. Errand work was beneath her, and she despised being reminded of how much her will in these matters was really worth. But she did enjoy the Americas, and seeing Kessler squirm when Persephone was in the vicinity would make up for the denial of her own pleasures she was facing when she left Beijing.

CHAPTER TEN

Barcelona

It had seen better days since the catastrophic explosion in the sewer systems twenty years ago, which had decimated the seaside half of the city and left precious little left of the rest. But humans were resourceful, and eager to restore their histories. And so Barcelona was still undergoing restoration, the recreation of its oldest and greatest structures, as well as a general revamping process, to modernize itself amidst the antiquities. Thus, it was no surprise to see one particular structure rising from the new Riviera strip: a scraper that was largely comprised of thick aluminium and steel bars that were spanned by mere glass panes, giving illusions of frailty, where in fact great strength existed. A narrow elevator tube ran all the way from the cultivated garden sprawl at the foot of the scraper to the middle section, where vacant glass spires and bars of metal became more functional by also encapsulating chambers and suites. But the most intriguing piece of work on the entire structure was a Gothic-style, twelfth century cathedral, complete with immense stained glass windows and modern amenities despite the medieval appearance. But for the cathedral, the skyscraper looked completely at ease amidst new designs of buildings and creative pieces of modern architecture and engineering ingenuity. It was the centre of attention, and yet also lacked the indomitable singularity to always stand out; at times it was hard to imagine the necessity of the tower, or to think further than mere constructive appeals. Few people ever truly quested for finding out what the tower was for, or who the occupants were. But there was a distinct reason for it.

Catherine Gilchrest was a tall woman, taller than most. She had a savage beauty that at times was terrifying and at other times less than impressive, if only because her features were sharper than average, more pointed and masculine, even a bit cruel. High cheekbones, a clear, icy complexion and short, ash-blonde hair that hung in tight kinks and coils beside her ears afforded her little attention from the opposite sex, but then, she hardly cared. The ice blue orbs that glared from a slightly slanted angle betrayed nothing but sheerest contempt and disdain for that which Catherine felt she needed not bother with. Dressed in a very mannish business suit that nevertheless offset her pristine figure and curves to some advantage, she waited, arms crossed, staring out one of the large windows that rested between the two large square towers of the highest level of the cathedral perched atop the scraper. From inside, the coloured glass could be screened to refuse the normally glorious play of colourful eddies and light beams from outside sunlight, instead serving as a normal window in spite of the appearance outside remaining the same. It was far easier that way for her to enjoy the sight of the slowly but surely reviving city.

"You are sure he has ordered this?" a man's voice, heavy with an Italian accent, asked from behind her.

"He seems to think it expedient nowadays for the more aggressively inclined of us to meet, or to be harangued into submission," Catherine said. "Though why he has played so openly in the last few months is beyond me."

"That man never needed an excuse to do anything," the man behind Catherine said. He moved out of the shadows of the largely illumined hall and closer to Catherine. Once there, she glanced sideways at him. "How many of us has he commanded into action this time?" he queried. She shrugged. Standing in the sunlight that also limned her, the differences between them could be made out clearly. Although he was an impressive man to start off with, Catherine's height detracted from the striking aspects of the man. Still, his wide shoulders and barrel chest, complemented by a dark tan and hazel eyes, made him as exotic and darkly attractive as Catherine was icy and unstoppable. The man, named Alessandro, shrugged. "You would know better than me," he ventured, and Catherine nodded.

"So it would seem," and left it at that, in spite of not answering his veiled question. She swung about and brushed past him, an oddly seductive motion for all that she showed nothing in her face remotely connectable to attraction. The man nearly danced back a single step, and then shook his head. Never mind that this remarkable skyscraper was his abode, and that Catherine was in fact his guest. But that was her way, he mused. It was why he preferred keeping her company than any others of the Changed, of the minions and associates of their great master. To her alone could he show any notions of trust and sharing, because the both of them were hardly as destructive and vicious as the others. He still remembered the one time Persephone had tried her wiles on him – she had almost succeeded – but then, when he had spurned her, the witch had cut him across the shoulders with a telekinetic blade, and had somehow left a wound where no wounds should ever have mattered. Catherine did not fear Persephone, though. It was safe to say that the two of them despised each other, but never, no matter how furious Persephone had been in Catherine's company, had Alessandro seen the telekinetic wench try and pull anything against Catherine.

Interesting had been the least of the concerns. Alessandro dealt with facts and backed-up assumption, and he thought it was hardly flawed to assume that Persephone could actually do nothing to Catherine, for inexplicable reasons. Alessandro followed behind Catherine, weighing the thought of her as he did so. He had always suspected many things about her. For a start, Gilchrest was hardly a very noteworthy name, so he suspected she hid her true name. Since he had met her, a century ago, she had been 'Catherine', but nothing else was forthcoming. She visited him often, and for some reason felt completely at ease to flaunt none of her powers where others could see, something none of the others ever did – they enjoyed parading their gifts all too often. Ten decades was a long time, and all Alessandro knew of her was that she was leery of open displays of power – another non-endearing item of dissent between her and Persephone. But Catherine was powerful, Alessandro knew. Her power was the quiet confidence that required unimaginable forces to break, and even then she would remain defiant and wilful. That she was old, he had no doubt. Possibly, he thought sometimes, she was as old as he was, if not older. As far as power contrast went, there was no telling what she was capable of, but if she remained under his reign even now, it meant her power was not great enough to challenge their master. Still. There were many things one did not find out simply by watching her.

"How is it that even you fear to speak his name openly?" she asked, breaking his thoughts. She had taken a seat at the large table to one side of the immense hall, and leaned with one elbow on the table top, eyes large and inquisitive, challenging him to answer. But she wasn't finished yet. "Did he forbid it, perhaps?"

"Do you always challenge everything?" Alessandro snapped, angry. Catherine was, as far as he knew, no empath – other mentalists had said so – and yet she still managed to pick exact, key thoughts from the minds of others. At the sight of his outburst, Catherine's eyes hardened, but she didn't rise.

"So you are angry because of his domination, is that it?'

"There is no telling what he can do to any one of us!" Alessandro fired, becoming belligerent. "You must know how he keeps track of us!"

"Ah," Catherine said, a long indrawn breath following, as her face assumed a relatively merciless grimace. It was contempt and condescension that clothed her face, and her mouth, held slightly slack and open, seemed ready to launch a world of sarcasm and ridicule. Alessandro stiffened, preparing for the retort. Strangely enough, when it came, it wasn't aimed at him. "Still up to the old trickery it seems. Such callow methods to quell the ambitions of the small-minded. I have never held truck with his regime, you know this." Alessandro paled, a sight for one so bronzed.

"Can you say these things without his retaliation?" he asked, almost a whisper. Catherine's smile was a perilous winter sky.

"I have never served because of terror, my dear," she said slowly. Alessandro's mind raced to compute, and the result he got forced an involuntary gasp from him. He stepped closer, keeping her in sight, and she replied by doing the same, her mirthless, knowing little grin in place. "But what Graven does and what he knows, and what he intends, that is what I wish to know, and that is why, every now and then, I serve, or give the semblance thereof." Alessandro flinched at the mention of the name, and Catherine's laughter simply exacerbated the experience.

"He can hear you, he knows where you are," he whispered.

"He always does the others, and you. But not I, not always," Catherine replied. "And I don't care." She rose, and began to walk towards the large double doors at the back of the hall. Alessandro waited for a moment, mired in his own thoughts and the ramifications of what she had said, before he rose as well and trotted after. "I will see you in New York."

"Why do you tell me this now?" Alessandro queried. "I have known you for one hundred years, and yet you tell me this now. Why?"

"Why not?" Catherine replied, shrugging. "I do not know why he summons us there now, but it cannot be for nothing. And I mean to see what his agenda over the centuries has reaped, if only to determine whether I am still interested in following in his wake." The doors closed behind her, leaving Alessandro alone in the silence of the hall. He shook his head, astonished at what he had learned. He knew, of the Greater Changed, that they were nine, including him. He knew of Persephone, of Catherine and Amorphia, and with himself included they were five. But he had heard rumours of the others, hints and names. A cruel being named Kessler, and a sinister Changed by the name of Amal. That made seven, and it unsettled Alessandro that he had no idea who or where the other two were, or if they even existed. Catherine, apart from the intense pleasure he invariably found in her company, and the wit and calculating, cynical charisma she exuded, was also a massive source of untapped information, and he treasured her insights like he would a vault of gold. Because of those insights in the past, he had unlearnt many things and corrected more, becoming stronger and more aloof from the seeming maddened rage that drove the other Greater Changed, the Chosen. But he was nowhere near powerful enough to challenge their master, the First amongst equals.

His gifts lay in calculation, in the ability to, through an immensely fast and undiluted force of will and mental skill, plot eventualities and calculate matters that would take anyone else weeks, even months. He was also a cybernetic expert, an Integrator, capable of sending his mind and senses speeding down and into any electrical device, no matter how primitive. At that level he was also a matter assimilator, capable of integrating his physical form with almost any material, and once integrated, able to change the material at will to serve his needs.

His calculation was what endeared him and bound him to the First. He breathed a sigh of relief, not yet feeling that very subtle and almost undetectable pinprick that signalled a response, an oversight, of the master when his name was mentioned or alluded to in any direct way. But the title Alessandro had long since given the master, and the pronominal diminutions that all the others also utilized to avoid his immediate attention, worked like a charm. It was better this way, because it guaranteed that he could think and reckon without the First finding out too much. And what Alessandro desperately wanted to figure out was what exactly the First was doing that suddenly required the presence of five of the Greater Changed, and what the First's agenda was actually about.

CHAPTER ELEVEN

Violated...

That was how he felt. He couldn't describe the turmoil that raged inside by any other means, or the sense that his world was upside down. He knew somehow that there was hardly anything he could do, but he still felt betrayed. Danny was the friend he'd never lose, his 'second brother'. Of that much he'd been so sure, the one person in the world that would always remain close and in confidence, no matter what. Apparently the 'what' had never seen the implications of what was happening now, of what had happened. Now Danny was as alien to Nathan as any stranger on the street: accessible yet unknown.

He turned on his other side, facing the large window. Night was falling fast, and it played gloomily along with the overcast white clouds that obscured the sky. Nathan sighed in frustration and sat up, trying to quell the unease he felt. He had never felt so lost before, so unhinged despite most everything in life remaining secure. The feeling curled his lips and twisted his stomach. He needed to get away. He suddenly felt the urge to just grab Joanie and fly off, back home, away from GOA and Danny. He knew somehow that convincing Luke to leave the organization was next to impossible, but then Luke was his superior in years, and could make up his own mind. So maybe Luke would stay, and in time, Danny would be Danny again, and just fine. But right now, Nathan felt that he would never be close to his estranged friend again. And Nathan knew his future wasn't here. He needed to get away.

Leaving the bedroom, he began looking for Joanie. She hadn't come back since leaving him to his misery, and there was no telling where she could be. He began sweeping the house, peering into the rooms with open doors. He passed the main bedroom as well, and hearing voices from within, he fervently hoped he would avoid Danny. The gap between them was just too great now, and anything else would be immensely awkward. He remained outside the main bedroom door for a few moments, hoping to identify anyone talking within, but then moved on, opting for that rather than be caught snooping. He made for the lounge.

Like the rest of the house, there was a feeling of gloom and an impending storm from outside hanging thick in the air. The dark was banished by a solitary lamp, and Nathan halted. Jamie was seated in a chair beneath the lamp, a newspaper open in his hands. The stocky man remained oblivious of Nathan's presence, or if he wasn't, he didn't venture any greetings.

"Have you seen Joanie about?" Nathan asked.

"Nope. She went walking on the beach a couple of hours ago, but I haven't seen her since," Jamie said, turning a page.

"Crap," Nathan breathed, and darted towards the doors leading to the terrace. He swept through, eyes searching the narrow garden and the pathway he had seen earlier. He took its winding course down to the beach, descending, swearing when he hit his foot against something in the dark, muttering under his breath. As he neared the beach, he began calling for Joanie. He walked onto the sand and began casting about, looking up and down, trying to discern any figures or shapes. He walked five minutes in one direction, then back to the starting point and five minutes in the opposite direction, but when he couldn't make out anything in the continuing gloom, he became frustrated and more than a little frightened. He stopped, feet kicking in the sand, one hand against the nape of his neck, and looked about one last time.

"She's not here, not now. She's in the house." Nathan spun, fervently glaring all around him. The voice, he knew when he saw no one, had sounded right into his head. For a moment he thought it was Charlie, and anger flared.

"Show yourself!" he yelled at the dusky sky.

"Why?" came the reply. "You don't trust me, and I am wary of you, to say the least." Nathan gasped, a sharply in-drawn breath. It wasn't Charlie.

"Danny," he whispered. As if on cue, a small sound, like a gust of wind, sounded to his left side, and Daniel materialized, wrapped in darkness, light blue eyes fading to obscurity as his power died down. Despite the distance of a few feet, Nathan took a step back.

"You say my name with such familiarity," Daniel said. "As though you're used to saying it. Or have been."

"I'm going back to the house," Nathan said suddenly, the feelings of awkwardness and latent anger at the whole situation rising again. He made to move past Daniel.

"Charlie said you're here for a reason," Daniel replied. "I know the reason, and so do you, so where are you going?" Nathan halted but didn't turn to face Daniel. "Joanie said she, you and I were friends once, and yet I can't remember you. I can recall my family, and some other folks I know, but not you, or her."

"Whatever," Nathan almost barked, and continued walking.

"I can't imagine I would be friends with someone like you, someone so uncaring," Daniel added, and Nathan stopped again. "Something tells me you don't like me in any case," Daniel finished sardonically.

"You nearly killed me you little bastard!" Nathan grated, swinging about and drawing close to Daniel until he towered over him. Dark green eyes stared up at him, unfazed.

"You threatened Charlie," Daniel replied calmly.

"You know what? You forgot about us! We were looking for you for the last year and you didn't even have the decency to remember us! We were this close Danny-boy! This close! You were my brother!" Nathan snarled, holding up two crossed fingers. "And the first thing you do when you see me is choke the life out of me and threaten to do worse!"

"Then make me remember!" Daniel challenged. "If we were so close, why are you running away?"

"Because you forgot about me! About Luke and Joanie too! You betrayed us!"

"And how would I have stopped what happened to me?" Daniel fired back, eyes ablaze, posture belligerent to match Nathan's coiled antagonism. "You think I wanted to forget? Or do you actually think I like being like this, a man with hollow memories?" They stared at each other, and Nathan swallowed, upset and unsettled by Daniel's outburst. "I remember almost nothing from before the Change, because of the Change, and here you stand, accusing me!"

"You say Charlie's your friend," Nathan went on, "but he's the guy who's covered all of this up! He knew all of these things, about me and Joanie and Luke searching for you, and he kept you and all of us in the dark. That's why I hate his guts!"

"This isn't about Charlie, Nathan," Daniel said. "Maybe some of it is, and maybe what you're saying is true, but the real reason you're upset and angry is because I forgot about you. And the bottom line is I don't even know why, or what about, really." Daniel seemed to deflate out of sheer weariness, and the two of them faced each other, estranged family. Nathan still felt cheated somehow, even though he knew better, in light of Daniel's account. But it didn't help at all that Daniel could be so completely divorced and unlike the person Nathan had known, and then out of nowhere would speak Nathan's name as companionably as if nothing had ever changed. Sighing, Nathan turned away and stared at the ocean. For the longest and most awkward moment they stood apart and in silence. "I spoke to Joanie this afternoon," Daniel said eventually.

"About what?" Nathan queried.

"She tried to tell me things about the past, our – my, yours and her – past together. High school, university." Daniel gave a dejected step forward. "I couldn't deal with it." Nathan listened, hurt and almost unwilling to listen, but intrigued also. "When she spoke, some of what she said began making sense, ringing true. I know who she is, and that alone should tell me that I should know you as well."

"So what do you want me to do?" Nathan asked. "Tell you stuff? See what fits and what doesn't?" Daniel shook his head.

"When Joanie tried that, I thought my head would explode. The memories aren't gone, not completely, but they're... damaged, somehow: when things begin making sense, the pain becomes worse, until I can't think straight, or think at all. I just couldn't listen anymore." Nathan turned his head. Daniel wasn't looking at him, and it gave him a moment to observe. Even in the almost-dark he thought he could make out the pained expression on Daniel's face, and the harsh sense of loss that accompanied it. "Going about it that way won't work."

"Then what will?" Nathan asked finally, dreading the answer he might get. Suddenly he was afraid of what might happen, of what Daniel might propose. When Daniel sighed, he steeled himself.

"You probably know by now what I'm capable of," Daniel began. "And not just because I threatened you."

"Alice calls you an Nth Prime, and the way she'd said it made it sound scary," Nathan answered. Daniel nodded, an affirmation more than arrogance.

"You're not an empath, are you?" he asked. Nathan shook his head. "So what I'm gonna ask requires your express permission, because it will hurt. Me a lot more than you, but that is the risk I'm willing to take from my end." Nathan looked away for a moment, then back again. Daniel stared out over the ocean, and Nathan was suddenly filled with a poignant sense of sympathy. The anger and frustration was still there, that he had lost his best friend, and that Daniel had gone as far as hurting him, but now, seeing Daniel stand there, body posed in a way that hearkened back to the old Daniel that Nathan recalled, he felt his heart and resolve soften. Daniel's simple explanation of his own perspective in the matter made Nathan realize that Daniel had indeed received a raw deal. It didn't make up for the way things turned out, but it had blunted the excess rage and the sense of betrayal Nathan had felt before. But it had also added a deepening sense of foreboding.

"You probably know, from Joanie, that an empath gets it pretty rough from physical contact," Daniel said, bringing Nathan back to the situation. "Some people say that an empath's entire nervous system is a network of thought relays: you touch any telepath's arm and you're given a glimpse of surface thoughts. If you touch any telepath's arm, and you are one yourself, a connection of greater ease is formed. I'd say they're about right on that count, but I don't know how it works between empath and non-empath. Probably nothing should happen, but if I touched your hand now I'd recoil, and that means I can sense your thoughts unbidden." Nathan listened, adding facts to information he already had. He did know that Joanie wasn't the most physical girl, and that she often shied away from him if he became overly affectionate. What Daniel said made sense. Then something else sidetracked him, and he frowned.

"Can you read my thoughts right now, without touching?" Daniel nodded, and Nathan shivered.

"I could, but I won't," Daniel said. He sighed and lifted his head. "There was this one woman at Headquarters. Her name was Marris – she's a cyber-specialist – and after the first time I met her, she refused to meet me again. Charlie told me later it was because she's said I'd somehow ripped her thoughts from her mind. Doing something like that is a severe violation, if you're an empath, and Charlie told me never to do it again." Daniel looked at Nathan and started, noting the horrified expression. He coloured – thankfully unnoticeable in the dark, and nearly reached over to Nathan to reassure him, but instead drew his hand back and chuckled apologetically. "Sorry. Guess you don't need to hear stuff like that."

"Not really, no," Nathan added, sounding choked.

"But you have to understand that I would never do something like that. The one thing I am definitely not is a wet-behind-the-ears recruit. I am well in control of my gifts. If you don't trust me, ask Alice, she did the last check-up on me herself."

"But Alice is also a telepath," Nathan said.

"Which is why I'm not entirely sure how I can best pull this off."

"What exactly do you want to pull of?"

"I need to enter your mind," Daniel said, and it sounded as though he felt as leery as Nathan knew he himself did. "I know you trust Joanie, and you love her. That goes a long way to helping, so she can steady you, if you allow her to. Charlie can steady me, and then..."

"Then?" Nathan insisted, when Daniel remained silent.

"Then I scan your mind and hope this works." Nathan sighed, and placed one hand on his hip, rubbing his mouth with the other. He was terrified of the entire empath situation: he'd seen from the start how bad it could get, especially with Luke being three years his senior, and a thirteen-year-old Nathan disallowed and unable to tell their parents or to help his changing brother in any way. And with Joanie, even after two years together, she could still get edgy and depressed in ways that Nathan couldn't really understand. But this was different: Luke was his brother, his blood, and Joanie was the girl he wanted to spend the rest of his life with, as things were now. Even though Daniel was as close to a brother as made little difference, the recent divide made Nathan's decision harder. And yet looking at Daniel now, noting the changes and all the things that were supposed to enforce the feelings of alienation, he couldn't help but feel himself reach out to him.

"You've made a decision?" Daniel asked, looking Nathan in the eyes. Nathan, on some impulse, raised one eyebrow and grinned.

"You can't read it from my mind?" he quipped, and shockingly, Daniel fired back a bemused, belittling stare, a gesture that was as familiar to Nathan as Joanie was. He couldn't help but laugh out loud out of a sense of relief, and snaked an arm out in the usual reply of jocular camaraderie. His amusement became shock when his arm connected with an invisible force, and Daniel's nearly deadpan expression stood as warning.

"Shit, sorry!" Nathan apologized.

"That's okay," Daniel returned, not sounding offended. "Just cautious, that's all." He tilted his head in the general direction of the house and began walking. Nathan fell in stride beside him.

"So when do we do this?" he asked.

"Whenever you're ready," Daniel replied.

There was really no point in delay.

Nathan sat at the breakfast table with Joanie and Jamie. He had risen late, after having a long talk with Joanie, and listening long hours into the night to her advice on how to deal with empaths when you weren't one yourself. Jamie merely listened to them now, relatively unperturbed by it all. He did add a few insights of his own every now and then, but not too much.

"Whatever you do, don't touch him if he doesn't order it," Joanie said, and Nathan rolled his eyes.

"You've said that already. Four times."

"I'm concerned!" Joanie countered. Jamie snickered.

"Hope you know what you're doing," he said, as usual, a newspaper open before him. Nathan bridled. The last few days, the man had turned into some gleeful bystander, grinning whenever something happened. If he recalled, Jamie had smiled when he'd walked in on Nathan, helped upright by Joanie, after Daniel had nearly throttled him.

"Care to elaborate?" Nathan asked snidely, and Joanie too stared intently.

"Nah," Jamie replied. "Let's just say that this could go either horribly wrong or very right. At least, it would have the desired effect Charlie wants on Daniel."

"What?" Joanie asked sharply. She frowned mightily at Jamie, but the man merely stared at her with a very calculated nonchalant expression rife on his features.

"What, he forgot to tell you?" Jamie challenged. Nathan looked at Joanie, his face turning red again. Joanie held up a cautioning hand to delay any outbursts.

"What exactly is your part in this?" she asked Jamie. "Apart from getting on everyone else's nerves nowadays and working up conflict?" Jamie quirked his mouth askance and actually seemed to give Joanie a slight nod. He folded the newspaper neatly, placed it on a chair beside him and put his hands together, regarding Joanie silently over them. For the moment he appeared to be ignoring Nathan, who was still gathering himself and defusing his fuming.

"Okay, ask a direct question, get a direct answer," Jamie countered. "We know how this one plays out. You two have reason enough to dislike Charlie already, and the sooner that clears up, the better."

"So you fix this situation between us and Charlie by dangling another fault before our noses like a carrot?" Nathan burst out.

"Maybe you two should just go back to preparing for the big test," Jamie remarked. "Maybe once Daniel regains his memories, you can skewer Charlie for his past mistakes without the immediate rage of Daniel interfering afterwards."

"Meaning?" Joanie queried.

"C'mon, use your heads!" Jamie snapped. "A thought transmission from one empath to another is easy, but even the most skilled telepath can only handle so much information from a non-telepathic source before he or she gets a meltdown."

"That's what'll happen to Daniel?" Nathan asked, horrified. Jamie looked at him and nodded curtly.

"Most probably, yeah. Nothing permanent, nothing lastingly damaging, but a mental explosion as his mind retakes control. Which is why Charlie and even Alice are willing to allow this to go on." Joanie gasped, sparing a startled look for Nathan, who frowned, unsure of what he was hearing. "What, you thought I liked this? I'm here to make sure of Charlie's discretion when it comes to Daniel doesn't go beyond the acceptable."

205

"You're Charlie's keeper?" Nathan asked, and couldn't help a sly snicker from escaping his control. Jamie shook his head.

"Too simple, a keeper. Let's just say I get to make sure Charlie's hold on Daniel doesn't intensify, for reasons I'm not at liberty to tell you."

"How? What can you do against Charlie? Phase?" Nathan asked snidely

"I have this barrier, this inbuilt defence, against mental intrusions and attacks," Jamie said, tapping his head. "Charlie can do jack-shit against me, beyond throwing me out a window telekinetically. Which is also why I get to steady the two of you when Daniel does the mental injection thing."

"You still haven't told us the real reason for Charlie wanting Daniel to do this."

"Maybe he just wants to let Daniel get to rekindle old friendships."

"Bullshit!" Nathan spat, actually startling Jamie in turn. The man laughed, a strangely appreciative sound.

"Okay, fine, have it your way." Jamie leaned forward. "As far as any of us can tell, Alice and Charlie are working to some sort of level, with Daniel's gifts. I don't know what Alice knows; hell, I bet she knows a lot more than all of the rest of GOA's Changed put together, and she ain't telling anyone anything, except maybe a few snippets to Charlie."

"What would Alice really want with Daniel?" Joanie asked, eyes dreamy and expression one of far-off introspection. Jamie shrugged.

"Lots of theories on that one, and none of them make sense. But come on, if you were in charge of something like GOA, and you get your hands on the first Nth Prime Changed in almost seventy years, wouldn't you work a little behind the scenes as well?" Jamie looked from Joanie to Nathan, then back to Joanie. "Still haven't figured it out yet, huh?"

"You're saying Alice can't be trusted," Joanie said after a while.

"Who knows? Maybe I should just come right out and tell you."

"We're all ears," Nathan said snidely. Jamie ignored the barb and continued.

"In the last two months, Daniel's progress has hit a standstill. He used to grow in strength daily, small increments or even big ones, and every now and then he'd show up a new power. He was scared shitless – I think I'd be also – but Alice and Charlie watched with barely contained elation as their pride and joy proved over and over that he was indeed an Nth Primer, a GenneY of massive skill. So you can imagine their surprise when Daniel stopped showing them new things. They didn't know what the problem was until about two months ago, when Daniel's headaches resurfaced. I don't know what happened then, but from what I've heard, Charlie did the usual mental link thing, and found out something real interesting."

Nathan and Joanie listened, raptly mesmerized by the narration. "Daniel's memories, the ones that are broken, so to speak, are causing problems. He can hardly engage in the usual bouts of the mental tomfoolery he did before, without straining a blood vessel. Wouldn't surprise me if he'd actually suffered a stroke, or got a tumor." Seeing the expressions of pale horror on Nathan and Joanie's faces, Jamie swallowed. "Not that he really did, I mean." Jamie sighed.

"I still don't get your part in all this," Joanie said after a while. "You're a GOA employee, and you speak highly of Alice and even Charlie, but right now you sound as if you're against them."

"I'm all for them, but that doesn't mean I like what they do all the time. And I obviously don't know Daniel the way you guys do, but I'd like to, because I like him and I bet there's more to him than you can tell right now. So I'm gonna stand by you two when Daniel does his lawful breaking-and-entering stuff, and keep an eye on Charlie, just in case."

After Jamie had left the breakfast table, Nathan sat staring at Joanie. The far-off look in her eyes told him she was using more than simple thoughts to think, so he waited for her to snap out of it herself. Only when she did so did he pay attention again, his own mind idly jumping between thoughts. A shiver alerted him to her return to full awareness.

"You still want to do this?" she asked him. He nodded.

"You heard Jamie. I think more than ever now we can't turn our backs on Danny. He needs this."

"But this is also exactly what Alice wants," Joanie said critically. "I've met her only once, and she seemed nice, even with the slight mental touch we experienced, but Nathan, she's an empath on a level I can only hope to be like one day. There's no telling what she can do, and what she can hide, even from another empath. And from what Jamie said, she and Charlie aren't all that open with dealing with Daniel. Giving him back his memories might further whatever agenda she has with him." Nathan stared directly in front of him, clasping his hands together even as he fidgeted uncomfortably on his chair. He took a few deliberate breaths, then spoke.

"You still remember Danny, right?" he asked Joanie.

"What do you mean?" she asked.

"Like we knew him, not like we've experienced him these last few days. Good old Danny, the cool, calm one. The guy who's never caught off guard, and when he is, gets to laugh it up with the rest of everyone, because he doesn't really care either way. Moody Daniel, depressed Daniel, outrageously funny Danny-boy, the guy I'd trust with my life any day, and you would too." Joanie listened attentively, still uncertain of what Nathan was driving at, but allowing him to go on uninterrupted. "If this goes right, and Danny gets back those memories, everyone wins, even if Alice does too. We get him back, like he used to be, and there's even more trust then, because not only is he like us, Changed, but damn!" He left the thought hanging.

When Joanie still appeared unconvinced, Nathan leaned forward, lowering his voice almost emphatically, trying to make her see sense. "Don't you see? What's the one thing Danny always said about himself? The one thing he hates above all else for people to do to him?" Joanie thought for a while, but not too long: it wasn't all that hard.

"He hates it when people try to control him, or force him to do something he doesn't want to."

"More so than usual," Nathan completed, sounding almost joyful, completing Joanie's statement. "He finds this out from me when we do the mind thing, and you can bet he won't take Alice and Charlie's meddling lightly!" Joanie managed a smile for Nathan, a brave attempt that hid her own feelings. She hoped Nathan was right, and that everything went as he thought they would, or else nothing would come of it, and they would have wasted their time, all the effort of finding Daniel again, and reopened the wounds for nothing at all.

"I hope we can trust Jamie," she said.

"He's no empath. You'll have to take care of the screening thing," Nathan replied, leaning over and placing his hands on her shoulders. "Hey, you trust me on this?" He waited for Joanie to nod, even though she had let slip the smile. "This'll work out fine, you wait and see. Just wait and see."

CHAPTER TWELVE

Adaptation

"It's fascinating, really, the way they go about it."

Alyssa pursed her lips, not responding to Margaret's comment. She was raptly attentive on the scene below, in the secluded gardens just behind the west wing. Another safe location where the careful Changed could explore and enhance skills, because it was away from prying eyes, and there was very little that could be damaged, beyond the odd bit of vegetation here and there. The garden was walled all around by topiary hedges, and sported several concrete walls in between. No, there was little that could go far wrong in there.

More, the view from the large windows in the south-facing lounge on the second floor of the west wing served admirably for any observers. And Alyssa had found herself gravitating here every time Luke and Alex began their sessions. Today though, Margaret had accompanied her, and she felt strangely suffocated by the older woman's presence. She wanted to enjoy this by herself. She wanted to stare at Luke without anyone else chirping in by her side every now and then.

"I admit I am impressed with the girl," Margaret continued, and it was all Alyssa could do not to start fuming. "She turned out alright, or at least, not nearly as troublesome as Alice had averred she would be."

"It's only been two weeks, Maggie," Alyssa protested, hardly bothering to hide the impatience in her voice. A slight twist on Margaret's lips went unnoticed, as Alyssa returned to watching the goings-on below them. She leaned a little closer, elbows supported on her knees, face close to the window pane, as she watched Luke assume a ready position some few feet from Alex, facing her. Alex in turn had an almost voracious grin on her face, an expression Luke had come to be familiar with, and Alyssa detested. It meant the little hussy was about to throw everything she had at Luke. Usually the bout ended with Luke rolling about to dodge the flying objects sent by Alex: he didn't have Alex's skill yet, and there was no telling really what his exact potential would be. It vexed Alyssa that she couldn't tell in any case, because she had absolutely no empathic gifts. It made the constant company that Luke and Alex had even more frustrating, because the two of them connected on a level that Alyssa knew she would never have. She sighed dramatically, ignoring Margaret's presence.

Below them, six clay plates lifted from behind Alex, and they spun freely in the air about her, rotating swiftly. Her smile indicated her intent, and Luke's stance became more pronounced. The first set of three plates flew towards him, juddering and careening in mid-flight, fast enough to break skin and cause bloodshed if they were to connect with flesh. Luke danced aside from the first one, lifted a hand that sent another plate flying away from him and made a crushing gesture with the other hand, causing the remaining plate to explode. There was hardly time for him to recover before three more plates whined their way towards him, coming wide and from three different angles at different speeds. Two of them bent away from Luke at weird curves, a sure sign of deflection. The third one came within inches of his body before he made a hasty chopping gesture that stopped the plate in mid-air and dropped it to the ground. Alex jumped up and down, clapping her hands, a clear indication of her own approval, and Luke, affecting a gracious smile, placed his feet together and made her a bow from the waist up. Alyssa scowled, hardly impressed by Alex's display, and entranced anew by Luke's performance. She would have liked to sit outside with them and watch up close, but three times up and running of that and she knew Alex was becoming suspicious of Alyssa's intentions. So Alyssa watched from afar, thinking enraged thoughts concerning Alex even as she practically swooned over

Luke. Fortunately she wasn't completely brainless: she never showed any sign of how she felt towards him when they were in each other's company. And heaven knows it took every ounce of her resolve to remain aloof when Alex was also in the area. Alyssa became incensed almost by default when she remembered how Alex had filched stray thoughts from her head, just a week go, simply out of spite and to show what she was capable of.

Another bout was underway below. This time, Luke also had a set of clay plates beside him. Alyssa liked these sessions more when it wasn't just Luke that had to dance out of the way of Alex's attacks, even if she was the teacher and Luke the pupil. Luke had never landed a hit before, but Alyssa always enjoyed the possibility of it happening, and she often visualized how Alex got knocked out by a stray clay shard. She could get hospitalized, sent away for a while, have a nice time recovering.

"Oh now that's something new!" Margaret said suddenly, causing Alyssa to jump. She speared the older woman with a venomous glare, then looked back out the window. She too gasped. Between Luke and Alex there was a shimmering screen, undulating in the light like a soap bubble. It seemed to buckle and shake for a few moments, a foot from Luke's outstretched fingertips. The looks of surprise on their faces remained even when the bubble finally shook and vanished. "Well?" Margaret asked gravely, looking at Alyssa. "You might as well go and find out what happened. I'll be along shortly." Alyssa, still not stymied enough by Margaret's incessant interference, nodded at the order and engaged her own gift of speed, which took her outside and down to the garden courtyard within seconds. When she came to a halt, Luke and Alex were talking animatedly, both of them still caught in the excitement. On noting Alyssa's presence, Luke grinned.

"Did you see what I did?" he asked, elated. Alyssa nodded. Even Alex seemed more buoyant and more tolerant of Alyssa's presence. "I've never done that before!"

"It's a shield!" Alex chortled happily, and Alyssa wanted to sneer that she knew that. She refrained from doing so, though. "But can you do it again?"

"Dunno," Luke replied simply, shrugging, but his face was optimistic. He frowned and held his hand in front of him, brows furrowing in concentration. After a while, when nothing happened, he lowered his hand and pressed his lips together. "Okay, it might work if I can recall what I thought the moment I did it."

"How about 'shit this is it!'" Alex ventured, and this time Alyssa did roll her eyes.

"Nope." Luke's eyes lit up. "Ooh, throw more tablets at me, and fast!" He jogged a short distance from where Alex was standing, back to his usual spot. Alex nodded and complied, standing beside her arsenal of clay plates. She waited for Luke to give her a ready signal, then lifted the plates and threw them as hard as she could, the telekinetic energy seeming to whine with the plates that rode with them. Alyssa drew in a sharp breath and stepped back at high speed, out of harm's way. She watched as first one, then another plate flew towards Luke. His frown of concentration was heavily in place, and each plate exploded several feet from his hand, or simply lost speed and fell to the ground, rolling off. "This isn't working!" he yelled at Alex. "Throw everything you've got!"

"You sure?" Alex asked, sounding, of all things, a little cautious.

"Yeah!" Luke replied, and Alyssa bunched herself together, in case something bad might happen. If needs be she could probably destroy the plates before they all hit Luke – she was that fast – but she wouldn't get them all. Still, she could save his life if she managed to target and eliminate the crucial ones that –

The sound of ten plates lifting at once and beginning to spin broke Alyssa from her train of thought. She almost protested the event, glaring intently at Alex, who ignored her flat, intent as she was on keeping all the plates fixed and ready to fly. Luke was breathing heavily, not from exertion but from adrenaline, one arm to his side, the other ready to lift at a moment's notice. With a sharp cry, Alex released the plates, and each one of them began spinning alternately, rotating and curving about, each one aimed at Luke but taking a different, tortuous path. With bated breath Alyssa watched, her senses gearing into overdrive to prepare her for the accident waiting to happen. When the first plate began its inward curve towards Luke's head, she moved forward, her speed on the brink of readiness. The plate swooped in, mere feet from Luke now, and Alyssa ducked low, engaging speed.

She stopped short suddenly, as the plate exploded. The rest of them followed, and connected hard with the bubbling field, as it rippled into existence, a curved dome trailing into nothingness around the edges, buckling slightly around the plate impacts but staying, crushing all incoming clay tablets. The shards and dusty debris that remained over from the impact fell uselessly to the ground. Luke whooped a cry of triumph, and Alex once more resorted to her undignified clapping. Alyssa merely watched, her gifts dying down, her mind in turmoil. She had really thought that Luke wouldn't get it right again, and that she could save him and earn his gratitude. Feeling thwarted, she prepared to congratulate him and leave, when Margaret showed up, slowly clapping her hands and walking like a grand dame. Alyssa turned back around, rather than try and school her mortified expression fast enough to avoid Margaret's scrutiny.

"Wonderful, just wonderful!" she said clearly. "A new gift is always a welcome one!"

"Thanks," Luke said, actually almost blushing from the compliment.

"I am so pleased by your progress, both of you," Margaret said, spreading her arms to encompass Alex also. "Even in such short time." Alex looked away for some reason, her face unreadable. Margaret didn't seem to notice, or care, so she clasped her hands together, a beatific smile on her lips. "Alexis, dear, I have arranged for us to go shopping this afternoon in the city. I have a very large and extravagant soirée planned in a month's time, and arrangements need to be made."

"A month from now?" Alex asked, incredulous. "And you want to start planning now?"

"She does that sometimes," Alyssa added, trying to keep the amusement off her face. "It gives her great pleasure." Alex speared Alyssa with a critical glare, then looked back at Margaret.

"When I plan a party, dear, I do it with all the style and flair imaginable," Margaret said, eyes twinkling. "And I don't leave anything to chance, so earlier it is, rather than rushed." Margaret gave a last, amused and obviously pleased look which she directed at Luke, then turned about and sauntered off with a graceful gait. Alyssa, knowing she would be treading on awkward domain again soon, didn't even look at Alyssa and Luke, and marched off after Margaret as fast as she could without engaging her gifts.

"You must be the first woman I've met who dislikes shopping," Luke said to Alex, when the other two were out of earshot.

"It's not that," Alex replied. "I dread shopping with Margaret. Who knows what would happen?"

"So go, have fun, enjoy yourself!"

"And leave you alone with that little twit Alyssa?" Alex countered, making Luke frown.

"Alyssa? What's she got to do with this? I know you guys don't like each other, but she and I get along just fine."

"Exactly," Alex breathed, and walked past him.

Luke watched the limousine pull away.

From the window that faced him, he saw a pale expression of long-suffering already spreading over Alex's face, as she waved weakly goodbye. Behind her, Margaret was more animated, her gloved hand waving eagerly. She looked, as far as Luke could tell, the epitome of city style, although he would hardly credit anyone for decking themselves out in an outfit like hers, with the massive, wide-brimmed hat overshadowing her face, and the large sunglasses hiding her eyes. A picture of snooty wealth. Old snobbery. Luke grinned, lamenting Alex's case but also secretly amused at what she would have to endure, and if it would really be all that bad.

He retreated from the front entry stairs and returned inside, making for his suites. He felt a slight twinge of trepidation, wondering where Alyssa was. Since Alex's small foray as to Alyssa's intentions, he had unwittingly found himself looking for her everywhere, suspecting she could jump him from any place, considering what her gifts were. Thankfully, she didn't appear when he went into his bedroom, and he gratefully closed the doors behind him, locking them. No doubt a locked door wouldn't deter Alyssa – for some reason he suspected she never really had problems like that – but it might still give him enough warning of her presence or entry.

He felt weary, but pleased. Despite his tiredness it was still hard not to jump up and down all the time, thinking of what had happened today. For the first time in two weeks he really missed his brother's company, because Nathan would have been the first one he'd tell. He was walking towards the bathroom when he stopped and chuckled. There was an antique-looking phone right next to the large couch in the comfortable sitting room adjacent to the bedroom. He picked up the handset, giving it a quizzical look, then dialled the small digit buttons beneath it. Strange device, outdated, and yet when he had input the number the sounds of electronic transmission could be clearly identified. But it was still an old device, so it took longer than normal for the connection to go through. Luke listened avidly, and snorted angrily when the receiver transmitted his brother's 'can't talk right now' message. So, no civilian calls came in or out of GOA, it seemed. Still, even the sound of his familiar voice soothed Luke somewhat, and he felt less lonely. He spoke into the phone and left a message.

He sat on his bed for a while, deep in thought, musing on life. For a start, his was turning out a little different from what he had expected. He hadn't thought, a month ago, that he would find himself here, in New York, and doing what he was doing. He missed his parents, but for all intents and purposes he couldn't live on their largesse for the rest of his days. He had finished studying just the previous year, and hadn't found a job right away. But this, GOA, Alex. everything had changed so rapidly, and he still felt as though he had to wake up at some point, or suffer some sort of shock to his system.

After a while, he got tired of the bedroom, even though it was as sumptuous as any hotel suite he'd ever seen. The novelty wore off after a while though, even if the setting was becoming more and more familiar. He left his suite and descended again, temporarily forgetting Alyssa, but remembering her when he passed the doors leading to her chambers. He halted and listened if she was inside, and nodded to himself, satisfied, when he heard the sound of music coming from within. Hopefully it wasn't some ruse. As he walked away he chuckled, mentally berating Alex for placing such notions in his head.

"What, I get blamed for pointing out the obvious?" her voice travelled to him, and he started, nearly losing his footing down the stairs. He righted himself and continued with a slower tread, before replying.

"Won't Margaret suspect you're talking to me?"

"Puh-lease, as if I can't do lots of things at the same time. In case you're wondering, I am prancing around in a very large dress. It's more like a blimp than anything else!" Luke laughed at the comment, then narrowed his eyes and focused on the distant origin of her voice. It took some effort, and a lot of strain – Luke was getting better at distance viewing, but it still took a lot of effort, and it grew immensely hard after a distance of a kilometre, for some reason. He strained against the limit, making it across but then feeling himself grow dizzy with the effort. *"Luke honey, don't strain!"* Alex warned. She wasn't all that much stronger than he was at remote views, but more experienced. It was startling then when he felt her own mind infuse his own stretched probe, helping it

onward and pulling it towards her. He smiled, still standing at the bottom of the stairs, when he noticed, through his connection, how she twirled for Margaret's approval. He felt the layers of dark amusement within her, even though she wasn't smiling, and giving every appearance of being made to suffer. The dressers clapped hands and made comments on how marvellous she looked, but Alex stopped, looked at no one in particular and pronounced in a very bored voice that she didn't like the way it fluttered about her legs. Margaret, not losing a single moment, clapped her gloved hands and ordered another bevy of dresses to be brought forward. The frustration, tinged with secret excitement, flowed through the connection to Luke.

"Careful, we never know if Margaret might catch on," he warned. At the mansion, he entered the west wing lounge and took a seat, idly tapping a fingertip across the small panel inlaid on the armrest of the chair. The wooden panelling flushed open and revealed a large wide screen, which buzzed to life and began displaying a stream of small mosaics, each square large enough to indicate which show it represented.

"Whatever will happen if she realizes you're actually enjoying this?"

"Like I care! Ow!" A small amount of pain flared across the link, but it was relatively mild. An outfitter had drawn the bodice too tightly, and Alex scowled angrily at the woman, who kept her eyes downcast. *"I'm gonna let you go now, otherwise we'll have headaches for the rest of the day, and we can't have that at Miss Maggie's shopping quest, oh no!"* The visuals faded, and Luke maintained only the communication relay. *"She might really suspect something if that happened."*

"How long are you still gonna be?" Luke queried, making a selection from one of the mosaics. The screen divided into four larger scenes, each one indicating current events and news headlines.

"Why, is Alyssa bothering you?"

"Nope."

"Aha!"

"What is it this time?" Luke sent back, puzzled.

"I was right! Again! The silly little tramp knows we're on to her, so she's playing coy. Or scared."

"Maybe," Luke added neutrally. Alex relayed her derision at the next gown she was to parade, and told him she was going to sign off. *"Wait! You think maybe you could ask Margaret if I could contact my parents, let them know where I am? Guess they're a little worried by now, and I can't get hold of my brother."*

"You mean tell Margaret that we've been talking mental-like and spoil my fun?" Alex replied.

"She never said anything about forbidding us anything like it."

"Fine, I'll ask. See you later, but don't hold your breath, it'll probably take a while." The connection fizzled away, and Luke focused fully on the screen before him.

"You were talking with him just now?" Margaret asked.

Alex nodded. They were temporarily free of the presence of the four dressers, who had gone to modify the gown Alex had chosen. Margaret looked a little flustered, as though she was upset by the revelation.

"Yeah. Why, isn't that allowed? I'm really careful, and no one would know if I did the telepathy thing anyway. Why, did you suspect?" Alex asked, pulling on her shoes again.

"No, I did not. But try not to do it often; one never knows who may be overhearing."

"Why, you know of anyone who would?" Margaret shook her head quickly. "Anyway, he asked if it was alright to contact his parents. He tried his brother but got no answer."

"He may," Margaret replied, but she looked as though she had her reservations. "As long as he warns them not to come here. I'll give you the secure frequency just now, it should bypass HQ protocols."

"Why don't you want them here?" Alex asked

"I am hardly in the mood to field the inquisitive nature of parents who are aware of their children's gifts. Questions get asked of the host, and the less people know about me or the people I am in contact with, the better. For them, I might add. Now, are you really satisfied with the gown?" Alex nodded, and a smile replaced Margaret's look of trepidation. "Then on to the next store. We need some shoes for you – several pairs, I think – and we mustn't neglect your makeup."

"Do we have to?" Alex whined, and Margaret drew short, shock on her lined face.

"Of course we do!" she snapped. "Take care of every aspect! And since you're so close to young Luke, you might as well pick out a tuxedo for him." Alex frowned.

"I don't know what would fit him!"

"Of course you do, the two of you spend enough time with each other to warrant more than passing awareness of each other. And he doesn't strike me as a young man too intent on the finer details of shopping. I'm going to pay for the gown." Margaret marched off, and Alex stared after her, thinking her the maddest and most eccentric old bat for miles around.

CHAPTER THIRTEEN

Chaos

Persephone lay on her bed, her mind in turmoil. She was filled with rage and howling remorse, and sobbed quietly. It had been two weeks, and still no sign of Sirtis. The other aides – who suffered for Sirtis' absence with a much larger workload – badmouthed her when they thought Persephone wasn't listening. Still, it would be childish in the extreme to punish them for it, especially since Persephone herself wanted to crush the very life out of the woman. Sirtis had simply not shown up the next day after Persephone had ruined the Circuit in front of her. At first Persephone had chalked the absence up to terror, and recovering from such a sight. Had it been so simple she would have berated Sirtis for cowardice, or a weak stomach, but after two days it had become apparent that something was wrong. So Persephone had sent a batch of people to Sirtis' apartments, after she had scanned the entire city and found her missing.

The rage had set in then. It had become clear then that Sirtis had betrayed her, had fled, either to someone else or just away. That was the price of Persephone's lenience, it seemed, because Sirtis, more than the other aides, had access to the secret files Persephone held secure in her own systems: files about the others, and about certain individuals. It galled Persephone that her foremost employee and most trusted aide should do this to her, and it didn't appeal to her at all that she could find out from the others if they had seen or gotten hold of Sirtis: the alliance was uneasy, and lies abounded when *he* wasn't in the vicinity, so any one of the others could have hold of Sirtis and be arrogant enough in their own power to lie blatantly to Persephone's face.

Frustration had followed the rage, accompanied by the slow escalation of fear. Fear that Sirtis had betrayed her and joined forces with someone else, one of the others who despised Persephone. Fear that Sirtis was busy right now, somewhere, unmasking the terrible power and secret existence of the Changed. Heaven knows it was hard to remain in the presence of someone as powerful as Persephone herself and not be jealous and covetous. What if Sirtis was undermining the Changed? Was she a spy? Had she always been?

The questions gnawed at Persephone. Maybe the bitch was still covering her tracks, securing a hiding hole for herself before she struck. Somewhere inaccessible, where it could take Persephone months or even years to unearth her, as Sirtis deliberately sabotaged all she had worked for and towards. Howling again, Persephone arced off the bed, screeching her anger at the high ceiling of her inner chamber. She didn't care if any of her aides heard her. They were terrified of her. When Sirtis' betrayal had become apparent they had all undergone screening, and Persephone's vicious temper had made the experience a living hell for them. She had their systems, at the office and at their homes, searched completely, even their personal files, and apart from the usual inanities and little pleasures, had found nothing of note that was either incriminating or damaging to Persephone herself. Needless to say the aides were horrified and cowed into absolute submission, after swearing anew their oaths of loyalty to Persephone. Satisfied, she had set them after Sirtis' tracks, as well as shouldering Sirtis' workload. One aide, Henrico Jerome, had fallen to his knees and begged Persephone to elevate someone else from just below them in the hierarchy as another aide, to shoulder part of the work. Persephone had backhanded the unfortunate aide, then told him quite firmly no, and that he was to get back to work. Then she had commanded the other two aides to make room for one more task, and had watched as they quietly absorbed the command, their faces white and drawn.

Now she waited, miserable, not caring how she looked, despite getting up every morning and making herself beautiful, as she always did. She would never admit to anyone that in Sirtis she had found something magnificent that made her hate the inferiority of humans less, that Sirtis, for all her minor ambitions and quiet defiance, had been as close as Persephone had ever come to being companionable with anyone. Sirtis had been above the term 'minion', even though she was – had been – one, for lack of a better term. But she had been treasured, like a very prized possession, and her loss was like the loss of a very valuable artefact. It vexed Persephone to the point of manic destruction, and twelve people in her employ had died in the last two weeks, struck down for defiance, ineptitude and just Persephone's general pique. Fortunately satisfaction came with every death, and though Persephone knew that the losses were in fact quite damaging to her methods of operation, she had felt it necessary, if only to calm herself.

So now she spent day after day lying on her bed or on the large chaise in the middle of her domed audience chamber, musing on what had happened and lashing out at her aides, depending on whether they brought her any news. It had been two weeks since she had received any good news.

Her foremost aide, the one that now held Sirtis' position, entered with a fawning attitude and closed the door behind him. Jerome approached almost reverently, a fact which made Persephone less inclined to slash him to ribbons. He actually bowed to her before approaching closer, and when she made no reaction beyond staring at him through puffy, red-rimmed eyes, he came to within ten feet of her chaise. Persephone glared.

"Well?" she demanded imperiously. Jerome swallowed.

"Mistress, I have news," the man began. He was a forceful person, and strong, but now he seemed unsure of himself. Persephone despised such lapses, but she could trust no one else to shoulder Sirtis' workload. Of the three aides, Jerome had been the closest to Sirtis, and also the one just below her in rank, so he remained the natural choice to replace her. Persephone sighed, then indicated that he continue. "The assignment you gave us twelve days ago."

"Yes?" Persephone grated.

"We've found something." When he received no further reply or imperative, he went on. "We've followed up on Sirtis' –"

"Do not speak her name!" Persephone screamed, rising in a single fluid motion, almost towering over Jerome, if not in physical size then certainly in anger and belligerence. He flinched from her, shoulders hunching.

"Forgive me, mistress." Jerome waited for the blows to come, but they didn't, and Persephone remained standing, eyes piercing and dark. "We've followed through on the data left by my predecessor, and we've come across information regarding a powerful Changed who we believe lives close by, at the very least outside the city."

"And what do you want me to do about it?" Persephone snarled.

"Mistress, this is the woman S – my predecessor had tracked down for you, when you had commanded her to. The contact for other Changed in and around New York." Persephone stared levelly at the aide, until he swallowed and began sweating. Then she held out a hand, and Jerome nearly jumped, before realizing his mistress demanded the pad storing the information. Persephone watched the contents file over it, then frowned.

"I will deal with this personally. You may go." Jerome backed away. "You have done well," Persephone added, not quite feeling the conviction of the words but adding them nonetheless. Sometimes one had to deal kindly to the lesser beings in order to soothe and enforce them. Jerome nodded, but the relief in his face was clear, and Persephone glowered. That she had to sink to the level of kindness to give her employees and minions the incentive they needed to feel better. But she realized then that she was beginning to feel better. She looked at the pad in her hand, and her mind began to roam, breaking free of the physical shackles of her body. She would search for this woman herself, knowing now where she was.

She telekinetically shut and locked the doors to her private sanctum, then draped herself across the chaise again, mind expanding under the onslaught of empathic searching. She expanded her radius exponentially, feeling her limbs become languid and flaccid with the effort of so massive a use of her resources. It was a slowly growing ache of pain she savoured, like the physical aspects of rape made empathic, as she always enjoyed her sexual exploits, and so she was no stranger to it.

Her mind was about to jump from the city – the pad indicated the woman lived outside the city in a large estate – when her mind latched onto something rare: a telepathic communiqué, between two Changed, a very rare thing for New York indeed. Very few Changed were powerful enough for communication across such a distance. Persephone located the point of contact within the city, on Fifth Avenue itself, and nearly reeled at the audacity. But she reined herself in and followed the trace to the point of origin, careful to remain aware only, not to listen in. She rose involuntarily from the chaise when she found it. Opening her eyes, she looked at the details on the pad. For the first time in two weeks, she smiled.

CHAPTER FOURTEEN

Unlocking

She shook her head in amazement.

In the five days they had been here, she had taken time to get comfortable in her surroundings. She loved exploring, and since that day on the beach she had been fascinated with the place. But she hadn't seen every place here, and she hadn't been prepared for the safety precautions and security instalments that seemed to abound, once she found out about them.

She had to do it herself, since she couldn't filch it from anyone's mind, and because it was against her principles to do something like that. Still, the thought had crossed her mind, and then died down again when she realized who she was up against. The exploring she had done when Nathan didn't need her, which was rarely; he wasn't clingy, and neither was she, but the union of opposites that defined their relationship made it hard not to be in close proximity to each other. In the rare moments of solitude she snuck about and roamed the part of the island where Charlie's house, the house they now occupied, sprawled. And sprawled it did, because from the outside viewpoint it was deceptive. Once inside, you got to see things differently: the house had three levels, not one, as was visible from the street that ran several hundred yards from the front door. The flat, cubic approach to the place made it seem misleadingly flat and close to the ground, when in fact the ceiling was never less than four feet above your head. The abundance of large windows and their intelligent tinting, which blocked excessive sunlight and could even adapt to the mood of the room's occupant, made for a spacious and airy feel. There were several bedrooms, each with its own en suite bathroom. But what intrigued Joanie was the space which was there, but to which she had no access. And when the day arrived for Daniel and Nathan to meld minds, and they accompanied the two following Charlie, Joanie was thrilled by more than just the prospect of having Daniel recover all his fractured memories.

It was a way to pass time, and to get her mind off the immediate matter at hand, though. She had been shocked when Charlie had walked towards one large and relatively empty part of the wall in the lounge area and had taken a small remote device from his pocket. When he activated it, the wall vanished. He called it a clever use of modern technology to blend the secret with the obvious: a field of energy, hard as the wall itself, and dusted with fine colorants and particles to leave a seamless blend between wall and field. The corridor that led from the cunningly disguised wall-field was dark, and lit up when the presence of people was detected. Joanie watched, awed, as the entire stretch of empty hallway lit up, and a couple of doors became visible near the end. Charlie seemed completely willing to share with them all what exactly this meant.

"Guess I don't have to explain exactly why such precautions are necessary. Only me and Daniel have access to this section beneath the house. The door to the left is the transmissions chamber, as well as the monitoring facility for the electronic load that passes to, from and through the house. The door right ahead is the hangar bay."

"Hangar bay?" Nathan asked. Joanie smiled slightly at the dependability. Nathan would always be interested in anything that could be found in a hangar bay. Charlie nodded.

"There's a skimmer plane, four jet-hover pads and a couple of cars in there," Charlie said. Joanie wondered if Charlie knew of Nathan's enchantment with anything mechanical and automotive, then decided not to pursue the thought. For a start, Nathan had something more important to do right now. The group halted at the right-side door, which Charlie palmed open at an access terminal against the wall. "And here's where we go about today's business." The door swung open, and he led the way in.

It was a room roughly similar to the one where they'd first seen Daniel again. The floor was tiered and circular, with steps seemingly cut into the sides of the smoothed stone surface. The room was large enough to comfortably hold a hundred people. It was empty and unrelieved otherwise, with only a large window spanning one wall, overlooking another vista of the sea. Dense shrubbery to the sides alerted Joanie as to why she had never seen the window from the sea, when she had gone walking on the beach. That, and she had a strong feeling that something like an illusory barrier on the outside wasn't out of the question, not after she'd seen the wall-field in the lounge. Charlie allowed them all entry, then closed the door behind them. With this done, he told them to get comfortable, at which point he took the remote out again and fiddled with it before putting it back in his pocket.

"And that?" Jamie asked critically.

"Neuronull field," Charlie said.

"What?" Joanie and Jamie asked at the same time, incredulous. Nathan, startled by their response, quirked an eyebrow at Joanie.

"It's a damper," Charlie added.

"And what good does that do?" Jamie asked critically.

"It keeps all activity on a mental level within this room. Nothing gets out."

"Why?" Nathan asked.

"Because of me," Daniel entered, stepping towards the middle of the room. He turned around, eyes roving across the ceiling as though he could see the actual field. He looked at Nathan and Joanie. "Because of the telekinetic energy that I can harness."

"It keeps him from ripping the foundations out of the house," Charlie concluded, then joined Daniel at the centre of the room. He took him by the shoulders and looked him in the eyes. "You ready for this?" he asked Daniel, who gave a quick nod. Pursing his lips, Charlie took a moment longer to also nod, then turned to the others. "Alright. Nathan, please take a seat in front of Daniel. Joanie and Jamie, wherever you want next to, behind or beside Nathan."

Charlie waited for them to do so, then sat down beside and behind Daniel. "When you're all ready."

Nathan sat down facing Daniel. He crossed his legs as well and watched Daniel for anything else. Daniel merely spared him a wan smile and held out his hand. Nathan felt Joanie squeeze his shoulder on one side, and Jamie patted the other before taking hold as well. It was an awkward event, and Nathan felt strangely speared by Daniel's piercing gaze. The green eyes held nothing but the faintest hint of apprehension, which was largely eclipsed by a look Nathan remembered from before Daniel's Change: determination. It burned like fire there, a prelude to the blue glow he knew would soon envelop every pair of eyes in the room. He felt, for the first time now, despite former misgivings, that maybe this wasn't such a good idea. "You want to back out?" Daniel asked, a tone of reproach growing in his voice. Nathan shook his head. "This is your last chance, if you want to," Charlie said.

"No, I'm good," Nathan added hastily, not really feeling that way. But the reproof in Daniel's voice, and the faltering in the face, jerked him back to the real reason they were here. He realized anew that there was more at stake than simply his own discomfort. Taking a deep breath, he wet his lips and held out his left hand. Daniel did the same and took Nathan's hand in his own, closing his fingers around Daniel's. Swallowing, Nathan looked up again.

"Keep eye contact for as long as you can," Daniel said.

"Why wouldn't I?" Nathan fired back in a strained attempt at lightening the mood. Normally he would succeed admirably, but now, under pressure and with his estranged friend's fate in his hands, literally and figuratively, he felt so uncertain that all pretenses were stripped away before they could even take shape. He took a deep breath and readied himself.

"Concentrate on nothing but what you hear and see in your head. I'm going in now." The green eyes went from their natural tint to something between sea green and aquamarine, glowing surreally. Nathan watched as Daniel frowned, and then, though his eyes were open, he felt as if he could see nothing. In his head, Daniel's voice sounded.

"How are you doing?" Nathan wanted to speak, but it felt wrong, as though he would be breaking some sort of trust. Daniel's voice went on. *"Think what you want to say, I will hear it."* Nathan nodded and tried it out.

"Like this?" Daniel nodded in turn.

"Yeah, like that. If you can't form the words, just make impressions, I can read those too."

"What can't you do?" Nathan asked, the last shred of his intent forming an image of sorts, though he couldn't place it or give it shape other than an impression of odds stacked against each other. Daniel's reply conveyed a slow sense of mirth.

"Unlike you, I don't know yet. Okay, whatever happens now, you tell me if you feel pain or great discomfort. Whatever you do, don't hold out on me."

"What do you mean?"

"If you feel great or increasing pain for one second and you don't tell me, I could kill you."

"What?" Nathan fired back mentally, or at least, made the disbelieving word in his head take form. He felt placation streaming from Daniel.

"All the more reason for you to stay honest here."

"Can't you just tell me whether I'm lying or not?"

"Why do that when you can do it yourself?" Daniel replied acerbically. *"Okay, here's the scary part now. Concentrate. When I show you something which you remember or recall, add whatever you can remember to it. And before you ask, yeah, I could do it myself but I could hurt you badly if I did, so help me out here and it'll go smoothly and painlessly for both of us."* Nathan nodded. For a moment there he had regained conscious control of his senses, and he could see again. He shied away when he did; Daniel's eyes went from luminous sea green to a violent miasma of gold-tinged blue that swelled and vibrated like a physical aura over and outside his

eyes. Swallowing, Nathan wished to retreat. He had felt a certain sense of doom and destruction in the virulent ripple of that gaze just then. Fortunately he was ripped back in quickly, losing control again. He was aware only of everything inside his head, which wasn't scary at all, considering he knew what it was like, and had known for the last twenty-odd years. Daniel's presence – he did feel him there – was as ephemeral and transparent as mist burning away before the sun, but didn't go completely. Nathan was still feeling around – he'd never experienced this kind of mental clarity and calmness before – when Daniel's voice assumed a more commanding presence, growing stronger within his head. *"Show me the first day we met."* Nathan thought a moment, then latched onto the image. The fact that his head was seemingly clear of the clutter brought on by other senses aided the process, and with unreal clarity the images began taking shape in his head. He saw everything from his vantage point, saw the young eleven-year-old kid walk into the house for the first time, eyes wide and unsettled, disturbed by the new surroundings. Nathan had been the first to say anything polite and bright to him, the first to welcome Daniel to his new home. Luke on the other hand was close-mouthed – he had stayed that way for the first year, until he and Daniel had –

"Concentrate," Daniel's voice snapped tightly in his mind, and he righted himself. He let Joanie go – longingly – and focused on the new scene unfolding there. Daniel was introducing Nathan to Joanie, in university, where Daniel had been a year before Nathan had joined him there – Nathan had taken a gap year, and Daniel, a ravenous young scholar at all times, had finished high school two years earlier than normal, which had been no small accomplishment - as well as Joanie Stratford, whom Daniel had said was his best friend since high school. Nathan had vaguely remembered her from a few times, seeing her at the house, doing some study time with Daniel, but back then it had been Nathan with his friends, Luke with his and Daniel and his own group of select few, and the bunch had never really mingled. A slight throbbing ache momentarily threw

him off track, but he dulled it. He sent image after image into the visual cornucopia, feeding the presence just behind his sight. After a while, Daniel spoke again.

"Show me a day at class." Nathan complied and began streaming all he could recall of the classes he, Daniel and Joanie had spent in each other's company. The info was short and sporadic, but it was there nevertheless. He began lacing the images with times after class, when they'd gone to the dorms, or to their old hangouts. For some reason, images of Joanie kept cropping up as well, and Nathan realized, unwittingly, that her hand was a little tighter on his shoulder than before. He wondered if she was simply stating it as affection, but then a slight dull throb began returning to the back of his head. He righted himself and sent a sentence into the void that now comprised the whole of his existence.

"Why are there so many images of Joanie?"

"Because she's linked with you, and I had to tie her in because she's also part of this."

"What? Does she know?"

"She does. She consented the moment the images became too involved with both of you. Any pain yet?" Nathan paused. The small pain at the back of his head was almost minor. He decided against telling Daniel about it. Mentally he shook his head, and actually rustled up a smile.

"Shoot," he said. The images began to continue streaming ahead then, and Nathan watched, an observer in his own head, as the images somehow began flitting by faster. He could barely make out what Danny was accessing, but a lot of the visuals were of scenes of Nathan's parents, scenes where they and Daniel were talking, once of them consoling Daniel about something or other. After a while even those blurred into incoherent colour streams which Nathan couldn't follow anymore, but which Daniel was obviously going through. He grew more anxious as they sped by, and after a while tried to slow them down. When it didn't work, he began wondering about it, and sent the query to Daniel. He waited

for the reply, patient, hoping that nothing was up. When Daniel gave no answer, he sent another sentence.

"Hey, you still there? What's happening?" Still nothing. Frantic now, he kept sending sentences at the presence that still hovered just out of sight. Nothing. With great effort he regained control of his senses, and felt the crashing, crushing deluge of his senses return with it. Sight blinded him, and his eyes began tearing; sounds assailed him and nearly made him cry out, and when he did cry out from too much of the renewed cacophony, the sound of his yell nearly deafened him. But he maintained control, and felt Joanie's presence behind him. Her hand was still on his shoulder, as was Jamie's. He strained to hear something, and became aware, gradually, that Joanie and Jamie both were breathing more heavily than normal. Surprised, he wanted to turn around, but remembered Daniel's warning to retain eye contact for as long as possible.

Squashing the urge to turn around and make sure Joanie was still fine, he narrowed his eyes to allow less light in, steadily making sense of what he saw.

He wished he hadn't.

Brought anew into understanding and light, he was completely caught off guard by what he saw. Charlie, seated beside Daniel, was breathing as though he had done ten miles at a flat run, sweat pouring off him, making his clothes and hair cling to his skin. His eyes seemed unfocused, staring way beyond Daniel or anyone else. But what bothered Nathan was the hue. It was dark, like a stormy sea. The blue veered between midnight hues and sparks of lighter azure, but they were afire, like Nathan had never seen any Changed's eyes. Startled, he reined in the sharp needles of fear, and looked at Daniel. What he saw there made him rip his hand away in terror. Daniel's eyes were wide and sightless, lacking whites or pupils, exhibiting as a single field of riotous blue colours. In the middle they grew darker, streaming waves of actinic light in concentric inwards spirals, like a slowly turning hypnotic wheel made of blue tints. What was more, Daniel's expression remained in place even when Nathan had sheared the connection. He had half expected Daniel to recoil, to fall back, to do anything, but instead, he remained there, hand still outstretched, face a rictus grimace of vacant observation. And yet there was no mistaking the shocking lucidity of that vengefully intelligent stare that spearheaded from beyond the maelstrom of blue.

Regaining control of his senses happened to be far easier than simply resuming control of everything else. His body refused to budge, as though his action of pulling away his hand had been spontaneous and involuntary beyond his control. He tried to focus on pulling everything together, studiously avoiding Daniel's expression. He realized that everything was slower, for some reason, and not just his awareness. It was as if time had slowed throughout the entire room. When he turned around, he realized he was in fact more in control than he had thought. For one, Joanie and Jamie both had expressions of mounting shock and horror growing on their faces. And yet, they were only just starting to appear. Joanie's eyes were also flaring sharply, but the glow was fitful, and so slow he could make out the oscillations! Jamie's eyes were the same as they always were; a greyish blue without relief, but pulsing just enough to remind that there was indeed gifted activity going on in there. Nathan, startled by the slowness, steeled himself and turned to Daniel and Charlie. Even they were slowed down, with their expressions frozen. Daniel, despite the wild surge of blue light that flowed from his eyes like beacons, was also prey to the dilated time.

It hit Nathan.

This was no uncanny revelation, no unearthly dimension inside his head. He had broken the contact, and unwittingly engaged his own powers, as a reaction to get away from what hurt and scared him. It was a reaction as elemental and primal as all of human nature. So, what to do. He looked at the slowed-down people all around him, at the slowly moving leaves outside. He had never noticed just how vivid and lucid the surroundings became when he

234

engaged his gifts. But the beauty was eclipsed by the need to place distance between himself and Daniel, at whatever had happened just after their last communication. He made as if to rise, finding that his body was more willing to comply to express orders this time. Faster than he could imagine, Daniel's hand snaked out and grabbed him behind his neck, pulling him closer. Amidst the sluggishness of everyone else, Daniel's movements were suddenly as fast as Nathan's. His eyes, still blazing violently, were almost murderously intense, and his face held nothing but brutal purpose. Nathan placed a hand over Daniel's and tried to pry it off his neck, but the hand remained fast, and Nathan winced when it clamped down harder. Daniel leaned close, placing his mouth near Nathan's ear, and Nathan could swear he almost heard the crackle of Daniel's eyes.

"A recoil reaction. But it won't get you anywhere." He leaned back, hand still clamped on Nathan's neck. There was an eerily disembodied element to Daniel's voice, as if it came from very far off.

"What are you doing?" Nathan asked. His eyes grew wider when he realized that nothing was moving. Everyone else was frozen solid now, their expressions horrified, their motions frozen in time.

"I am not doing this, I am simply here, with you. You drew me here when you broke the connection before I could shut it down from my side," Daniel said. Nathan started, marvelling at the sudden double image of Daniel, one moment stationary, then folding apart like a slowed motion blur, face rolling from side to side, smearing lightly across his field of vision. It was nauseating to watch.

"Let go of me!" Nathan grated, and tried to push Daniel away from him. Instead, Daniel slapped aside his hands, brought Nathan closer to him and placed his other hand over Nathan's forehead. "Danny, stop!"

"You made a deal. Close it!"

Nathan felt slammed back into his own head, and Daniel was there with him, only this time his presence dominated almost overwhelmingly, without taking absolute control. Nathan fired back a swathe of angry swear words, and screamed inside his own head. When this brought nothing, he tried reason, though it was the last thing he felt capable of in the escalating nightmare.

"You said you wouldn't do this!"

"Do what?" Daniel asked, and the sheer nonchalance and almost-innocence in his words momentarily terrified Nathan more than the maniacal gleam that had preceded it. It went beyond that, though: there was an utter lack of emotion.

"Violation!" Nathan flung back, but received nothing in return. *"Answer me, damn you!"*

"I'm sorry it's come to this, Nathan, I really am. But I'm this close, and I don't think even you knew of this little secret of yours." Intrigue derailed Nathan, and he fell back onto it, seeing as it was the only sane part of him within range.

"Secret?"

"Something you don't know of. Luke and Joanie knew of your premonitions, your gut feelings which always turned out true and trustworthy. I can see a little deeper than that. There's something else there as well. very faint, but promising more to come. Marvellous!"

"Tell me what it is!" Nathan demanded.

"No." That single word rocked Nathan beyond description. It was a denial of food, water and air, all at once, so grave was the response from Daniel. *"You'll find out eventually. I'm surprised, it caught me off guard completely. But it won't keep me from what was agreed on."* Multiple thoughts flashed through Nathan's head. On one hand he felt triumph, that even Daniel, a supposed paradigm Changed, hadn't foreseen it, and had nearly failed somehow. But then the sobriety returned. Whatever it was that had thrown Daniel and nearly allowed Nathan to escape whatever dark terror had momentarily lurked in Daniel's presence, Daniel had simply stated that he would not be dissuaded. Nathan almost knew what would happen next.

"Give me everything," Daniel's voice resounded in Nathan's head.

"No," he said, even though he knew it wouldn't help.

"Not a problem." That statement sent Nathan reeling again and again, as he felt control ripped from within his own head and torn from his fledgling grasp; something beyond his will to comprehend, even to mentally 'see', walled him off and ripped open his head. In the moments before the world went white and he drowned everything else in his own screams, the world beyond him resumed its pace. He vaguely heard Joanie scream, and Jamie and Charlie yelled as well. And then the world exploded. He knew it as he felt the warmth of a heatwave roll into him, slamming him to the ground, dousing the light and giving only darkness in return.

She came to with someone helping her up. Bewilderment followed, and when she found her bearings she was looking about her, wildly looking for stability. She looked at the person helping her up, both hands around her arm. Jamie, she vaguely recalled. Her mind felt as though it was swimming through fog, and she was finding it hard to stay focused. She was shaken gently, and she looked at Jamie, whose face registered insistence and urgency, as well as dark smudges of dirt, and a few cuts. Vaguely she heard her name being called, and sound returned as though it was through a funnel. At last she found her voice.

"I'm okay," she managed weakly. "I'm okay." She looked down, and her heart stopped. She shook herself loose of Jamie's grip, falling down again next to Nathan. She placed both hands on him, alarmed at the stillness of his pose, and aware of how her hands were shaking. Jamie hunkered down next to her, but he was looking across the room, eyes narrowed, scanning through the haze that hung all around them. Joanie, flustered and frustrated, and growing ever more frantic with Nathan's quiet, snarled angrily and cleared the mist, sending her mind roaming, gathering the haze and dispelling it. It evaporated in billows, revealing the entirety of the chamber. Nathan was looking up, but not at her, eyes wide and staring. For a moment hope died, and she thought he was dead, but his chest was jerking in spasms, and his mouth fluttered with rapid bursts of expelled air.

Across from them, Charlie was cradling Daniel in his arms, his face creased with anguish. He seemed oblivious of the gashes on his brow, or the blood that leaked from them and down his face. Daniel's eyes were closed, and his complexion was almost too pale for words. Joanie, shocked and appalled at the scene, began sobbing, then looked back down at Nathan. She was only distantly aware of Jamie leaving her side to go to Charlie. She placed a shaking hand on Nathan's forehead, then started when he reacted, a jerk of his head. He still remained staring aimlessly at nothing in particular, above and beyond her. She bit her lower lip, to stop it from trembling, and rubbed an arm roughly across her eyes, to clear the damming tears. Then she did something which she had never thought she would do. She steadied the hand on Nathan's forehead and sent her awareness inside, hoping against hope that she would find him sane and healthy.

He jerked violently and threw her back, but it had the desired effect. He blinked owlishly, eyes focusing and dimming, and it was with visible effort that he maintained focus after that. He looked at her, and his face crumpled, and he began sobbing as well. Joanie, distraught and overwhelmed, lifted him to her and folded him in her arms, trying to stop the wracking shudders that ripped through his body. She held him close, her eyes darting to Daniel. Charlie's hands were shaking incredibly, and he seemed incapable of any action. Jamie gently disengaged his grip on Daniel, then lifted Daniel off the ground. Charlie seemed as one bereft of will, and his eyes followed the motions, although he remained in place. Somehow Jamie had gotten the remote from Charlie, and he pressed the dials, opening the door. A flood of fresher air swamped the room immediately, and he marched past, Daniel in his arms. Only then did Charlie seem to regain control, and he rose like a marionette, following with unsteady footsteps. Joanie wanted to rile against him for simply leaving, but her words died down when he detoured and settled down next to her, concern odd on his bloodied features.

"Can he walk?" he asked in a cracked whisper. Joanie, taking an even firmer hold on Nathan, nodded curtly, then whispered in Nathan's ear for him to get up. Charlie waited patiently as the two of them struggled upward, Joanie, still unsteady, more or less supporting Nathan's weight as well. When she was sure of her footing and Nathan's as well, they began the slow, almost surreal walk towards the door, Charlie following.

She took Nathan to the bedroom and laid him down on the bed. His eyes followed her every move, and remained fixed on her when she sat down next to him, taking a breather. She rubbed a hand through her hair, pulling it back over her head, not really caring that it was unkempt but that it was simply out of her eyes. This done, she looked down at him, and voiced the question that nagged her.

"What happened?" He only remained looking at her. "Nathan, what happened?"

"Violation," Nathan whispered, almost inaudibly. Joanie's ears perked at the word. For an empath it had added meaning. Joanie swallowed.

"Did he do that to you?" Again, no answer. Joanie sighed. "Will you be alright?" He closed his eyes in answer. Knowing she would get little else out of him, she rose and went to the bathroom, cleaning herself up as she stared into the mirror. Thoughts and impressions came back to her gradually, of everything going fine. She recalled Daniel mentally asking her permission for a joint inquiry, of her memories of events joining with his and Nathan's. After that, things had gone horribly wrong. All she remembered was an insane azure glow suddenly erupting from Daniel's eyes, of Charlie's face registering shock as his own eyes went haywire. She had seen very fast movements then, first from Nathan and then, strangely, from Daniel. The next thing she had seen was Nathan rearing back, yelling, Daniel's hands clamped on Nathan's neck and forehead, and of Daniel's face distorting into a grimace of absolute pain. That was when the explosion occurred, and all she could remember after that was Jamie helping her up.

She needed to know what had happened. Nathan was uncommunicative, and as much as she hated leaving him alone, she knew she had to talk to Charlie. She went back into the bedroom, and found Nathan's breathing rhythmic and stable. He had fallen asleep in the minutes that she had been in the bathroom, but at least it was peaceful. She left him to it, and made for the lounge.

Only Jamie was there, and he had a very worried expression on his face. It was replaced with concern when he saw Joanie.

"How are you? How's Nathan? You guys okay?"

"I'm okay," she answered. "Nathan's asleep. He barely said a word to me."

"Charlie took Daniel to bed as well," Jamie said. "He said he'd be out shortly." The two of them looked away, both of them somehow embarrassed. They waited in silence until Charlie emerged, still walking shakily. When he noticed the two of them, he took a deep breath and leaned with one hand against the wall. "Get on with it then," he said, voice sounding harsh.

"Well I guess the one that bears on us all is what the hell happened in there?" Jamie snapped in reply.

"Isn't it obvious? I mean, I can't speak for Nathan. But Daniel did something which he shouldn't have even considered, and I bet he's paying for it somehow. I can't get anything from him, he isn't speaking, he isn't even awake, and his mind is completely closed to me." A look of puzzlement entered Jamie's face, and Charlie shook his head. "Completely."

"I thought that was impossible," Jamie breathed, sounding awed. Joanie mused on what she knew. She knew the mental bond between Charlie and Daniel allowed Charlie to know Daniel's thoughts, inasmuch as Charlie was willing to delve in there.

"I've never been shut out like this, ever," Charlie added. "I can't even get a read off him by touching him, and that says far more than I'd like to think about."

"Guess you'd better think about it then," Jamie said, overriding him. "Because we have a serious situation here, and Alice is likely to have a field day if this entire operation has failed."

"You think I don't know that?" Charlie snarled. He still hadn't cleaned the blood from his face, and it gave his expression a feral look. "I had no control whatsoever back there! None!"

"You think?" Jamie antagonized further. Joanie felt sorry for Charlie, suddenly, and was about to protest, when Charlie went on.

"Don't you get it? He reversed the link! He turned my control safeguards back on me, and I didn't even see it coming! Do you have any idea what this means?"

"What?" Joanie asked, feeling fear build up. Charlie didn't sound happy at all.

"The explosion in there? That was him, shorting out the neuronull field. That field is state of the art, tested on the first GenneY seventy years ago, perfected until now until it's even stronger than it was back then, and back then, it had held under everything that Nth Prime had." Realization dawned, and Jamie paled. Nodding, Charlie went on. "Yeah, Daniel did that. He single-handedly destroyed a device which held one of the most powerful Changed of all time. It took everything he had but he did it, and the question that bugs me is why."

"Why?" Joanie queried.

"Daniel didn't lose control, at least not of his gifts. He loosed them, but not at random."

"How can you tell?" Jamie asked worriedly.

"Because even when he began shutting me out of his safeguards, his thoughts were moving with crystal clarity. It was calculated, but I didn't get any idea why. I could almost see the control he was executing."

"But he's okay?" Joanie asked, another question which bugged her. Charlie looked at her, as if seeing her there for the first time, and his expression softened.

"I don't know yet. Nothing I do gets through, not even a body scan. His skin might as well be made of water, or dirt: teeming with life, but that's it. Nothing intelligent gets through, from my side or his. But he's still breathing, if shallowly. Its like a trance, almost like the first time I saw him, only this is way deeper."

"Hope you don't have to re-educate him again," Jamie replied offhandedly.

"How's Nathan?" Charlie asked.

"He said one word to me," Joanie replied, feeling that they should know exactly where things stood. She noticed them waiting attentively. "Violation".

Jamie only frowned, but it was Charlie's turn to pale. With the blood still on his face, he looked like an animated cadaver, eyes draining and turning a lacklustre hue. He sat down heavily and dropped his face in his hands. When he spoke it was audibly enough despite his posture.

"Why would he do that? After all he knows, after all the lessons, after everything I told him!" he ended, rising swiftly and turning away, the last part of the sentence erupting angrily from him. Then he turned back to Joanie, and there was an unspoken demand of trust on his face. "What was he like before the Change? Bare facts, personality, intellectual application, anything! You have to tell me now, because if it falls anywhere in the assumptions that I've made then it may explain some things."

"He was forceful. Always on the ball, always one step ahead unless he was being tricked or taken for a ride, and then he always drew back and won anyway. He never lost with anything really, and when he did, he did it graciously."

"What else?"

"Determination!" Joanie replied hurriedly. "He was determined beyond anything I've ever seen, and defiant. But kind, and generous, and reliable when you really needed someone to trust."

"Defiant and determined," Charlie breathed. He sat down again, eyes far-off. "Defiant and determined," he repeated. "Hell, that's vague."

"You said you wanted basics," Joanie replied reproachfully.

"I know. I'm sorry, it's just… dammit! How defiant and determined?"

"You could never force him to do anything he didn't want to. Show him, persuade him, but never force him." Joanie watched this sink in on Charlie. He was slowly compiling the facts. When he was done, he spoke.

"I tried to force him to calm down, to back off," he said, and his voice sounded unsteady, as though he was admitting to something atrocious. "Right before the usual moment of acceptance, he slammed a block onto me so hard I'm amazed my eyes didn't pop."

Joanie listened carefully, and was surprised when she felt an involuntary twinge of triumph. Whatever had happened, whatever was going to happen now, she somehow knew, simply from Charlie's retelling, that Daniel, the old Daniel she had come to know and love as her dearest friend, was back. Or at least, the best part of him. She didn't know if she should shout for joy or cry because of what the whole episode must have done to him, judging by his reaction on the beach several days back, when she'd simply tried telling him of past events. What had a full mental access done to him?

"So now what?" she asked, and Jamie looked at Charlie, mirroring Joanie's question.

"We take him to GOA, both him and Nathan. They're better equipped there to handle things further. I don't know if it's safe to move Daniel, but it's a risk we have to take."

"What about Alice?" Jamie asked quietly. Charlie sighed and leaned back against the wall with his head, eyes closed, resignation etched on his features.

"Time to face the music," he said simply. Again, Joanie was amazed at how sorry she felt for him. A few days ago she hadn't trusted him an inch, and felt more than a little mild anger towards him, even knowing what Nathan had told her about Daniel and how Charlie had featured there. Now, she felt only pity. As much as she hated to admit it, Daniel had played them all badly this time, with even Charlie taking a dive. And yet, until they'd heard from Daniel himself, she couldn't bring herself to cast stones and judge anyone. She rose, noting the afternoon sky outside. She felt bone-tired, and by the looks of it, everyone was.

"I'm turning in. Nathan needs me," she said simply, and returned to the bedroom.

Ancillary Documents

GOA X: Charles Avery

One of the very few people that Alice McNamara allowed into her closest confidence, even her friendship, was Charles Avery, or Charlie, as everyone called him. At the onset of Charlie's career in GOA, Alice took him for her protégé, mostly because she saw the great mental potential in the young man who had at the age of fifteen experienced the first fits of the Change.

Charlie was born on March the 25th, 2037 in Dallas, Texas, the eldest son of Virgil Avery and an unknown mother, or at the very least an undisclosed one. Charlie's youngest and only sibling, Jeremiah Avery, was born four years later in 2041, to the same parents. After Jeremiah's birth the mother vanished, and Virgil never seemed to yearn for her or try to find her, by all appearances content to raise his two sons alone. Charlie, being the eldest, was at first closest to his father, but Virgil began taking more and more to his youngest, up to the point where, by the time Charlie began to Change at age fifteen, a very strained relationship between the two had developed.

Virgil began taking heavily to drinking, no doubt a side-effect of being a fairly unsuccessful businessman and resultantly failing his fatherhood duties in the process. At this point Charlie, in spite of his uncontrollable surges of telepathy, began taking over the care of his younger brother, growing to love and care for him deeply despite childish resentment at Jeremiah being the obvious object of their father's attention, and the two saw fit to try and raise their father from his slump.

When Jeremiah Avery died in 2053, just a month after Charlie's sixteenth birthday, in a freak car accident involving a drunk Virgil – another business deal gone sour and Virgil had taken to the bottle again in spite of his sons' urgent pleading not to – Charlie blamed his father, but his raging mental potential had begun branching into coercive domains, and he managed to bring his father back from the brink of further disaster. Although Charlie effectively took care of his father for the next two years, helping him with business ventures – some moderately successful – he never stopped blaming Virgil for Jeremiah's death. Neither did Virgil forgive himself, despite outward indications to the contrary, and he took up chain-smoking as an unconscious result. In 2055 the combined effects of guilt and another small and relatively insignificant business transaction falling through the floor drove Virgil Avery to a final drunken binge. Charlie had been out of town taking care of some of his father's clients, and on coming back found his father, comatose, in their house. Virgil was rushed to the hospital, but despite the care taken and all efforts expended to bring him back from the brink, Virgil Avery died from severe alcohol poisoning that had cascaded to a colossal failure of the liver and subsequent chain-reaction breakdowns of other organs, notably emphysema in the lungs and heart failure as a result of the short but impressively dedicated two years of intense smoking.

In the aftermath of losing his family so swiftly within two year's time, Charlie allowed himself to be institutionalized, letting his mental faculties – an oddity he considered as a kind of karmic repayment for the devastating losses he had suffered thus far in life – dwindle with non-use. He remained in a mental health clinic for the better part of two years, until a chance meeting with Alice herself, who in 2055 happened on the clinic in search for another potential Nth Prime. She found the lead to be quite unfounded, and instead identified Charlie's suppressed abilities. It was both a measure of her pity for him – after more than sixty years as an operant psychic, finding mental aberrations and reading into disorders and their cause intensely was an easy task – and the fact that he had nowhere else to go that drove her to convince him to oust himself from mental care and join her at GOA. Alice's personal life can also be compared to Charlie's in many ways, regarding deep losses of intense closeness (see File GOA IX: Alice McNamara).

At Headquarters, Charlie was identified as a CCT Prime, with M-class empathy, P-class telepathy, M-class telekinesis, I-class coercion and a better-than-human regenerative faculty. Under Alice's personal guidance and attention – lavished almost freely despite her tight schedule as GOA's Director – Charlie became a highly-skilled and accomplished field agent, second to none in expertise and unparalleled in achievements save for Alice's own long stint of field work prior to her ascendancy as Director. Many considered her keeping close watch and confidences with Charlie as a sign that he would possibly, even eventually, be groomed to take her place as Director, a job which despite Alice's long term in office had nothing to do with hereditary earning. (Alice's skill and immense capacity as GOA's Director made her the constant candidate for the job, and she never once refused it when the GOA Board of Oversight in charge of appointing the Director every five years kept choosing her for the last eleven consecutive terms.)

In the last half of 2061, after more than five years of exceptional GOA field work, Charlie was recalled from his most enjoyed pastime as a GOA employee and immediately placed in charge of a project which even he had thought Alice would oversee personally, possibly even give up her seat as Director in order to pursue it to ultimate success: the discovery of a second GenneY Prime, Daniel Mercer.

Instead, Alice showed her own intense participation from hand and placed Charlie in charge of coaxing the catatonic Daniel back to health and stability, a job which he at first resented, then finally grew to enjoy far more than his forays in field work. Consequent inquiry into the matter revealed Alice to be as dab a hand at handling the subtleties of her employees' moods and needs as she was at orchestrating successful conclusions to massive diplomatic and political issues of great delicacy: despite her own surprise at Charlie's reaction, he had played his part willingly and unconsciously, nursing Daniel back to near-complete recovery and comfort, and in the process healing his own unresolved wounds from the death of his cherished youngest brother and his father. Some people would argue that Alice did it as purposefully and coldly efficiently as she did everything else, but even the most jaded of these speculators would agree that Alice had always harboured a very large soft spot for Charlie, not just because of his potential but because his losses echoed her own personal ones, and in this they found a strange and disjointed comfort in each others' happiness and life achievements.

CHAPTER FIFTEEN

Preparations

"So they say you're fine?"

Chris lifted a rock and threw it, watching it skim across the dead calm of the lake. He and Nathan stood there, biding their time and yet waiting for nothing in particular, except enjoying the still, grey-sky morning at the lakeside. Nathan swung back and loosed the flat pebble he had in hand, but he didn't stare at the rippling effects for very long. His face was forbidding and taut, but he nodded.

"They say nothing's wrong with me except some minor trauma to the brain. It should heal in a couple of weeks tops."

"Life ain't complete without brain trauma every now and then," Chris replied, refusing to be shaken by Nathan's mood. He was always in an unflappable mode, never quite taken to dark moods, even when he was angry or depressed by something. So he took Nathan's temper in stride like he did everything else: grinning. "Care to place a bet?"

"On what?"

"On who throws the most bounces with this here rock, that's what!" Chris hoisted a fairly large pebble, one which looked as though it would hardly do the job of just one bounce. Nathan eyed the stone sceptically, not really taking into account the wide grin on Chris' face. Nathan shrugged, but he was intrigued nevertheless. "Okay then, where to start? Ten bucks?"

"Do it," Nathan replied, his voice still lacking conviction. Chris remained standing for a moment longer, then with one sudden motion he threw the stone as far out as he could. Surprisingly, it bounced four times before flopping to the depths. He loosed a crackling guffaw, staring at the ripples. Satisfied, he turned to Nathan.

"Your turn." He lifted a stone of the same size and handed it to Nathan, who regarded it without emotion.

He then looked out over the lake, narrowed his eyes a little in the sharp white glare, drew back and threw. It was half-hearted at best, but managed three jumps before sinking unceremoniously. Chris turned to him, smiling wide. "Guess you own me ten big ones." Nathan merely nodded. "You know, it would really help if you cheered up a little."

"What?" Nathan frowned, caught off guard by the sudden statement.

"Yeah, it might help. So what, you got violated. Roll with the blows and deal with it."

"Easy for you to say," Nathan retorted.

"Yeah it is," Chris went on. "You think you're the only guy who's had that done to him? Danny did that to me so many times I've lost track."

"You're lying," Nathan rejoined disbelievingly.

"Really? How'd you know? There's a reason I don't visit the kid anymore, and not because I hate him, just because it's turned into a game for him. With me, that is. Light stuff. Yeah, maybe not as bad as he did to you, but you get tired of having your brain filched, and then having him tell you he just did it. Creepy at first, and then you start to adapt. I'm not an empath, but I can shield the brainpan better by now." Chris tapped the side of his head. "I guess he's just eager, and he wants what's his."

"That didn't give him the right to do what he did to me," Nathan snarled. He picked up a rock and simply threw it with a lot of force, not caring if it jumped or sank. "I trusted him, and he repaid me like that!"

"Guess it is a tough one to swallow," Chris admitted. "And I'm not saying I take his side, because I ain't. I'm not taking anyone's side."

"Kinda lousy of you."

"Maybe. So ask what's really important then. What'd you get out of the deal?" Nathan thought for a while. He remembered now, a week after they had returned to GOA Headquarters and the testing had been done, the day he'd gone for a particular test. Alice had been there, and Nathan had been asked to give a full account of what had happened, what he had felt in the mental link and if he had anything left over after that. He hadn't told anyone about what Daniel had said to him, about the 'neat little gift' Nathan supposedly had. He realized it was one of the reasons he still felt so resentful, because Daniel had withheld that from him. It chimed in with him placing his trust in Daniel, giving him a chance, and not getting one in return. "You haven't spoken with him yet, have you?"

"They won't let me. I don't even know if he's conscious yet." Daniel hadn't been conscious at all in the trip back to Headquarters, or so Nathan had heard. He had refused to ride in the same plane as Daniel, so Jamie had taken him and Joanie in one skimmer plane, and Charlie rode with Daniel in another. No telling if Daniel was actually awake or not, yet. Nathan found himself not really caring. Then he sighed. He did care. He just didn't know what to make of the whole situation. He had bluntly refused Alice any mental access to his mind, and the woman hadn't been pleased. Still, she wasn't foolish, or arrogant enough, to bypass his decision, and she had expressed it as such. Despite the frustration there, Nathan had found himself strangely drawn to the woman, mainly because by her actions – in spite of the thwarted looks and grimaces – she had proven that at least one empath played by the rules. That revelation had shaken him, because he had actually doubted Joanie. But then it had been easy to discard that one out of hand. Two years of everyday proof gave him the right to do it. Charlie was a conniving bastard, but he never once broke into Nathan's memories, or tried to, as far as he could tell. Only Daniel had done that, and after Nathan had foolishly placed his mind in Daniel's hands. The betrayal stung greatly, more so than the memory loss had, and it fuelled him to a new level of anger. He yelled, startling Chris. "Dammit! I don't even know if I wanna see him! First the amnesia thing and now this!"

"Hey, give the guy some credit, he had no control over the amnesia stuff," Chris interjected, voice placating. "You know that one's true, you just haven't gotten over it yet."

"Maybe I don't want to. Maybe this whole business is a crock of shit! Or turning into one." Chris shrugged.

"I say wait until you can see him again. You've come this far, haven't you?"

"Right now, I just want out. I want to take Joanie, get to Luke and vanish. Screw GOA, and screw the whole 'I can fit in here, with others like me!' gig. Me and Joanie are better off alone, and I bet so is Luke."

Chris let him rage. He simply remained on standby, in case Nathan posed a question. That was the only reason he was with Nathan now, and though he liked the younger man well enough, he did it out of pity, not out of obligation, or because Alice had deemed it necessary. Nathan would never find out about that, and Chris was doing his best not to feel soiled again. Maybe if Alice hadn't turned the thing into a command, and simply asked if he would see to Nathan, it wouldn't have felt so wrong.

"So you're just gonna turn your back on all of this. Your brother, the people here who wanna help –"

"We don't need your help!" Nathan fired back. "And I don't even know if Daniel is still trustworthy! I can't trust him, not after what he did!"

"Like I said, maybe you should talk to him before you jump to conclusions."

"There's nothing left to talk about!" Nathan riled angrily. "I've made up my mind! We're going." Nathan stalked away angrily, leaving Chris alone. Chris didn't watch him go, he simply waited, breathed a deep sigh and leant down again, picking up another stone, which he hefted in one hand before throwing it as far out as he could manage.

"Sorry Alice, guess you have to figure this one out yourself," he said quietly.

Nathan strode into Headquarters. He ignored the polite nods from the people around him and marched along to the elevators, angrily punching the buttons. He waited impatiently, wound-up, for the tubes to reach the level he had ordered, then continued his march to the guest quarters. Sweeping into the suite he shared with Joanie, he looked about for her and found her at a terminal in the study area. She noted his arrival, gave a winsome smile and returned to the screen.

"I've been going over some of the declassified files in GOA. Nathan, this place is amazing!"

"That's nice, but we're leaving." Joanie looked up again, frowning.

"What? Why?"

"I realized I'm fed up with all of this. Yeah, so these people are great. Just amazing, like you've said. But we don't belong here."

"This is about Daniel, isn't it?" Joanie queried, rising from her seat and moving towards Nathan. "You haven't told me everything about it yet."

"What more is there to tell, Joanie? He screwed us over, even his precious Charlie, and hell, if it weren't for the nasty one he pulled on me I would have cheered, right there and then. But it's over. End of story. We're leaving."

"But I don't want to leave," Joanie said plaintively, almost meekly. She recognized she was going to fight him on his decision, and that she would probably lose in the face of his rage. More, this could fast escalate into something horrible. "These people care about us."

"Joanie, come on!" Nathan snapped. "Alice is gonna use us, like she uses everyone here! She doesn't care either way what happens otherwise, as long as she has willing subjects who would do whatever she says. And I don't care what you think about her.

She can be Mother Theresa the Second for all I care, and as pleasant as a Sunday drive, but she has her own little agendas and I bet you she's ruthless as hell to boot."

"So you're going to leave Daniel here, under Alice's ruthless agendas?" Joanie challenged snidely.

Nathan's face drained of colour with suppressed rage building. "I don't care about Daniel anymore."

"But I do!" Joanie snapped back. Her sudden shift into anger startled Nathan, but didn't derail him. He had seen Joanie angry only once, and he'd been impressed, but he wouldn't give in to her this time. "I care what happens to him because he also happens to be my friend. Don't I get a say in this?"

"He didn't pick your mind clean after he promised he wouldn't, did he?" Nathan nearly yelled. "Violation, that's what you empath people call it! Well now I know what that feels like, thanks a lot Danny-boy, you've at least taught me something!" He turned away from Joanie, attempting to end it right there, but she followed him.

"What was it you said? 'If Danny gets back his memories, everyone wins.' Isn't that it? Everyone wins? Well guess what? What you're saying now goes against the reason you agreed to do the mental link thing!"

"So what?" Nathan sneered. "Don't you get it? I don't care about what happens to him anymore! He can rot here for all I care!" Joanie's slap temporarily spun his head, and completely broke his tirade. He put a hand over the stinging spot on his cheek, staring with malevolence and hurt at her. Joanie's lower lip was trembling, but her eyes were hard and resolute.

"So that's it then. Just poor you, all the time. How hurt you got when Daniel forgot us! How badly you were violated, just because Daniel was desperate to get back the memories that got damaged when he Changed! Violation is bad, but it could have been worse. I've read in GOA records what happened in the past when people got seriously hurt by mental intrusion. They lose their minds, they go ape-shit and serial killer! Their brains explode, their bodies get traumatized and they lose function in their limbs! What happened to you? You told me you're actually better now, your gifts improved!" He remained quiet, still stung by the blow, immobilized by Joanie's outburst. And it wasn't finished yet. "And yeah, I believe you about Alice, and that's why we can't leave Danny here! I can't! Because we have to find out what she's doing to him, what she wants from him! I don't think, even if he's back to normal as we knew him, that he's a match for Alice! So you go if you want, Nathan Hirsch, but I'm staying here." Finally done, she began trembling, and to hide it from him she spun about, returned to the terminal and sat down forcefully, ignoring Nathan, eyes fixing on the screen and the information that sped by.

He didn't know what to do. He had thought it was bad when Daniel had threatened to kill him, back at the house on the island, but this was worse. Not only was he still enraged at Daniel, but Joanie had added her case to the mix as well, and it wasn't for Nathan, but against him. He wanted to scream and cry, and to rail against her for what she said to him, and for the slap. But he couldn't, he was too distraught, and he wouldn't cry, because he would get no sympathy from her, not this time. So he stood there, tears almost pooling in his eyes, absently rubbing his cheek where she had slapped him. For the first time in his life, there was truly no mercy in life. And all he could do was stand there.

Night again.

Alice enjoyed the feel of her own office most at night time, when everything around her was shutting down and employees were going home, or exiting the buildings and switching off the lights. It was like watching the death of an illumined empire, slowly decaying, but instead of loss, she always felt a sense of peace, of the clockwork efficiency of a massive machine winding down to a slower pace, awaiting the hands of the workers in the morning. She also felt, sometimes, like a spider in her web, a web of unified fronts and collective intentions, which she regulated day in and day out. It also chimed in weirdly with her job, because of some of the things which she had done, and what she was doing, and, with a sigh, she knew she would keep doing. It was her job, and she was utterly dedicated to it, irrelevant of the cost to herself. Or to others. And she felt this way now, seated on her desk, facing the large window that was usually behind her, watching the start of the early morning hours. Charlie was seated next to her; in a rare show of sympathy she had told him to do so, right after she had berated him for ineptitude and scolded him like a teacher would scold a small boy. He had looked suitably chastened, even when presenting his own arguments in defence of what had happened. It hadn't taken Alice long to figure out what had happened, after Charlie had given her a step-by-step retelling of the mental link disaster. And from her viewpoint, it wasn't as disastrous at all.

"He doesn't have control yet," she said. Beside her, Charlie shifted, still a little uncomfortable on his perch, which he would never have conceived of doing, never mind that Alice, the staunch adherent to propriety and business-like proceedings had done it first and then kindly ordered him to do the same. "He broke the field in the training room in a moment of heightened ability, nothing more."

"How can you be sure?"

"Because he hasn't broken the field where we keep him yet," Alice replied. "Granted, he isn't trying very hard. The technicians said he was probing and prying – they could detect fluctuations in the field grid monitors, but nothing too strong. So we have a dilemma, albeit a relatively benign one." She knew he was listening attentively – one positive response from those who accepted their reprimands with equanimity and dealt with it – so she went on. "On one hand, it means we have no change, even with the severity of the happenings in the mental link, which means square one again, which means," she almost couldn't conceive of it, not with the harsh reality of what she had told Margaret on the rise, "that in a short time, sooner rather than later, we might lose our young progeny to the ravages of his own mental awareness."

256

"What?" Charlie asked sharply. Of course it would sting, that one: Charlie's dedication to Daniel's safety and wellbeing was tempered in no small amount by his projected sense of love, the love he had transferred from his dead brother to Daniel, and would maintain at any cost.

"A repeat of the Nth Prime GOA monitored seventy years back," Alice confirmed. "Charlie, if that is the case, an intervention from every single empath I can get my hands on may become necessary, even if Daniel is hurt in the process."

"Why are you saying this? You would hurt him for your own ends?" Charlie asked, anguish rising in his voice. Alice shook her head slowly.

"There are things moving out there that will swallow us whole, if we don't act. Losing someone as powerful as Daniel, as capable as he could be, would doom us the sooner. And sometimes I wonder if he might stem the tide for only a little while anyway."

"I don't understand," Charlie answered, and Alice smiled wanly.

"Never mind. This is all speculation anyway, the worst case scenario of one possibility. And it isn't the most prevalent one either. Probably something else, something a little more mundane and emotional is eating at our gifted young genius." She didn't need to see Charlie's face to know he was catching her drift.

His reply confirmed it.

"Nathan."

"Yes, Nathan Hirsch, and young Joanie. Points of great attachment for Daniel. Who knows from what motives Daniel's sense of dedication and love towards those two springs? Maybe it conflicts with how he feels towards you; make no mistake, Charlie, Daniel is almost as dedicated to you as you are to him, but in the turmoil that makes him what he is, it can be hard to delegate attention to such things. But they cannot be allowed to leave. Daniel's return to what he was before the Change, emotively speaking, is crucial, that cannot be denied."

"So you're saying he's depressed," Charlie ventured.

"Lacklustre eyes, slumped posture, erratic but lengthy sleep patterns, the signs are there. He is listless and unresponsive unless compelled to add something to a conversation held with him. And there is that incomprehensible field he's forged around his mind and himself. I've dealt with massive telepathic responses and fields before, Charlie, with you, Jamie and even Alex, not to mention our first GenneY, but what Daniel has erected around his mind defies even my experience. And to think he made it so because of the one thing he can't bring himself to ask of Nathan, and Joanie. But mostly Nathan." Alice smiled wide when Charlie replied, thrilled by his quickness.

"Forgiveness," Charlie breathed.

"Yes, the quintessential cornerstone to human emotional progress. Daniel needs to ask it of them, and be forgiven, even if it is for something he had no control over."

"What about the other brother, Luke? Wouldn't he be able to help?"

"Luke is doing admirably under Alex's care and tutelage, not to mention it actually calms and stimulates that overactive head of hers to do so. No, bringing Luke back wouldn't help. I've spoken only once to him, but he revealed – willingly – enough in his actions and his mind, to warrant a forgiving spirit. To such an extent that he would forgive Daniel anything short of physical rape and murder."

"Won't that help Daniel? Make it easier for him to approach Nathan and Joanie?" Alice closed her eyes momentarily, quickly scanning for a very shallow emotional depth, aiming it at Joanie. She was angry – she and Nathan had fought about something – but concerning Daniel, she was inquisitive, worried and anxious. There was little anger there. Alice nodded, then shook her head in answer to Charlie's question.

"Joanie harbours Daniel no ill will. That leaves Nathan. Joanie and Luke will forgive in a trice, but Nathan was hurt too deeply by the pile up of screw-ups he thinks Daniel is the architect of."

There was silence for a few moments between the two of them, Charlie wrapped up in his own ramifications, and Alice sparing a moment from the intellectual rationalization to look at the lights of the Main Office section go off. Only GOA Proper remained lit now, and it always stayed that way.

"And what of me?" Charlie asked suddenly. "I don't need Nathan's forgiveness, but I can't retract the bond I've made with Daniel to stabilize him. What happens to me if he dies?"

"Back on that avenue again?" Alice asked dryly. "There is a reason I do what I do here, Charlie. Why I am so dedicated and efficient, so absorbed in GOA and what it is about. Because almost forty decades hasn't yet dulled fully the loss I felt at losing my husband." She knew she was going out on a limb with Charlie, telling him, a mere boy of almost thirty years, compared to her century-plus lifetime of experiences. But it was merited here, because his concern wasn't aimed at anything but Daniel's wellbeing, and Alice knew it completely and irrevocably. "You find something else to consume your passions and you go on. I said the pain isn't completely dulled yet, but Charlie, the bond I had with my husband was a willing contract, and forged in the understanding between a married couple, bound by absolute love on all levels. I don't demean your bond with Daniel, or deny its potency, but from a bond such as I had there is almost no chance of recovery, and yet here I am. If Daniel dies, you won't, unless you foolishly ascribe too much love to what you've felt for him, and commit suicide. It sounds far-fetched, but it has happened before. Such a waste."

"So it means nothing to you that I could hold you to blame for forcing me to bond with Daniel."

"I never forced you to do anything, Charlie," Alice countered.

"You all but commanded me to do it!" Charlie retorted. Alice snorted.

" 'All but commanded,' the very words that refute you. I never forced you on pain of anything to bond with him."

"I would have lost my job!" Charlie said.

"Maybe, but I doubt it. GOA cannot simply throw away its employees, especially ones like you."

"Flattery now?" Charlie added, and there was a slight hint of amusement in the question. Alice took it in stride.

"Don't get cocky," she warned, but not unkindly. "You agreed to it because of how you felt towards your brother, and his death. And I know what happened there, Charlie, not because I have to but because I needed to know what drove your devotion to Daniel. Your brother was a conflicted young man before he died, and you wanted to help him, but he refused." Alice continued, despite the twinge of regret she felt at bringing this into the equation. She could practically see the sobering effect this was having on Charlie. But it was necessary. "Forgive me for being so direct, but now you know the lengths to which I will go to make sure nothing happens to Daniel."

"I have your word?" Charlie asked, voice almost hoarse-sounding.

"My word?" Alice asked, surprised. "I cannot give it here, because if Daniel dies I would have broken it. But I will give it on account of minimizing anything that might happen to him, if we were to intervene. If it came to that."

"So now what? Sit back and wait?" Charlie asked. "Daniel won't speak to me, but I don't hold anything against him. He didn't ask for my forgiveness but I gave it anyway."

"He knows, that's why he doesn't ask for it," Alice replied.

"Then why doesn't he talk to me, or confide in me?" Charlie asked critically.

"Because of the conflict of interests. He knows Nathan dislikes you, and that you don't hold vice versa in any case either. A remarkable start, if indeed he is restored to his former, pre-Changed emotional self, because Daniel would have killed Nathan for your sake, if asked of him before the mental link. Now, we have him preserving the peace, even if it furthers his own crusade. So rest assured, I doubt we are losing him. Mere speculation, that was all."

* * *

"You like?"

Luke stepped back and gazed at the tux. It was a momentary distraction, even though the tux Alex and Margaret had picked out for him had been an overwhelming gift, and a marvellous surprise. But a distraction it was, because Alex had chosen, either by her own craftiness or simply because she knew, somehow, how he felt concerning her, that he would much rather stare at her instead. She sat with one leg on the side of the couch in his bedroom, the tux held high in one outstretched arm. She was wearing the gown she had gotten for the upcoming party, an impressive brocaded array of silk, miniscule embroidery and sheer swathes of black. In the daylight it looked out of place, but it was ravishing on her, a perfect accompaniment to her dark hair and round blue eyes. He had been thinking about her a lot in the three days they had been gone, staying in a city hotel while they did the shopping spree.

He could stare at nothing else but her porcelain child's face and the immaculate picture she cut in the gown. But he knew it was called for, so he effected a nonchalant smile and unwillingly ripped his eyes from her and stared at the tuxedo. He tried to think of words to describe it in his head, but all he could say was that it was black, svelte and that he would hopefully look suave in it, considering that he'd never worn one before. A bright spark of hope flared in his head: it fitted perfectly with Alex's gown.

"The tuxedo or the dress you picked out?" he asked, remembering to talk. She smiled almost coyly, even shyly, and tilted her head back, appraising him with mirth-filled eyes.

"Either one would do," she said, a slight inflection in her voice. Luke grinned, playing along.

"Okay, the tuxedo is amazing." He suppressed a grin when he saw her face fall, and then he laughed. "But only because it'll go really nicely with your dress."

261

"You clever buffoon!" Alex retorted, breaking into laughter, and would have thrown something at him if she had anything handy. Instead she draped the tux over the back of the couch and sauntered closer to him, feet clicking in the new shoes she also sported. "And here I thought you didn't know a thing about cheering a girl up."

"I don't, I'm just teasing," Luke replied, still grinning.

"Oh? Then tease away," Alex remarked, swung about and walked the other way, looking at him over her shoulder, a secretive grin turning her mouth into a voluptuous flower. "And now give me the skinny: to dress, or not to dress."

"Definitely to dress," Luke said, almost softly, mesmerized by her walk. "Definitely."

"Well then today wasn't a total waste, I guess," Alex said. Her almost playful mood was turning a little more relaxed, and she undid the earrings, taking a velvet box from the table next to the couch and delicately replacing them inside. "Margaret isn't the vengeful, vicious old bat I thought she was, except when two twits in the boutique stuck needles into me, trying to fit the dress perfectly. I've never seen an old woman get so worked up and spin a massive tantrum. Honestly, it shouldn't be legal to have that much money and have people fall over themselves when you've insulted them."

"She insulted them?" Luke asked absent-mindedly, using every opportunity to sneak glimpses of her.

"Yeah, it took every shred of self-control not to laugh out loud. I think she actually enjoyed doing it. An old woman's folly, she calls it." She sat down gently on the sofa, careful not to wrinkle the dress overmuch. "Although the make-up part of the shopping spree was boring, to say the least. Not the application and stuff, or the sorting, but damn, finding the right shop, according to Margaret, and traffic, was murder. The shoes I liked looking at and fitting, and the jewellery. Well, what can I say? Diamonds." With a characteristic whoop of delight she held high her right hand and threw back her head, arcing one leg through the slit in the dress.

Luke was almost beside himself, and swallowed, forcing himself to look at the ring on her finger. And a massive ring it was. He took her hand and stared at it, eyes widening.

"Shit, the woman is insane. She bought it?"

"Yup. Said I can keep it. Can you believe it?"

"And you were afraid she'd turn you into a lady," Luke snorted, unable to stop himself from rolling that one past. She glared at him, the smile not leaving her lips. "It's true!"

"Oh shut up," she said, and took the hand back, gazing admiringly at the large stone perched on her finger.

"If you'd come along she would have fussed over cuff links till kingdom come, and you would probably have liked it."

"I seriously doubt it. Shopping isn't in my nature, and I've been told style is a topic I should avoid at parties," Luke remarked, taking a seat on the chair opposite the sofa. So he could continue looking. "Hope a tux counts towards some sort of redemption. I have to go and thank Margaret for it, though."

"Ooh, I'll come with you!" Alex said, and jumped up, belatedly remembering what she was wearing. She halted, gasping, and spun about, trying to look over her shoulder and down her back as far as possible, seeing if she had torn anything. "Crap, did I tear it? I could've sworn I heard a zipping sound."

"Probably the slit," Luke said tightly, not wanting to play the lustful admirer and look down.

"Help me check?" Alex asked, and he thought he would have a fit. But he did it, schooling his features into detachment and making a pointed if hasty pass with his eyes, before assuring her it was nothing.

"Oh good," Alex breathed, relieve. "Gotta get out of it." She reached back and unzipped the artfully disguised zipper that laced the bodice together and began slipping out of the dress. Luke, mortified and turning bright red, intervened.

"Aah, you should do that in your room!" he managed, and her saucy grin returned.

"Why Luke, is that a blush?"

"I have no idea what you're talking about!"

"Its like an exploding tomato!" Alex crowed devilishly. "Relax, I've got a very sheer but wholly covering lace slip on."

"Go to your room!" Luke boomed to the sound of her laughter, and she took off the shoes, running out, and dress half undone at the top. Luke waited for her to be gone before he breathed deeply, hoping the colour in his face was going down. That, and he clamped down as tightly as he could on his thoughts, in case she added the final ignominy of filching the full truth from his head. He waited a minute, calming himself, before leaving the bedroom and searching for Margaret. He found her and Alyssa in the parlour, both of them taking their tea. He spared Alyssa a courteous smile.

"Ah, Luke, is the tuxedo to your liking?" Margaret asked, voice amiably prim.

"That's why I came down, I'd like to thank you. Umm, do I return it at some point, or –"

"Dear heavens boy!" Margaret snapped, not unkindly. "It is a gift, and one which you will keep and take away from here when you leave. It is the least I could do."

"I, ah, don't know what to say, except thank you. I didn't expect a gift."

"Call it a minor incentive for your remarkable progress," Margaret said, lifting her cup. Before she took her intended sip, she eyed him over the rim. "And what of Alex's gown? To your liking?" Alyssa suddenly spluttered, a little tea spilling down her chin, and she leaned forward, avoiding eye contact with Luke and glaring almost murderously at Margaret, who ignored her. Luke, slightly peeved at the open display, put it behind him and smiled.

"She's beautiful in it." With Alyssa's response in the open, he decided not to rub in his obvious feelings for Alex, and turned to her. "Didn't you get a dress as well?" The question sounded remarkably gauche and flimsy, but it was the only thing he could think of asking to divert the topic.

"Oh, I have lots of dresses already. Maggie foists them off on me at intervals," Alyssa replied, grimacing. Margaret's beatific smile remained in place, and Alyssa threw herself headfirst in drinking her tea, looking remarkably absorbed in the simplistic process of sipping it and not looking at anyone. Luke felt strangely upset by her reaction, wondering why Alex always had to be right, somehow, concerning Alyssa. But there was nothing he could do about it, and frankly nothing he wanted to, except make Alyssa's plight easier. Courtesy, then. He bid them farewell, thanked Margaret one last time for the tux and left the parlour, once more breathing a sigh of relief. It was remarkable, how quickly relief came onto him today, he mused.

"Oh, Luke dear, did Alex give you the bypass code to contact your family?" Luke ducked back inside, nodding. "You may call your parents and brother if you wish," Margaret said, and he thanked her, before being off like a shot, away from the tangled web in the parlour, only too glad to put distance between him and there.

CHAPTER SIXTEEN

Party

He woke up to the sound of activity outside.

He rubbed the sleep from his eyes and rose, ambling to the window to look out. He was hardly surprised that there was already activity out there, even though it was only nine in the morning. On the massively sprawling lawn, awnings and verandas had been set up for the grand soiree. Near the lake edge there was a massive pavilion with platforms set aside for the live entertainment, the dance floor and the outdoor kitchen from which all the food would proceed. Next to that, a massive fireworks stand was already being constructed as well, to finish the evening's proceedings. He was amazed at the event, mainly because he had only seen such things on television, and the fact that he would be present at the event itself was still a little overwhelming. But it was still early, and he mused on the proceedings as he went to take a shower to get cleaned up for breakfast.

At the table in the kitchen, he found Alex, who had also just risen and was idly gazing over the newspapers as she dragged the large mug filled with coffee closer to herself. She gave him a lopsided smile by way of greeting, then indicated the pot near the fridge. He sat down and stared at it, not in the mood to go through the motions, so he telekinetically pulled a mug closer, lifted the pot and poured. He grinned, extending a minute thread to add two sugars and milk, meeting Alex's quirked brow as the spoon stirred the mix without him touching it.

"What?" he challenged.

"A bit early for that, isn't it?" she asked.

"What can I say, I'm lazy today."

"Just so long as you remember not to do any of that stuff tonight, or Margaret, Alice and the collective might of GOA will make sure you disappear off the face of the planet," Alex said. She downed the remainder of her own coffee and set the mug down. It sped off to the sink almost before it even touched the table surface, and she smiled without looking at Luke, daring him to add anything about her own reply to his telekinetic exercise.

"I know," he said simply. "And the same goes for you."

"Are you teaching me now?" she asked slyly. "No training today, too many stragglers and curious people about. But I suppose you know that."

"Yup. So what else is on the agenda for the day?"

"Nothing, except take it slow, relax, all that. I don't know what you're gonna do, but my supposed stylist arrives at twelve and starts my ministrations. Hair, makeup, dress sense, all sorts of crappy details to make sure I behave myself while careening around on the dance floor in high heels. Gotta look my best for a bunch of people I don't know at all." She smiled indulgently though, and Luke knew she actually enjoyed every moment of it.

"So knock 'em dead!" Luke quipped. "I think I'll take a relaxing shower before then, laze around the pool and be half-man half-couch until it's absolutely necessary for me to join the fray."

"Show-off!" Alex retorted, the yearning to do the same clear on her face. "Don't let me see you at the pool while I get my hair yanked out by the roots, or it'll go badly for you!"

"I look forward to it," he replied with a wide smile. Whatever dance they had initiated at some point in the past few weeks was taking a turn for the best, growing ever more intricate. And Luke knew more than ever that he was falling madly in love with her. He only held back because he didn't know if she felt the same, and if she didn't he refused to make the first move unless it became blatantly obvious that she did.

The day proceeded as lazily as he had thought it would. At twelve Alex departed the kitchen – they'd chatted up a storm about everything imaginable, from GOA to the weather – and went to clean herself up.

Margaret and Alyssa were nowhere to be found, so Luke went back to his room, got into swim trunks and began an indolent reclining session on a deck chair next to the pool, diving in when he became too hot and drying off in the sun afterwards. By four he became bored, a little more than curious as to why he hadn't seen Margaret, or Alyssa, but he supposed they had to undergo the same process that Alex so deeply resented, before they could be seen by the public eye in their entire well-prepared splendour.

At five-thirty he was in the tux, staring at his own reflection in the mirror, turning this way and that. The suit was a perfect fit, and he mentally – not so she could pick it up – praised Alex for her superb taste and eye, because he wouldn't have been able to do the same were he in her shoes and forced to pick out a tux. Or a dress, God forbid.

On going outside, he was suddenly surrounded by chaos. The entire house staff was about and scurrying around, probably at Margaret's behest, tying up inevitable loose ends and helping the hired caterers and chefs with last-minute preparations and minor disasters which would always accompany such events. Luke ducked and weaved past and between them, nodding politely whenever someone greeted him. He was amazed at how easily the snooty behaviour came to him, after a month of living here, and not because he spent an inordinate amount of time with either Alyssa or Margaret. Upsetting, the shift in attitude, but then he thought that tonight at least he could enjoy himself, seeing as he was Margaret's protégé, or so everyone would be told, and thus think.

He went outside and stood on the higher level, at the top of the multitude of steps that led down to the terraces, gardens and the general concentration of the party. The place had changed dramatically since the morning, and lanterns hung between tree branches and large metalwork poles. Surprisingly, some of the guests had already arrived, and were sitting either in the parlours or outside beneath the trees, on comfortable chairs, sipping bourbon or rich, imported coffees. The tables near the main party area were already decked out in a massive selection of silverware and crockery, and the chefs and their assistants were standing about nervously, eyeing the entire scene and chasing underlings off to check on the dishes in the mansion kitchen, the ones which couldn't be brought outside until the time was right.

"Wow, can I pick 'em!" Luke spun around on hearing Alex's voice, and grinned. She was gorgeous in her gown, and her hair was a tight mass of curls and intricate little pieces of jewellery that brought out the colour in her eyes. Her face was a picture of perfect beauty, with enough make-up to highlight her features without overwhelming them. He walked closer and was shocked when she came in close and planted a lingering kiss on his cheek.

"And that?" he asked, incredulous.

"Because you are so cute in that tux, and because you think I'm pretty."

"I didn't –"

"You didn't have to say anything," she said, and that secretive smile played over her face again. "And even if you didn't think I'm pretty, I still am."

"Well then, from my very mouth, I think you're the most beautiful person here right now."

"But you're holding out for someone else?" Alex asked coyly.

"Now you're being foolish," Luke ventured, and her mouth opened wide, curving at the edges, and she slapped his arm.

"Why sir, the nerve!" she joked. "The audacity!"

"And what if the other guests saw you slapping me? What then?"

"Oh shush, I bet all these rich bitches slap their husbands around, and get slapped around in turn. It's the new thing, domestic violence, it gets the juices flowing and it makes sex afterwards all the better." Luke coloured – he didn't need Alex's twinkling amusement to know that – and kept his mouth shut, impressed for

269

the untold time by her mercurial mood shifts, and how she could always force him to laugh. This time she had come a little close to being very forward. That, or he was paranoid. When she didn't add anything to the statement, instead turning away and walking slowly to the stairs, he hoped that was the case, and followed politely after.

By seven-thirty the guests were almost all assembled, and either dancing a few rounds before starters and the grand supper or mingling in socially accepted circles, either sharing friendly chitchat or fawning after their peers. Luke didn't recognize anyone, apart from a few high-level names. He and Alex were seated beneath a tree close by, watching high society move past deep in conversation or breaking into gales of laughter.

"Nope, I don't know anyone here at all," Alex said.

"You're not the only one. Hope we're not expected to mingle."

"I don't know, Margaret didn't leave any instructions with the room service tray this morning." Luke snickered at Alex's comment, which she had delivered with deadpan seriousness. "Although Alyssa seems to be making friends. Or capitalizing on them." She directed Luke's attention to where Alyssa was gliding across the dance floor, accompanied by several young men and one or two women. "Guess she knows how to play this game. An old hand. Or it's the gown." Luke didn't miss the insinuation in Alex's voice. Alyssa's deep scarlet dress was very simple but incredibly elegant, like Alex's outfit matching every aspect of her features and physique. "Shameless hussy."

"Hey, lay off," Luke remarked, and Alex glared at him.

"I'm getting bored already and you want to deny me my only real pleasure right now."

"Thank you, I like being a wall ornament." This time Alex laughed.

"Sorry! I didn't mean it like that, its just that she annoys me, and the fact that she is so damn skilled, obviously, just aggravates me further. Look at her; she's practically twiddling that old fart around her pinky!" Luke returned his attention to where Alyssa was artfully simpering at an agedly rotund man with a walrus moustache and his old wife, who leaned back in her laughter at whatever Alyssa had just said. She then bade them goodbye and moved off, her coterie following, as they moved right into another bevy of richly dressed snobs and their affiliates, immediately worming their way in with cheerful greetings and remarks about the lovely dresses, or so it seemed, from the way Alyssa stepped back and appraised an older woman's dress, then leaning in and saying something which made the woman smile widely.

"Jealous?" Luke asked, joking.

"Jealous? Maybe," Alex admitted, strangely enough, but Luke picked up the mischief there. "I wonder if she'd know it was me if she got pushed into a punch tureen, or very saucy gravy."

"Alex!"

"Oh, the temptation. Quick, hold my hand." She didn't wait for Luke to comply but latched onto his hand, surprising him. She didn't look at him, but he was marvelling at how her hand felt in his in any case. "I can't look at her, she's making me sick. Let's go somewhere else." She rose suddenly, tugging him along. They went to the bar, where they ordered red wine. Luke never really liked it, but considering where he was, he supposed it was almost called for. After his first sip, Alex rolled her eyes and proceeded to show him how to smell the aroma, take a liberal sip and roll it around in his mouth before swallowing.

"Seen Margaret anywhere?"

"She likes to make a big entrance," Alex said moodily. "She always does, or at least, that's what she 'insinuated' all the time we were shopping and getting a dress for her. So I suspect we'll probably wait another half hour. I'm surprised she didn't invite anyone else from GOA to this shindig." Taking a very liberal gulp from her wine, Alex shook her head as though it would clear the taste, then downed the rest and ordered the waiter to fill her another glass. Luke stared, and then thought better of saying anything, opting for making his wine last longer. No sense getting lightheaded this early, unless Alex intended to make a smashing first appearance by endearing herself to all around. He suddenly suppressed a grin; he'd never seen her drunk, and he wondered what she would do.

Margaret's arrival was preceded by all the pomp and splendour of a very carefully timed preliminary fireworks display, gallant fanfare from the orchestra at the lakeside pavilion and a cavalcade of gracefully stampeding older women who were dying to see what 'Maggie' was wearing, and to be the first to congratulate her on the start of another successful evening. Luke stood on tiptoe trying to gain a glimpse of his and Alex's supposed patron, and could just barely make her out before she was literally swamped by well-wishers and social climbers. He hoped there were at least a few real friends in there, otherwise, he thought, he would have gone insane long ago.

After the big arrival, Margaret ordered everyone to find their seats beneath the draped pavilion. She caught Luke's eye at some point and jerked her head in the general direction of the main table, and Luke took Alex's arm and bodily dragged – she was on her third glass already, and more than halfway through – her towards the table, caught between amusement and trepidation at what Margaret would say if he saw her. So he decided on something relatively below the belt and told Alex, who was wildly protesting that he unhand her before she really made a scene, that any moment now Alyssa and her party cronies would arrive and treat her to all the condescending stares they could muster. This seemed to have an immediate effect.

"That's mean," Alex said, pouting.

"It's also true," Luke fired back, and watched, relieved, as Alex smoothed her dress, schooled her face to calm and assumed a very haughty and deliberately snotty attitude. This immediately garnered her the attention of several attendants, who led and cleared the way for Alex and Luke to the main table. Luke nearly wilted under Margaret's tight-lipped smile and reproving eyes when Alex all but tottered – elegantly – to her seat, two spaces away from Margaret

272

herself. So he shrugged and avoided eye contact. "You are embarrassing yourself," he whispered furiously to Alex.

"Myself or you?" Alex snarled back, frowning. She seemed more or less in control, but more belligerent than was usual.

"Pick one," Luke said, ending the argument before it could go further. Fortunately Alex remained quiet the whole time during Margaret's thankfully short opening speech, and she remained mostly quiet during the starters and supper, although she did refill her glass with champagne. Luke, feeling protective but not wanting to intervene, found himself caught between checking up on her and fielding questions from the people seated opposite him.

"There's a woman staring at me," Alex nearly drawled, when dessert arrive. Luke, finally reaching a point of being relatively fed up, confiscated the bottle of champagne she was fondling and placed it out of reach.

Alex almost tried to grab it back from him, and the bottle began shaking slightly when he deposited it. Shocked and mortified, he leaned into her.

"Are you insane? Don't do that!" he whispered furiously. She smiled half happily, then ignored the reprimand. Luke sighed, thinking he hadn't drunk nearly enough yet to level her mood of flighty, bubbling happiness. "There's a woman staring at you?" he asked, exasperated. Alex nodded, inane grimace on her face. She almost pointed, then let her hand drop, brought to a little reason by her own doing, and leaned closer to Luke. She nearly dislodged the dessert tray the waiter tried to deposit before her, and Luke apologized. The waiter gave him a knowing grin before moving away.

"She looks kinda Chinese. Oriental, or something. She keeps looking this way." Alex whispered conspiratorially, furiously and like a teenage girl with a secret. She glanced surreptitiously in a particular direction, and Luke waited for a moment before he too glanced that way. True to Alex's word, a breathtaking Asian woman was seated at the third table from them, a champagne flute held in one gloved hand. She seemed unaware that they were looking at her, and then she did look at them, nothing cracking the pristine porcelain smoothness of her face. Alex looked away and snickered. Luke frowned instead; the woman had blue eyes, and although he supposed such things weren't exactly uncommon nowadays, it had been a strangely unsettling gaze. But the dessert arrived, and Luke dug in, refilling his own flute with champagne. Alex went on as if nothing had happened, and she appeared to be sobering up somewhat.

The evening proceeded a little more calmly and without incident, until the orchestra began playing livelier music, almost an hour after everyone had finished eating. Such being the case, most of the people not embroiled in deep conversation rose and went to the nearby dance floor. Alex stared after them, a mild pucker on her forehead. Luke had denied her more alcohol, and though she had glared venomously she hadn't made an outcry whenever he told a waiter to take away the bottle after she had ordered it. She sighed, then stood.

"C'mon, let's dance."

It was a strange moment. One moment he had been quite angry at her for her behaviour, no matter that she disliked such gatherings – he didn't know exactly where she had picked up the dislike – and yet here he was, thrilled to hold her so close as they danced slowly to jazz tunes a century old. She was content to lean her head on his chest, and he was more than content letting her. The moment filled his head, and for a long time he simply thought of nothing but her closeness and how terribly in love he was. After a while the music became a single solemn roll into hypnotic similarity, and they simply moved slowly to the beat. When the music picked up again, people everywhere began filing back onto the floor, engaging in more energetic dances. Alex lifted her head, casting about her almost vacantly, and then looked back up at Luke. "I'm gonna go get a drink," she said, giving him a slightly drawn smile. He nodded and watched her go. Seeing as there was no one to talk or dance

274

with where he was he decided to return to the table and idle away the time, making polite conversation with anyone interested enough, or anyone who spoke to him first. Before he could take two steps though, he was accosted by someone's hand on his arm. He looked down and was surprised to see the Asian woman, staring prettily up at him, her face demure but still self-assured.

"May I have this dance?" she asked, voice liltingly caressing, accent plain but invoking shivers. Luke swallowed, uncertain of what to do. This was a defining instant of being thrown head first into high-class society and not really knowing what to do. But there was nothing to it. He looked about, wondering where Alex was, and knowing she had been gone too recently to be back so soon. He suppressed his sigh and smiled at the woman.

"Of course, Mrs..."

"It's Miss. Miss Sung," she replied almost daintily. Luke nodded and whisked her away. He thanked his mother for teaching him how to waltz, and though he was by no means skilled or even moderately good at it, Miss Sung aided admirably, as though she was in fact a skilled dancer. Belatedly Luke wondered if it had been rude to call her 'Mrs.', and if he shouldn't have stuck to madam, or ma'am. No, not ma'am.

"Are you here with anyone, Miss Sung?" he asked, aiming to avoid getting tongue-tied or acting sheepishly. He hoped the question wasn't forward.

"No, not tonight," she answered, and leaned back elegantly at a slight dip in the music. When she came back up he spun away, amazed at how easily the steps felt with her. "Aren't you Margaret's new protégé?"

"Umm, yes, as a matter of fact," he answered. A simple question, but one which felt wrong, somehow. And she didn't miss a single beat, not even a slight one. They continued dancing. "Do you know Maggie?"

"Oh, yes, she's helped me so many times, when throwing small but select little parties of my own. You really should come some time when I have another."

"I'll keep that in mind, thank you."

They finished the dance in relative silence, regarding conversation, and Miss Sung only demanded one dance before she gave him a bow and a smile, then left. Luke watched her go, puzzled by the strange incident. He looked about for Alex, but didn't find her. Alyssa was still plying her social skills and was dancing continuously and consecutively with the young men she had begun trailing after dessert had been finished and the champagne had flowed in earnest, and was enjoying herself immensely, by the looks of it.

Margaret was sitting with several other elderly-looking people at the main table, and by the looks of it was deep in some sort of discussion. She paid little heed to any of her three supposed protégés.

He left the pavilion and went searching for Alex. Fortunately it didn't take very long. She was at another bar, a much smaller one near the awnings on the outskirts of the main pavilion. On seeing her Luke nearly assumed she was getting drunk again, but she was talking casually with the barman, and her glass – more wine, albeit white this time – was still full and sparkling with the crisp coldness of it.

"Where've you been?" she asked. "I thought you would have followed me."

"I got a request for another dance."

"It wasn't Alyssa, was it?" Alex asked, eyes widening, and she actually spilled some wine over her wrist.

"No, it was your mysterious Oriental woman. She's a good dancer. A bit weird, though."

"How weird?" Alex began walking back towards the pavilion, with Luke falling in beside her.

"Dunno, just weird."

"Luke you have to be a little more specific than that."

"What do you want to know? She's Asian, she's beautiful, she dances really well, her eyes are blue –"

"What?" Alex asked, stopping short.

"Didn't you see earlier when you first told me she was looking at you?"

"I was drunk, I didn't pay attention to details," Alex said, waving one hand and taking a sip of her wine. She grimaced, looked at it and shrugged before taking another. "A blue-eyed Asian woman."

"What exactly is so weird about that?" Alex regarded him with a piercing gaze for several uncomfortable moments, then thanked the waiter for her drink, took hold of Luke's arm and hastened them away from prying eyes and ears. Her voice was low when she spoke.

"It could be nothing, but you know I used to hunt the hard copy archives at Headquarters, right?" Luke nodded. "One of the files had a really juicy murder case concerning a Changed, a man named Jorgen, in 2038. There was a witness who was later killed, but not before he testified: he saw a blue-eyed Oriental woman."

"Coincidence?" Luke asked with longsuffering. "Are you still drunk?"

"Hey, I'm being serious here," Alex snapped angrily. "Lets go in closer. The witness had taken a photograph. Not a very good one, but good enough to make out differences. I saw it, so maybe if we can get closer I can tell if it's the same person."

"Alex, you are being paranoid. Its weird, considering you aren't, really." But he followed as she strode off, as fast as her dress could manage. She stopped at the outside of the pavilion entrance facing the long paved walkway up to the house and began scanning the inside crowd for the mysterious Asian woman, placing the wine glass on one of the tables. Luke helped with casting about, even though he felt it was a wild goose chase, and that Alex was quite possibly on another stage of her drunkenness. Still, he humoured her.

"Where is she?" Alex asked.

"Don't know," Luke replied wearily, not caring to hide his boredom with the whole thing. Alex ignored the jibe and turned around. She narrowed her eyes, and then they widened. Luke, ready to give up the charade and go back inside the pavilion – he wanted to dance with Alex again – also turned around to see what she was pointing at. He gasped, more out of shock than anything else. The Asian woman was standing halfway to the top of the steps, talking with two other people. One, a woman, had a stunning Mediterranean cast to her, with long dark-brown hair and glittering dark eyes. The man had a face like some strange boy, with wide-set blue eyes and thin, cruel lips. While he was staring, they turned their heads almost as one.

"Well that's weird," Luke remarked.

"The woman in the middle is a Changed," Alex said, her face draining of colour. Her voice actually squeaked into nothingness. Luke, half-impressed by the assumption – he doubted for some reason that Alex was wrong – and half-uninterested, frowned.

"So?" He then frowned, made a little aware of his own increased mental sluggishness from drinking too much champagne. Belatedly he added. "How'd you know?"

"Remind me to teach you how to low-scan people, it picks up Changed traits as well," Alex said, and her hand tightened on Luke's arm. "Now we have to go."

"Why, it's not like –"

"Now!"

"Alex you have to explain yourself," Luke said, as Alex tried to drag him away from where they stood.

They both jumped, startled, when the fireworks began going off, making massive coronas of intriguing patterns in the night sky. People began cheering and clapping hands, mostly because of their inebriated states. Luke watched, amazed at the seeming closeness of the display, then got shaken again by Alex.

"The guy standing next to the woman is also a Changed. I bet you the Asian woman is Changed as well."

"Alex, what's your point?"

"That while you're standing here, gawking, something is up!"

"Or, like I said, you're being paranoid," he reiterated.

"You know what the perks of being an advanced empath are?" Alex chopped back, growing tetchy. "You don't need premonitions to tell you something bad is about to happen." She hurried away from him, and he followed.

They hadn't taken five paces when a shrill scream rent the air. It had come from one of the awnings near the pavilion. Luke and Alex strained to see, and then were startled by another scream, this time a man. All of a sudden people everywhere were screaming, and began to run as well, even though the fireworks were in full force and the orchestra was still going about it. "You see?" Luke, too shocked to protest, felt a shiver running down his neck. Startled, he looked slowly over his shoulder. The three were still standing there, but the man was smiling widely, and the Asian woman was looking straight at him. But what shocked him to the core was the dark-eyed woman in the middle, her eyes flaring vivid blue even from the distance he stood. And then she too looked at him, and her smile turned cruel.

"I think maybe you're right," he said to Alex, whose face was drawn and pale. She looked at him, and then over her shoulder as well.

"There's only one thing we can do," she said, breathing heavily. She didn't tell him what, she hiked up her skirts to an otherwise inappropriate height and simply started running towards the pavilion.

"Well, I hope you feel like talking today."

Daniel's only response was a slight tightening of the mouth. Alice crossed her legs and leaned back in the chair. Despite the fact that Daniel wasn't exactly a prisoner, they had dispensed with too much comfort in the holding chamber. The almost imperceptible hum of the neuronull field filled the air when there was silence. It was a sound that disturbed Alice, although it never had before. It had lent security before, an unbreakable field of energy that disallowed empathic emanations from within, and access from without. And yet Daniel Mercer had broken through one. Granted, the report Alice had filed, after Charlie had told all, had included the notion of the event occurring as a result of heightened senses and awareness. Now, as she sat staring at him, she was inclined to scoff at her own inscribed words: he wasn't even doing anything, and she was afraid. But she squashed the sensation.

"That all depends," he said, remarkably. She hadn't expected a change at all in his attitude to these little questioning sessions. He leaned forward, lacking all earnest, face neutral.

"On what?"

"What the topic of discussion is. Are you going to drone on about Charlie? Or is it gonna be Nathan this time?" Alice quirked one eyebrow. This was definitely different from the Daniel she had met and spoken to before the mental link. Back then he had been shy, almost retiring in her presence, and always ready to smile. Now his tone of voice was biting, even if his face betrayed nothing.

"The sooner this is over and done with, the better. Daniel, I don't like keeping you here," she said, trying for sympathy. He snorted.

"No, you don't. But that doesn't mean it isn't necessary. I know you Alice, you're driven by convenience." It was all she could do not to bridle. The remark was one she would have expected from no one but herself, after a lot of buttering up, selling the concept to herself. Coming from a twenty-year-old, progeny or not, was unsettling, and not a little offensive. "And you're really pissed off I said that." More change, a gleeful quirk to his lips. He was amused! Enjoying this!

"So is that how you want to play this?" she asked, her voice hardening. Most people in GOA knew that tone of voice. Disdain and contempt went hand-in-hand when Alice grew annoyed. Daniel, though, merely stared, that half-smile on his lips. "Small-minded games and petty little displays of superiority?"

"Why thank you!" he added, and grinned, although the mirth didn't touch his eyes. "You think I'm superior."

"Why are you doing this? This isn't the Daniel I know, the boy I've grown to like," Alice protested.

"That guy was a lie, a small fragment of the real deal," Daniel said, deadly serious. "That was the nicer part of me, but in general, Alice, I've never really been nice. Caring, kind, sympathetic, but not all that approachable. Dark, but in a good way."

"I don't understand." Alice frowned, truly mystified. She had expected tears and recriminations when Daniel finally deigned to talk to anyone, and yet now she found defiance and open hostility. She looked at him, and was surprised when his face softened. His words were measured and less antagonistic, but nothing she could refute.

"I dislike it as much as you do, but the fact is that I would rather be me, as I used to be before the Change, than live that hollow existence from before."

"Does this mean your gifts are unfettered again?" Alice asked, unable to stop herself from pouncing on that query. He rolled his eyes.

"If you mean to ask whether I am having a ball as an energizer bunny with a new trick every day, then yeah, probably." Alice sagged a little, relief clear in her reaction. If Daniel saw it, he didn't comment thereon. "But since we're on the topic of me being me again, how about you?"

"What of me?"

"What do you get out of all this? I mean come on Alice, you're not one for love and charity."

"Please refrain from commenting on things you don't know," Alice remarked icily, and once more elicited a grin from Daniel.

"People's reactions are so easy to read when you're Changed. And I was good at it even before I Changed, so I guess that makes me an instant shrink, now. I don't intend on hurting you with what I say, Alice, but the truth is better than fawning lies." Alice could only stare at him. His responses to her words were astonishing, and not because they were bordering on rude. He was matching her, will for will, and doing it with impunity, it seemed. She tried to reassure herself that he was a GenneY, after all, but this time it didn't help. "So, what do you intend to do with me, your pet Nth Prime?"

"I cannot tell you. The information is classified."

"Bullshit." There was no anger, no outrage, only a quiet statement. "You know, and it's hidden in a part of your mind which I wouldn't be able to access unless I had both my hands on your head." Alice paled, and almost rose. He merely stared at her, completely nonchalant, even cheerfully so. "What, you think I'd do it?" And there she saw her opening. Anything, to unbalance this unstoppable calm tirade against her.

"Like you did with Nathan?" It worked. Daniel's eyes hardened, and for a moment she thought he would actually jump her and force her mind to confess what she wouldn't do with words.

"I should have known you would ask that," he said. "One thing I do know about you Alice is that you are always an opportunist. You wouldn't have this job if you weren't." She was caught between castigating him for his arrogance and simply letting him rile against her. But in the next instant her earpiece chimed, and she looked away from Daniel.

"Yes?" she asked. She had put in an earpiece in case something important came up, seeing as telepathy was out of the question inside the field. She rose, for the moment forgetting about Daniel. It was her secretary.

"Slow down," Alice said, and then her eyes widened. "What? When? Right now? I see. Dispatch a team immediately, use the slipstream boomers." Her secretary signed off. Alice, deeply shaken by the news, sat down slowly, her legs feeling numb.

"What is it?" Daniel asked. His strange sincerity saved her from slipping into unwelcome thoughts, and she looked back at him, marvelling that his almost-sneers and almost-smiles were now replaced by earnestness.

The sarcasm and antagonism was gone. Alice wanted to say 'nothing', but for some reason she told him the truth. "Margaret de Witt-Emerson's mansion is under attack from unknown Changed." She was about to continue explaining who Margaret was, but Daniel rose suddenly.

"Your friend, to whom you've sent Alex. And Luke." Alice nodded mutely. "Where is it? The mansion?"

"Outside New York city, just south of Manhattan Island." Alice frowned, then stood, concerned. "Why?"

Daniel didn't say a word, but his eyes flared suddenly, the green turning azure in a flash of brilliant light, forming misty coronas.

"Daniel, what are you doing?"

"One way to find out, if the gifts are good to go once more," he said. Around them, the room began to shake to the rising crescendo of the neuronull field's whine. It was growing sharper, higher and more intense, and Alice gasped. She backed away a little, afraid of what could happen, but also horribly mesmerized by the fact that Daniel was actually overloading the field, right before her eyes. She watched spellbound for the earth-shattering explosion that would possibly cave in the ceiling, but instead, Daniel seemed to grow lightly transparent, before a horizontal slash of stripy white energy engulfed him.

He was gone.

Alice cast about, sending out her mind. She tried to find him, looking for any clue as to whether he was still inside the room, but found none. She sent her mind outward and found it blocked by the neuronull field. Stunned and puzzled, she tapped the comm button on the table.

"Where is he?"

"We have no idea, ma'am. He vanished off the scope."

"And the field? Is it disabled?" she asked. Stupid question, seeing as she could feel it still there, but she needed to know what had happened. The techs replied quickly enough.

"The field is still active, ma'am. It surged, wildly, but it didn't short. He vanished when it spiked." Alice sat down again. This was bad. She had expected a quiet talk with Daniel today, maybe a little comforting from her side, but her estimates had been way off. There was no doubt about it now: Daniel Mercer was restored, in mind and power.

And she had just lost control of him.

"Get me Security," Alice said to the techs, and waited a few seconds before she was tapped into the main GOA Security Bureau office. "Hold that boomer, prepare a strike team and wait for my arrival there. I am going with them. And bring Charlie."

CHAPTER SEVENTEEN

Counter-Offensive

Mayhem, that was all there was, amidst the screaming people and the crackle of flaming trees, exploding debris and general mayhem. Luke held onto Alex, fending off recklessly fleeing people in their tuxes and stately gowns. Some of them were burned, manic and hysterical, and they lashed out at anyone who came in their way, happenstance or otherwise. It was hard keeping a lid on his abilities, especially when one woman came storming past. She would have missed them by far, but out of sheer panic she snaked out an arm and practically backhanded him across the face.

"Do you see Margaret?" he asked Alex, who was frantically scanning the milling hordes of people for their patroness. She shook her head quickly but kept looking. Luke held his head a little higher and tried to see if he could spot Alyssa. There was more success in that department. The woman, for all that she was hardly tall enough to reach Luke's shoulder, stood high and almost proud, surveying the chaos. She caught his eye, her own face lighting up with relief, and she trotted over to them.

"Where is this coming from?" she asked, looking down at Alex when she halted. There was only concern on her face.

"Three people: two women, one man, on the steps. Or they had been," Alex replied hastily. Gone was the mutual animosity, replaced by the necessity of working together. Alyssa frowned and looked at Luke. "One of them is a Chinese woman, or someone Oriental at least. You can't miss her, she has blue eyes, apart from the flaring." Alyssa nodded, as though she was assessing the info and planning something. "Have you seen Margaret?"

"No, she vanished in the commotion. We have to go, inside the house, find a safe place," Alyssa said. Luke and Alex fell in step with her and they dodged incoming people, making for the house the long way around, avoiding the large stone steps.

"What about all the people? We can't just leave them here!" Luke protested. Alyssa spared him a glance over her shoulder, not shortening her stride or slowing down.

"I care more for these people than you do, Luke, but we can't help them. Most of them are gone already, and the ones still here will figure out soon enough to take a hike, as fast as they can. We have to find Margaret and then contact Alice. Bet she knows what to do."

They entered the house by a service entrance, stealthily making their way to the deeper bowels of the house. But their route would take them into the main foyer. Alyssa swore loudly, and ducked back behind the open door they had been passing. She pressed Luke and Alex back with her, spun about and held a finger to her lips, cautioning quiet. She leaned in close to Luke and whispered: "You can read minds, right?" He nodded. "Can you read mine? It'll be easier that way."

"But you're not receptive to our minds," Alex objected.

"Doesn't matter, just follow my lead," Alyssa said. She looked up at Luke, waiting.

"Hear me?" He nodded. *"The Oriental woman you talked of is standing at the top of the main stairwell. I can get past and create a diversion for you to get past."* She glared when Luke almost opened his mouth to protest, then turned away. In a flash she was standing, in full view, in the middle of the central foyer, right in front of the stairwell. The Oriental woman started and smiled.

"What are you doing in this house?" she asked, voice heavily accented but remarkably amicable.

"It's my house," Alyssa said defiantly. "You're trespassing."

"Your house? Then perhaps you can help me." Luke dared to peek a little past the doorframe. The woman was slowly descending, acting as though she had all the time in the world. Alyssa remained in place, and he mentally berated her for being so insolent in the face of obvious danger. "I am looking for an older woman. Margaret, I believe you call her. Where is she?"

"Who wants to know?" Alyssa challenged back. The woman's eyes hardened, though her face remained pleasant.

"We have unfinished business with her, my colleagues and I. We need to see her, now."

"Guess she's not around," Alyssa replied, cocking her head askance, eyes ablaze, but not flared. The Oriental woman stopped two steps above the floor and remained there.

"You are one of them, are you not? One of her supposed protégés. A Changeling. How many of you are there?"

"You ask a lot of questions for a trespasser," Alyssa said. "I think you should leave!"

"Oh, I think I'll stay," the woman said. The next instant she extended a hand, and Luke could see the impossibly fast spray of dark lines shooting from her fingertips. He gasped and started when Alex's hand clasped over his mouth. He looked back at the scene in the foyer.

As fast as the woman had shot those things, Alyssa had been faster. She stood several paces to the left of the woman now, further from Luke and Alex, and she was coiled and ready for action, brown eyes lightly limned in blue. The woman looked at her, an expression of amazement on her face. She hadn't expected the particular response. It didn't deter her for long, and she sent another spray of the black darts Alyssa's way.

Alyssa dodged them again, so fast that she appeared to be going through stop motions. The woman began to grow more agitated and animated in her gestures as Alyssa kept ducking and diving beneath the projectiles, slowly but surely moving towards her. When Alyssa stopped scant paces from her, the woman held up a hand.

"I admire your perseverance, but it will not avail you," she said. Before Alyssa could fire back some snide query as to why that was, the woman simply dissolved. It wasn't a simple vanishing trick, or a teleportation, because her features darkened terribly, fading into a pitch-black vapour that billowed monstrously, discarding her shape and resorting to a cloudy expanse of jet-black, oily smoke that was as dense as the bottom of a lake. Alyssa's eyes widened, and she was momentarily caught off guard, facing the unimaginable sight before her. She ducked away as an arm – there was no other way to describe it – coalesced and slashed towards her, somehow faster than the projectiles had been. More, the smoke wasn't contained to two hands firing now, and multitudes of arms snaked out, almost reaching Alyssa before she danced nimbly out of the way. When the smoky mass had almost covered the entirety of the floor, leaving her no room to jump to, she did the next best thing. Even Alex gasped when Alyssa bunched herself together and threw herself into the air, but instead of a second of suspense she hung there, levitating, eyes roving quickly for a safe space to land.

"We have to help her," Luke mentally sent to Alex. Alex nodded, and she took her hand off Luke's mouth and prepared to step into the foyer, her eyes already starting to blaze.

A sound from behind them caught Luke's ear, and a split second of distress saw him grab Alex and shove her hard, away from him, not into the foyer but into the lounge opposite where they stood in the corridor.

He yelled as he was lifted off his feet, held immobile for a moment and smashed against the wall behind him, before he dropped to the floor, jarred by the blow.

"I can read minds also," a commanding voice said, and he looked up. The other woman was standing at the opposite end of the corridor, the one whose eyes had blazed first, outside. The cruel-looking one. Her face looked bored, and her eyes were dark now, but there was no mistaking that the attack had come from her. "I had no idea there was an entire nest of Changelings, right under my nose. But I will enjoy myself, at last. I have so few amusements nowadays." Luke rose groggily, not daring to look at Alex for fear of the woman redirecting her assault towards Alex. "Margaret de Witt-Emerson, where is she?"

"Can't tell you what I don't know," Luke said, and before he was finished speaking the next unseen blow snaked out. He fielded it, but barely, gasping with the effort. The woman was horribly strong! He felt a moment of despair. She was walking closer, as lazily as the Oriental woman had, contempt on her face. Her eyes remained dark. The possibility of that simple fact was enough to make Luke want to run: no Changed could engage their gifts without the flare, it was impossible. Or so he thought. He scrabbled to right himself and prepared to battle for his life. He hoped Alex was gone, hoped she was running as fast as she could, or had teleported away and had located Margaret, so they could get away. He hoped Alyssa had gotten away from the Asian Changed. He hoped he survived, but it seemed unlikely.

The next blow threw him off his feet, even though he had put all his mental capacity behind blocking it. Through the spinning haze of mental torture so much exertion was putting on him, he heard the woman speak.

"Perhaps I shouldn't kill you. You lack the finesse but you have potential. I can feel it, sense it. It has been a long time since anyone could come close to dispersing the brunt of my attacks. Do you do it easily, or does it take a lot of effort?" Luke nearly gaped. The woman was making polite small talk while she routed him, inquiring about his skill. It was almost as though she was fishing for a compliment!

"Maybe I won't kill you. But I will break you." Another blow, and one he largely avoided by ducking low and letting his own mental defences send it overhead instead of blocking it. The woman stopped short, a pensive gaze on her immaculate face. "Now that was interesting. You didn't block, you passed it." The look turned feral, devilishly enjoyable. "This is getting more and more interesting."

Another blow, lifting him from his horizontal crouch on the ground and slamming him to the ceiling above. All he could do was buffer himself from hitting the ground too hard on the fall downwards, and he landed softly enough. But he could taste the blood bubbling in his mouth, and the dull throbbing in his chest. The woman was going to kill him, and she wasn't even trying very hard, with only the faintest haze of blue filming over her eyes. He was going to die, he knew it. He couldn't even muster the rage to fuel a new effort in hopes of fighting back.

Fight back.

He didn't care if she got incensed and maybe went into overdrive. He was dead anyway. Snarling, he rose shakily, as fast as he could, and sent as large a destructive telekinetic field towards her as he could muster.

The blow didn't land, but he could see the effects of her dispersal clearly. She halted, almost bounced a little, and a motion like a passing breeze ruffled her loose hair somewhat. Her eyes widened, filled with shock and outrage.

"You insolent little cur!" she snapped. An arm snaked out, and Luke couldn't block the piercing punch that dug into his shoulder and spun him in chaotic cartwheels, throwing him several paces back. "Killing you would be a mercy!" He lay there, the breath knocked out of him, body aching in too many places to give attention to, and mused on the sad ending to his life. He wanted to cry, to rant and rave. He thought of his parents, and of Nathan and Joanie, and how he never really got to them again. And he thought of Daniel.

He missed Daniel, and he would never see him again.

It was at that exact point that he was proven wrong.

The woman, angrily marching towards him, arm still outstretched, eyes finally flaring, stopped short, a frown creasing her flawless skin as she stopped dead. Luke felt rather than saw someone standing next to where he lay. For a moment he thought it was Alex, and he wanted to yell at her for being stupid and coming back. But it wasn't Alex who rolled him onto his side. It was done too easily. Despite his imminent doom he looked at the would-be helper, and his eyes widened.

"Yeah, I missed you too," Daniel said, a light film of tears over his eyes. They flared light blue, and Luke was about to ask why – pointless question at a crucial time – when the same back draft breeze he had seen affect the woman when he had attacked her roiled around Daniel, ruffling his hair. He frowned. "Lie still, I bet Alice is on her way."

"Daniel you can't fight her, she's too strong," Luke cautioned Daniel, before coughing up a small clot of blood. Daniel actually smiled.

"More people telling me what I can and cannot do." Before Luke could protest further, Daniel rose and stepped towards the woman, who was still staring at him as though he was the most impossible thing that could happen at that moment.

"Another weakling?" she challenged, mouth twisting in a sneer. "Two of you won't match me at all!"

"I don't need his help," Daniel said, quietly confident, pointing at Luke. Eyes flaring, he made a chopping motion, and the woman danced back, face a mask of shock. Luke wanted to grin at what he saw, but it was too painful. He had almost felt the massive assault the woman had sent flying towards Daniel, and apparently, so had Daniel, because he had sliced it in half before it could reach him. Slicing was hard, Luke knew from experience, because it involved completely disarming the willpower that drove a telekinetic blow. And from the looks of her, the woman knew it. Her bored demeanour was gone completely, face glazed now with wary concentration. She sent blow after blow at Daniel, but he didn't even flinch as he dodged them or simply halted them. The woman's face was twisting into an enraged mask, a petulant response from someone who had obviously never been thwarted before in such a way. More, her eyes were flaring vividly now, a sure sign of mounting rage and growing power.

"I need to find Alex," Luke whispered, when Daniel had loosed a blow that sent the woman sliding backwards on her behind. Daniel looked back.

"Go outside, she's with Margaret." A massive tremor shook the walls of the hallway, and the floor beneath their feet buckled. A ceiling caved in somewhere, and there was fire in one of the smaller lounges leading from the corridor they stood in. Daniel snarled as he turned back about. The woman was angrily poised, her fists clenched, face twisted into an almost feral smirk of rage. Coupled with her eyes, it was a terrifying sight, one she compounded by making a pushing motion with both hands. Daniel crossed his arms but got pushed back a full pace before halting the blow. Luke rose unsteadily, hands on knees, leaning against the wall.

"I can help you," he began, but Daniel wasn't looking at him. When Luke tried to muster what was left of his resolve into anything that could aid Daniel, the black-haired younger Changed gave a curt look back over his shoulder.

"Go!"

"But I –"

"Lucas Hirsch, don't make me force you!" Daniel snapped, strain clear in his voice. The woman stared, flabbergasted by the exchange, probably because Daniel was capable of holding her at bay whilst talking, albeit under pressure. Luke remained immobile, wracked with indecision. Daniel breathed deep. "Go," he said, almost sounding more kindly. Nodding, Luke lifted himself up and walked painfully away from the fight scene. Everything felt incredibly wrong; him leaving Daniel to fight the woman, the way the evening had turned out, everything. But he kept walking, somehow amused by the woman's awkward squawks of rage and frustration as Daniel joined in with snickering humour, denying every blow she sent. He looked back once, and gaped when Daniel made a sweeping, throwing motion, sending the woman flying through a wall.

* * *

"Alice is on her way."

She could see Margaret relax visibly when she said that, and she knew she felt the same. It would take about ten more minutes for the arrival, but at least it would happen. Now all she worried about was Luke. She had sensed rather than 'heard' his unspoken command that she leave, even though she had felt so strongly that she should have helped him. Her face nearly crumpled when she thought that he was probably already dead.

"Cheer up my girl," Margaret said from one side, patting her reassuringly on the back. Alex wanted to lash out at the woman and then thought how much more Margaret had lost. For a start, the house was on fire, in several parts, and wouldn't last very long. The garden also was aflame, and the entire party scene was in ruins. She refrained from looking at the few motionless bodies that lay close by, feeling her gorge rise. She took a deep breath, swallowed her tears and whipped up a bleary smile for Margaret's sake. The woman replied with an almost beatific one, marred only by the smudge marks and tattered finery she wore. Even so, the older woman still looked regal. "I wonder where Alyssa is."

"She was fighting the Asian chick when Luke and I got attacked by the other woman." Margaret's face darkened, and she rose. She ordered her house staff – the ones who had searched for her and hadn't bolted – to hurry off the grounds, silencing any protests. Without waiting to see what Alex would do she all but marched towards the house. Alex cursed and darted after. "Where are you going?"

"I will not let these upstart delinquents run amok with my people!" Margaret snapped.

"You can't go up against them, you're –"

"Too old?" Margaret interrupted, imperiously climbing the steps. "That's just it, I'm too old, or so they think."

"I don't understand," Alex said.

"I am not defenceless, girl, so stop acting as though I'm daft as well!" Margaret snarled. She reached the doors and threw them wide open. "I have a few surprises up my sleeve." Alex didn't know what to reply, so she marched along. She did think Margaret was too old, and she didn't want her going up against either one of the two female Changed inside the house. But there was no stopping her, so she trotted after, hoping she could field enough damage until the old woman could see sense.

Margaret strode through her ruined domain as though the priceless antiques and the well-used but immaculate furnishings in tatters meant nothing to her. She swept through the lounge opening up to the back gardens and out the one door leading to the foyer. When the doors opened, the old woman's face fell. There on the floor was Alyssa, seemingly unconscious, with the Asian woman bending down beside her.

"Back off, cretin!" Margaret demanded haughtily, causing the woman to look up. Alex tried in vain to stop her but she shook her arm loose.

"Ah, I take it you are Margaret, yes?" the Asian woman asked. "Your party was impressive; I got quite a few pointers." As if to insult them, she reached down, fingers elongating into sharp, thin prongs which she jabbed into Alyssa's chest, much to Margaret and Alex's horror. Alyssa gasped, her eyes rolling and her chest heaving, before she fell back down, breath fluttering. "I wonder why you are so important, but then you do seem to have a few surprises prepared for us. My colleague in the corridor is amusing herself, smashing the handsome blonde man, who danced so protectively with me, into pulp."

"What?" Alex demanded, and this time it was Margaret who held her back. But Margaret couldn't hold back Alex's gifts. With fury born of wrath she loosed her strongest imaginable telekinetic blow at the woman, and watched her flung hard against the front doors, landing heavily. She rose shakily, her flawless face impassive despite the undeniable rage that boiled in her gaze. Alex swallowed.

A blow that strong should have crushed the woman to a sodden bloody mess. As it was, the woman rose slowly, back straight, eyes fixed on Alex.

"So, he meant something to you? Then perhaps I should join the little session in the hallway, add my condolences to the cause." The woman made as though to walk towards the corridor, and when Alex loosed again, her body simply rippled, almost assuming that terrifying oily smoke she had done before, but maintaining her shape. She smiled at Alex, who screamed furiously. She diverted her attack to a telepathic assault, but found nothing at all. Whatever the woman was doing, even her mind turned to smoke and mist when she did that. Unchallenged, she kept walking.

Margaret darted past. Frayed skirts in hand, she moved faster than Alex would have thought possible for her age, practically sprinting – in very ladylike manner – towards the shimmering Asian woman. The woman stopped and chuckled derisively.

"And what will you do? Punch me?" Margaret stopped just before she would have gone through the woman – Alex thought going through that wouldn't be too hard to accomplish – and lashed out with one hand. The Asian woman's eyes widened in shock, the natural blue rippling in tune with her body, but her face registered amazement, of all things. Margaret's eyes were narrowed and her mouth set.

"There's always something different!" the old woman fumed, and lowered her head, her arm immobile. The Asian woman's mouth formed a cruel moue, but it was also an expression of concentration and focus.

Alex moved in closer, ready to loose at any moment, puzzled by what she saw. The next moment Margaret cried out, and so did the Asian woman, and they both shot backwards, away from each other, the Asian woman fully materialized again, and looking dazed. Margaret was first to rise, getting quite steadily to her feet. The Asian Changed had newfound wariness in her eyes. She lifted a hand, and before Alex could make an outcry, the fingers elongated again, shooting straight for Margaret.

Somehow the old woman managed to get out of the way, even though one of the sharp needles nicked her arm. She was about to elongate the other hand when Margaret raised her chin and shook her head.

"None of that!" she said commandingly, and the prongs juddered and stopped halfway to her, jerking before recoiling and shooting back into the Asian woman's hand. The sound it made sounded like a slap with a wet hand, and Alex winced involuntarily, watching the woman cradle her hand, black ichor seeping through the fingers clutching the injured hand. The woman looked at Margaret, pain evident on her face. "You *imprinted* me?" she demanded, and Margaret's small, mirthless smile confirmed the accusation.

"Feel free to join in at any time, Alexis," she said tightly. The woman, roaring angrily, ran for the closed hallway door, ripping it open with one hand before darting through. She was gone before Alex could respond.

"What just happened?" she asked Margaret, who hunkered down beside Alyssa. She placed two fingers against Alyssa's neck and felt for the pulse. She waited for a few moments and then nodded, apparently assured that Alyssa was fine.

"Like I said, I have a few tricks of my own up my sleeve."

"What did she mean, about the imprinting? What is that?" Alex queried.

"When we have more time I will indulge your questions, but we still have two other people to worry about," Margaret said, and moved to the hallway.

"What if that Asian cow comes back?" Alex asked, stumbling after.

"I doubt she would, and she didn't look stupid," Margaret said, of all things amused! Alex could only shake her head and follow.

She desperately hoped Luke was alright, and that the woman had lied.

* * *

Luke was outside.

He hadn't found Alex or Margaret anywhere, and he had even done the distasteful job of scanning the faces of the bodies outside. He had spewed the contents of his stomach twice, but he still went on. Now he was on his way back to the house, wondering if maybe there wasn't some secret hiding hole beneath the mansion where the two of them could have gone. He dreaded returning to the house. There were fires in there – smoke was filtering in from somewhere near the kitchens – and he didn't doubt they would spread quickly. He didn't worry about the telekinetic monster in there, if she still was – the mental punch she had taken from Daniel would have thrown anyone, no matter how big, at least a hundred feet, if not done through a wall, so the odds were the woman was outside and unconscious, or even dead.

He was amazed to find he hoped she was dead.

At least Daniel was in there. It was amazing, seeing him again, even under the terrible circumstances, and Luke wanted to talk to him. It blew his mind, how casually Daniel had faced the woman, and it opened up all the questions he had thought of asking when he finally saw Daniel again. There was no time for it now, though. He was hardly surprised to see the back doors ajar, and he went inside.

Alyssa was lying on the ground, unconscious but otherwise seemingly unharmed, save for five small bleeding spots on her chest. Luke felt for a pulse, was relieved to find one and dragged her away from the floor and into the lounge, depositing her on a couch. He wondered if leaving her alone was a good idea, then thought better and quickly rushed outside with her, gently laying her down near a tree on the front lawn, away from the burning house. He hadn't seen the male Changed of the three intruders yet.

297

"Daniel where are you?" he said aloud.

"Hunting the male Changed," came an aloof mental reply, shocking Luke. *"Leave Alyssa where she is, Margaret and Alex are out front, also looking for the guy. I can't find him, but if they do… Let's not find out what happens, okay? Bring them to the front of the house, outside. I'll be there shortly."* The presence vanished, and Luke charged for the front doors, throwing them open. He cast about him, frantically hoping to catch a glimpse of either Margaret or Alex. The front garden where he'd left Alyssa was intact, even though the house was burning in multiple patches now.

"Luke!" Alex yelled, coming out from the side of the house, running headlong towards him. She jumped and enfolded him in a tight embrace, burying her face in his neck, sobbing. "I'm so glad you're alive!"

"I got helped," he said, wincing. She laid off, placing a hand on his cheek, looking up at him. "Daniel's here."

"Really?" Alex asked, startled. "Where is he?"

"Where's Margaret? Daniel said you two shouldn't look for the male Changed."

"Why not?"

"He didn't say. Get Margaret."

She teleported, leaving Luke in an agony of waiting, hoping she didn't run afoul of any one of the two Changed women. Mercifully, he didn't wait too long, before Alex and Margaret arrived, with Margaret dirty and covered in dark smudges, her gown spoiled. She smiled weakly when she saw him.

"I'm glad to see that Asian cow, as Alexis called her, lied about your death," the older woman said meaningfully.

"Where were you the whole time? I've been looking all over for the both of you," Luke replied.

"Margaret got rid of the Asian bitch –"

"Alexis!" Margaret snapped. Alex just went right on.

"– and the other woman vanished, so we went looking for the guy."

"Daniel took care of the other woman," Luke said, sitting down, on the lawn beside Alyssa's prone form.

"He killed her?" Alex asked, eyes wide. Luke shrugged.

"I dunno, but he did throw her through a wall. He said he'd be here shortly." He looked back at the escalating conflagration, and grimaced when one of the windows facing front exploded in a shower of glass, a fountain of fire screaming hungrily outward. "Margaret, your house," he began, but Margaret scoffed.

"It is just a house."

"But all your beautiful things," Alex chimed in, looking upset.

"I am far more concerned with the people who lived in the house, and with those who lost their lives today," Margaret replied. "I hope Alice has a story ready to explain this one to the world." Even as she said the words, a low boom echoed overhead, and a sleek, wide craft moved in lower, engine ports whining, slowly hovering to a more open spot on the lawn.

"Cavalry," Alex breathed, relief clear in her voice. Luke sighed, bone-tired and aching everywhere. No one got up to greet the people climbing off the jet. They were too tired.

"I do wish my bedroom was still intact," Margaret said with a weary grimace. "I look a mess."

CHAPTER EIGHTEEN

Recriminations

The vault was empty save for them.

It was like being inside an old Gothic cathedral; the scope was not so grand, but the stonework detail, arches and buttresses ribbed overhead like the inside of a whale's chest cavity. A single sarcophagus dominated the centre of the chamber, and though it was half underground there was a set of tall, slit windows, ground level, that allowed some garish morning light inside. Amorphia sat on a rail that ran parallel to the rectangular casket, eyes wide and unfocused, staring at nothing. Kessler leaned casually against the wall, mouth thin and compressed into a faint sneer. Only Persephone walked about, angrily yelling and ranting, but nursing her broken arm like the most precious of possessions. Her face also had a cut above the forehead, marring the normally effortless beauty that adorned her. Her gestures and reactions were the most animated of the three, and she was doing most of the talking.

"Inconceivable that this could happen! We were challenged, and we failed miserably!"

"Well, the two of you failed miserably," Kessler said, holding up one hand and staring at the nails. He lifted his head and smiled mirthlessly at Persephone. "So much for your arrogance."

"You are on thin ice with me, Kessler," Persephone warned. She could always cow the man's incessant dark cheer, but this time he merely watched her as though she was far beneath him, even his contempt.

"It could have succeeded, had you actually joined in," Amorphia snapped, words half-hearted, but her eyes glittered as she raised her head and fixed Kessler with a baleful glare. "Were you afraid? Is that it? Or did you know something we didn't?"

"I was commanded to remain in New York pending further orders. I went along because it was amusing, but neither of you ever so much as asked whether I would join in." He smiled. "So I didn't." He looked at Persephone, speaking before she could react. "Don't throw me the tired lines, woman," he snarled. "I am not your lackey, and I certainly don't do your bidding."

"Then perhaps you should be reminded why you are here, and not with one of the others!" Persephone lashed at him, and he recoiled, hand to his cheek. He held it there, momentarily thrown, and then the smile returned. He took his hand away slowly; underneath his cheek, the cut healed seamlessly even as the others watched.

"Weakened from your struggle?" Kessler asked sarcastically. "My, my, what a perfect opportunity. It is rare that you are so weakened that you can't even fend for yourself."

"You wouldn't dare!" Persephone snapped, glaring.

"You know what you are without your powers, my precious?" Kessler crooned, taking a single step forward. "You are a weak little human, just like all the others." Another step.

"Enough!" Amorphia yelled and threw herself from her bench. "Even if this exercise failed, there is something we've learned and seen."

"And what would that be?" Persephone griped.

"Save your contempt for someone who cares," Amorphia fired back and settled for ignoring the outraged anger on Persephone's face. "This woman, Margaret, is a powerful Changed. Under other circumstances I wouldn't have cared, but while you," she turned to Persephone "were off amusing your petty interests, I searched the house. The woman has ties to the government."

"Oh? How interesting," Kessler said snidely.

"The government knows about us," Amorphia overrode him. That brought them to attention. Even Persephone was shocked, but Amorphia thought that it was because she was weak now. Looking at her, even she was tempted to crush the life from the woman, silence her tantrums and pride in a black blanket of poisons. But it wasn't allowed. "About the Changed, about what we are and what we are capable of."

"It's only one government," Kessler said. "Although the Americans have an annoying habit of working well behind the scenes with the bodies of other countries, I admit."

"Do you wish to become the hunted?" Amorphia challenged both of them. "That old bitch touched me and imprinted me." Amorphia whirled to face Persephone, who broke into a fit of laughter.

"She imprinted you? Well then she was worth the scare after all, if she could do that. But I am less worried about her than about that thing that attacked me!"

"That broke your arm and threw you through a wall?" Kessler couldn't keep the genuine amusement from his voice. "I would like to meet this young man. Who knows, maybe I can coerce him to finish the job." He laughed at Persephone's murderous glare.

"It doesn't matter, they are gone now," Amorphia said. "We have wasted time and effort, ultimately, and all because you have this little thing about every other Changed in 'your' city," she snarled at Persephone. "Perhaps next time you will get killed and save us all the trouble of enduring your childish outbursts."

"How dare you!" Persephone began, but Amorphia held up one hand.

"I know I may not kill you, but I have never been one for killing when I could wound and maim. If you value that precious face of yours, I suggest you keep quiet."

"This isn't over!" Persephone fumed, the hand of her other, unbroken arm clenching and unclenching.

"Oh but it is, for now at least," Kessler said from his side. He walked towards the door and opened it. "I am going to Boston."

"To do what?" Amorphia asked critically.

"None of your business," Kessler said, then was gone. Amorphia turned to Persephone.

"Make no mistake: I will tell him of this, if only to amuse him." Persephone's face drained of colour, even as Amorphia smiled. "Until we meet again, try not to overreach yourself. There is no telling what could happen to you, as weak as you are." Dissolving into dark, liquid smoke, Amorphia dissipated herself and vanished out of the tomb, leaving Persephone to muse on her misfortunes.

There was a private lounge above the Mess level. It was accessible only from the saloon and from Alice's private entrance, which was locked by her at all times. There was no real reason other than keeping Alex from snooping about, but since Alex had been gone for more than a month, Alice had grown used to not keeping the door locked at all times, because everyone else understood the concept of privacy. She would have to be careful now that Alex was back in the area, but apart from her, it was a private seclusion spot, a nice retreat after an enjoyable meal in the saloon, and any Changed was welcome to enter.

The lounge was on two levels, with an antique spiral staircase winding from the second floor to the first one. The entire room was done in a very strange early twentieth century style, since Alice preferred the Art Nouveau coils and minute details of the almost organic, Celtic motifs dating from that era of architecture.

The lounge was mostly for her personal use, but it had enough space there to seat thirty people at most. But she wasn't in there as she gazed from the one-way window, down from the second level and onto the main couch arrangement. From inside the upper chamber – the one which led directly into her office suites – she regarded the scene below her. Nathan and Luke were talking animatedly, and though she couldn't hear a word she was certain it was about the daring rescue orchestrated by Daniel, and how he had beaten the disturbingly powerful Changed woman who had all but decimated Margaret's mansion.

"I wouldn't have thought them brothers, at first glance," Margaret said, drawing close to Alice as she too looked out from the window. "The other one looks surer of himself."

"And that's supposed to define their being brothers?" Alice asked absently. Margaret scoffed.

"Personal certainty is a sign of maturity, in most cases. Although young Luke has remarkable fibre to him, which no one sees on the surface."

"Nathan in turn is very likeable, but I think he is hardly as sure of himself as he lets on," Alice added.

"Those two may prove instrumental in Daniel's willingness to cooperate with us."

"He's not cooperating?" Margaret asked, quirking one eyebrow. Alice looked at her old friend. Margaret was still looking a little bruised, but it was a testament to her remarkable regenerative gifts that she was almost completely mended. There was no telling yet how she was taking to the destruction of her home – the older-looking woman was very stubborn; some things you couldn't unlearn from old age, even when you received access to gifts which lengthened your lifespan indefinitely.

"He's secure, I sent him to one of the safe houses after we came here. Hardly said a word on the return trip, but was amiable and friendly enough when pressed. He disturbs me," Alice replied.

"Disturbed? You? What changed so dramatically?"

"His reawakening – lets call it that – to his memories from before the Change has restored something…dark, to his personality. A pragmatic edge of directness, even harshness, at times. He moves, speaks and operates as though nothing is beyond him, and yet he shows no arrogance at all about his gifts."

"A terrible mixture," Margaret agreed. "Great power without the pitfall of pride. I can see why you are so troubled. Do you think he can be convinced to stay?"

"That depends on Nathan Hirsch." Alice said, and for a few moments there was silence in the room, as both women watched the two brothers talking, Luke still in animated discussion, Nathan smiling wearily, failing to completely hide his discomfort at talk of Daniel. It bothered Alice, because she knew the younger brother distrusted her as well, else she would have intervened and spoken to him about mental violations. Now Daniel's one lapse could cause him to regress, should Nathan scorn him.

"You haven't tried weaning Daniel from his friends, have you?" Margaret asked at length. Alice shook her head, sighing.

"It would no longer work, and they were never just friends, remember," Alice corrected, and Margaret nodded quickly, remembering Daniel's deeper connection to the Hirsch family. "Retrieving the brothers and Joanie Stratford was a last-ditch effort to restore Daniel's fractured memories, and now that he has them back, he cannot forget that these people are his friends and family. And you've never seen the boy react to the people he loves, Margaret." Alice's voice sounded wistful, almost melancholic. "I have rarely encountered such a bastion of trust, even amidst his general paranoiac reactions to unknown outside factors, like people he doesn't know. I've seen it with Charlie and with Alex – they were closest to Daniel before the reawakening – and to some extent even with Chris, which takes a lot of effort."

"How extensive would the damage have been? Had you failed to reawaken the memories?" Margaret continued. "If bringing in the Hirsches and the Stratford girl was a last ditch attempt."

"We would have lost him, Maggie," Alice said, and the fact that she used the diminutive for her old friend's name spoke volumes about the close sharing. "He would have self-destructed, and no doubt caused a national incident in the process. And there is no telling how long we would have waited for another Nth Prime." Margaret narrowed her eyes, watching Alice with shrewd interest. She looked away and closed her eyes, her hands trailing on the inner sill of the window. Below them in the lounge, Nathan was leaning back, eyes far-off as he talked, with Luke listening this time.

"How will you explain my mansion?" Margaret asked. "I don't blame you at all for what happened – an old woman's folly gone too far – but there is little one can do to explain away the events that happened there. And there's no telling if anyone saw any one of us go about doing our Changed theatrics. Not to mention it had taken four GOA agents with psychic coercion abilities almost four hours to track down every fleeing guest, and emplace the regrettable but necessary mental shuns to forever block the truth from their minds "

"I am already working on a press release. I leave for Washington in the morning to debrief the President, and hopefully to salvage the potential disaster. Preliminary cover-up reports and some misdirection's are already in place on the media channels" Alice added.

"Potential?" Margaret snorted. "Maybe you should take Daniel with you, give the man a glimpse of the truth."

"Out of the question," Alice snapped imperiously, not meaning to do so but on the defensive nonetheless. "It is enough that the President and his closest cabinet members know what I am capable of. If the less informed of people in the government figure out that we have a massively powerful human weapon in our control they will most likely demand Daniel's presence at every single counteroffensive sortie outside the country, and blow GOA's cover if we don't acquiesce." Alice leaned forward, the strain clear in her face and posture. "The world isn't ready to know about us yet, Maggie. Many people do, but not enough to warrant widespread hysteria or pogrom propaganda. We must work towards that goal, but it isn't in reach just yet."

"What is your agenda, Alice?" Margaret asked suddenly, drawing herself up. "The last time you visited me you confided your fears about a threat on the horizon, and from what happened in New York, I'd say you are dangerously close on the right track. But your actions make no sense! You practically raise and train a GenneY for something but you won't say what, you theorize – correctly! – about

306

extremely powerful Changed individuals at large who may threaten GOA itself and you keep everyone in the dark, even me."

"The fewer people who know, the better," Alice said.

"Oh, rubbish! You take the world on your shoulders and leave none to shoulder for anyone else! How long before you burn yourself out?"

"Concern, Margaret?" Alice asked, looking at Margaret through half-mast eyes. It was a warning, and Margaret drew herself up, huffing, annoyed by Alice's closemouthed tactics. But she wouldn't presume to press her further. She withdrew slightly, tightened the soft woollen shawl about her shoulders and frowned.

"I hope you know what you're doing, girl. You say the fewer who know, the better, but you go gallivanting off to retrieve your 'human weapon' and risk capture. What happens when you are found or incapacitated? Where does GOA aim then?"

"I was out of harm's way, and no one knows of me," Alice protested. Margaret pursed her lips.

"I wouldn't be so sure. You know I imprinted the Asian woman, and though it was fleeting only, the woman has a mind like a coiling viper; I could practically access her surface thoughts like a filing cabinet."

"What did you see?" Alice asked, suddenly intrigued.

"She was working at the behest of the dark-eyed woman who attacked young Luke. They were looking for me, but there was a vague impression of me simply being a crossing point."

"For what?"

"For finding someone else." Margaret's expression hinted at the obvious. "Someone higher up."

Alice turned her head slowly back to the lounge below, thoughts in turmoil. She gasped when Luke lifted his hand, and a small sphere of rippling mauve energy formed there, like a very thick and less glossy soap bubble. Margaret smiled. "There have been some interesting discoveries, before the attack."

"Alex?" Alice asked, stunned.

"She was instrumental. Quite the young teacher."

"One more thing that's changed," Alice remarked with a wry smile. "At least for the better."

From where they sat, they couldn't see the two women looking down on them.

Nathan listened carefully as Luke retold of the harrowing happenings at the New York mansion where Luke had been the last month or so. He listened carefully, because it was important to Luke, but he was more concerned with his older brother's safety. When he had heard there was an attack on the de Witt-Emerson mansion he had demanded to speak to Alice, only to find out that the woman was already on her way there, with Charlie, and because of that, probably Danny as well. Nathan had been furious at being excluded, and it had taken Joanie, Jamie and Chris to calm him down and to make sure he didn't do anything rash. But Luke was safe, as well as Alex, Lady de Witt-Emerson and everyone else who mattered. All thanks to Danny.

The thought twisted his mouth. He was growing angrier at him with every mention of his name, for all kinds of reasons. But this was Luke's time now, and he was actually interested in hearing what his brother had to say. So he listened, putting a lid on his emotions and affecting a smile or a grin of appreciation every time Luke emphasized something fantastic about the whole experience. His ears perked when he heard something he thought was improbable, even unlikely.

"You like Alex?" he asked, and Luke blushed, smiling sheepishly.

"Like her. Well, more than like her, actually," Luke amended. The grin spreading on Nathan's face was a very genuine one this time, and he leaned forward a little, as if he couldn't wait for the details to come rolling in. "We've gotten really close in the last two weeks."

"How did this happen?" Nathan asked. He remembered Alex as a loudmouthed but very pretty, porcelain doll-faced girl, barely older than himself, and that she was generally annoying.

"You know I went with her because she asked me along for moral support and all that. But there isn't much you can do there when Margaret isn't throwing a party or shopping, so Alex began training me." Nathan nodded, strangely elated in the midst of his own inner turmoil. "I don't think I would have lasted two seconds against that woman if I hadn't gotten the preparation Alex gave me. Oh, and this also happened."

With a wide smile Luke lifted one hand, and a bubble of filmy energy formed about it, rippling in the light.

Nathan's mouth fell open, and he reached for the bubble, feeling the almost electric current travelling just beneath his fingertips. He pressed a little, and found the bubble pliant, but otherwise unbreakable. "I can make it big enough to hold two people inside, but no bigger yet."

"Amazing," Nathan breathed. "Wonder what mom and dad will say about it."

"How are they anyway, I haven't gotten time to call them yet!" Luke interrupted, face filled with concern.

"They're fine. Worried about you, angry that you didn't ask them whether they thought it a good idea for you to go off alone to a strange place, but fine."

"Guess I'll face the music eventually," Luke said, sounding none too happy about it. "You've kept them updated on Danny?" Luke was surprised when Nathan's face darkened, as though a cloud had passed overhead. Nathan sat back, eyes angry.

"No, I haven't."

"Why not? I mean, you've spoken to him, right? You and Joanie were somewhere up north was the last I heard from Alex, and you've gone to see him. I mean, I saw him in New York, but there was hardly time to catch up on old times." Luke's face lit up with the thought. "Guess he's somewhere around."

309

"I don't care," Nathan said simply.

"What do you mean you don't care? That's why we came here, remember?"

"Like I said, I don't care," Nathan repeated. Luke frowned, mightily puzzled. Nathan had been the foremost voice in demanding to see Danny. Something was wrong.

"That doesn't make sense. Did something happen while I was gone?" he asked, intent on discovering the truth.

"I'm not in the mood to talk about it right now," Nathan said, face growing stubborn as he shifted uneasily in the seat. "Can we just forget about Daniel for a while and talk about lighter stuff." With visible effort he grinned. "Like you and the irritating chick!" He leaned over and landed a punch on Luke's shoulder.

Luke, not really mollified, absently rubbed the spot on his arm where Nathan had hit him. He realized that something was seriously out of place, but Nathan was remarkably stubborn sometimes, and pressing him now would only anger him and make him leave. Sighing, Luke pursed his lips and gave in to the forced change of topic.

"She's not irritating," he protested.

"Maybe to you she isn't," Nathan snickered. "I just recall she loves shooting her mouth off."

"She's changed since then," Luke replied mulishly, mind diverted to defending Alex.

"So where is she? I should congratulate her for netting my bro, the one guy who's never interested in things like love!" Nathan joked. "Guess it is easier, what with her being like us. Look at me and Joanie."

"Maybe it started out as that, but it didn't last, the whole Changed attraction thing," Luke said. "She's just an incredible person; witty and clever, and she *is* attractive." Against his will he found himself responding to his brother's insistent joking, and he did enjoy talking about Alex, even boasting about her.

"So are you two an item, or is it just another flight of fancy of yours?" Nathan asked. Luke bridled a little, but let it slide.

"I haven't asked her yet, but I think she feels the same."

"So ask her. C'mon, it'll take our minds of things!"

"What, now?" Luke asked, incredulous. Nathan rose and made a following motion to his brother.

"Yeah, why not?" The idea horrified Luke – being forward and flirtatious in the presence of other people wasn't his style – and Nathan just loved doing stuff like it. He shook his head.

"I'll do it when I'm comfortable with it," he said.

"Afraid I'll embarrass you in front of her?" Nathan quipped, jumping from one foot to the other.

"That, and maybe I want to check on Danny first." He hadn't wanted to resort to mentioning Daniel in order to get out of a sticky situation, but there it was. And it was the truth, really: Alex was still sleeping off the better part of her ordeal – she had just wanted to be alone for a while, actually – and she had demanded absolute privacy, so Luke was left with moseying about the complex, talking to Nathan and Joanie or finding out where Daniel was. He steeled himself and looked his brother in the eye, and was rewarded with a blank stare. There was absolutely no show of emotion on Nathan's features. For what felt like an eternity they watched each other over the uncomfortable silence. Then Nathan shrugged.

"Okay," was all he said, and then he turned and left the lounge.

Luke, stunned, watched him leave. He stayed there for a while longer, a vicious frown marring his forehead, trying to figure out what had happened. It was only three days after the attack at the mansion, and he had been in recovery for two days, the medical staff in the hospital section adjacent to Headquarters making sure he was fine, tending to the cracked ribs he had suffered from being forcefully thrown about like a rag doll. He still felt a little woozy, and fragile, but he was recovering. He wondered if he could ask Charlie, if he found him, or Jamie or Chris, depending on who would know the most. Talking to Alice didn't really appeal to him;

she intimidated him too much. But he needed to know, and in the process find out where Danny was.

Charlie would know, then, about everything. Sighing, he rose gingerly from the couch, wincing at the numb patch on his shoulder where Nathan had punched him.

"Would have thought he'd respect the injured," he said darkly, and left the lounge.

Alice was gone. He had seen her off on the boomer, and she had barely had time to bid him goodbye and leave a few confidentialities in his care – an almost unspoken accord that he was in command when she left, which was almost never. But this, meeting with the President and working on a suitable cover story, as well as integrating it, required her presence in Washington, and she would be gone for a couple of days. He disliked handling things anyway, and delegated most of the work for someone else. Fortunately Margaret was still here, and she sat just across from him, in Alice's office, sorting through some paperwork. Charlie looked up from what he was doing once, amazed by the woman's unflappable strength and her resilience.

She intimidated him also, and even from where he sat, in Alice's chair, it felt as though he was sitting on the other side, facing Margaret, who was in fact at the head of matters. Sighing, he looked back down, going through some crucial information regarding the integration of a defunct branch of a mothballed military project with the rest of GOA.

"Oh Alice, you clever minx," Margaret said, half startling Charlie. More, he was completely unused to someone even daring to say such a thing about Alice. Margaret was snickering, looking at some paper in hand. "You never do leave anything for us to sniff around at."

"Something wrong?" Charlie asked. Margaret looked up, sheer features composed, but slightly watery eyes twinkling with amusement.

"Oh now, not really. I am just curious as to how Alice manages to run this project and juggle security protocols as well. I was actually looking for some dirt."

"That's very honest of you," Charlie replied, shocked by her frankness.

"Be sensible, dear boy, I am not undermining her as a leader." Margaret actually seemed to square her shoulders, as if preparing to dive back into something. "But as a woman she does tend to upset me at times with her closemouthed tactics. Hence, dirt!"

"I doubt you'd find anything," Charlie qualified, still looking at her even though she had looked back down again at the files before her. "She's very efficient."

"No one is that efficient. Ooh, I wonder if Alexis can be of service, Alice was always going on about how the girl was an irrepressible snoop!"

He couldn't help it. He burst out laughing, even when she fixed him with a critical glare. He waited for the mood to pass, then shook his head.

"I'm sorry."

"Really? About what? Did I say something funny?" Margaret asked dryly.

"Yes!" Charlie protested. "You are actually considering breaking into the Director of GOA's personal files to look for dirt? I think it's hilarious. Not to mention saying someone else is a snoop when," he left the thought hanging.

"There's no need for condescension," Margaret said airily, with a hint of disgruntlement. "I merely wish that she would delegate some work from herself. She's too burdened by everything. She needs to delegate."

"And what about you?" Charlie asked, bemused. "What happens now that your home is gone?"

"What does it look like I'm doing here?" Margaret asked derisively. "I may not have a home at this very moment, but it was never the only one I had, just the one I loved the most." Charlie, eyebrows raised, looked at her. "Well? I am filthy rich, boy! I don't need to be here, but I am, and you know the reason for that."

"You seriously want to crack Alice," Charlie breathed.

"Crack her? We can't have that, we need her strong and determined. Not crack, no. Maybe soften a little."

Charlie returned to working on the screens, shaking his head. He had hardly considered it unwelcome when Alice had ordered him to have Margaret about all the time, helping him to sort out the necessary details and to generally manage things. He had at first levelled the usual protests about not being capable of handling her job, and she had told him he only needed to worry about matters pertinent to the Changed in GOA, nothing else. He knew there was a non-Changed Director somewhere, someone who handled the uninteresting things, as Alice called them, and rarely made contact with her or any of the Changed unless necessary. A faulty little setup, but one that somehow worked. Charlie was thankful for that; he hardly needed some discontented non-Changed riding his ass for things he had no idea about. Charlie knew the only reason he was the prime candidate for taking over the reins from Alice for a while was because he was her most trusted employee, and there really wasn't anyone else who could do the job in any case.

"And how is your young protégé?" Margaret asked suddenly.

"Daniel? I don't know, Alice has him around here somewhere," Charlie replied, refusing to be drawn into any conversation which could derail him. Just hearing Daniel's name made him start worrying again. He had barely spoken two words with him since they returned from New York, and then he had simply vanished, no doubt somewhere where people under Alice's direct orders and control could monitor him. Maybe that was another reason Charlie was cooped up here, in Alice's office with Lady de Witt-Emerson, keeping busy and out of trouble.

"You don't care at all about him?" Margaret queried. Charlie looked up, not amused by her directness.

"Do you care where Alyssa and Ryan are?" he asked pointedly.

314

"No need to get fresh, young man," Margaret said dangerously. "I know perfectly well where my two are: Alyssa is recovering from her ordeal, still, and Ryan is no doubt gone with Alice – he's quite taken with her, and they work well together, Ryan being a business-like young man after all. Do you even know where Daniel is?"

"No, I don't!" Charlie snapped, getting frustrated and showing it. "I don't have the luxury of knowing wherever Daniel is, what he's doing or how he's doing! Alice put me here so I could keep my mind on things other than Daniel, and since I am the Changed currently in charge of this division of GOA, I say she succeeded neatly!"

"You poor child," Margaret said immediately after his outburst. For a moment Charlie thought she was mocking him, but when he glared at her, he saw nothing but sympathy in her eyes. "You have no idea at all?"

"No."

"The woman walks a fine line," Margaret said, sounding critical. "And you think I'm snooping to break her? She has too much control over everything here because she can't let go."

"Let go of her dead husband?" Charlie asked snidely. The only indication he got of Margaret's surprise at him knowing of it was a slight widening of the eyes.

"I am not a psychologist, and I don't intend to play one," Margaret replied tersely. "But whatever she is planning, we need to know."

"Why? Why do you need to know so badly?" Charlie asked challengingly.

"Because it involves young Daniel in almost every aspect," Margaret said, sounding condescending in turn. "You may not know where he is right now, but do you honestly not care what happens to the boy, now or in the future?" Charlie didn't answer. He wanted to run from the office and go home, if only to get rid of the gnawing feeling that something bad was going to happen to Daniel, and for some inexplicable reason Margaret was right, and they needed to go behind Alice's back and figure out what her agenda concerning Daniel was. Sighing, he rubbed his eyes with two fingers and took a deep breath.

"We'll have to wait for Alex, she gets out tomorrow. I can't help much; I have to oversee the running of the place while Alice is gone."

"Perfect, then she can't blame you for betraying her trust," Margaret said with a wide, conspiratorial smile. "Better, she might even think you knew nothing about the dirt at all, cooped up in here as you were." Margaret winked, a disconcerting gesture from that regally creased face.

"And you have no qualms about doing that yourself?" Charlie asked, deadpan.

"What can she do, send me home?" Margaret challenged, lifting her shoulders and grinning.

CHAPTER NINETEEN

Interaction

A day after Margaret DeWitt-Emerson's mansion burned down,, almost all the Changed employees presently at Headquarters were immobilized before a single viewer-screen in the saloon, wide-eyed, watching the footage playing on the selected news channel. Among the images, a scene of a large conflagration in an opulent mansion south of New York, the blaze rising into the night sky even as fire trucks and the police came swarming in. The reporter's running commentary remarked of a massive fireworks display gone horribly wrong, with some tragic consequences for a few unlucky people. They listened attentively to the news report, any of them trying to discover whether there were any lapses, or mention of 'Changed', or people using superhuman powers. Nothing followed, and the employees moved back to their work, with only one or two remaining behind, scanning all other news channels for any variations on the broadcast, all of them aware just how close a thing it had been and breathing sighs of relief that Alice had once again worked her magic for a plausible cover-up.

Charlie also sighed, relieved that Alice had managed to cover their bases. He had only once met with the President, and had been vaguely daunted by the man's stern features and no-nonsense policy of minimal conversation. Apart from that, he knew from Alice that the man, though hardly a staunch supporter of the Changed, nevertheless upheld the facade of keeping the Changed away from the public eye, and funding GOA to do so. Charlie, satisfied when he saw nothing else from the other channel transmissions, turned around and vacated the saloon lounge. Alice would return today, and he was all too happy to be rid of his job. More, he could start pressing her about Daniel's whereabouts, since the woman had promised to tell him once she returned, and matters hadn't gotten out of hand. He scoffed to himself that the chances of that happening, no matter how he disliked taking over, were slim to non-existent.

He thought back, as he returned to the office, about when he had last seen Daniel. There was no doubt in his mind that Alice hadn't moved him from Headquarters – she wouldn't do that without Charlie's say-so – so Daniel was probably held secure in a Neuronull field. It nagged at Charlie that Daniel hadn't seen fit to escape from his confinement and come to him, but if Daniel's behaviour had been any indication, on the boomer back to Headquarters, then Charlie wasn't a very high priority to Daniel at the moment. It hurt him to think that Daniel would feel so little about doing anything about his worries.

He was about to enter the office when he saw Luke coming towards him. Charlie sighed, not truly in the mood to entertain the obvious barrage of questions the older Hirsch brother would have for him, but there was no avoiding it. Patiently he waited for Luke to approach, then opened the door and indicated for him to enter and take a seat. Thankfully Margaret wasn't in there; she was no doubt off terrorizing some or other employee for information, or had descended on Alex to all but command her aid in ferreting out Alice's agenda with everything. He closed the door behind them telekinetically, proceeding ahead of Luke to take his seat behind the desk. Luke sat down, hands fidgeting a little, no doubt trying to think of something to say. Charlie watched the minute gestures. It bothered him, now that Luke was this close. For some reason feelings of resentment and jealousy came up unbidden. When he thought of Nathan as well, the reason for his discomfort became clear: Luke was the eldest of the two brothers, and exactly three years older than Nathan. Charlie had been four years older than his own brother, but the grating closeness of the similarities were there. And there was more. The sensation of resentment came because of Daniel, because of how highly Daniel was held in the regard of these two Hirsch brothers. Or at least, that was the case with Luke.

318

Nathan seemed not only to hold Daniel accountable for everything bad happening in the recent week, but also avoided mentioning him like he would a plague.

"I don't know where Daniel is," he said simply, forcing Luke to refrain from the gestures and to listen attentively. Charlie was in no mood for small talk, so he cut right to it. "Even if I did, I wouldn't have had the time to go see him."

"Okay," Luke replied, unsure of what else he could say. "But you're sure you don't know where he is?"

Charlie fixed Luke with a pointed stare, but the other Changed mentalist stared back, if with no intent other than the discovery of the truth. Charlie wanted to snarl. This was how he paid for his own way of protecting Daniel: everyone suspected him of deceit, now, because he had lied to protect his charge. Biting down on an angry retort, he shook his head. This seemed to satisfy Luke, and Charlie was amazed to detect nothing in Luke's eyes but quiet concern.

"I didn't get a chance to talk to him on the boomer back from New York," Luke explained. "I was hoping I could find him somewhere, or that you'd know where, maybe."

"Daniel didn't speak to anyone on the boomer," Charlie said. Daniel in fact hadn't spoken physically to anyone: his expression had been one of pensiveness, and he had remained staring thoughtfully ahead for the entire half-hour long trip back to GOA Headquarters. But there had been a few moments, after Charlie had tried to prod him for information, when he had been sure Daniel's eyes had assumed the vaguest shimmer of blue. "At least, he hadn't spoken to anyone." Charlie was surprised when Luke frowned.

"Did he transmit anything mentally to anyone?"

"Maybe," Charlie replied ambiguously.

"What do you mean? Aren't you supposed to be in constant contact with him?"

"I tried it, but he's somehow learned how to block me," Charlie admitted. "Nothing goes in but what he wants in." This seemed to unsettle Luke, and Charlie reflected on the younger empath before him. From what Alice had said when she had briefed Charlie, Luke would eventually move beyond his cursory GOA classification, considering that he was making excellent progress with his training. It wasn't unheard of for such a heightening to occur, but it was rare. Luke would, with full training, become one of the more powerful GOA empaths. "Even I don't know all the places in Headquarters where Alice might keep him."

"But she comes back today, right?" Luke asked, and Charlie nodded. "Do you, uh, think she'd talk to me?"

"I don't know how she'd feel when she came back, but it's worth a shot." Charlie admitted to himself that Luke asking after Daniel would probably yield better results than if Charlie did it. "I'll let you know as soon as she returns." Luke blinked, then realized this was his cue to go. He nodded once and rose, vacillating between saying goodbye and simply waving or smiling. So he just nodded again and left the office. Charlie leaned back in his seat, sighing. He hadn't expected Lucas Hirsch to turn out as an unlikely ally. But Charlie was growing increasingly desperate. Margaret had awakened a growing enmity in him towards Alice, for keeping important information from him concerning Daniel, and though that was the primary concern, Charlie was also growing increasingly disillusioned with Alice's leadership. She was a superior leader, no doubt, but her motives and agendas were secretive beyond comparison, and no one knew for sure what she intended, or how much she knew. Charlie fervently hoped that she would tell him where Daniel is, and that Margaret and Alex would figure out what Alice was about.

Alice sighed.

Daniel was seated across from her at the table, in a room that was remarkably well-lit and similar to the one he had been confined in at Headquarters. But it had been necessary to take him to a secure GOA sub-station, several hundred miles north of Seattle and the rest of GOA's domain. Charlie could not get hold of Daniel yet, that much Alice had been sure of. There was a battle of wills that was drawing closer to a conflict between Daniel's adopted family and Charlie, and Alice intended to let the worthier of the two win. She refrained from assuming there was anything worth winning, and that Daniel was in fact still a human being. But she had come too far now, risked too much and allowed leniencies where none were normally to be had, and all for the boy who sat before her, ignoring her flatly with his vacant stare. He wasn't catatonic at all; he simply refused to acknowledge the presence of anyone. Alice had given up trying to break him out of it. Instead, she had ventured a minute probe of his thoughts, something which considering his capacity required the very greatest of her skills and a vast amount of focused concentration, simply to brush the surface thoughts. But she had succeeded, and Daniel had given no intention of him either noticing or caring that she had dared to do that. What Alice had seen had at first disturbed her, because of the magnitude of mental processes Daniel was maintaining, and of the scope of his speeding intellect. And yet, she had found what she had been looking for: the probing had revealed a very small yet definite overtone of what his thoughts were really about. The maelstrom was in fact not just a defensive barrier against all but the most skilled empath tactics, but also a symptom of the emotional turmoil that Daniel was feeding through his own head. It was as though he was forcing himself to experience the anxiety of uncertainty, the prospects of failure and the most insidious levels of his own fear, all things which Alice knew little or nothing of and could only guess at, but which Daniel was seemingly forcing himself to confront. And all the time he sat there, eyes vacant, face etched with a total lack of movement and body held as though he was a statue.

It baffled Alice that he didn't even blink, or that his eyes didn't water or close involuntarily against dryness, especially here in the cold. But the smallest minutiae that only an empath, with heightened senses and extended awareness could detect, told Alice that Daniel was awake, well and completely lucid. His silence and refusal to notice anything or anyone was self-imposed, and he would break it once he felt like it.

There were no windows here. It was an old military fallout shelter, complete with blast doors and cold, concrete interiors, alleviated only slightly by the comfortable glistening surfaces of modern technology and all the comforts it could provide in the colder climes. Alice had enforced a neuronull field in the chamber where Daniel had, on arrival, taken a certain liking to – he had refused to leave it, standing there, giving no indication that he would do ought else – and had sat down and entered his semi-conscious state once they had brought a table and chair. For the last three days, he had remained thus, the techs and GOA observers had told Alice. No mental activity had been detected inside the room, nothing that could say that the attractive young man in the room was in any way a Changed. Alice looked at the ceiling. She would have to leave today, back to Headquarters. She had stopped over at the sub-station the previous day, and apart from the obvious reason for being here, she had used the spartan surroundings of even her better-appointed quarters in the base to clear her thoughts and live for the day without the luxury she normally associated with her position. But Charlie would no doubt start fidgeting, and there was a nagging feeling at the back of her head that Margaret would be up to something that would turn out to be completely frivolous and benign if she failed, or malignant and far-reaching if she got what she was looking for. That was why Alice had sent Ryan ahead on a flight just before her. Ryan would probably be almost back to Headquarters right now. Alice hadn't felt it all that strange for the young man to be so inquisitive, and he had indicated no intention to bother her overmuch. He had enjoyed accompanying her, but he was far from unpredictable, as he had shown when Alice had spoken about Daniel. No, that was Margaret's skill: one could never say which way she would go. Closing her eyes momentarily, she leaned back her head before opening her eyes and turning her head from side to side to relieve the growing tension in her neck. She was surprised when she looked forward again and found Daniel's eyes seemingly fixed directly on her. She frowned, and after a few moments lifted her hand and waved it before his eyes. The eyes remained seemingly fixed on Alice's face, despite her response, and when she rose, Daniel's head tilted slightly to follow.

"Daniel?" Alice asked tentatively. No response. She pursed her lips, and moved again, becoming a little unsettled by the bright-eyed stare that followed her, when nothing else was forthcoming. She moved towards the door of the room, his eyes following, and when she opened the door, Daniel's face turned away, staring ahead at where she had sat again, once more refusing to be disturbed by her presence, or the fact that she was leaving.

Outside, Alice went to the monitoring rooms. The techs assured her that nothing was coming in or out of the room, and Daniel's reaction, though recorded, revealed nothing that the auric profilers could detect.

When she asked what the profilers had detected, the techs smirked and shrugged. Alice frowned mightily. Profilers were rare individuals, capable of reading hints and traces, so it was declared, that led either forward or backward along the space-time continuum. If a profiler could see such traces days after or before an event, and remain relatively accurate, they were completely accurate when looking right at someone or something. If they couldn't see any potential relevancies in Daniel, and if he betrayed absolutely nothing to their senses, then Alice knew she had greater cause still to be alarmed.

"Prepare my boomer, and make sure this stopover remains undocumented and erased from the directories. I don't want anyone snooping after my presence here, or Daniel's." The head tech nodded curtly, used to such orders and also completely uninterested in questioning them. Alice, satisfied, ordered her luggage brought to the boomer and walked slowly towards the hangar, deep in thought.

There had been a time when she had also been idealistic, when the world hadn't been so bent on crushing her with its indifference and its discrimination. There had been times where she found herself stopping and wondering at the lengths she had gone to preserve GOA, and more, to preserve the people who worked with her, and to prepare them. Inevitably that was what she answered, when people asked her straight away – and she deemed it fitting – what she was doing. It was so simple, really, when you looked at it her way.

Daniel, as sweet a boy as he was, or had been, would play his part in whatever scheme she spun to save GOA and the rest of humanity from whatever monstrous regime lurked out there, ready to assail them at a moment's notice. If only Charlie or anyone else would apply themselves to figuring it out, then she wouldn't have to beat around the bush so much. But no one else, save for Margaret, and then only marginally, knew of the threat, would pinpoint that threat as the reason for the subtlety and the nearly inhuman demands she made, not only of Charlie but of others as well.

At times like this she was forced to confront, once more, her rationalizations. Was it really necessary to keep everyone else in the dark, or would it serve to have someone else know about her ploys and her intentions? But the usual support reason came flaring to mind again: the more people who knew, the greater and more plausible the potential cover being blown. Anyone else who knew of Daniel, and the extent of GOA, would be a liability. Today, though, she wasn't so certain anymore. She scoffed silently to herself as she entered the boomer and took her seat inside, strapping herself in. She blamed the Hirsches; they complicated matters, and yet Daniel would have died, had it not been for them. Or at least, for Nathan. But what effect would Luke have on the now-enigmatic young progeny? The thought jarred Alice. Nathan reviled Daniel now for his mental violations, but someone like Luke, who by his nature was more retiring and relaxed, and an empath also, would possibly have more success in breaking through to Daniel, to figuring out what was happening to him. Tapping her lips thoughtfully, a light frown marring her brow, Alice called for the pilots to halt the boomer. It took her only a moment to gather herself and make the necessary calculations. It was risky – very much so, but she thought that desperate times required more radical if erratic measures. She ordered the flight sequence to stand down until further notice, and then waited for the head tech to arrive in the hangar.

"Change of plans," she told the man, who nodded sensibly. "Sedate Daniel, if he will allow it. Otherwise, prepare a secondary null web in the boomer and prepare him for transfer with me."

"You'd risk moving him?" the tech asked, not challengingly, but pointedly, as if to make doubly sure of his orders. Alice nodded, not in the least perturbed by the man's frank directness.

"Necessary," she replied, and the man nodded, turning around and barking out orders to his own entourage of intermediaries and aides. Alice watched the proceedings, then returned to just outside the boomer, waiting. Within half an hour, the tech team had installed a neuronull field inside the boomer. Daniel had refused to be sedated, a response elicited by a medic attempting to press the vacuspray to his neck; the man had apparently passed out when he had begun brandishing the spray, and the other medics, by now alert to Daniel's history of minimum displays of repulsion techniques when he chose, decided against trying again and informed the techs of their status.

Daniel seemed in no way averse to his plight. Still in silence, refusing to acknowledge anyone or anything, he walked almost casually – eyes still strangely vacant – between four armed guards, all four of them wearing neuro-damper gear, just in case. Alice deplored the precautions, but Daniel was unpredictable, and hardly trustworthy since his reawakening. He paid them or her no need, and walked up the ramp into the boomer, taking a seat and allowing himself to be strapped in. Alice thanked the tech team and ordered them to cast off, and to make for Headquarters. The flight would take only about ten minutes, and there was no one else in the civilian seating section.

Alice watched Daniel's immutable facade for two minutes into the flight, and then, knowing that no one else was with them or could hear them, she began talking to him. "You know, we can't help you if you don't speak." Nothing. Alice went on. "Do you wish to talk to anyone else in particular? Charlie? Luke?" She bunched for the clout. "Nathan?" Surprisingly, nothing. "Then what am I to do? Do you want me to spill the beans on everything?" That was a long shot, but she had to try.

"What makes you think I care?" a reply flared in her head, and she smiled, suppressing triumph.

"Just tell me what I can do for you, that is all," she spoke the words aloud.

"What I want no longer features, does it?" his mental voice fired back, sounding downcast. *"I've become this...ah, never mind!"*

"No, continue," Alice prodded. Remarkably, Daniel was still outwardly engrossed in nothing, his body rigid, shaken only slightly by the minor turbulent currents outside the boomer.

"I wish to speak to everyone, but not at once."

"That is why we're going back to Headquarters."

"Among other things. And there is no need for a null field, I won't run again."

"And how do I know I can trust you?" Alice asked. Daniel's eyes regained their certitude, the burning green flame that spoke of his attention, and as he lifted his head, he fixed Alice with a critical glare.

"I give you my word. I haven't done that before, so it should count, still," he said, also out loud. "Other than that, you will just have to go by faith."

"I am not a very religious person," Alice said conversationally, pleased with the fact that she had somehow shaken Daniel from his self-imposed silence. "But it's settled then. I will lower the fields once we reach Headquarters. Who would you like to speak to first?"

"Charlie, I think. He is very concerned," Daniel replied. Alice felt a strange wariness creep over her. Again she was faced with how mercurial Daniel's moods were. Granted, they were spaced far apart, over several days, but still, he had gone from a meek and bright young thing, to a vengefully cynical and dark being, to a pensive and tentative mind, almost dejected in its conflict. It bothered her to no end, and she gave her trust with a heavy hand, not willing to throw all caution to the wind. "Luke next, I haven't had time to talk to him yet either." And there it was again. Alice nearly gasped out loud when she saw the faintest sheen of moisture in his eyes, at the mention of Luke. It was fondness, such as he had never shown for anyone or anything. His emotions were ranging across his face, and she could see the scope when his face darkened, and his eyes went large, seeming to float in tears. He was thinking of Nathan, no doubt. He didn't say anything, but wiped the heel of one hand across his eyes. Surprised anew by him, she let him recover in peace, her own thoughts rambling. "And then maybe you can add me to your charter." Alice nodded, but she wasn't done.

"Would you mind another question?" she asked, when the pilot announced their arrival at Headquarters within a minute. He looked at her, and then shrugged.

"Nothing stopping you," he replied, a little too casually for Alice's taste.

"How is it that you can feel Charlie and block him from your mind at the same time? A bond doesn't work that way, one person cannot selectively ignore the other, no matter how unequal the partnership of strength between the two is."

"Shows how much you know, Alice," Daniel said, a small wry grin twisting the corner of his mouth. Alice, startled to almost show amusement, bit back a scathing retort, becoming aware that he would say more on the matter. "How can I explain it to you? Maybe it's another gift, or the perfecting of one. Suffice it to say that," he sighed, frowning, struggling with the explanation, "one mind only can't grasp the scope of another mind on multiple levels."

"Meaning?"

"There's no other way to explain it, really. Charlie's connected to me, but I get to decide when and whether he stays in contact. More I can't say, and not because I don't want to." The boomer landed softly on a helipad, and the harnesses unlatched themselves, leaving the two passengers free. The doors opened and the ramp extended, and Daniel rose, staring at Alice. "I hope you don't mind, but I'd like to take a walk now. I haven't been here for a few months, and I want to have people around me now. Lots of them." Alice nodded silently, allowing the strange request. She followed him outside and was about to ask whether he would accompany her to the main section of Headquarters, when he vanished, a thin trail of discharged energy alerting her to a teleport. She quashed a snarl, but was rewarded for her tension with a swift, short missive from him, placing him at the doors of the Mess Level. Sighing, she shook her head.

"Ma'am?" the tech asked, noting her expression as he hefted her bags.

"Nothing, really," Alice said, sparing the man a smile. They left it at that, and Alice walked slowly down the ramp, in no real rush. Her known world would come rushing at her anyway, when she reached her office. Margaret would start nagging again, Alex would no doubt be off snooping, Charlie would start immediately harassing her for Daniel's whereabouts and Jamie would simply smile, wave and go about his own business, not bothering to be bothered, so to speak. Chris was never around much anyway, always fidgeting with gadgetry. It almost caused Alice to smile, the accepted familiarity she was walking towards.

He walked through the crowds, and they paid him little heed. He was frowning, but he knew he looked nothing much out of the ordinary. It pained him greatly, these people, the fact that for all their smiles and their pleasant greetings – the ones who did so – they would never know how much he wished he could be just like them again, free of the burden of his gifts. There had been a time,

328

when he and Luke had joked about such things, still, and the whole business with the brothers being Changed hadn't arisen yet, that he had wished for such gifts, for the ability to do what he could do. But never in his wildest dreams had he thought it would be like this, and that he would cause so much harm.

The fact that he had saved Margaret DeWitt-Emerson and everyone at her mansion worth saving didn't feature. It was a small thing, and fighting against that woman – he had somehow discarded her name, but it was still in his head, somewhere – had been taxing at first, until he had pushed himself harder and found that she was really no match for him at all, despite her prodigious strength. But it all meant nothing to him, and it felt hollow, to think such things as a standard by which he could measure his life.

The train of thought led him down a now-familiar path, one he had gone over again and again, in the security of his distanced thoughts, safe from outside interference unless he wished it, and he let it flow freely within him as he walked past the people and the shops, stalls and doorways to conferencing halls and entertainment areas on the Mess Level. These people paid him no heed, even though, in a flash, he could no doubt rip the foundations loose beneath their feet, or send them all flying through the walls, like wind-blown leaves. And if they broke, he wondered, would he care? Would it hurt or appall him, if he simply loosed his gifts and began killing indiscriminately?

He didn't want to think about anyone who loved him. It was easy to think of Alice, and Chris, and Jamie and Alex, who were friendly with him, but only because they were actually terrified of what he could do otherwise. But Charlie. Charlie was devoted to him in a strange way which both soothed and upset him, because he was unused to such a deep level of commitment. He looked forward to talking with Luke again, even though he had no idea what he would say, or whether he would dissolve into tears. And Joanie would probably enjoy seeing him again. He was aghast at how little he had spoken to any of them, right after the reawakening. But the bottom line had been that he had seen the rejection in Nathan's mind, the revulsion his one-time best friend and closest confidante had practically broadcast as a scream into his mind, at the violation. It hadn't been intended to happen, but the prospect of everything restored, every memory filled with life and meaning and wholeness again, and Nathan's obstinacy in the way, had made the task more appealing than daunting. And now he would possibly pay for it for the rest of his life. And more than the thought of nothing touching him, of nothing upsetting him and reaching his sympathies, he feared the final confrontation, the battle with Nathan, the scrabble to explain himself in the face of Nathan's wrath. He couldn't avoid it, he knew that, and that rejection, that denial from the person he had trusted most in all his life, would send him over the edge, would open up a place of dark agonies and vengeance.

Daniel stopped in mid stride and closed his eyes, as though to shut out the consecutive thoughts that nagged at the back of his head. They always rose to the fore when he began thinking of the confrontation with Nathan.

"Excuse me sir, have you been helped?" Daniel looked to his side, where a pleasantly smiling girl in the military-style uniforms of GOA employees, gently tugged at his sleeve. A million thoughts went through his head, accompanied by a million replies, and it took moments only for him to find the one he thought would serve best. He smiled, even though he didn't feel like it, and placed his hand over hers, allowing nothing through from either her touch or his.

"I actually work here," he said. Instead of intimidating her, she nodded, the laughter clear in her eyes.

"Are you one of the Changed, then?" she continued, undaunted. He nodded simply. "Ah, I thought I didn't recognize you as one of the non-Changed staff." Daniel knew how incongruous this looked, but he was strangely drawn to this woman's gentle, unperturbed manner. "I never know, and I've always had so many questions, always." She delivered the statement without preamble or eagerness, as though she meant every word but didn't need to invest fawning with them. Charmed in spite of his tumultuous plight, Daniel turned to her.

"Would you like to get something to drink?" he asked, for a single moment amazed at his own forwardness. Or so he thought. The young woman nodded, and another dazzling smile played over her face.

"I have some time off." Taking a slightly firmer hold on her hand, Daniel led the way to the saloon. When the staff saw him, some of them whitened a little, but Daniel merely nodded at them, gently and easily dispersing any tears, and also distracting as many people as possible from fully recognizing him, before leading the woman to a seat inside. He sat himself down opposite her. "And I've never been in here before."

"It's a weird discrimination, really," Daniel replied. "I don't think that most non-Changed people care about it though, either. Not many people find us pleasant." They halted a little as the waiter took their orders.

"Why not?" she continued. "Are you all that different from us?" Daniel was amazed by her almost naively innocent queries, despite the fact that he knew she was far from ignorant.

In answer, he grinned. "You have no idea."

"But you look the same, and you're still human," she replied with some conviction.

"I don't know," he said, feeling a little of his despair return. "There's so much distance between us. Have you ever wished to be Changed, to have powers and gifts?" She was silent for a moment, and then shrugged.

"I'm a little ambivalent on that one. Part of me would love to be able to do what you can, to experience life on such a level, and the other part of me is just grateful to be alive, and to be me, really."

"I'd recommend you stick to that one," Daniel returned, and thanked the waiter when he brought their drinks. "I guess to a lot of us, life is enjoyable. To others, it's burdensome."

"How so?" Daniel checked himself, aware that he was becoming frank and informative with a woman who was probably either a fresh recruit from wherever, or someone not privy at all to the workings of the Changed within GOA. He gritted his teeth, hating himself for what he intended to do, and then did it, lightly scanning her mind for her surface thoughts, attempting to discern her intentions. He was relieved to find nothing overt or subtly manipulative there, just curiosity, the kind that knew of things in theory but was excited to gain practical, personal insight. More, she wasn't just a clerk or a low-level officer, but someone in charge of Changed and non-Changed relations. Her interest was natural, and it had endeared her to her job posting. Relaxing visibly, Daniel picked up the conversation again. "No Changed starts out as Changed. As far as I know, we aren't born Changed."

"That's right," she stated, reinforcing his assumption. "Although some of you reach the Change earlier than most."

"I reached mine a little over a year ago," Daniel confided. "I'm almost twenty-one, and I've gotten used to being normal, if you'll ah, pardon the –"

"I'm not offended in the least," she reassured him, reaching over and touching his arm. She leaned back again and took a polite sip from her beverage. Daniel remained toying with his own, unconcerned and uninterested with it.

"Well, no matter how much you wish for it, for gifts and neat powers and stuff like that, nothing prepares you for the real thing. I guess I'm just still adjusting."

"If you don't mind my asking, what do you do? What can you do?" Daniel checked himself again, in spite of what he knew about her. There was no point in alarming her by spilling all the beans and telling her she was probably in the presence of the most powerful Changed on the entire base. He settled for a downplayed answer instead.

"I'm an empath, mostly. Not average, really, but empath gifts are the worst."

"Do you read minds or move objects?"

"All of the above," he said ruefully, chuckling. "But enough of that, if you don't mind. I don't even know your name."

"I don't know yours either," she replied amiably. Daniel nodded, then extended his hand to her, smiling.

"Daniel Mercer," he said. She took his hand and gave it a gentle shake.

"Irene Townsend."

"Pleased to meet you, Irene."

"Daniel Mercer. Daniel Mercer. I've heard that name somewhere," Irene said, tapping her lips. Daniel started, hoping she wasn't in the real know about him. She shook her head and pursed her lips. "No, I can't remember where I've heard it. But then, I'm more a liaison for the non-Changed working with the Changed than the other way around. Who knows?" They sipped their drinks for a while, and then Irene's irrepressible curiosity resurfaced. "I don't mean to pry, but just how far does empathic skill go? I mean, I've worked with a Changed named Charlie Avery before, do you know him? He's a remarkable man, if a bit close-mouthed and business-like, but he's an empath. I always wonder if you can read our minds as easily as snapping your fingers."

"I know Charlie," Daniel replied heavily, but it didn't alert Irene to anything overt. "Charlie's a strong empath, but I don't think he reads minds unless ordered to, or unless it's necessary. At least, that's what he taught me."

"Oh, Charlie's your teacher?" Irene asked.

"Sort of. I haven't seen him for a while now, though. But to answer your question, yeah, we can read thoughts pretty easily, but it's considered rude."

"Can you read my thoughts right now?"

"Do you want me to?" Daniel asked warily, a little unsettled by her own directness, though he felt nothing but earnest intrigue coming from her. "I mean, yeah, I personally can read the mind of everyone here without much effort. For other empaths it's more difficult without permission, or they simply can't manage without touching that person." Irene drew her hand back.

"Oh, I am terribly sorry! I didn't realize you could do that!" She looked appalled by her actions from before, and seemed to regret placing her hand – quite reassuringly – on Daniel's arm. He shook his head and put on a winsome smile for her sake.

"Don't worry about it. I can shield my own mind from yours, so touching doesn't have to be a hands-off affair." He realized how it sounded and chuckled, and she also smiled, as if her recoiling was completely forgotten. "No pun intended."

They finished their drinks in relative silence, stealing glances at each other without investing them with deeper intentions. After a while Irene took Daniel's hand again and shook it.

"It was so nice meeting and talking with you. Refreshing, since most Changed don't have the time to be a little casual, or in the mood for mingling."

"No, I think I have to thank you," Daniel replied, rising with her. "It was nice, being seen again."

"Seen again?" she asked, puzzled.

"When you're Changed, and other non-Changed people know it, they tend to steer clear, or deal with you as though you're either diseased or way beyond reproach." He thought back on his life over the last year, recalling it as well as the renewed memories of life before that. Unlike who he was now, with previous instances in HQ, his blithe unconcern had not stopped him from noticing the veiled aversion some non-Changed people had towards the Changed ones in their midst.

"Ah, I get it," Irene said. "Well, I hope I didn't come over as a sycophant."

"Not at all," Daniel assured her, and walked outside with her. "It was nice meeting you, Irene Townsend."

"And you, Daniel Mercer. I suspect I'll see you again."

"Who knows?" Daniel shrugged, settling for an ambiguous ending.

"There's Mr. Avery now," Irene said lightly, gaze momentarily darting over Daniel's shoulder. Daniel frowned and looked where she nodded at. Charlie was indeed walking towards them, a determined look on his face. "He's headed here."

"I know," Daniel said softly. He turned to Irene. "See you again, whenever. Oh, and don't scream."

"Don't scream?" she asked critically. Daniel nodded, sent a fast signal to Charlie and teleported. He vanished before he could see the complete look of surprise on Irene's face, but his lingering thoughts found her flustered but otherwise unaffected by his display. Charlie though, would reach him soon. He hadn't wanted to talk with him in the saloon, or where other people knew they were, so he stepped out on the rooftop just above where he had stood in the Mess Deck. Charlie would join him soon.

Charlie kept himself from running towards the roof.

Daniel had said he would wait there for him, in the last mental splinter before he had teleported. So it was with some trepidation that he opened the door, deciding to take it slow rather than actually ripping the door open. He did it slowly and with measured intent, letting the light in.

Daniel stood with his back to Charlie, arms folded across his chest. Charlie bit his lower lip, an uncharacteristic gesture of indecisiveness he deplored in himself, but couldn't stop right now. He moved slowly, ignoring the impulse to run and simply spin Daniel about and –

"Sorry for teleporting. It's considered rude, I know," Daniel said, and turned around. Charlie breathed a little less quickly, strangely soothed by the slow, calm cadence of Daniel's voice.

"You look good," he said, walking until he was within a foot of Daniel. "Considering that I haven't seen you in a while. And that evening in New York was too rushed to count."

"I can take care of myself, thanks." Charlie frowned.

"I didn't say that, I simply meant that the last time I saw you, Alice nearly had a heart attack, just at the state you were in. You had everyone scared there. And you pretty much ignored me flat in the boomer back from New York."

"I'm touched by your concern." More calm, as though he was screening. Charlie tried to reach through the link, and met a wall head-on. He gritted his teeth.

"Is it really necessary to block me? How can you even do it?" he demanded.

"Its not that hard," Daniel began. "I can't tell you how I do it, words won't do."

"Why do you do it? You've never done it before, and not just because you couldn't." Daniel was silent, simply looking at Charlie. "Well?"

"Because you're so concerned. Because you never stop worrying, and because of it you don't ever let up and relax a little. Because I no longer know just how trustworthy I can be with you. Need I go on?" Daniel asked. Charlie swallowed, shocked and amazed at Daniel's insight.

"If I was overly concerned before it was –"

"You were looking out for me, yeah, I know. But you don't have to anymore."

"Will you let me finish, dammit?" Charlie snapped. Now it was Daniel's turn to look surprised. "In case you didn't notice before, you were never just my ward!"

"What do you want me to say, Charlie? I'm turning into the centrepiece in GOA's mutant arrangement, and people all around me start pandering after what their superiors tell them, not what I want. And Alice is playing this link between us like a string quartet. You realize that, don't you?" Charlie nodded. It appalled him, the radical change in Daniel's demeanour, his words and his assumptions. It was official, then: Daniel Mercer, the kid he had trained and nursed through the most intense and violent adjustment periods of the

Change, was no longer there. No more sweetness, no more clever generosities and wide-eyed child-like musings on everything and anything, no more outrageous bouts of mischief. He saw nothing but calculation and dark insights in the green eyes. It nearly caused him to choke up, and he turned away. "See? Even you don't like what you see. Would you have stood by as the innocent, naïve teenager you saved from the brink was paraded in front of the knowing world as an icon of power, and eventually a lodestone for every adventurous and reckless Changed who would try their luck against me?"

"I'm sorry," Charlie said, closing his eyes.

"What?"

"I'm sorry for doing this to you! For letting Alice get a hold of —"

"Stop!" Charlie drew up at the swiftly commanding drive in Daniel's voice, looked at his young ward. Daniel's body was drawn up in a belligerent pose that was echoed in his facial expression. "You don't get to play the martyr, the responsible one! Because you weren't to know!"

"Then what the hell is this about?" Charlie queried. He expected some sort of flighty battle of wills, a contest where he ducked and dodged as best he could against the one person he never thought would be so invasively offensive. But what he saw moved him again to emotion. There were tears in Daniel's eyes as well, pooling in his enraged eyes. He was breathing heavily.

"The people close to me get hurt, and I'm doing it right now! I am tired of it, I want nothing of it!" Daniel yelled. "I've driven away my best friend – my brother! – with one stupid mistake and I doubt I'll get to fix it! The people who knew me shrink back in fear and revulsion, and you." He halted momentarily. "You are so close to me it hurts just to look at you! To know what I've done, because I didn't know better back then, and to know all of it now. And there's no way out." Daniel spun around and strode angrily towards the edge of the concrete rail. Charlie followed, and attempted to place his hands on Daniel's shoulders, but the boy shook him off. "I would give up all of this, just to be like those people in the Mess level, just going about their business, not having to worry about hurting the people they love through their gifts. Gifts!" He spat the last word. "If this is mankind's idea of a gift then this world has been shot to hell!"

"You can't change what you are, or what you've become," Charlie interjected slowly. "Is that what's bothering you?"

"Why me?" Daniel demanded. "Why do I get to be the strong one, the guy so endowed with gifts that others will probably never achieve even a fraction of the understanding that goes with it? I would have been happy to be a weak. Something! Nothing would have been better. Just ordinary."

"And when you can't have that?" Charlie continued, keeping his questions low-key.

"Then I become what Alice wants," Daniel replied, darkly sullen. "I get to play the great destroyer, the monstrous enforcer of GOA's peace, and the world's safe space from those freaks out there, like that woman at Maggie's mansion. A glorified cop with no friends. Who can live like that?"

"Why do you think your friends won't stay just that? Friends?"

"Because they are out there now, wondering why they came here in the first place!" Daniel snarled, jerking one arm at the general expanse of Headquarters below them. "Luke is with Alex – he got the good part of this deal. He can't wait to see me, but he's scared. Joanie is petrified of meeting me again, and Nathan…Nathan would rather drown himself than look at me, let alone talk to me. Don't you see, Charlie?" Daniel turned to his keeper. "I can't win!" The statement was a heart-wrenched admission, one that caused Daniel to start shaking with repressed emotion. "I've even driven my family from myself! Maybe you should have just let me die, allowed me to go out of my mind with suppressed memories and died a peaceful death in my sleep." Charlie had had enough. He reached over and drew Daniel to him, folding him to his chest and holding him there. He felt the tensing muscles in Daniel's arms and shoulders, the small jerks of somatic response, of Daniel unconsciously trying to deny the gesture. Instead he gave in, and Charlie felt the fight go out of him, replaced instead by racking sobs. He lowered his head, placing his cheek against the top of Daniel's head.

"If you ever think like that again I will give you a reason to mope, you get me?" Charlie asked, choking back his own tears. "There is nothing wrong with you, and there was no way you could have reacted differently."

"If I hadn't melded thoughts with Nathan he wouldn't have –"

"You can't always be the bright spark to everyone. And heaven knows you're a great kid, Daniel Mercer. A bit too hard on yourself, but great," Charlie said, managing a chuckle in spite of the situation. Daniel sniffed and drew back from Charlie, rubbing his hands across his eyes hurriedly, as if ashamed of his outburst. Charlie placed his hands on Daniel's shoulders and wasn't shrugged away this time. He lowered his head slightly to look Daniel in the face. "The people down there may be afraid of you, but they don't hate you. Not even Nathan. I guarantee it." Daniel gave no response, and Charlie let him simmer down a little. He didn't let go of him physically, though. "So, what do you want to do first? I can go with you when you talk to him –"

"No, I have to do it alone," Daniel replied, taking a slow, deep breath, calming himself. "And don't get any ideas about kids growing up and being all parental, either!" Charlie grinned.

"Ah, I missed you!" he said, pitching his voice a little higher and more congenially flimsy, almost mockingly. He jerked Daniel back to himself and hugged him again, ruffling the dark lazy curls on Daniel's head. Daniel retorted with a sharp cry of surprise, then broke free, but he was smiling.

"Yeah, I think I missed you too," he said softly. Charlie gasped as the blocked access to Daniel's mind opened a little, letting the familiar presence back into his head. There was a dark aspect to the return of info, but it was ameliorated, in part by Daniel's own mental doing, Charlie thought, but also by the genuine warmth and affection, even halting love, that Daniel felt for him. It soothed him, and he knew the sensation he felt was transmitted back to Daniel, who regarded him with a wan but fulfilled look on his face. Charlie draped his arm across Daniel's shoulders and rotated the both of them towards the door.

"Who's first?" he asked.

"I think Luke. I need to reconnect a little with older brother number one for a change."

"Older brother number one?" Charlie queried, sounding disparaging and outraged.

"Hey, don't force me to get technical!" Daniel protested. "You know how I feel, so don't act hurt and sidelined, please!"

"Gotcha," Charlie added, and left it at that. He was only mocking, after all.

CHAPTER TWENTY

Devices

There was little she could do but scoff inwardly.

Alessandro walked beside Catherine, and noted the indrawn hiss as she regarded the gear strewn almost haphazardly across the table. He could make little sense of it, but then that was why they were here, why *he* had summoned them both. Catherine had, on one of her rare instances of being forthcoming with what she knew – which he knew was an immense amount more than most people did – remarked offhandedly that he had summoned Alessandro for some menial purpose, no doubt, and her mainly so he could gloat in the face of his impending triumph. What triumph? Alessandro had asked, but had received that icily disdainful stare. He should have gotten used to it by now, the responses he received when querying her after such tidbits were dropped.

They had been taken to a large building in the middle of the Boston sky rise, an incongruous monolith of carved stone and immaculately decorated relief work that smacked of a cathedral. Outward appearances seemed to confirm it, but the building was, in fact, the work of some renowned contemporary architect out to revive the antiquities of the Middle Ages, so the man had made a statement and had constructed a massive cathedral-like edifice, in the middle of the modern and high-tech structures all around. Of course, the building had been destined to be a museum of sorts, and Catherine supposed it was that, but it was also Graven's favourite place to stay at when he stopped moving about all the time. He lived here, and in the bowels of the place – another medieval ingenuity: the dungeon-like expanse of the basements were complex and easy to get lost in – he stored his most precious belongings and ordered the expanse of his multi-conglomerate empire. Catherine simply sneered at the blatant display of power. Alessandro couldn't stop taking everything in.

This room had no one inside it, save for a few technicians, and the people were either schooled to be extremely non-conversant with visitors, or they bore the not-so-apparent stamp of Graven's trademark mental dominion. Alessandro had heard of their master's techniques, and he shuddered, now and then. "What exactly is he doing here?" he asked Catherine eventually. When she made no sign of replying, he began fuming, until finally he sighed. "You have to tell me something!"

"And spoil his fun?" she retorted, snorting. "No my dear, if I tell you and you fail to look sufficiently impressed at his words, he will begin riling at me."

"Your relationship is more complex than anything I've ever encountered!" Alessandro grated moodily.

"And you're Italian, so I will take my compliments where I can get them," Catherine returned, amused. At present they passed by all the rough-hewn stones with their ancient-looking motifs and the bizarre and brooding statues of Babylonian seraphim and other divine creatures, arriving at a large stone door. Catherine stood squarely in front of it, hands on hips, and sighed. "I am not knocking." On cue, the doors slid open silently, belying their appearance. Catherine practically stalked through, Alessandro in tow.

"That was never necessary," a cultured, petulant-sounding voice echoed from within the chamber. Inside, the chamber was vaulted by a flying buttress ceiling, but that was where the adherence to antiquities and their recreation ended. The room was decked out in the most basic-looking of appliances, and the floor was a polished block of singular jet-black stone, reflecting the dense blue colour of the massive water-tanks built into the walls. The floor sloped upward on a natural curve, towards an unassuming if large desk, where a shadowy figure sat, limned from behind and yet receiving by contrast no light from the front, leaving the figure cloaked in darkness. Two women whom Alessandro recognized stood at either side of the wing-backed chair, and he only noticed a rawboned, weirdly effeminate-looking man standing beneath the surreal aquamarine-blue glow of the thick glass divide, far to the side of the desk. The women Alessandro knew, and secretly disliked.

"Such excess, Graven. And you sit there like a monstrous spider." Catherine stated it like she disapproved, and Alessandro was reminded again who they were dealing with. "What have you got to show off this time?" One of the women, the oriental-looking one, hissed and actually leaned forward, but a casually dismissive hand rose from the chair, ordering her silence.

"You never did like me ordering you about, ma cher, but I never do so without good reason," Graven said.

The chair rotated to one side – to the oriental woman's side, Alessandro noted, if only because the other woman, Persephone, drew in breath suddenly, and seemed to inflate into a pout. Alessandro had never seen Graven face to face – always in the shadows, his power and gifts and their use preceding him and leaving nothing physical to discern – and he was unprepared for the relative ordinariness of the man. He was hardly as tall as either of the women flanking him, but he had wide shoulders, a sharp face and features resembling a ruthless predator's, with a high forehead and hair drawn back tightly across his scalp. "Please, join me."

Out of the seamless expanse of the floor, a duct opened, and a chair lifted swiftly and silently out of it. Only one chair, and two sighs of petulance this time, one from each woman. Catherine inclined her head slightly and strode forward, taking the seat despite the obvious dislike radiating, even in the relative gloom, from Persephone and Amorphia's faces.

"Yes, I do hope I am not wasting my time," Catherine said, as though she were dealing with an inferior.

Graven seemed completely unfazed by what the others and Alessandro considered a gross breach of etiquette and respect.

"Why is she here?" Persephone snapped, her voice husky with scorn.

"Because I said she could be," Graven replied, not turning his head to look at Persephone, but the displeasure clear in his voice, along with a marked French accent. "And because without her, this whole thing will prove useless."

"And the boy?" the man from the edge asked, not turning around. Alessandro wondered whether he had ever seen or met the enigmatic character, and then realized he was the topic of discussion.

"Excuse me?" he asked, and Graven snorted.

"The young puppy seems to dislike the description you've supplied, Henreik. Perhaps he has taken offense, non?" The mockery was emphasized by slow rolling laughter of an undeniably condescending variety, and Alessandro bridled despite knowing whom he faced. "Yes, the young hot-blood is angered by your words. No, everyone here has a purpose for my ends, and soon we will all be present and ready."

"Ready for what, Graven?" Catherine asked impatiently. Alessandro felt slightly relieved that she had intervened, if not for his sake per se then at least because it took the attention of everyone off himself. "I do hope these imbeciles you've gathered won't be wasting my time either."

"And what have you got to do that takes so much of your time, cher?" Graven asked coyly, smiling. The lighting level seemed to rise a little, and with it came a harsh reality to the man's face, even as it softened and embellished the obvious seduction and allure of both Persephone and Amorphia. Alessandro could also make out the man, Henreik, and was struck by the inordinate cruelty and seeming lack of any compassion whatsoever on the stark face. The light blue eyes seemed cold and dead.

"Knitting," Catherine said simply. Amorphia and Persephone snickered, and even Graven tittered a little.

"Knitting? Surely you jest," he said, truly perplexed despite his response.

"Am I a jester?" Catherine returned, and Alessandro almost grinned at the distinct displeasure in her tone.

Even the others seemed to sense it, and their smiles faded into obscurity out of sheer embarrassment. Graven seemed unperturbed, as though he were dealing with a troublesome and obstinate relative. It was an amazingly convoluted web of intricate social detail, and it all centred somehow on the man standing close to Catherine, and Catherine herself. Alessandro knew Catherine was a powerful Changed, possibly one of the most powerful ones, and to see even Graven, reputedly the most powerful of their kind in existence, seemed more intent on mollifying her than subduing her spurts of erratic moodiness. He listened intently, watching as he was apt to do, trying to piece together a coherent picture.

"Truly, you have always been such a character, my dear," Graven said, sounding fond, of all things! "But the time for games is at an end. Time for more serious matters." More perplexingly, Catherine seemed to accept this, and though she showed no outward sign of agreeing, her silence spoke more voluminously of acquiescence. "Good. Now, if everyone will be so kind as to follow me." Graven swept from the room, passing close by Alessandro, who tried his best not to recoil. Catherine remained seated even when the man Henreik stalked past on deliberately slow and languid steps, hands clasped behind his back, ignoring everyone else flatly. Persephone spared a look of great dislike for Catherine, and Amorphia seemed content to simply walk as seductively and beguilingly as possible. She did look pointedly at Alessandro as she passed him, and though her face was all smiles and invitation, her luminous slanted blue eyes were cold and distant. The four of them had left the room before Catherine rose, smoothing her business suit and taking up position next to Alessandro.

"Whatever you do, do not annoy Kessler."

"Henreik?" Alessandro asked quizzically, and received a curt nod.

"And remain as aloof as possible. Persephone or Amorphia, trollops that they are, will do you more harm than good."

"And what about you?" Alessandro asked. Catherine sneered.

"I? I have nothing to fear from any of them, but Graven. Now come, before he grows irritable."

Outside the room, they were joined by three others.

Alessandro knew none of them, and they all looked, in spite of first impressions, as though they were lethal in the greatest sense of the word. Graven was talking quietly to a man seemingly hewn out of stone, a massive giant towering over even Alessandro. The darkness gave a little, and Alessandro could make out the man's dark, bronzed skin and similarly bronze gaze, as the appearance of stone receded from his skin. Still, the man seemed quite intelligent, not defined by his appearance. Another woman, a flaming redhead, looked flighty and wayward, but her green eyes burned with a fire that seemed echoed in her hair and the brisk whiteness of her face. British, Alessandro mused, by the looks of her. The man next to her made Alessandro's skin crawl. He had first thought it another woman, albeit a very handsome and boyish one, but was surprised when he noted no breasts and a manner that defied femininity. A boy-man was the closest description he could come up with, and those long-lashed eyes held no warmth either.

"Ah good, all here," Graven said congenially. "This way." They walked again through the hangar-like expanse where the statues and archaeological pieces stood like a giant display of a temper tantrum. Graven walked briskly, the other eight people in tow. Alessandro and Catherine lagged behind. Graven led them down one of the side corridors, the lighting increasing as they progressed further and further down a slow descending slope. Alessandro had little by way of empathic gifts – he could manage a basic contact stream, and his awareness stretched more into the realm of machinery and manipulating them, but it was only as he paid more attention to the finer subtleties of the people about him that he realized Graven was triggering undetectable machinery all around them, building them up into something, preparing them before they reached their destination. He realized he was right when that arrogant French voice flared briefly in his head.

Yes, little Italian man. Wait and see. As simply as that the contact ended, and they had reached their destination, another vault. The door weighed several tons, of that Alessandro was sure, using the most rudimentary of his inanimate object-driven divining skills, but with no noticeable effort, or even a gesture to betray the action, Graven forced the door back without letting it make a sound. More disturbing.

Alessandro hadn't noted even the slightest flare of blue when Graven had obviously made use of his gifts. The darkness beyond the open doorway was banished suddenly by a surge of light, a reaction from the red-haired woman, who had raised her hand. Light danced there, remarkably not hurting the eyes of the onlookers but banishing the shadows into the furthest reaches of the chamber. Alessandro wasn't the only one who gasped when he saw what lay before them.

He knew instinctively what it was, when he noted the circular layout. There were zodiac-like markings all around, but the detail of the symbols were horribly intricate, like interlocked strings of mathematical precision, compiled of smaller sigils and combining to form larger symbols, until one could only see a relatively solid line stretching through each segment of the divided circle. In the centre of the circle was a small round pedestal, with four minor protrusions about it. Alessandro swallowed as he recognized the dark stains over the protrusions.

"Yes, it is blood. Old blood," Kessler said, and Alessandro was shocked to discover the man staring directly at him. He thought he detected a hint of relish in the man's voice.

"I would advise none of you to get too close to the centre," Graven's voice cut across the eerie gloom of the chamber. The redhead lifted her other hand and another light blossomed there. She sent them trailing upward, where they hung, casting fitful if prevalent light, like immense candles in a light breeze. "I deplore the loss of good servants, but then, carelessness is often a step closer to death." Graven chuckled, hardly bothered by his own allegation. "A messy death, if one without blood. The death of the mind is a terrible thing." Alessandro wondered what that meant, but he was also loath to inquire more. Graven seemed to take his inquisitiveness in stride though. He fixed Alessandro with a piercing stare. "You are a diviner of the inanimate, yes?" He didn't give Alessandro a chance to respond. "Place your hands on the circle and tell me what you feel."

Alessandro did as he was ordered, aware of the looks of frank appraisal he now received, even from the people he mused disliked him, though it was for no apparent reason. He placed both hands against the grainy surface of the stone and sent his mind racing along the incomparable paths of transcendent lines, of ancient magnetic forces and inherent elemental barriers across the spectrum of all known elements, manufactured and natural. He plumbed the stone for answers, and was perplexed when the deeper he sent his mind to search for clarity, the more evasive those answers became. In the end, after what felt for an hour of desperate seeking, one single finality gathered in Alessandro's mind.

Unknown.

"Well?" Graven asked. Alessandro, anticipating displeasure, sighed and answered.

"This circle isn't made of any known element." Instead of anger, Graven surprised him with a snicker that could only be called 'knowledgeable'.

"Yes, its maker was a very clever man. More clever even than the scientists of our own time."

"Meaning?" Catherine demanded. Graven shrugged, then stepped onto the circle, or rather, a scant inch above the surface, walking on nothing as though there was actually a floor. Alessandro tried again to fathom the man's gifted aptitudes, but came up with nothing, including the absence whatsoever of a signal blue flare denoting usage.

"This circle is my most recent recovery. I had it dug up from beneath a mountain near the source of the Nile, and it took me a century to do so. Still, all things considered, I know enough about it; enough to demand respect for its creator."

"And that would be?" the effeminate-looking companion of the redhead queried.

"It is older than the ancient Romans, older than the Greeks. I would go as far as to say that ancient Egypt was still in its Old Kingdom phase when this device, this marvel of ancient engineering, was crafted. And it is made from an element unknown to us even today. Tell me," Graven said, turning to Alessandro, "what does it feel like, this 'sense' of awareness, this plumbing of the mystery?"

"There is nothing there, except a denial of natural cohesion," Alessandro said, caught between Catherine's sharp looks and the expectations of the others. "No elemental uniformity, no affinity to any known elements. Compared to other objects, this circle is…"

"Dead? Yes, it is dead," Graven said, and Alessandro resented the Socratic angle of the man's debate. "It requires something else to activate it. Something, elementary, if you will pardon the joke." No one laughed, but Graven seemed more intent on pressing on with his point. "And as you can see from the protrusions, there is a clear indication of what is needed."

"You didn't bring us here for some bizarre and disgusting blood ritual, did you?" Catherine challenged. Again, Graven treated her to that fondly enigmatic smile.

"Not your blood, no. None of you have blood remotely resembling what I've unearthed there." He pointed at the dark stains in the centre of the circle. "My scientists are baffled, by the blood as much as the elemental disparity of the circle itself. But there is a key to it, you see. My own blood, it has certain properties similar to the blood and DNA on the circle. Not nearly enough, which means even I lack the sophistication to make use of this device." Graven couched the admission in false bravado, but Alessandro noted the strained level of frustration in the man's voice. The point was that no one seemed either willing or reckless enough to remark – in any way – on the statement. It was then that Alessandro realized something important.

No one wanted to be here.

By the sheer force of his will, by his ambition and drive, Graven kept each of the eight other Changed in check. Through intimidation, through fear, through like-mindedness, whichever way one put it, Graven inspired those around him. Were he to leave, a bloody struggle would ensue, and almost no one would survive. The other Changed despised each other, and their mutual fear of Graven, and what he could do, fuelled the enforced peace. Alessandro felt himself go completely cold with icy fear on his insides. And yet here they were, all of them uncomfortable to some extent, but horribly mesmerized by Graven's conversational explanation, mutely astonished and cowed by his callous acceptance of the fact that some insane and barbaric ritual of blood sacrifice was required to somehow make the circle work. No one would object. Not even Catherine. But even in the low light level of the chamber, Alessandro noted that she had turned paler than usual.

"So we have a circle, and we know nothing of it save that it boggles the minds of even the most skilled inferior scientist," Kessler said, distaste for the general human masses implied. "We have a blood ritual ready to happen, but no way of finding out who is required to complete this process."

"That is where you are wrong, my bloodthirsty friend," Graven amended. "This circle is merely the culmination, the apex, of my lifelong quest. You see, I have no name for the creator of this device, but I have more of his works here. To the outside world he is an unknown, but his mark is on every single piece of stone and useless clay shard beneath this structure. So very simple, really, once you unlock the easy ciphers he used to disguise himself. Three small initials, couched in convoluted and seemingly random combinations, but discoverable across all the languages the man came across!" Graven's voice climbed as his conviction and excitement did, until he seemed ready to launch into a narration of accolades.

Alessandro, enrapt, could do nothing but listen.

"How do you know it was a man?" Persephone asked, and Graven treated her to a stare which screamed multiple volumes of sexism and condescension, mixed in with the obvious displeasure he felt at having her close by.

"Simply put, my dear," Graven began, voice dripping sarcasm, "the blood, though denying all of our modern tests any more access than cursory explanation and identification, denoted masculinity. And if you must question further, the initials are inscribed, in his blood, on the central dais." A light flared more brightly above the central dais, and there, amidst a faded stain of dark red, thin lines were visible. "Ancient cuneiform, in no way discernible as the creator's original signature and thus unreliable to prove the actual length of his existence, but still a truly ancient sign. Translated into English, we are left with three initials: KAR." Even though Alessandro knew only Graven himself truly appreciated the scope of whatever he had just revealed to them all, he was drawn along with the charismatic exuberance and respect for such historic data that Graven's poise broadcasted. "Nothing else, but recognizable everywhere, on all the other artefacts I have gathered to this point: KAR, in Egyptian hieroglyphs, in the earliest Greek and Phoenician scripting, in Latin, in Norse runes, everything! Whoever created this device, and all the other records, documents and inscriptions I have here, is ancient beyond our ken. To put it simply, my friends, I have good – very good – reason to believe that all these things, the artefacts and contrivances, are the works of the very first of the Changed." He looked at them, head lowered slightly, dramatically increasing the menacing aspects of his features, as he pronounced the final statement: "Possibly even the progenitor."

"So you've finally come across something concrete."

"Mais oui, ma cher," Graven answered. He eyed Catherine askance, almost coyly, his right hand holding the large wine glass at an angle, observing every gesture she made. She in turn refused to look at him, and her glass was more a trivial thing to toy with than for enjoying the beverage. They were standing on the ramparts of the cathedral – call it that for lack of a better description – staring out over the lower domains of the structures about them. It was night time, and though the central city never really slept or turned off its dazzling display of lights and traffic, it was peaceful, this high up. Graven never tried to read her mind, mainly because her greatest strength was almost like his own: there was, as far as he could tell, no sign whatsoever of a mental barrier that kept him out, but screening her was like blaring white noise into your ears. She noted the particular glance he gave her, and shook her head.

"Always up to your old games," she said, disproving. He shrugged.

"I have often wondered whether your mental resistance is somehow tied in with your stormy disposition. A natural weather barrier of mental proportions, to match your gifts."

"And so you gnaw away at what you don't understand."

"I am merely a scientist, l'etudiant d'histoire, call it what you wish. If I must make the world pay in blood for furthering the cause of others like us, pour quoi pas? They would destroy us if we miss-stepped, even once, and you know it."

"We have not miss-stepped once in the past, and you and I go back a long way," Catherine said, and took a generous sip of her wine. She twisted her mouth, eyed the wine and snorted. "Long enough to lose taste for the supposed vintages they make nowadays." Graven chuckled appreciatively and stepped a little closer.

Catherine's next statement rooted him to a standstill. "And you never worked under pretenses of furthering the cause of the Changed before. What has made matters different, or do you think I wouldn't see your lies?"

"I have never harmed any of our kind, unless they got in my way," Graven protested lazily.

"An easy thing to do, from what I hear."

"And what is it you hear in your far-away chateau in the French mountains? Does the wind carry you word?" he asked, and there was no denying the harder edge to his query. "You never will agree with me on anything, Catherine, but you will be a part of this." He gulped down the last of his wine and threw the glass into the open night air, where some distance out it shattered into dust-fine fragments.

"I seem to have no choice," she replied wearily, but only because even she would only go so far to thwart him. "But under one condition."

"And that would be?"

"You will tell me everything. Every single detail of what you intend. I am not as callous and arrogant, and as disrespectful of all life, as these underling buffoons you've gathered here are, and I will not stand by as you waste life for your own schemes."

"Always the humanitarian, the staunchly bleeding heart."

"Don't patronize me!" Catherine snapped, and threw both glass and wine over the edge. A gust lifted it momentarily before it crackled, shattered by a sudden burst of static, disintegrating the glass into fragments as tiny as his glass had become. Graven quirked a brow at the display. "You are as reckless as the others, but you get away with it because you are older and wiser, if that is even plausible! They will act at your behest, and you do nothing when we come ever closer to being revealed for what we are." She stepped towards him, eyes narrow and wrathful, as her voice climbed with anger. "Can you face the entire world, Graven? Can you halt a war, as powerful as you are?"

"I have done it before," he said dryly. She barked mirthlessly.

"In a time where they used wooden siege weapons and you could still evade crossbows! Even you are prey to bullets, when you can't see them."

"This discussion about what I can and cannot do is pointless!" Graven said, spreading his arms. "But you have my word. I will tell you my intentions, if that is satisfactory. You should be honoured."

"I would destroy every shred of what you've gathered here, for my own peace of mind," she retorted angrily. "I have hated you since the day you first launched yourself after this progenitor Changed and his collected works. And that blood on the circle is not as old as you made it out to be. What have you done?"

"I have implemented a very useful subject," he said simply, but he sounded cornered, and his displeasure was plain.

"You found a Changed with blood even richer than your own," Catherine whispered, appalled.

"If you will, yes. A remarkable occurrence, but his blood was not enough. It activated the circle – it set some of the symbols alight for a few moments and then connected a few of the lines. A remarkable display, seeing ancient stone shift itself so, to have those lines undulate as though they are alive. It fills me with such excitement!"

"Did you kill him?" she asked, dreading the answer.

"Such a thing, though possible, would be a waste," Graven continued, as if he were discussing gardening tools. "He lives – a remarkable regenerative combination in his DNA which makes him at least as old as we are, which is astonishing! You have to admit it!"

"I admit to nothing! I deplore your barbarism!" Catherine hacked viciously.

"Tut, tut, do not lose your temper cher, it is an unbecoming sight." His words, his mockery, suddenly calmed her, restored her icy facade and composure. "He is safe, because he is useful, and it will stay that way, because he is more than simply a fitting pre-subject for what I think the circle will do." When Catherine gave no reply, he went on. "A link, to another, a Changed of unforeseen power. He eluded me when I captured my subject."

"And you hold the grudge even now," Catherine remarked snidely, goading him.

"Irrelevant. I wish to find him again, because that is where the other facet of my test subject's usefulness comes in: a link, possibly an emotional one worth exploiting." He ignored the clear disgust in her eyes, knowing full well that she would use any pretense to reopen the subject of his atrocities. "If I can somehow leak information on certain channels, I might bait the elusive fiend, possibly trap him and substitute him for his unfortunate friend."

"I grow weary of your lording over such things," Catherine said, and made to leave. "But I suppose I must weather it, if you are to maintain your end of this deal."

"Yes, life and all its pleasures, everything. Bear with me cher, you might learn something," he said, snickering close-mouthed. The bottle of wine appeared out of nowhere, a new glass ready, and he began pouring. "Another?"

"I already know too much," Catherine said, and stalked off.

"Suit yourself," Graven said to her retreating back, took a whiff and then a delicate sip, murmuring appreciatively.

CHAPTER TWENTY ONE

Reflections

The shield rippled dramatically.

Luke gritted his teeth and focused his mind on keeping the barrier intact. Alex was vigorously attempting to break past the defence, and her face also was strained with the effort. She had admitted cheekily to him that he didn't really want to keep her out, but it had been a deliberate ploy, one he had paid for in pain, when one telekinetic blast had managed to get past the field and punched him in the shoulder. The shield had nearly come down then, but he had maintained it, much to Alex's renewed glee and admiration, which had been soothing enough for the pain in his burning shoulder.

He hadn't been the only one with an increased potential. Alex's telekinesis was becoming almost too much for her to control – he had noticed vases and glass objects shatter at the slightest emotional outburst from her – but she was learning to rein it in. Where Luke's shielding was becoming increasingly easier to create, maintain and enforce, Alex's mental assaults seemed to achieve a hardened tangibility, as though it could almost be seen. That, or Luke mused he was becoming more adept at recognizing mental attacks in any form.

"Ready for the big finale?" Alex asked him. He nodded, biting down on his lower lip. "Ooh wait, maybe you should try and see how big you can make that sucker around you!"

"The bigger it goes the harder it is to maintain," Luke replied.

"I won't attack when you try it, I just think you should experiment, now that you're on a roll, and before I tire you out." She winked at him, and seemed to deflate a little, a sure sign of her backing off a bit. Luke positioned himself correctly – the shield was not that finicky, but he had found he could better align whatever energies constituted the barriers when he stood with his legs apart and his arms outstretched, as though he were reaching for the overcast sky and the biting little autumn breeze. As he did so, the shield rippled and then stabilized a little. With a grunt he began extending it, watching it expand slowly about him. It could hold two people inside without much effort, and he held it like that in any case, but now it could hold four…six…eight.

"Keep going," Alex coaxed from the side, stepping closer somewhat, eyes glistening with excitement.

Luke's jaw began aching, but he extended it further, the bubble expanding more slowly, but still expanding nonetheless. It grew to a prodigious size, but a low whine began to grow as it approached a twenty capacity. Alex, amazed now, drew back a bit. "Whoa, slow down, don't hurt yourself!"

"If I let down, anything can go through it," Luke said tightly, face white and bathed in sweat.

"You mean you're holding it this big at full strength?" Alex asked, alarmed. "You have to let it go!"

"In a moment," he croaked, but a strangely triumphant grin was on his face. "Just one more."

The bubble suddenly popped, a vicious explosion that would have sent Alex crashing into the rock face behind her, had she not managed to hurl up her own unseen, cursory barrier. As it was, she simply rolled away over the grassy ground, jumping up the moment she came to a standstill. She looked anxiously over to where Luke was resting on his knees, one hand supporting him, the other clenched in a fist that was shaking.

"Hey, don't you dare scare me like that again!" Alex snapped, moving in fast, walking angrily towards him. He looked up, face still white, but shining with excitement amidst the sheen of sweat. He ran a hand through his hair and rose shakily, holding Alex from supporting him.

"Did you see what happened?" he asked.

"Yeah, you sent me for a roll down the grass, in a way that reminded me of my childhood," Alex muttered.

Luke's face instantly turned concerned. "Did I hurt you?"

"Relax," Alex said, shrugging. "You're not the only one with barrier capacity here. Mine just don't look as pretty as yours, and they're see-through."

"Did you see it then?" Luke asked after a while, assured that Alex was fine. "It can work as a weapon!"

"Weapon?" she asked, then frowned. "Honey, you lost control of the shield. That hardly counts as a weapon, unless it's your last effort to take out someone who's beating your ass, and you have no way out," she explained. He shook his head.

"No, I can do it again. I'll show you," he began.

"I don't think you should try it again, you're stretching –"

"Take cover and watch," he commanded, startling her. "I won't make it as big, but I'm gonna put everything I have in it!" He walked away from her, still shaky, but buoyed up by confidence. Alex sighed, shaking her head and muttered darkly about stubborn men, but complied and ducked behind an outcrop that was low to the ground. Only her head peeked over the rock, and she placed a barrier in front of her face, in case he did manage to do it.

The shield shimmered into place, vibrant mauve, barely undulating in the sunlight. Alex frowned more deeply; every time Luke seemed to overreach himself, something improved in spite of the possible burnout waiting to happen. The shield had never been so stable, as far as she could remember. It grew a little, and then began to thicken. It was the only word she could think of. The shield became so dense that Luke was obscured from sight, lost behind a screen of wildly playing streaks of dense purplish energy ribbons. For a moment his voice echoed to her, still filled with enthusiasm.

"Wanna see if you can break through this?"

"How certain are you that it'll hold?" she sent back, and heard his laughter. Tilting her head askance, she readied a monster strike, galled by his cheek. She sent the strike, forming it fast and focused, like a lance of energy. For a moment she was sure it rippled, like a heatwave, and then it scattered, breaking against the impervious curve of Luke's shield, which didn't even buckle. Gasping, Alex nearly left the safety of her cover, but Luke's voice came to her again.

"Wait, I'm gonna let it go!" he warned. Alex ducked back, barrier in place, and watched as the energy began roiling about over the shield, as if it was becoming agitated. Suddenly the thing collapsed, exploding outward like a bursting melon, blasting back the grass and leaves on the nearby trees, and actually scorching the ground bare where Luke was standing. The lashing wind burst against Alex's shield, and she was vaguely shocked when she noted the rocks near where Luke stood crack and expel tiny plumes of dust. When the whipping gust died down, Alex moved out from behind her shelter, and was surprised when Luke ran up to her and lifted her off her feet.

"See? A weapon!"

"Yeah, and boys, I guess, will be boys," she quipped, snickering. He put her down, and she surveyed the light devastation. "Trust a guy to come up with a weapon of mass destruction."

"C'mon," he protested. "This'll hardly cause any of those super-Changed freaks we fought at the mansion to break a sweat. I bet with practice I can make it stronger."

"But not today," Alex warned, spinning about to face him. "Right now, I need a bath, a cup of coffee and a very large and soft bed in front of a roaring fire."

"Sounds nice, can I come?"

"Bath or bed?" she asked, and quirked a mischievous brow at him. He noticed and grinned.

"I get only one?"

"Oh damn your boyish allure!" Alex snapped. "Both, as long as you wash me as well as yourself!"

* * *

"For how long exactly do I need to keep this up?"

"For as long as you can."

Alice disliked that she couldn't follow Daniel's trains of thought. She disliked that the only way she could actually follow anything he was doing was by observing his outward reactions, and of course the cursory mental allowances Charlie had politely ventured for her convenience. At Daniel's urging, of course. She and Charlie watched as their returned and seemingly recovered – mentally and emotionally – progeny and ward sat in the middle of the room at GOA Headquarters, a sealed chamber several hundred levels below the main complex.

"How is he doing?" Alice asked after a short interval of silent observation, when Daniel seemed to be in a low trance of sorts, the only indication that he was using his gifts a slight blue sheen to his eyes. He didn't respond to her question either, in spite of the fact that it was addressed to Charlie – Daniel loved playing games, and fielding people's questions not directed at him seemed to be a favoured pastime nowadays. Cheeky little bastard, Alice thought, hiding the thought deep, in case Daniel did catch it. Charlie shook his head slowly, a look of wonder on his face.

"I would have thought since we're this far underground he would have trouble projecting, but I'm not detecting any obstacles in his thoughts. We might as well be in a room at the top of a skyscraper for all he cares." Alice nodded, hiding her own amazement. She knew her own capacities, knew that telepathic transmission of any kind, receptively focused or simply loosed in general, was almost impossible, if not improbable, when underground. She herself would be hard-pressed to send her thoughts roaming further than a hundred miles from their current position, if she strained herself to her limits, and Charlie admitted that he would maybe manage coherent stream topside. Daniel, though, seemed exempt from the restrictions associated with telepathic communication in general: subterranean depths greatly hampered such communiqués, and simple roaming was technically out of the question, but there Daniel sat, in a pose of relaxation, leaning with his back against the low seat he occupied; according to Charlie, Daniel was presently observing a fishing flotilla off the coast of Newfoundland.

"And the flare isn't even all the way present," Alice added, shaking her head. Partly she was amazed at the scope of Daniel's powers, and partly shocked and horrified that any one being could have such strength. Not even the GenneY that GOA had secured seven decades earlier had been this skilled, although it could be argued that the woman had been out of her mind, her powers made sporadic by her lack of focus and mental stability. Daniel appeared, in spite of many pitfalls and – according to Charlie – regrets about certain things he had done, to be in full control of his obviously prodigious gifts. She ran through the tests she and Charlie had performed on Daniel, with his willing cooperation, strangely. He seemed more at ease with the role he perceived he had to play, with regards to Alice's input and his own insistence that he remain at GOA and become a part of it.

"There really is no need to delay this further," Alice had told Charlie and Margaret several days earlier. "He appears to be ready to join us, and apart from testing his abilities, the technicalities of registering him with us and erasing all government records of him outside of GOA alone needs to be done."

"Testing his abilities?" Margaret had queried.

"More to the point, recording for posterity the progress he's made," Charlie had added, and Alice had nodded her agreement.

Now they were seated in the deepest suites within GOA itself, running perhaps the thirtieth test on Daniel's abilities. Daniel simply went at it the whole time, not really mincing words but also at times making it abundantly clear that he thought some of the tests were trivial. He showed his disdain by performing the required tests with alarming alacrity and skill, unfettered seemingly by whatever personal restrictions Alice and Charlie had thought he might have. In the last four days they had tested all of Daniel's abilities, some of them involving careful surveillance with the most advanced scanning technology that mankind presently had at its disposal. It was an established fact that Daniel's telekinetic power was unparalleled by anyone in GOA – he had shown just how strong he was by crushing a twenty-ton concrete block to dust, and he had done so from within the chamber where they now were. The block had been outside, on the surface. They had tested his teleporting – Charlie had sat in on that one, since Daniel had allowed the mental link between them to operate once more, and a GPS tracking nanite in Daniel's clothing had been the backup: Daniel managed to teleport from within the chamber, and the signal had picked him up again just south of US-Mexican border, close to the Gulf Coast. On returning he had appeared without the jacket where the tracker was secured, grinning wide at the flabbergasted looks the technicians registered at the duality their screens had picked up. It had been another massive improvement on his skill with teleporting, since he could now apparently manage to transport himself wherever he wanted without actually seeing where he was going, as opposed to before, when he needed line of sight.

Testing Daniel's other abilities had been easier, though. The closest GOA classification came to describing Daniel's unique capacity to affect almost anything about him was dubbed Manifestation, a new alteration to be made in the CC: it included his ability to reassemble whatever he had destroyed – granted he did not obliterate the object into dust or even tinier components – as well as his ability to extend his phenomenal mental might and literally direct it into a wave of energy. The chamber walls, despite the tight-fitting shielding that kept the structural integrity of the inside chamber intact, as well as preventing the chamber to be damaged from the inside, bore scorch marks of various kinds, some of them the result of vicious pyrokinetic lashes, some from Daniel's gleeful displays of jagged bolts of lightning arcing from splayed fingertips.

His last fully displayed gift was phasing, of course, which Charlie had mused would be a problem, since Daniel became violently nauseous whenever he engaged the particular ability. But none of that seemed to be a problem when they tested him for it: Daniel had phased inside the subterranean chamber and had levitated himself through the ground and upwards to the surface, where he had reassumed his corporeal shape. He also managed to phase through the class-5 shield in the room, which meant that relatively very little of GOA Headquarters was safe from him if he were to go looking for something in restricted areas. Alice had frowned at Charlie's barely-contained amusement at the thought of Daniel using his gifts to steal or spy, and had remarked that he could probably teleport through a shield in any case, since he had shown that he could do so with apparent ease.

They left his telepathy, mainly because Alice had a certain personal flare for saving what she considered the most intricate and delicate of abilities for last. Charlie wondered whether she merely wanted to be present to see exactly just how advanced Daniel had become, and because her actual job kept her from being present at all the tests.

"Satisfied yet?" Charlie asked Alice suddenly.

"Why, is he growing tired?" she queried, and Charlie snickered.

"He's actually getting bored. Just as well, he seems to be enjoying himself."

"What is he doing?" As Alice fired off the last question, Daniel's eyes closed somewhat, staring ahead through half-mast eyelids, but the blue glow increased, obscuring the green of his eyes completely. Alice looked back to Charlie, who also seemed wrapped up in thought, delving into the impressions and visions he received through his mental link with Daniel. He smiled slowly, eyes lighting up with merriment. "He's at Niagara Falls, roaming about the ferry next to the waterfall. He's..." Charlie guffawed suddenly. "He's rocking the boat!"

"Tell him to stop!" Alice snapped, alarmed and annoyed. And secretly exuberant, thinking on what this meant: Daniel had just demonstrated a talent for something no one but she herself had managed, and only after decades of practice and experience: he could meld his psychic gifts, use one to offset or boost the other, depending on the necessity. Charlie nodded, still grinning, placing a hand slowly on Daniel's shoulder. Daniel lowered his head, and when he looked up, the flare was gone, replaced by a muzzy green stare that became clearer with each passing second. Alice couldn't help but smile, even though her words were meant as warning.

"If you must show your facility at something, try to do it constructively," she said. Daniel looked at Charlie, who was smiling wider now, and Daniel too seemed to bite down on breaking into a fit of laughter.

"Okay," was all Daniel said. Alice turned to look at the section of the room just behind her, near the ceiling. The wall shimmered, revealing a wide window, where several technicians were observing everything below them.

"High-level Mental Fluidity aptitude," Alice said to them, knowing they would hear her and add the cited gift to the already exceptionally long list. She turned back to Daniel. "This concludes testing."

"Do I get a gold star?" Daniel asked flippantly, and grimaced when Charlie punched his arm.

"What you get is full GOA membership," Alice replied. She allowed herself to smile warmly and inclined her head slightly. "Allow me to be the first to officially welcome you, Daniel Mercer, as a GOA employee." She extended a hand, and he took it without further ado, giving it a firm shake. In the crossing, Alice quickly spoke telepathically. *"I hope you know this means playing by the rules, and abiding by them."*

"I'll try my best," came his reply, but it was riddled with undertones of mischief. Knowing she would not get more from him, Alice disengaged.

"Tomorrow we will discuss the details of your contract, benefits and other formalities. For now, please feel free to go about as you please. Except," she said, halting his hasty dash for the door. "I would appreciate it if you would not go gallivanting around the world. Heaven knows you can do it, but it would be inadvisable."

"I was actually thinking I would like a decent meal, maybe an insanely large amount of alcohol," Daniel said straight-faced, and summarily teleported away, ignoring the dash for the door. Alice shook her head.

"He's still your responsibility," she said, turning to Charlie, who was rubbing a hand across his forehead.

"I didn't think that would change, really," he replied, smiling.

The circle was silent.

The whine still filled the air of the chamber, a strange counterpoint to the snap and twang of the torch fires lit in their sconces. Graven floated a foot above the floor, next to the edge of the circle, pensively staring down at it. His face was drawn together in a frown of concentration, as though he could figure out the mystery of the circle simply by glaring pointedly at it. Close by, the effeminate-looking Changed, a man named Amal, watched and waited, dark eyes scanning both the circle and the floating man.

"I am sure you have tried these things before," Amal said to Graven. He had a high-pitched voice, almost nasal. It made him sound far younger than he actually was, as did his fine, delicate features. He was careful not to allow disrespect into his voice – Graven was a dangerous man, and Amal knew for a fact that he himself had no might whatsoever to pitch offensively, successfully, against Graven. Those were not his strengths. Graven's head snapped to the side, to fix Amal with a piercing stare. "Is there a reason why you have gathered us all in one place?"

"Yes, it amuses me to see how you all squabble!" Graven snapped snidely, mouth thinning in spite of the almost-smile of cruel enjoyment he displayed. "Of course I have tried these things before, but any single event of power could trigger the circle!"

"And then what?" Amal asked slowly. He dared a step closer, the light catching him strongly from behind now, darkening his face. "What will this circle do, exactly?"

"I am not interested in what it can do right now," Graven replied. Amal frowned, stunned by the strange statement.

"Isn't this what you are trying to figure out?" he asked.

"No," Graven retorted, voice dripping with long-suffering. "What I am trying to do is configure the damned contraption so as to use it."

"Use it for what?"

"Must you ask so many questions?" Graven fired back, and his voice assumed an icy edge. Amal swallowed, aware of his precarious perch between annoying the man and causing him to outright recoil and incinerate Amal. Fortunately, the outburst let Graven continue, and Amal wondered again whether Graven didn't already actually know what the circle was for. The First was a great keeper of secrets, and always knew far more than anyone gave him credit for. But then Graven sighed, resigned to explaining his actions. "The circle itself will do very little, I think, except act as containment." Graven held up one hand, and a very slight sheen of glowing blue raced across his eyes. Amal strained to see what the man was doing, and tried to mentally force himself to awareness, but he detected nothing. And yet, slowly the whine he had heard earlier, when the circle had first been afloat, filled the room again. It intensified, and then recoiled, making a sharp snap that manifested as a physical flare of light blue, screaming like an infuriated hornet's nest as it died down. Amal physically started at the sound and sudden added brightness, but Graven merely smiled slightly. "It almost has a mind of its own, or at least an attunement beyond mere technological scope that guides such defences. It cannot be destroyed, it cannot be lifted by anything man-made and it recoils against excessive empathic actions." Amal listened, fascinated. "And yet it doesn't object when a live object is placed at the centre dais. It begins draining the life from the unfortunate creature –" Amal noted the total lack of mercy or compassion when Graven said that – "and will kill anyone not Changed."

"Catherine had said that you have someone ready, someone to use," Amal ventured. Graven's smile failed slightly, as though the mention of Catherine's name somehow brought him down.

"She did, yes?" he asked, voice becoming neutral. An awkward silence followed, Graven returning to his pensive state, staying afloat and bobbing slightly. Amal watched the circle. He schooled his thoughts, marvelling that such an ancient device remained intact. If what Graven had said was true, then the circle could not be broken by any force, and neither could it be lifted by anything man-made. He tried to picture a fork lifter or an industrial crane attempting to lift the circle and fail. It was staggering. But Graven managed. The circle had, several minutes ago, floated at vicious speed, turning around and about under Graven's power, seemingly unfettered by anything. Graven's face had beaded with sweat after a while – a terrifying thing to behold, Amal had thought at the time – and he had put the thing down, with nothing but that whining sound as reward for the exercise.

Amal hunkered down on his knees beside the artefact, eyes scanning the symbols in the light. It was an unparalleled combination of uncounted small sigils and signs, and depending on how deeply they were engraved, they formed darker congregations that evolved into new symbols and objects, which in turn did the same. Graven had said the smallest symbols were only visible with microscopes, and that each one was unique and different from the one next to it, like a collection of countless snowflakes. Amal stretched a hand reverentially towards the circle, and stopped when Graven's voice cut across his thoughts.

"Do you wish to die?" Graven asked.

"At your hand or by the circle's?" Amal asked, daring a little defiance. He knew what he needed to do, and he didn't want Graven stopping him. Although there was nothing he could do if Graven decided it was a waste of time, and Amal was insubordinate. "You allowed that Italian whelp to touch the circle."

"When he uses his gifts he becomes separate from his body. He would hardly have felt the beginnings of the draining effects," Graven explained.

"Then perhaps you will allow me to indulge in one of my own gifts. Think of it as my contribution to the cause," Amal said. He didn't wait for Graven to reply or deny, and instead placed both hands on the circle. He felt a momentary stab of pain lance through his splayed palms and into his arms, but he ignored it. He had felt far worse before, and a little pain would not deter him now. He lifted free of his body, but it wasn't as though he was projecting his mind outside of it. This was far more complex, a method of power only he could employ so accurately that it garnered him respect from even Graven himself. Amal had encountered other, far weaker Changed with this gift before. They called it 'profiling', reading backwards into the past, but the most competent Changed Amal had come across with, sharing his gift, could only do so a few weeks backward. Amal smiled, thinking of the man's astonished look of horror as Amal had shown him centuries past flash by, before he killed him.

"If you die, I will be most displeased," Graven said, sounding nonchalant. Amal wondered if it was whether Graven would then have to find another old Changed, if any of them still remained. It was definitely not because Graven had any particular affection for him, that Amal knew. And Graven did like the number nine, so it was purely technical.

"I intend to outlive even you," Amal replied, and before he could hear Graven's outraged retort, his mind soared backwards into the past, feeding off the incredible variety and richness of the etched stones beneath his hands.

CHAPTER TWENTY TWO

Brothers

There was an aftermath the next day.

Daniel, overjoyed at finding himself part and parcel of the GOA Changed family, had never imagined just how many other Changed snooped about Headquarters, or how many people knew him and what he was capable of. His exuberance had taken a turn for the alcoholic, as he had intended, and by the time night fell he was drunk to the point of slurry speech. It had the desired effect. For a start, a lot of the other Changed had joined in, Chris and Jamie included, and the latter two sat side by side with Daniel, on one of the couches, trying to outdo each other with complimenting and welcoming him into the family of GOA.

Daniel, amused and mentally sporadic, laughed in spasms and joined in every now and then to further derail a train of thought, or simply to thank them in turn, until finally, Chris broke into tears, expressing his admiration for Daniel, who regarded the spectacle, drunk as he was, with some trepidation, whispering after a while to Jamie:

"He'll be fine, right?" The innocuous query set him laughing again, and the mood was lifted that quickly as Jamie joined in, shaking his head to clear his vision.

"Chris is a feeling kinda guy not given to deeper things. But not stupid, no, no, no, no, never stupid!" he cautioned with a peremptory finger, and Daniel nodded, snorting back a guffaw. Jamie, noticing the expression, broke into more fits of laughter, and steered himself and Daniel to the bar counter, where the waiter looked at them expectantly. Jamie frowned, and in his inebriated mode he leaned onto the counter, staring straight at the waiter. "Whassa matter? Never seen a drunk Changed before?"

"Sir?" the man asked, startled by Jamie's frankness. Daniel, still merry and amused by Jamie's unheard off and never-before-seen – at least not by Daniel – displays of raucousness and rowdiness, leaned in beside the stockier man, who swayed belligerently.

"Never mind," he managed, and shivered as his mind rallied to keep up at normal speeds. "Keep the drinks coming," he told the waiter, who nodded and ducked away, seemingly all too happy to be out of some uncalled-for line of fire situation. Jamie belched and pardoned himself, face momentarily caught between the indecision of feeling embarrassed and resorting to gales of laughter at the antic.

"Stupid unchanged people. What, we can't have the same fun they do?" he said moodily. Daniel shook his head.

"Relax, it's not that bad."

"Really?" Jamie snorted. "You never saw my parents' reaction to having a mutant freak for a son!" Daniel, shocked for a moment beyond his own intoxicated haze, narrowed eyes and stared at the normally staunch and unremittingly jovial character. "Would have shot me right there and then," Jamie continued, his seeming admission couched in a strange aura of guilt and remorse evaporating in the face of a stupid grin, "if I hadn't blown the gun up in the bastard's face!"

"Wow, never heard that story before," Daniel opted, knowing somehow that this once, his sarcasm and discomfort would escape Jamie's usual concise notice. Jamie shuddered, leaned his head back and momentarily closed his eyes, mouth set in a wan smile.

"Hmm, yeah, I did that. Then I ran away."

Daniel looked about for anyone to foist off on Jamie. He was drunk, in a celebratory mood and not ready at all to play the dapper hand of sympathy and understanding to a man he was accustomed to having the kind of unseen character fibre that denied even the possibility of such strange stories. And Daniel didn't doubt for one second Jamie was speaking – revealing – the truth, in a rare moment of lacking inhibitions.

Fortunately Chris arrived at that instant, face and body completely devoid of any sign of former drunken emotional outbursts, as he sauntered through the small crowd that comprised the Saloon party, winking at women and cheering along with any guy who somehow got his attention. In this way he reached the bar again, drawing level with Daniel and Jamie and watching them both with an almost slack-jawed camaraderie.

"Hiya kids, what happened when I was out?" he asked. Daniel drew closer to him when Jamie didn't respond, and trying not to sound mischievously conspiratorial he whispered to Chris: "Jamie's a little sad about something, or maybe just a little weird. I dunno what's got into him."

"Did he tell you anything about how he blew his dad's gun up in his dad's face?" Chris asked quickly, shushed halfway to a finer whisper by Daniel's insistent gestures. Daniel nodded, and Chris's face split into a wide grin. He placed a hand on Daniel's shoulder – Daniel hardly thought he would feel anything from Chris, and he didn't – and shook his head, winking. "I can handle this one. You go and find someone to sleep with, or have a drinking contest with. Something like that!" he finished sheepishly, snickering. "I'll talk to Jamie, poor guy. You go and have fun, bucko!" Daniel nodded, thankful for the timely intervention, as he meandered into the crowd beyond the bar, not really caring that he was jostled or waylaid by scores of people who didn't really know him but knew of him. He kept the exchanges as short as possible, but being drunk was something he remembered well from before the Change: he'd always enjoyed an active social life, when it came to booze, much to his father and brothers' delight, since they also indulged every now and then in alcohol binges, much to Mrs. Hirsch's and Joanie's prevailing horror. The thought forced Daniel to smile, even when he felt the surge of loss and remorse at how he had possibly ruined that bond.

He stopped in mid stride, waved away a beleaguered apology from some woman being jostled away by three others and went to take a seat close to the spread of the window looking west, in one of the saloon alcoves where no one else was seated. He sighed, concentrated a little and cleared his head of the excess of the alcohol.

Jamie's strange predicament had sparked off Daniel's thoughts. He wanted to go back, to rejoin Jamie and Chris at the counter, possibly even race around at breakneck speed on some or other gadget which Chris no doubt had stashed somewhere close by for just such an occasion. Daniel snickered by himself: he didn't need tales of previous parties at any of the GOA Changed personnel's houses to tell him that this was exactly the kind of stuff Chris was reliable for – a very dangerous but adrenaline-filled, scold-worthy and exciting blast at the end of the evening, when everyone was either passed out, gone home or mellowing down to sobriety, in the company of other likeminded, matured drinkers. Later, Daniel mused, for the nonce letting his own thoughts take over.

"Penny for your thoughts?" someone asked.

"Which thoughts in particular?" Daniel fired back before thinking, or registering who had spoken to him. Startled by way of delayed reaction, he twisted his upper body around and found Charlie watching him from the edge of the padded circular seating of the alcove, a smile on his face. "Hey. Thought you'd never come."

"I had no idea I was invited," Charlie said, and Daniel scoffed, moving inwards to leave Charlie some space.

"What kind of excuse is that?" Daniel challenged back. Charlie grinned, sat down and winced. "And what's wrong with you?"

"You make a lousy gatekeeper when you're drunk, you know that?" Charlie replied, tapping the side of his head. Realization dawned on Daniel, and he held hands to mouth, eyes wide.

"Shit, sorry!" was all he managed. Inadvertently his alcohol escapade had let slip his control of the otherwise tightly sealed containment that was his end of the mental bond he shared with Charlie. "I forgot!"

"I know, and I'm not angry," Charlie amended kindly. He treated Daniel to a lengthy stare, and Daniel cast about, first uncomfortable, then exasperated and finally settling for showing it, and demanding an explanation. Charlie shrugged. "I've never seen you drunk before, and by the looks of it you're not exactly a wet-behind-the-ears rookie at it either."

"How can you tell?" Daniel asked, relieved the stare hadn't been for anything critical or serious.

"I have your hangover, waiting to happen," Charlie replied. "Like a dull ache behind the eyes, threatening to make me regret your shenanigans!"

"I had no idea mental linkage was so much fun," Daniel snickered, the full weight of intoxication striking him squarely again, and he burst out laughing. Charlie grinned widely, amused at a side of Daniel he had never seen before. "I honestly think there's only one solution."

"And what would that be?"

"Drink till you're as sloshed as I am," Daniel replied, sounding like a slurred pro explaining elementary basics to a raw trainee.

"In the hopes that you might get my hangover?" Charlie asked, and Daniel nodded happily. "Can't see why not, then."

"Christopher Bellman and James Arden, report to alcove." Daniel leaned closer to the tabletop in the alcove, peering at the ornate bronze numeral standing alone in the middle, "eight, and bring as much booze as you can find!" Charlie started, astonished by Daniel's booming voice, amplified no doubt by some or other minor use of his gifts. When he stared quizzically at his young charge, Daniel winked at him, and started clapping hands when Chris and a very much cheered-up Jamie arrived, each bearing at least three bottles in each hand.

"Good evening Mr. Avery, what's your poison for the evening?" Chris asked, peering down at Charlie from beside his nose like some souped-up, snotty butler.

"Whatever will get rid of Daniel's hangover," Charlie replied a bit snidely, ears still ringing from Daniel's uncalled-for shouting. Jamie guffawed again as he took a seat, but Chris, strangely enough, caught the gist of the joke.

"Wait, you guys even share hangovers?" He all but screamed his laughter for all to hear, much to Charlie's increasing discomfort. "What else do you share?" he asked suddenly, face deadpan.

"In a few more moments, our joint enmity at your delaying the celebrations further," Charlie grated between gritted teeth, and Chris, catching that one loud and clear, hid his placating behind a quick bow of his head and one hand raising some bottles.

"Alright then, guys and guys, drinks all around! We'll run this on Alice's tab." Even Charlie joined in the laughter at that particular crack, and the night picked up further to the revelry of close friends, associates and nearly unstoppable alcoholic rivers.

Luke surveyed the scene. He hadn't joined the impromptu party in the Mess Saloon the previous evening, although a part of him had wanted to. It had almost been too hard to pass up the opportunity to join Daniel in some well-remembered partying indulgences, to possibly reminisce on old times, and see if Danny-boy was still himself. But it had been too tempting to snuggle down with Alex, to enjoy the simplest gestures and to feel her slumbering body beside his. And he had seen the smile on her face as she had drifted off to sleep. He had been careful to shield his thoughts on wishful thinking to join the party, not wanting her to consider giving him the option of going there. He hadn't known if she would have been open to joining him, but something more overriding had told him that she wanted him to herself, without having to share him with anyone else and to possibly lose his close interest to catching up with Daniel.

Most of the debris had been cleared, and the tech teams were salvaging some larger pieces of the sled, but the thing was a write-off, as the scorch marks and the dark streaks stretched like drunken doughnuts for a long area before ramming into the wall indicated. He hadn't met the owners of the house where Chris had crashed the sled, but he wondered whether they were livid, or whether they had been part of the gaggle of people who had ridden on the overtaxed, overloaded craft. Needless to say, Chris was in Alice's office, Luke had been told by a gleeful Alex, getting a massive dress-down for consistently and recklessly endangering lives and also for demolishing a prized prototype sled, never been tested and now destined to never be.

"Who else was on the sled?" Luke asked, sounding both concerned but also buoyed up by Alex's infectiously mischievous mood. She stood next to him, snickering at odd moments as another stray thought of some kind, concerning the previous night's missed action, crossed her mind.

"Jamie," she said. "Bet Alice is cracking his balls real badly for his part. There's a tree back there that's sheared in two, and it wears his bio-blast signature like a neon sign."

"Really?" Luke asked, shocked and amused. Alex nodded vigorously.

"And from the looks of it, he was too drunk for words! Jamie! Never thought I'd see the day! And Daniel, of course. And three other guys." Luke stared at Alex.

"Daniel?"

"Yeah. Don't sound so fond, I wondered last night if you had wanted to join the party," Alex said. Luke waited for a moment, and then shook his head, knowing she was watching him out of the corner of her eye.

"I was with you, and you didn't ask, so I left it at that." Alex turned her head, her own eyes carefully scrutinizing, and she seemed to nod almost imperceptibly, then shrugged.

"You might have been on the sled too, and I think one of the others got hurt. Not too badly, but enough for Alice to really reel the culprits in this time. Wonder what she'll do to Danny. Bet he'll get off easy, since he's new to the ranks, and he's her poster-boy." Luke refrained from saying anything to Alex, not knowing whether she knew he might take offense at something like that, or whether she knew Daniel's actual history with the Hirsch family. He let the topic slide, rejoining Alex's tranquil observation of the cleanup. "How did they all get off before the thing crashed?" he asked at length.

"One of the other Changed on sled's a low-level teleporter, got them clear. Danny took care of Chris, by all accounts, though how he could teleport straight or even at all is kinda mysterious. I mean, the low-level guy barely managed – I asked him, and he was real sheepish about the details – and Daniel was so drunk that Charlie went to bed early with a pre-binge hangover! The one guy who wasn't so lucky got hit on the arm by a piece of flying shrapnel."

"I bet Charlie isn't happy."

"Wouldn't know," Alex replied wistfully. Luke smiled. He knew by now that she hated not knowing choice morsels on everyone, and that it would irk her to her dying day that people like Charlie, Daniel and Alice had mental barriers and blocking techniques that defied her most potent inquiries, both innocuous and mental. "Anyway, I've got to go. Margaret wants to talk to me, dunno about what, but it should be interesting." She turned to leave the scene, and Luke accosted her before she departed.

"Kinda weird," he mused. "Two months ago you would have been spitting, just thinking about her."

"She's not that bad," Alex said, and she seemed embarrassed. Luke smiled and reached out to squeeze her shoulder. She placed a hand on his and squeezed back, leaving him with a mysterious smile of acknowledgement, before leaving. Luke remained, watching the techs remove the last piece of equipment, the marks on the wall removed. He sighed, narrowed his eyes and lifted his mind free, letting his attention focus into a broad general scan of Headquarters, trying to pinpoint his brother's location. He wondered if Nathan knew of Daniel's escapades of the previous evening, and what his reaction was. He found Nathan's presence in one of the rec rooms near the Saloon, watching the vid screens. Joanie was in their room.

He decided to join his brother. Today, he felt, was as good as any day to press Nathan for details on why he was so close-mouthed whenever Daniel was mentioned.

He stopped when he was at the Saloon entrance, and marvelled at the lack of anything remarking on the party of the night before. He hadn't been there, but he knew what a raucous party was all about, and a place rarely looked so clean after one. Still, he supposed it was fitting, since the Saloon serviced the Changed throughout the daytime, and it wouldn't do to close the place for too long. He moved past and joined Nathan in the rec room.

"Morning," he said. Nathan greeted him with a wan smile and nodded, and Luke took a seat on the long couch beside his brother. They regarded the screens for a while, and then Luke thought on how to broach the subject. He never read his brother's mind, simply out of courtesy, and because in an almost childish way it seemed disgusting to do so, even though Nathan had no mental barrier to speak of. "What's new?"

"Nothing," Nathan replied absently.

"Thought you might have joined the party last night," Luke said, aiming for the dark and hoping for better.

"Nah. Me and Joanie just chilled."

"It's not like you to miss out on a bash that successful," Luke continued, forcing himself to sound jovial.

"I just didn't want to go, that's all," Nathan explained, not looking at his brother. "You weren't there either." Luke sighed, tipped back his head and prepared for the worst.

"I was with Alex, and she didn't really want me to go. Didn't say as much, but I assumed as much." Nathan remained silent. "Bet there's another reason you didn't go, and I bet Joanie wouldn't have minded."

"You bet all that, huh?" Nathan asked.

"Is it because of Danny?"

"What if it is?" Nathan retaliated, immediately on the defensive.

"What happened, at Charlie's place up north? Alex managed to get a few details, but no one else is talking, not even Joanie. She looks uncomfortable, and it isn't because she doesn't want to talk about it. You told her not to tell me, didn't you?"

"What if I did?"

"You owe me the details!" Luke snapped, leaning forward and turning to Nathan, who regarded him with icy disdain. He hadn't risen yet, which was a good thing: Nathan usually left when faced with a confrontation he didn't feel comfortable with. "Dammit! He's our adopted brother, and you talk about him like he did something unforgivable!"

"He did," Nathan said softly. He did rise then, and without excusing himself he made as if to leave. Luke snarled, and the doors flew shut, locking Nathan and himself in the rec room. Nathan's eyes hardened further, belligerently fiery. "Open the doors."

"No," Luke said simply. He was unprepared for Nathan's retaliatory action, which saw him lifted off his feet and held upright, Nathan's hands fastened on his shirt lapels, face close to his own.

"Open the damn doors!" he insisted. Luke, hating the situation, but also knowing that he would be nowhere near fast enough to counter his brother's speed, agility or strength, did the only thing he could think of, short of telekinetically immobilizing Nathan. He extended his awareness and formed the shield bubble, forcibly disengaging Nathan's grip on his shirt and shoving him backwards. Encased in the shimmering indigo field, Luke regarded Nathan.

"Are you gonna break down the doors?" he asked quietly. Nathan watched his older brother, a look akin to a cornered animal's on his face. "Alice will like that."

"I don't want to talk about it!" Nathan fired back angrily, his hands clenching and unclenching. "Why don't you just read my mind?" he ended nastily.

"You know I won't do that," Luke replied, a little mortified at the challenge.

"Well Danny-boy didn't hold to your precious self-control!" Nathan spat. "The first thing he does is rape my mind, and I was stupid enough to fall for the whole 'wounded' routine!" Luke winced. Alex had spoken of such things, when she had played instructor at Maggie's mansion. Empaths called it violation, the forceful entry into another person's mind. It was an uncalled for act of invasion. He had never been subjected to something like it, but the thought of someone unasked-for rifling through his head twisted his mouth with disgust. Nathan nodded as though he was following Luke's train of thought. "Yeah, little Danny-boy did that."

"Why would he?"

"To fix his own head!" Nathan riled. He was so upset he began pacing. Luke felt awkward, with the doors sealed and locked by his mind, and the near-impervious field dividing him from anything Nathan might do. He told himself it was precautionary, but he knew his brother: Nathan wouldn't shy away from finding an opening and making a quick exit, if he thought it would extricate him from an unwanted predicament.

"I don't understand," Luke began, and Nathan rolled his eyes.

"He and Charlie are in cahoots, all the way. Danny was supposedly dying from some or other mental blockage, and the only way he could have been saved was to heal the memories of his past. Only me or you could have done it, but since you were off gallivanting after Alex's skirts, it fell to me!"

"Hey!" Luke protested, but Nathan overrode him.

"The next thing, Danny politely but completely fucks up Charlie's supposed superior control and tells me that whether I like it or not, what I know of his past with us is now his."

"And why is that so bad?" Luke asked.

"Because of the way he did it!" Nathan hacked furiously, as if he were explaining himself to a ten-year-old. "Because he felt no qualms whatsoever about invading my head and taking what he needed, without asking!"

"But you allowed him," Luke interjected.

379

"Yeah, and I get violated for the trust I show! Let Danny-boy rot here with his new pals for all I care, me and Joanie are leaving in the morning." Nathan seemed to subside a little, and he sat down, running his hand over his head. He rose again suddenly, face eerily schooled in calm, save for the eyes, which still seemed ready to explode. "Now you know. Please open the damn doors, and drop your shield, I won't hurt you." Luke watched his brother for a long moment, before the shield winked out, and the door opened.

"Thank you," Nathan added snidely and stormed past. Luke sat down, wondering about what he had heard.

By the time Nathan was long gone, he still sat in the rec room, oblivious to the screens and their visuals.

Danny was, apart from the technicalities of adoption, Nathan's closest friend. For him to have hurt Nathan so badly, for Nathan to have reacted so viciously towards the mere mention of Danny's name, implied a very intensive and personal invasion of Nate's mental privacy, to such a degree that uncompromising love and understanding was thrown clear and replaced by anger and even hatred. It appalled Luke. He shook his head, and did the only thing he realized would shed more light on the situation. And he didn't like it one bit, in light of what he now knew.

"Where are you?" he sent his mind as far-ranging as he could, hoping he was successful. A few moments later, he got his reply.

"Inlet near the north shore of the lakeside, twenty minutes," Daniel's mental reply returned.

Luke wasn't the first to arrive at the inlet.

Amidst the stretch of dark grey granite that lined the shore of the lakeside, and the few stray, stark trunks of the dead or dying trees, Daniel almost blended in with his surroundings. He wore unrelieved black clothes, making him austere-looking and forbidding. Not having had a decent interval to reacquaint himself with his adopted brother, Luke took in the sight of him. Daniel was indeed greatly changed, taking physical appearances into account.

His face, once unassuming, if passably attractive, now held handsome curvature and remarkable angles, sharpened into something more than the amiable curves of before. The green eyes danced with an unfathomable light, a spark beyond the prior intellect that was always a trademark glimmer of the highly skilled and mature young man. The dark hair, always curly and short-cropped before, now hung long beside the face, straight and shimmering like jet stone. The light breeze that swept in from the water tugged at the bangs.

Luke felt a spark of trepidation, seeing Daniel again. The brief stint in New York, exchanging a few words only, and the return trip back to Headquarters – in which no words and almost no cursory glances were exchanged – had been inadequate for the long-overdue reunion, and beside the apprehension Luke also felt the giddy surge of anticipation. Daniel didn't look at him approach, but Luke knew beyond a doubt that Daniel knew he was there. No empath that powerful could miss any arrival in close proximity. Luke drew level with Daniel, standing by his side, staring out over the expanse of grey-blue water, and they remained in unspoken oblivion for a long time, listening to the movement of the water and the light sound of the leaves moving in the wind. When Luke could no longer contain his mounting exuberance, he turned to Daniel.

"How've you been?" he asked. A million other queries vied for supremacy, but he started with the easiest one.

"I've been better," Daniel replied, voice the well-remembered mellow deeps belying his usually spare, rawboned frame. A small smile quirked the edges of his mouth. "Between Charlie's hangover and Alice's contained but eloquently obvious reprimands this morning, I suppose it could have been better. Still, all things considered." Daniel did turn to Luke then. "And you? How's romance treating you?" Luke chuckled, flooded with relief.

"Alex is, well, Alex. You'd know better than I would."

"I'm not caught in a relationship with her," Daniel added. "I always thought she was an annoying and nosy woman myself, but I suppose to each his own. Congratulations, by the way. I wish you the best."

"Thanks. And congratulations to you too," Luke said. "Full GOA membership. I guess I'll join the ranks soon as well." Despite the relief at finally speaking to Daniel, and not being hurried by other factors or divided by other demands, Luke felt an upwelling of dark discomfort. Daniel was aloof, even distant, and he had thought at least that his adopted brother would share his sentiments of long-time-no-see and show it.

Alex had filled him in on minor details regarding Daniel, like the bond with Charlie, what kind of person he was according to her – the image rarely matched with the one Luke remembered – and how gifted Daniel was. Alex had called Daniel a warm and affectionate kid, which Luke had doubted, if only because Daniel's backdrop history before joining the Hirsch family had been one of changeable homes and intermittent bastions of trust which were severed whenever he was foisted off on another foster home. The after effects of isolation and inherent distrust to people showing him any signs of affection had lingered well into the latter half of Daniel's senior years in school, broken only by the constant and vigilant attention that Luke, Nathan and their parents had lavished, without stinting or remission, on Daniel. Luke had factored in the fact that Alex was by her very nature more forgiving and positive about other people's attributes, but even her description of Daniel had seemed way off the mark. Daniel, always focused even when he was having a good time, had never struck Luke as exceptionally warm, even though he knew Daniel had every capacity to love and express himself emotionally that he or Nathan did: he just showed it differently. But warm and affectionate had never really featured much. Luke was both elated and a bit upset that Alex's story hadn't carried through: Daniel was more detached and controlled now than ever, even with his eldest adoptive brother, whom he hadn't really seen in more than a year. Luke thought back on that evening where Daniel had appeared like a Godsend and had rescued him, Alex and

Margaret from a certain doom at the hands of the vicious telekinetic woman who had nearly killed Luke. The look in Daniel's eyes then had been one of absolute recognition and tremulous joy, even tears. Now, there was nothing of the kind. It puzzled Luke. He sighed – he did that a lot today – and ventured something he had never tried before, both because Daniel had never been empathic, and because he could never let the unchanged Daniel of before know the full extent of his own telepathic gifts: he opened his mind, letting the surface thoughts and feelings surge forward, contained just enough so that Daniel could sense them. A quick turn of Daniel's head in his direction alerted him to recognition of the gesture. With skilled precision he felt the lightest mental touch swim forward through the imprecise domain of empathic awareness, as Daniel joined him in the mental dance.

"What happened between you and Nathan?" Luke sent, no holds barred with the intimacy of collected thought sharing. He didn't feel the need to glaze or ameliorate his intentions or non-vocally actuated thoughts on the subject, and his feelings on the matter paired the query, letting Daniel know that it was uppermost in his thoughts. The reply sensation of resignation alerted him to Daniel's reluctance, but the reply came in, upholding the conversation.

"I screwed up, Luke. I screwed up bad, but Nate won't let me have a single chance to explain myself, or apologize. And I have no idea what I could possibly do to make up for it." With the thought transmission came every ounce of regret and remorse that hid beneath Daniel's unbreakable outward demeanour, the upwelling of emotive darkness and despair that accompanied an uneasy and unwanted impasse between close, supposedly unbreakable friendships. *"I've heard that he and Joanie intend to leave tomorrow, as soon as he's thanked everyone and let Alice know."*

"Joanie doesn't want to leave," Luke confirmed. *"But she won't go against Nathan's express wishes, even if she disagrees strongly."* Luke couldn't delay the bitter mental chuckle that

followed. *"They should marry and finalize the contact, they're already at it like a married couple."*

"I can't do anything, Luke," Daniel continued. *"Any use of power would only drive him further away, so I can't just teleport into his presence, or send him a mental query. He would only leave, and the idea that I had resorted to such tactics would alienate him further."*

"Tell me what happened," Luke asked again, the implication and the demand for the actual details of the nettlesome event clearer. Daniel sighed, both physically and mentally, and a tightly contained and strained stream of the event unfolded as a sequence of painfully etched images of that day. With it came a barrage of imagery that explained Daniel's predicament before the restored memories, of the kind of life he had led in the year Charlie had trained him and coaxed him from his catatonic state. Luke gasped, seeing Daniel as he saw himself, and as Charlie and the others had seen him. Alex's story had been true: Daniel had been a warm and strangely friendly guy, operating without full memory of who he was or had been. With this basis in mind, the desire became awakened in Daniel to restore himself, to be the person he had always been instead of a hollowed-out, history-less individual. Charlie had a hand in that, both positively and negatively, when Luke, Nathan and Joanie had been brought in, hiding his own agenda – the full scope which was hidden even from Daniel – yet steering the course Daniel had taken. Luke watched as Daniel poured out his fractured soul to Nathan, on the Pacific shore of the Vancouver Island haven where Charlie lived, and as Nathan warmed to him, agreeing to the transaction of mental images. Luke started as the mental play of visuals darkened around the corners of consciousness, no doubt as a result of the pain Daniel experienced even now with sharing the images. From his end, Luke sent an uncompromising stream of reassurance, mediating a bond of trust. Daniel responded, whether out of recalled affirmation or simply out of sheer frustration and release. Luke pressed on, letting Daniel's

retelling reflect against the mirror of his internal template. He saw the rounded room, with Daniel seated in front of Nathan, their hands held against each other's. Joanie and Jamie were seated beside and behind Nathan, with Charlie doing the same for Daniel. Regulating the flow of empathic conduction, Daniel sent briefly, piercing the veil of images. Luke couldn't account for the stilled poses of all five, except for Daniel's and Nathan's spoken communication, and shreds of the mental communiqué Daniel had initiated with Nathan, who had no way of melding and sending his own thoughts in such way.

Luke watched and listened, and was suddenly immersed in Daniel's thought stream of that very moment, as he navigated the lines of memories presented him by Nathan, and to a lesser extent, by Joanie, who had by express invitation joined her own recollections to the equation. Luke watched as Daniel's methods increased and rose to a dramatically potent force of inquiry, scouring Nathan and Joanie's thoughts clean of every iota of restorative recollection. He felt Daniel's mind lock the patterns within the fractured shells of his own memories of the shown events, but then he felt the sudden, uncalled-for thrust of demand, as Daniel grew impatient with the pent-up frustration at having the process so laboriously executed. Nathan protested, mentally and outwardly, as Daniel lapsed into a silence both mental and vocal, his presence the only indication that he was still rifling through Nathan's memories. Nathan protested the sudden injunction into his private thoughts, and broke the physical contact. In the mental transmission he read from Daniel, Luke noted how time seemed to stretch, how the entire episodic visual blurred and smeared. Luke reeled back with recognition: Nathan had unwittingly engaged his gift of speed, seeking any means to disengage from the transaction gone wrong, and contrary to the success he had expected, Daniel had compensated, retaliating faster than even Nathan could react! He watched the scene unfold, darkened by exterior streaks of jagged black and purple – Daniel's mounting pain and anguish at replaying the event – as Daniel forcibly quelled Nathan's bid for freedom and release, binding him with horrific speed and mental precision into an unbreakable grip, as he siphoned further into Nathan's ravaged mind, demanding more and greater effects from the memories. As Nathan's eyes closed, and he and Joanie joined in a simultaneously rising scream of pain, Daniel's eyes flared so vividly and extensively blue as Luke had never seen in any Changed, a blinding flash of almost blue-white energy radiating from the nearly feral insistency that broadcast itself in full terror from Daniel's unremitting, unrelenting gaze. Charlie, behind Daniel, had closed his eyes, dripping sweat, mouth forming words but not uttering them, as he no doubt tried to compensate for the uncontrollably massive drive that Daniel executed. At some point, Luke was almost certain he saw something inexplicable. For a single instant, the vantage point of the relayed vision jumped, not to Charlie, or Nathan and Joanie, not even Jamie: there was no explanation, but Luke was sure there was someone else entrapped within the scene, an unknown observer. And from that vantage point, he heard Daniel's mental voice, speaking with a devastating clarity, echoing like a bell inside Nathan's head: *You'll find out eventually. I'm surprised, it caught me off guard completely. But it won't keep me from what we've agreed on.* And then the final clarion call that broke Nathan's resistance, and no doubt ensured the scarring of violation, of Nathan attempting a denial of Daniel's unstoppable demand. And Daniel's reply: *Not a problem.*

The mental transaction ended, and Luke reared back, physically unbalanced, breath coming in rattling judders. He shook his head, trying to clear the doubled vision that played havoc with his sight. When the feeling passed, he was surprised to see Daniel standing close by, a steadying hand on his shoulder, eyes filled with concern and unveiled remorse. And something which Luke had only in the rarest of instances ever beheld in Daniel's eyes: tears.

"I still can't explain what happened, why I did it," he said, voice shaky with emotion. "Luke, I lost control back there."

"It didn't look like it," Luke said, not unkindly. "All I saw was incomprehensible drive, and a kind of focus I can only dream of in my wildest fantasies." Luke breathed deeply, feeling the welcome sensations of returning control. He leaned back a little. "But I believe you. Somehow, for some reason, I do." The relief in Daniel's face was unparalleled. "Do you remember what you meant when you told Nathan about whatever secret he held onto?" Daniel shook his head.

"I should be able to remember it. There's nothing impairing my gifts anymore, my memories were restored by that invasive experience, but I can for the life of me not recall any reason why I would say something like that to Nathan. And I can't recreate the enactment of my gifts on such a level. I've tried."

Luke regarded Daniel. He felt mixed feelings of anger and commiseration: anger at Daniel, for the first time, at comprehending fully why Nathan was no longer amenable at all to Daniel, and why he wouldn't go near him, but commiseration, because he had felt, beyond a shadow of doubt, Daniel's strange rush of indescribable power, a power and skill beyond even his prodigious abilities. There was a mystery here that boggled his mind, and Daniel had no way of recalling anything beyond the depths of his mental awareness up to that point. The idea that something deeper, something hidden in the depths of unconscious recesses, could yet come into play with Daniel, terrified Luke, all of a sudden, but he clamped down on the thought. It didn't work. Daniel drew back his hand, a frown clouding his expression.

"You're afraid of me?" Luke snarled angrily at himself, drawing himself up to his full height, which made him a head taller than Daniel.

"Wouldn't you be?" he challenged, knowing anything less than being truthful would hurt Daniel. "Danny, you have more power and ability than ten of me could handle! Easily! And I have all the mental ability that goes with comprehending such capacity! I know how strong you are, and what you are capable of!"

"I never asked for it," Daniel breathed.

"But you can't shy away from it," Luke added immediately after. He took a step closer to Daniel, forcing him to look up at him. "This is what you are, and everyone will just have to make peace with it."

"Make peace, but not accept," Daniel said, a hint of anger rising to the fore. Luke shook his head vigorously, feeling the familiar brotherly urge of helpfulness and reassurances come into play within himself.

"Bull! You had no control over what you did, that much is clear. I think you should talk to Alice, have her and Charlie do some sort of deep scan into your head, if you're willing. I'll talk to Nathan – it should go easier, now that I saw what happened. Please Danny, trust me on this! I'll do anything to fix this!" For a moment more Daniel simply watched his older brother, then he bound forward and enfolded him, hugging him close.

"Thank you," was all he said, and Luke followed his example, strangely but incontrovertibly reunited on a familiar level with Daniel. He savoured the moment, wistfully wondering what their parents would say, when he spoke to them about Daniel. Never truly unaware of his brother's thoughts, Daniel looked up, determined amidst the welled tears in his eyes. "I'll come with you when you go to them. After your initiation, I think." Luke nodded simply, sealing the deal.

CHAPTER TWENTY THREE

Trigger

Luke ran for the hovepad.

The boomer was already prepped for liftoff, only waiting for its passengers to board. Luke forced himself to go a little faster, as he saw Joanie, Nathan and several other people prepare to board. He drew level with the boomer docking ramp just as Joanie hefted her bag. Luke dodged the other people, zipped in beside Nathan and took hold of his arm, forcibly dragging him away from the craft.

"Hey!" Nathan protested angrily, and Luke, also angry, jerked him away and shoved him backwards, where Nathan trotted unceremoniously to maintain balance, holding both his and Joanie's bags in hand.

"Very nice Nate, very nice!" Luke snapped furiously. "Not even a goodbye for your brother?"

"Which one?" Nathan retorted nastily. Luke reached over and pushed him against the shoulder.

"Helluva juvenile way to act for a grown man! What's next, name-calling? Are you going to try and manhandle me into submission, to force me to let go of you?" Luke challenged belligerently. He vaguely noticed Joanie arrive, concern and upset clear on her features. "Maybe I understand now why you hold such a grudge against Danny, but me? Figured on going home and lying to mom and dad? 'Luke's fine, he'll call in a couple of days!' Coward!"

It was too much for Nathan. Enraged, he dropped both bags and dived for Luke's midriff, catching him off guard and forcefully expelling the breath from his body, as they both went down in a sordid tumble, both of them trying hard to get on top. Nathan drew back one hand and slammed it across Luke's face, fury contorting his features. Joanie yelled for them to stop, and the people near the boomer stood by, astonished at the scene. Luke, head spinning and vision swimming from the blow, tried to get a grip, but another blow rocked him, as Nathan swung the other hand. He had secured his position on top of Luke, and was preparing for a massive salvo of blows. Luke sensed rather than realized that Nathan, enraged as he was, would resort to using strength. He could easily break Luke's face apart, and his rage brooked no mercy.

Stunned by the implication, Luke had a moment more to think on retaliation before Nathan's third blow landed, causing black flecks to dance across Luke's vision. Similarly enraged now, he forced himself to distance, focusing his energies. With ferocity born of necessity, he slammed a telekinetic blow into Nathan's chest, sending his younger brother flying off him, to land hard on his side, crying out in pain.

Luke was on his feet instantly, ignoring Joanie's plaintive cries for them to stop. Before Nathan could recoil – he was already rising despite the pain on his face, and a light flare in his eyes hinted at trouble to come – Luke, still striding purposefully towards him, lifted one hand, and Nathan was raised off the ground, to hang immobilized above the ground. The flare died, and the impotent wrath burned normally, as he treated Luke to a fully venomous glare.

"I get it now," Luke said, driven not only by need but now also by the fact that he held his brother in check. His own anger and sarcasm rose like bile, as he pressed onward. "You took a dive, your trust was broken, and all of a sudden Danny no longer features as part of the family. What did you tell yourself to make yourself feel better? That Danny's adopted? Not blood?"

"Luke, stop!" Joanie yelled, in tears, all but dancing in one place.

"You have no idea what he did to me!" Nathan yelled, body quivering with the useless effort to break free from Luke's telekinetic grip. It didn't waver, and neither did Luke's conviction.

"I do!" Luke yelled back. "He showed me, and you can't lie to an empath! Not even Danny can do that!"

"Why should I trust anything you say?" Nathan challenged, face contorted, tears of anger and frustration trailing down his cheeks. "You're all the same!" Joanie was silent suddenly, and her mortification drew Luke up short. Then it only fuelled him on the more.

"So that's it?'We're all out to get you', is that what you've made it? Nate, for God's sake, we're family! Danny had no control over what he did to you!"

"Lies!" Nathan snapped vehemently.

"You won't even let him apologize! If you never want to see him again, that's fine, but don't let it fester!" Luke pleaded, seeing that Nathan would not see reason. "Talk to him before you go!"

"No!" Nathan retorted, and his face crumpled fully under grief and nullified rage. Hanging immobile, arms and legs held rigid beside his body, he was a picture of apathy and loss to move any heart. Luke, astonished suddenly by his own anger, and what he was doing to Nathan, loosed the grip, and Nathan tumbled to the ground. He lay as he fell, not getting up, crying in the dust of the hovepad platform. Luke spared a momentary glance over his shoulder. Joanie, face still white from the shock of what Nathan had said, nevertheless rushed to his side. He didn't repudiate her presence, and endured her light touch of sympathy, even though he didn't acknowledge it. Luke drew a little closer, not daring to show the same sentiment for fear of reigniting Nathan's fury. Instead he held back, noting the people boarding the boomer. It would take off soon.

"What does he have to do to make up for it?" he asked quietly. Nathan gave no reply, venting his upset in tears. "Was it really that bad? Bad enough to make you want to forget everything that all of us have shared in the last nine years?"

"Luke please," Joanie begged, face hazed by tears. She wanted the fiasco to end, and badly, but she also wanted a moment's peace, for everyone. Luke hardened his heart, knowing that if he let up now, he would possibly lose any chance in the near future of healing the rift between Nathan and Daniel. He finally moved in close, and hunkered down beside Joanie and his brother. With a sigh he folded his hands on his knees.

"What will you do if you go back now?" he asked kindly, softly. "What will you tell mom and dad about me and Danny? You can't lie, and the truth will out eventually. Nate, you can't just up and go!"

"Why is everyone taking his side?" Nathan whispered amidst his tears. "He's the strongest damn Changed in history, and everyone treats him like an eggshell! 'It's okay Danny-boy; we forgive you for violating the closest people you have to absolute family!'"

"Nathan," Joanie began, but he overrode her.

"I didn't ask everyone to pity me!" he snapped. "But he gets away with it, and all everyone else can think of is how to heal the rift, how to fix the gap! I am sick and tired of it! I don't want to see him, and I don't want to talk with him." Luke sighed, defeated. That particular tone of voice was the be-all and end-all of it, he realized. Nathan was stubborn, unstoppably so, and his intransigence showed, both in his posture even as he was lying down, and in Joanie's stricken features. She didn't say a word as they helped Nathan up, cleaned up his face and retook charge of the luggage. Luke didn't say a word as he escorted them to the boomer, and he remained standing some distance from the craft as it lifted off. He looked up, at the window where Nathan and Joanie had taken their seats. From the oval curve, he saw Nathan's profile, an unresponsive mien turned away from anyone looking.

"I didn't intervene. I'm sorry." Luke closed his eyes, feeling dejected as he felt the inrush of air. Daniel stood next to him, looking up, an unreadable expression on his face as he regarded the boomer slowly lifting into the air.

"It might have gone worse if you had," Luke said, feeling the leaden impact of his words. He didn't open his eyes to see what their effect would have on Daniel.

"He won't speak to me for a long time, that much is certain," Daniel said, voice laced with the anguish he felt. He sighed. "I guess I owe him that." Luke opened his eyes and turned to Daniel, placing a reassuring hand on his shoulder.

"For what it's worth, I'm not angry at you. I won't turn my back on you." Daniel deflated somewhat, giving in. He nodded once, curtly, then forced himself to smile.

"Guess it's just you and me then. A small fragment of an unhappy family." The words were heart - wrenching, and Luke felt himself knot up inside. Daniel shook his head. "I'm due to report to Alice's office in an hour. Wanna get a bite before then? She did say you were welcome to join us."

"Join you for what?" Luke asked, head ablaze with countless thoughts on endless things. Daniel smiled wanly.

"My deep scan. Maybe once we're through, we'll all know just what happened that day." Luke nodded. He prayed for the best clarity and certainty. If they knew what had gone wrong, he could eventually begin working on Nathan again, explain to him the finer details, and hopefully salvage the broken bonds of their family.

The interior of the room was flooded with light. In the centre of the floor, the stone ring waited, showing no sign of activity at all, the myriad signatures and symbols silent and lifeless, showing nothing. In the excess of light, it looked almost harmless, simply another artefact of a bygone time, brought to the scrutiny of the ones that had uncovered it. Resting in the chamber, it assumed a pose of eerie disturbance, of ancient mystery unfettered by modern means, but by no means fully explored and deemed safe for use. This did not bother Graven at all, standing next to the ring, looking down at it. He had a pensive expression on his face, one hand rubbing his lower lip as he thought matters over. The testing had proven inconclusive, concerning the actual workings of the device, but the recent foray into Eric's mind had yielded some interesting insights, though even Graven couldn't completely smash aside the mental barrier that Eric had in place, not without killing him, and then there would be no bait. He smiled suddenly, at the thought of what would happen tonight. Sometimes the empirical methodologies failed, and trial and chance were the only recourses left. He hated resorting to hasty measures, preferring careful planning and certitude to rash blundering forward and reaping the possible but by no means certain benefits that accompanied such strokes of fortune. Idly, he scanned the people present.

He had brought them here from across the world, the eight other – known – most powerful Changed. Over the centuries he had played them off against each other, matching strengths with weaknesses, fears with arrogance, until all of them served him but would be at each others' throats, given a chance. Closest to him, acting all sultry as though he had forgotten her past transgressions, Persephone waited, staring at nothing in particular, those dead brown eyes of hers radiating the power she had. She had her uses, or at least, if all went as planned, she would again soon enough. Graven did not return her smile.

Persephone had conveniently taken up position opposite her most hated adversary, Henreik Kessler. Strange, considering Kessler feared her mightily, vulnerable as he was to her gifts. Graven shook his head, looking at the placid, devastatingly obvious cruelty in the man's face, even though Kessler never seemed to show facial expressions, save for a devious smile or a condescending sneer. Though Graven detested the man, he was far more useful than most. Kessler's feral lust after blood could be tampered by a cold-hearted meticulousness when it came to torture and maiming, and if needs be, tonight would secure the necessity for the man being present. Other than that, for the purposes of harnessing the power of the ring, Kessler would play bystander.

Graven looked at Amorphia, who considered – she would never admit it outright, but it was obvious – Kessler as her primary antagonist, and most certainly her nemesis. True, Graven mused, since her unique physiology and aptitudes failed utterly in the face of the man's indomitable regenerative power, and her more offensive gifts would hardly make Kessler blink. Her eyes darted about furtively, seeking any point of conflict or possible attack. Opposite her stood Alessandro, Catherine's young protégé. Of the assembled, the hot-blooded Italian man was the youngest, at a mere century of age. A boy, compared to the others, who had survived the trammels of time's passage across centuries. Graven mentally calculated the odds of someone like Alessandro surviving Amorphia's assaults, and came up with a favourable outcome. For Amorphia. He chuckled, and no one asked him why, even though Alessandro squirmed uncomfortably under Graven's close but passing scrutiny. His eyes roved to beside the Italian Changed.

Catherine. Graven couldn't help but smile as he thought on the woman he considered his equal in almost all things. He also considered her his age-old paramour, but she would never give in to his way of doing things. Her wintry gaze encompassed all about her, and by saying nothing at all she denigrated all. Her gifts would also be of great use tonight, in activating the ring, if such power as she had could in fact unlock – or aid in unlocking – the baffling artifact. Graven frowned momentarily, when he noted Catherine's eyes slip towards Enson. Yes, a woman of Catherine's intellect and might would frown on someone as belligerent, physically monstrous and supposedly stupid like Enson. At seven feet, the man was immense, and his massive musculature would make any man quail in fear. Enson was a cannon, to be aimed without precision but much damage at anything. He was a force of nature, a physical embodiment of everything feral and warrior-like the human race could conceive of, dressed in a tailored Armani suit, a fitting accoutrement to the <u>fact</u> that his sheer size also hid the <u>fact</u> that he had an impossibly powerful mental faculty for lasting tactile coercion. He too might become more useful soon.

That left the dark duo. Clarissa McFadden was a fiery Scotswoman, betraying her heritage with every fibre of her being: wild red hair, flaring green eyes and a pale complexion, with only the colour of her hair to give any indication that she could annihilate city blocks with the impact and destructive force of a nuclear weapon, were she given enough time to build up her might. And next to her, the man she often accompanied, though Graven hardly knew why. Amal – no other name had ever come from the man, and Graven deemed it beneath him to filch the exact origins from Amal's mind – was lithe, of average height and boyishly slim build. He appeared Arabic, with a woman's features and a slightly tan skin. Of all the Changed that Graven considered his weapons, Amal was the most devious, the most insidiously corruptive.

Why wouldn't he be, with a gift for shape-shifting that transcended mere morphogenic alteration: Amal could be anyone, and were he to touch, even for a moment, the skin of any of his victims – or of anyone in the room – he could self-imprint the very essence of existence of that person, effectively becoming the one he touched. But that would not be his task this evening. No, his use was determined by his other major gift, his ability to see into the past. Graven watched for a moment longer, as Amal continued some inane piece of conversation with Clarissa, possibly saying something amusing, because the woman laughed, a cruel sound born of arrogance and contempt.

"We will begin," Graven said suddenly, startling all. The assembled ceased whatever they were about and took up the positions Graven had previously outlined for them, studiously ignoring anyone else save for those who came within physical striking range, and speaking not a word. Clarissa and Catherine assumed places opposite each other, with the younger Scotswoman attempting to haughtily hold her own against Catherine's icy stare.

She failed – no one could radiate disdain and contempt like Catherine could.

Alessandro and Amal took up space beside each other, shoulder to shoulder, kneeling beside the ring, ready at Graven's command to place their hands on the device. Enson nodded and retreated from the room, to bring in the bait, whom he would then maintain in place, on the ring; Eric. Graven spared a glance for the strange Changed man he had captured more than a century ago. He would have done away with him long ago, had it not been for the information he held in his head. Eric was powerful in his own right – not a patch on the gifts of any of the assembled others, but nevertheless a nine-hundred-year-old witness to the passage of time.

The man looked miserably at Graven, who smiled toothily. "After tonight, mon amie, you may taste the release of death." Eric's eyes lit up with that fire of defiance that even after years of torture remained his in full, and he spat toward Graven. Enson, without making a sound, lifted a hand and casually – for him – landed a blow on the side of Eric's head, causing it to loll about. Graven bridled, concerned. "Careful! He must remain conscious for this to work!" Enson merely regarded Graven, then directed Eric to the edge of the ring, forcing him to his knees. Graven looked to Persephone and curtly inclined his head. She complied quickly enough, not deigning to smile, but the fawning in her step apparent. Satisfied, Graven stepped forward.

"There is only one chance for this to work, and it will require all of us – those of us capable – to work in complete unison, d'accord? I will start." He moved in closer, and before he stepped onto the ring itself he stepped over it, a scant inch above the surface. He walked to the centre, then indicated for Enson to bring Eric closer. The massive man, with his ward in tow, also stepped onto the platform, unperturbed by the repellent surges of vile nausea that seemed to affect everyone else who touched the ring. Eric, putting up a mild struggle, winced when Enson's grip on his arms tightened considerably. Enson deposited Eric in the centre of the ring, between the four protrusions. Eric grimaced as his bare hands and feet touched the ring, mouth already twisting with the uncomfortable sensations of growing nausea. In spite of himself Graven grinned, amused by the man's discomfort. "If you will not tell me how this thing works, I will force it out of you by demonstration, non?"

"I told you, I've never used it! I've never even seen it!" Eric protested, voice hoary and cracked from the solitude of disuse.

"Some of the blood on these protrusions is yours," Graven replied, and was surprised to note a genuine hint of puzzlement in the man's eyes. He shrugged. "No matter. Tonight will tell me exactly what this ring will do. All of you, begin!"

As one the Changed went to work. Amal and Alessandro simultaneously placed their hands on the ring, wincing with mixed urges of pain and revulsion. Their eyes flared blue, Alessandro plumbing and controlling the vicious intricacy of the elementary structure of the ring even as Amal fed him the past impressions he in turn received from the ring. For several moments they waited, and then Amal drew back with a gasp. He looked up, eyes finding Eric and narrowing. Eric, seeing the attention he got, winced, and Graven smiled. Kessler was a brutal torturer of the body and all things held sacred to the mind, an eventual breaker of the spirit, but Amal could get inside anyone's head, literally and figuratively, and Eric knew it: a century of torture had acquainted him with Amal's unique tastes and abilities.

"I will need to imprint him," he said, pointing at Eric.

"And why is that?" Graven asked critically, distrustful of Amal's intentions. In all the time Amal had had Eric under hands, he had never imprinted the man? Graven remained suspicious, but Amal merely smiled.

"I will know what he knows." Graven treated the boyish Changed to a long and hard stare, before nodding quickly.

"Make it quick," Graven replied, watching as Amal stood, walked across the ring and placed his hands on Eric's head. Eric gasped and struggled, but Amal was stronger than he looked, and it took a mere second for him to reel back, eyes momentarily vacant with the flood of new memories.

"Hurry up, this is becoming unbearable!" Alessandro snarled between gritted teeth. He was beginning to sweat, and turning pale as well. Amal ignored him, turning to Graven.

"Our friend is more powerful than we thought," Amal said. "He has used this device before, but had no memory of it. I think he wasn't in control of himself when he used it the last time. And I may also have an idea what the device is for."

"Hurry!" Alessandro repeated tightly. He was white as a sheet.

"Amorphia," Graven said calmly. The Oriental woman nodded, placed her hands on Alessandro's shoulders and closed her eyes. At once the area about herself and the Italian Changed darkened, as she assumed a non-corporeal form and shrouded him within, distancing him from the immediate effects of the pain. "Go on," Graven said to Amal.

"The ring is not a summoning device only, as you have suspected, although it is possible to use it as such. It is a substitution mechanism. From what I gathered out of Eric's experiences, it was used to… embody someone."

"Embody?"

"To create a physical shell for someone," Amal said. Graven's mouth opened, but he didn't speak. He looked at Eric, whose head was hanging, then back to Amal, and an eerie light of understanding filled his face. "This ring can shape matter, when directed by the correct level of conscious and unconscious control." Graven stared at Amal, equally stunned by the ramifications of such a thing happening. He smiled, the fullness of his schemes clicking into place within his mind.

"Your master was most clever when he created this device," Graven spoke without looking at Eric. "You called him Aidan, back then. Did he have other names?"

"He did not," Amal replied, ignoring the fast glare of irritation from Graven at his intercepting the question.

"If he did, Eric doesn't know them."

"No matter!" Graven snapped impatiently. "I will use this device for its intended purpose – my intended purpose tonight – only! And then your master and I can speak."

"You'll never...make it, against him," Eric said, softly. He looked up, eyes fixing on Graven's face, and he managed to crack a smile. "None of you can stand against him." Graven shook his head, long-suffering of fools clearly stamped on his harshly angled features.

"My foolish friend, who said anything about assailing him?" Graven challenged back, and snickered. He looked beyond the centre of the ring, first to one side, then the other. "Clarissa, Catherine."

The two women lifted their hands, placing them close to the ring. From Catherine, a concentrated glow of icy blue energy seeped, whereas Clarissa's contribution manifested as a ready streak of whipping flame, gradually going from orange to yellow, and then white, as the intensity grew. The ring symbols began to glow, tracing random sigils and connections between the delineated segments, as the device absorbed levels of elemental energy that would have easily fried and blasted everyone present to icy cinders. Graven nodded at Persephone, who joined him from beside the ring, her eyes flaring as her telekinesis aided Graven's own, lifting the ring off the ground slightly, before initiating a spin on the horizontal axis. Before him, Enson jumped back, off the device, leaving Eric alone, but the man was rooted to the spot, seemingly, and he retched, though nothing came up. Graven's laughter began building, as Catherine's eyes began to flare and her input began creating massive cold draughts, causing the others to flinch from the cold.

Clarissa followed suit, and the fiery back draft of her colossally focused energies whipped contrary to Catherine's, causing a general rush of conflicting heat and cold maelstrom eddies in the room. Amal retook his place beside Alessandro and Amorphia, revelling in the sensations his touching the ring now gave him, coupled as it was with his newly experienced memories from Eric. Enson went to stand beside Kessler, who watched the happenings with an unreadable expression, save for the inadvertent snagging that the winds caused.

In the centre of the ring, Eric began to scream.

Graven looked down, startled. Even he was unprepared for the whiplash tendrils snaking out of Eric's hands, his gift of manifesting physical kinetic energy weapons playing against him, seemingly, becoming thin filaments with razor edges that gashed open his wrists, which began spilling gouts of blood. The moment the blood struck the ring, all the symbols erupted into blazing colour and life, all but blinding the assembled, as the collective energy provided by Clarissa and Catherine, and the telekinetic spin Persephone had begun increased drastically, making Eric vanish in a blur of motion. Graven looked down, knowing what he had to do next. Calming his mind and aligning the very metaphysical forces that defined the universe about himself, he began spinning with the ring, slowly going faster, until he matched Eric's vicious rotation. He moved closer, improbably, against the pull of monstrous gravitic forces, his body buffered against them by his mind, which remained clear and precise in its intent. He listened to Eric's animal screaming of pain, as the blood flow began slowing but the ring began gaining in power, the pool of ichor between the four protrusions remaining astonishingly contained by some unknown force outside of the gravitic spin that would see it spattered against people and walls outside the ring's edge. Graven bent forward, ignoring the strain which even his mind, conditioned by the human response to external physical forces, could not fully bypass. He reached out with both hands and took hold of Eric's head, momentarily stopping the screaming.

"Let's see if your master is still at large in the world!" he yelled triumphantly, the words lost in the vortex spin of the ring and the cacophony of wind inside the room. Eric screamed again, and the world seemed to explode in glaring white light, as Graven's laughter seemed to fill the universe.

CHAPTER TWENTY FOUR

Alice's Office

Luke waited patiently as Daniel pleaded his case. He seemed ill at ease, for some reason, as though what he was asking Alice and Charlie – Charlie hadn't arrived yet, but if they could convince Alice of the necessity, then Charlie would hardly be able to deny the request – somehow upset him. As Daniel continued talking, Alice watched him with careful scrutiny. No doubt she was thinking partly of the hovesled fiasco two nights earlier, and Daniel's complicity therein, but Luke doubted she would shoot down Daniel's intentions simply because of some old-fashioned drunken fun.

"I will need a containment field, I suppose," Daniel remarked, thinking out loud after he had pitched his request to Alice. At that point, Charlie came running in, looking flustered and contrite for being late. He made his due apologies, and Daniel narrated the deal from the top again. Once that was done, he looked from Charlie to Alice; the two of whom were exchanging unreadable glances. Alice rose from behind her desk, slow and stately, weighing her options.

"You didn't mention this kind of sundered control, before. Any particular reason why not?" she asked Daniel, her eyes narrowing with scrutiny. He shrugged, unperturbed by her heavy attention.

"It didn't surface fully until I showed Luke what happened that day back home." His face clouded, as the thought of duality concerning actual homes struck him: with his memories restored, he hadn't been to the Vancouver retreat since he had been brought to GOA Headquarters, unresponsive, and the restored memories of the Hirsch house and his place there intruded. He cleared the thought, though, as his face reassumed its attentively focused cast. "I couldn't detect it on my own."

"Why would you need a containment field?" Charlie asked. Daniel sighed, preparing for more informing.

"I've been playing around with the idea for a short time only," he began, and Luke recognized the topic: when he and Daniel had eaten lunch in the Saloon before coming to Alice, Daniel had run the concept by him. "But I think that there's something else, up here, with me." He tapped the side of his head with one finger. "I know it sounds far-fetched, but it's the only logical explanation I can come up with."

"So you're saying that there's someone else in there with you?" Charlie asked, face caught in a frown. He was trying his best not to sound disparaging, and rallying magnificently in his efforts. Daniel nodded.

"Luke said he read a kind of focus, of my empathic gifts, that he thought didn't quite match my capacity. A directed intent beyond my abilities, as of this point in time."

"Though I don't doubt Luke's skilled assessment, I don't quite see how he can make such an assumption based on arguably limited experience," Alice said, sparing Luke a humourless smile. He felt like squirming under her irrefutable scrutiny, but he realized her remark was quite even-handed, and not meant to denigrate his own skill at empathy. "Granted, empaths deserve their moniker: empathy allows greater insight than simple intuition can give, so he may not be too far off." She looked at Charlie. "If this is the case, it must be sorted out now, before any more hiccups occur that might cause unforeseen complications." Charlie nodded, and left the office, Alice following after and indicated that Luke and Daniel follow suit.

They accessed an off-limits elevator and descended into the depths of Headquarters, the silent white lights and austere ambience lasting for several minutes as they made their way into the unknown expanse of GOA's subterranean expanse. When the elevator stopped they disembarked into an equally clean and sterile corridor, lined with running lights that banished any notion of gloom in the dark recesses of the earth. Alice took the lead, nodding politely at the employees marching past on their duties. She led them to a door that required an access entry, which baffled Luke, since there were no discernible keypad or identifier devices. Alice frowned slightly as if concentrating, and the door swung inward. She noted Luke's amazement, and chuckled wryly.

"We are nowhere near fathoming the full extent and range of telepathic transmissions, but we manage at times to harness what we know: brain frequency pattern identifiers are one of our best-kept secrets." She actually winked at him and pressed on. Luke allowed Charlie and Daniel to go in before him.

Inside was a narrow corridor, with consoles lining the one side. There were also several thick window screens facing into a darker expanse beyond. As Alice passed the consoles, they sprung alight, and the lights peaked to a higher intensity, revealing the view from the windows to be a massive domed chamber. Luke turned to Daniel, who nodded; he had been here before. "This way." Alice led them towards the door at the end of the consoled corridor, down a staircase and into the domed room. It was empty inside, until Alice activated a voice-recognition computer command system. With small, muted clicks the computerized systems inside the entire chamber began obeying her vocalized orders, and she commandeered a gurney, of all things. Luke was startled when the requested item rose from the seamless stretch of floor in the middle of the room. Alice turned to Daniel.

"The neuronull fields are active and at full strength. Daniel, lie down on the bed please. Luke, you may stand close by Charlie." Charlie stood next to Alice, and they waited for Daniel to lie down. Once done, the gurney tilted somewhat, leaving Daniel's head higher than the rest of his body. Alice assumed a position at the head of the gurney, holding her hands near Daniel's temples but not touching him. Luke's interest was piqued.

"Won't touch ease the thought transmission?" he asked. Again he got Alice's wintry smile, clouded by concentration on the task at hand.

"I am a long-lived telepath, Luke. With my kind of age comes a level of finesse, and experience. I can learn more from a person's thoughts without touching them physically, than I can when placing my hands on naked skin." She lapsed into silence then, and Luke deemed it wise not to interrupt anymore. He was surprised when Charlie placed a hand on Daniel's forearm, his eyes sparkling with a strange fondness which Luke found disturbing. His thoughts checked up short: to Daniel, Charlie was almost a brother, if not by blood then by goals and intentions. And deep affection. Luke realized the gesture irked him only because it was something he would have done, and seeing someone relatively unknown and unconnected by known familiarity or blood disturbed him somewhat, but he let it go. "You may lend some support, if you wish," Alice said to him. "Your experience of Daniel's allowed inspection of his thoughts of that day may prove insightful." Luke nodded, and placed his hands on Daniel's other arm. Daniel remained rigidly staring up at the receded dome overhead, not acknowledging either touch. Luke, feeling nothing come through his tactile contact, knew Daniel was shielding his thoughts.

Silence fell. Nothing happened, and Luke felt uncomfortable suddenly. He swallowed, and felt a feather-light mental touch reach for him. Alice's mellow, sultry voice reached him inside his mind. *Sense outwards with your mind, not your hands*, she advised, and Luke did so. Instantly he became aware of the deeper currents flowing within the room, juggled and balanced with astonishing equanimity and skill between Charlie, Alice and Daniel. Their thoughts flowed almost too fast for Luke to follow, but he was never one to shy from a challenge. He plunged into the transaction, catching glimpses of the visuals he had experienced the previous day when he had spoken with Daniel alone. Charlie's recollection also intervened, and Luke was treated to another perspective of the

406

events, feeling every sensation and emotive response that Charlie had felt and endured within that maelstrom of mental bereavement, orchestrated by Daniel and upheld by that unknown presence of mind that had seemingly enhanced Daniel's awareness beyond his abilities. Coupled with that, he sensed the fast-flowing observations that Charlie and Alice fired at each other.

There is a node of improbable synaptic overload in his mind at the time of the event, Alice said. Luke was astonished; the woman had managed to read deeper than simply the recollections: she had managed to re-enact and recapture Daniel's biological brain functions within the happenings! *I'm surprised we didn't detect the effects of scarring.*

His mind heals faster even than his body, Charlie added. Luke wondered at their observations. He had only heard of Daniel's vaunted empathic and spatial abilities, never that he also had, in fact, a regenerative faculty more vibrant than any average human. *What is the estimation of the healing rate?*

Exponential, as though something is covering its tracks. We must take into account that Daniel is in fact not a full GenneY.

Let's not jump to conclusions, Charlie's mental voice echoed, sounding almost defensive of Daniel. *How do you explain this level of focus? Coupled with the mercurial mood shifts?*

Common human emotional byplay. I think we can show it of hand. Alice's affirmation went mentally unvoiced, and they continued their inquiry.

If not that, then a Changed of unequivocal and unmitigated power. The latency factor is undocumented, unheard of, but it might account for the reverse of my former assumption: Daniel will in fact become even stronger than he is now. That remark stunned Luke. To think that Daniel would become even more powerful was mind-boggling. A mollified acceptance flowed from Charlie.

That leaves motive, Alice continued after a pause of silent further scrutiny. *Daniel would have no reason to voice a speculation of sundered control and still maintain that he didn't mean to invade Nathan's mind without preamble or lack of courtesy. Any alien intellect that may be harboured within his mind would account for such a disparity. But I cannot place where it might originate from.*

A siren sounded. It was an insistent beeping that shook everyone from their mental reverie. Alice was looking towards the upper level console room, face marred by a frown, her lips seemingly working soundlessly.

"The monitoring network is registering a dangerous rise in the integral structure of the neuronull field."

Both she and Charlie looked down at Daniel, who was seemingly staring at some point far beyond the dome above them. His eyes were focused, but didn't acknowledge any light shaking from Luke or Charlie.

"I can't read anything through the bond, except that he's here, with us." For a moment the statement sounded daft to Luke, before he recalled that the bond Daniel and Charlie shared allowed the one to pinpoint the other's location, even if they were miles removed from one another. The whining siren switched off, no doubt Alice's doing, but she seemed intently focused on narrating what the systems overhead were reading.

"It has to be Daniel. The field would hardly pick up either my own or your attempts to breach it," she said to Charlie. She looked down at her hands, still poised over Daniel's head. "I can't read anything coming from him." She looked up sharply, staring Luke in the eye. "See if you can't coerce anything from him." Luke, slightly disturbed by the idea of a forceful entry, no matter how benign the intent, swallowed again, shook his head and concentrated on receiving anything from his hand on Daniel's arm. After a few moments he gave up.

"It's like touching a stone wall," he admitted.

"I may need to break through," Alice said after Luke's pronouncement, and her hands touched Daniel's head. Instantly she recoiled, all but flung from her position next to the gurney. Charlie and Luke both gasped, as Daniel sat up. Various looks of shock and determination flitted across his face, in a disturbing parody of indeterminate emotions. He looked at Alice.

"Can't you hear it?" he asked softly, voice faltering between the betrayed fear of the unknown, and a dispassionate fascination. "Like a beacon. A white light, screaming across my senses, like watching two planes of reality." Mesmerized by the narration, the other three looked on. Daniel swung his legs over the side of the gurney, as if to stand on the ground and leave. "I have to go."

"Daniel, what do you see?" Charlie asked, in a voice that brooked no nonsense. Daniel looked at him, staring as though he was seeing Charlie for the first time.

"You can't see it because I've blocked the bond," he delivered in nonchalant tones of confirmation. "But maybe you'll understand now." On 'now' he reached out and touched Charlie's face. Charlie gasped, began to shudder and physically buckle, his eyes almost rolling back in his head as he struggled for air. Alice slammed Daniel's hand away, and Charlie fell backwards. Daniel, unmoved by the display, looked at Luke.

"I really have to go. It calls, like a siren song. I must go." Around them, a sound like an angered beehive began building up. Daniel's face betrayed a look of delight, as though he revelled in the sound. Alice, helping Charlie up, took a cautious step away from Daniel, and Luke unwittingly did the same. The whine achieved fever pitch, accompanied by Alice's wavering pronunciation that the neuronull field was at maximum containment, and would short out soon. Daniel, still looking up, was suddenly limned in soft myriad sparkles, like bent filaments of white light. His eyes suddenly flared, going from emerald green to glowing aquamarine in a flash. The whine became unbearably irritating to hear, and Daniel vanished to a soft inrush of air, filling the chamber with a slightly colder draft, filling the void where he had been. The whine died suddenly, leaving Luke, Charlie and Alice staring at the space where Daniel had been.

"The field is still active," Alice added, sounding inexplicably flustered. "He didn't short it; he shifted through the elevated frequencies."

"Meaning?" Luke hazarded, body flooded with adrenaline, and not caring for respecting proprieties.

"He began overloading the field, but he didn't need to break it: he simply slipped through the distortions created at high-yield wave transmission. Under that kind of stress, discrepancies become frequent but almost impossible to isolate and bypass." Alice's voice was filled with awe. "He's done it before, but never with such finesse." Her moment of contemplation lasted only a second, and then she was all command again. "Where is he?" she asked Charlie. Luke read the unspoken plea there: she hoped Daniel hadn't closed off the bond link between himself and Charlie. Charlie's eyes became unfocused for a moment, and he looked off into the distance. His face lit up, even though his eyes radiated troubled thoughts.

"East. On the seaboard." His eyes narrowed. "Boston." Alice didn't wait to make her orders known. She spoke directly to the computer systems.

"Execute primary tracking order five," she said. "Prepare three boomers for maximum velocity, order the crews on standby and prepare for immediate departure." She was silent for a moment more, then she looked at Charlie and Luke's expectant expressions. "We leave now. Alexis, Chris, Jamie and Maggie will meet us at the launch pads." She moved resolutely for the door, Charlie by her side. Luke trotted after.

"What about me?" he asked.

"You are not a chartered GOA employee, Luke. We cannot risk any harm coming to you," Alice said, mounting the stairs and talking at Luke over her shoulder.

"I'm his brother," Luke protested. He refrained from bringing up the fact that Alice had had no qualms about sending him, the 'non-chartered employee', with Alex to New York. And that he was nearly killed back there.

"You will stay here, and that's final," Alice snapped, mind focused on taking command of a possibly disastrous situation. Luke, helplessly frustrated, followed them to the elevator and endured their silence, knowing he wouldn't go with them. When they exited at the top again, and Alice stormed off, Luke grabbed hold of Charlie's arm, forcing the man to a standstill and rewarding Luke with a frown of thwarted intent.

"Bring him back safely," he whispered. Charlie watched him for a long moment, then nodded simply, a joint moment of deeper understanding passing between them.

"I will," Charlie said, and then he too left.

Ancillary Documents

GOA VIIIA: Null Fiends and Associated Research areas

It was only a matter of time before the human race developed technology that managed to bend both light and create particle barriers that managed to ward off incoming assaults and defend against such attacks. Shielding tech was already a relatively fixed field by the mid twenty-first century, and advancements were made quite easily, providing stronger and more resilient shields.

When GOA discovered the GenneY Annabel Swanson, and realized that they had little or no technological devices to counteract her violently powerful mental thrusts, they were forced to jury-rig something on the fly. This did not seem too hard at first, on principle, mainly because of the already stated successes in particle-field generators that could ward off physical and energy projectiles, and the fact that GOA Research itself had long since stumbled on a coherent manner to identify the unique mental wave patterns and energy streams that constituted brainwaves exerted outside the skull. The problem remained that even though a sigma wave detector – the waveform mostly identified with brain wave patterns – could be used to detect the slightest spike of errant mentalist intent, it still couldn't be modulated to perform the same function as a particle field; initial testing on empathic GOA employees yielded not even a slight ability for the first prototypes of sigma field inhibitors to deter any extraneous thoughts. Various alternatives were attempted: the concept of a generator was dispensed with entirely and attempts were made to create a device that would inhibit the empathic abilities directly inside the mind. Another attempt was also made in mental amplification techniques, in creating devices that could augment a mentalist's mental patterns to become amplified. The first alternative was later deemed unsuitable, being a step beyond the very technology they were trying to create, and as such, would not become viable until a particle-sigma field generator was in operation. The second alternative was deemed unsafe, even if it was more likely to be achieved than the actual problem: there was no telling what a reversal of the field enabling the mental boost would yield, if the mind of someone like Swanson managed to turn the intrusion back on the mentally amplified user's mind.

Within months of exhaustive testing, a solution presented itself. In spite of the relativity of waves and particles, the approach to solving the problem was found to be faulty. Instead of attempting to introduce sigma waves into the particle field generator, the generator was adapted to broadcast sigma waves, transmitting them through a converter that rendered them particulate and, with much further adaptation, allowed them to behave in a way similar to that of a plain particle field generator. The result was a very bulky device that at first failed to completely render a barrier to any strength of mental strikes, but with enough testing became a bubble of sigma particles that were so dense they disallowed any intrusion. Within two more months of experimentation the first sigma field generator was tested successfully, by Alice herself, and found to be capable of handling an immense counter-strike from any mental source. More to the point, Annabel Swanson was also subjected to the field, albeit without her knowledge, and gradually allowed the full reign of her mental prowess. Even at the height of her power, the field managed to hold, and GOA Research began an immediate subsidiary project within its ranks to permanently dedicate time and effort to further perfecting sigma field technologies.

By the time Swanson had died the first field had been upgraded one more time, and seventy years after Swanson's death, when the second GenneY Daniel Mercer was found, sigma field technology was in a stage of rapid advancement, to the point of small generators that not only broke any outgoing or incoming – dependent on the orientation of the generated field – psychic streams but also annulled them (previous sigma generators only managed to repel such strikes, rebounding the effort, often with painful results irrespective of the kind of mental technique employed). When Daniel Mercer was first placed within a field, even his untrained but enormous power failed to breach the barrier, and his most potent thrusts were negated. This led to the term 'null field'.

Such fields were also retrofitted with convergent particle fields that served as 'physical' backup for the null fields. Despite the major advances in this technology, Daniel Mercer still managed to find an incredibly small discrepancy in the wave cycles of the null generators, thus forcing a rethinking of current field technology. Regardless, his tactic had been cross-referenced and classified as a one in a million chance encounter, enabled only through a mental state that bordered on extra-dimensional psychic capacity, impossible to achieve by anyone less skilled and weaker than an Nth Prime mentalist. Regardless, the tireless GOA Research department immediately began reworking their technology for improvements and defences against even such unattainable prospects as Mercer had managed.

Another area loosely associated with Null Tech is the drug known as 'Neuronull', a pseudo-smart-drug that is laced with pre-programmable nanites. This catalytic agent allows certain pre-selected – via any neurosurgical access terminal - areas of any brain to be 'dampened'; effectively rendering the person taking the drug temporarily and completely ignorant of the blocked areas' memories and knowledge, but more importantly, rendering said sections of the mind virtually illegible and inoperant – seeming to any psychic intrusion and scanning.

The drug was initially envisioned and later created by Alice McNamora before her stint as GOA Director of the Changed began, in an effort to arm key political figures against a generalised surge of mildly psychic agents, non – GOA – affiliated, who cropped up every now and then in the higher government echelons. Although the initial, raw state of the drug in its earliest days of use prevented excessive use – over use promulgated intense and, in some cases, irrevocable hallucinogenic episodes and ultimately severe brain damage – the Neuronull drug has had several phases of dramatic and overall improvement since its creation in 2010, allowing for highly diverse levels of suppression, duration and half-life – regarding the benign decay and harmless expulsion from the body. The drug currently in use has little or no side-effects, and more advanced nanotechnology even disallows over use, shorting out all effects by dint of unbreakable, default protocols deeply embedded in both nanite programming and the drug's encoded cellular structure

CHAPTER TWENTY FIVE

The Hunt

He didn't know where he was going.

He had been in Boston before – one of his first foster home experiences, but that had been a long time ago, and he hardly remembered anything of the city. And yet here he was, observing everything with unveiled eyes, marvelling at what he saw, seeing the people stare at him for no apparent reason. He had teleported into a very public place, and yet before he had even considered throwing a quick mental damper over everyone around him, it had happened, and no one even noticed his arrival in a swirl of blurring light eddies. There were also no cameras or observational devices anywhere about, so his approach went unnoticed.

A strange need drove him, an indefinable urge that demanded his absolute and immediate attention. The white light still blared across all his senses, and he mused that if he hadn't had a mental awareness unparalleled by any of the people around him, he would have rolled on the ground, moaning and experiencing gut-wrenching agony. Part of him was appalled by his exit from GOA, by how he had seemingly shunned the people who had been in the process of helping him understand his own predicament. But the greater part of him was driven, spurred on by a necessity to find the source of the strange call. That was what it was, he thought: a clarion call, an echo across distance that had drawn him across the country at a moment's thought, teleporting without defined boundaries and regulatory mental preparation. It was an easy exercise, teleporting, but it required focus, and most of all, a sense of spatial awareness to determine the release point. Yet he had transported his body across an unknown distance, determined only by the insane demand placed on his psyche, to depart and find the source of the disturbance.

He walked into the night-time sprawl of downtown Boston, past the people still out and about in the streets, bathed in their glowing lamps and lights. Like some revenant he gravitated to where his mind assured him the source of the white light was. He walked calmly, strangely unhurried despite the urgency he felt. Whatever it was, it was stationary, and he doubted it would move. It encompassed so much of his thoughts that he knew he would find its location, even if it died down suddenly. But it didn't.

He stopped before a building that resembled some monstrous cathedral, a construct hailing from several centuries before, standing like some obscenely enlarged version of its nearby churches and holy places.

Once again he didn't care if anyone saw him, or if anyone noticed what he did. The doors to the place swung open to his merest telekinetic touch, and he swept inside, finding no one else around. There were desks and information centrals, and he thought it might possibly be an office space of some sort. Trivial details like names and company signage didn't feature highly in his priorities right then, and he doubted anything like security guards or employees would interest him either, so he moved past them, nearly as oblivious of them as they were of him. He moved on, the beacon in his head screaming louder now that he was almost at it. He hadn't teleported to the very spot where it came from, though considering what he had just done, how effortlessly he had gone to work escaping GOA and coming here with almost instantaneous alacrity, it wouldn't have been beyond him. The expedience of that gesture eluded him.

He walked into a large warehouse-type chamber, with a high ceiling. The cavernous room was stacked with ancient statues, from Ancient Middle Eastern civilization, by the looks of it. They would have had him quailing; enrapt with an eerie sense of foreboding, but now he watched them as casually as they seemed to watch him, faces etched with shadows, adding an unholy dimension to their miens. Past the boulevard of stone edifices he went, heedless, unaware of anyone else close by.

His mind could almost no longer contain the elation at finding the source. It was inside a room, just beyond the hall of statues. He could feel a pulsing vibration through the floor, and he had to curb his own immediate desire to gratify his curiosity and open the door, to see what was inside.

"You look different from when I last saw you," a voice behind him said. Daniel spun about to confront it.

He frowned, not recognizing the man. He was tall, head and shoulders taller than Daniel himself. He had an amiable face, with soft but strongly defined features, and round, child-like blue eyes that were covered in a thin film of tears.

"Do I know you?" Daniel ventured casually. The man remained rooted to the spot. He swallowed, then smiled wanly.

"Don't you recognize me? Its Eric," the man said, taking a step forward. Daniel remained impassively staring. "I'm so glad to see you escaped, but I was so worried. I activated the ring to call you, as you told me I should, in great need."

"Ring?"

"The ring you created, I don't know when Aidan, can't you remember?"

"Who's Aidan?" Daniel asked, puzzled out of his distanced reverie. The man, Eric, took another step forward. He opened his arms in a gesture of acceptance.

"Read my thoughts, like you used to when we just met. You used to read my mind back then, like you would a newspaper, or a book. It'll all come back to you." Eric came closer, until he stood towering over Daniel, a beatific expression of fulfilment on his face. Daniel recoiled slightly as Eric reached for him, the large hands closing over his own. Instantly his head was flooded with images, of a foggy morning, just before sunrise, as Eric waited, with a youthful-looking other man held protectively in his arms. The man appeared completely catatonic, mouth slack and blue eyes wide and unrelentingly dead. The visual sped onward, to where the blonde man was lying prostrate in the train tracks. Daniel felt an unfamiliar tugging at the edges of reason. The entire episode that played in front of his eyes buckled under some unknown force.

Daniel withdrew, but he could somehow not break the physical grip the man had him in. Drawing back, he reassessed the situation, letting the images play unchecked as his mind raced to figure out what was going on. Part of him actually recognized the blonde man lying there. Changed, came the unbidden thought. But it meant nothing to Daniel. More, to his mounting horror, something else surged through his mind, a dark presence, like a black shade that would suck him dry of life. Inside his head, a scream echoed, followed by a chorus of angry, upset shades protesting some dark act of unlawful, unwanted entry. He recognized the pattern immediately. It was a violation. The man before him was not Eric, even though Daniel didn't have a clue as to who Eric actually was. What lurked before him was an abomination, someone intent on violating his mind, his very essence. One word came searing through his brain like a glowing shard of metal.

False.

With a stentorian roar he threw the man away from him physically, falling backwards with the effort. He was on his feet immediately, breathing heavily. The man rose, an unreadable expression on his face. Then he smiled, folding his hands behind his back.

"So you're not Aidan. Why did you answer the summons, then?" he asked, voice completely different from before, sounding higher, more nasal. Daniel circled the man warily, ready at a moment's notice to assail the creature before him. "Who are you?"

"I could probably ask you the same thing," Daniel replied. The man smiled, a cruel grimace that all but distorted the amiable features, making them darker and less discernible. "What is this place?"

"You will find out soon enough," the false Eric said.

The boomer was flying high.

At the speed they were making, they could hardly afford to crash into something at maximum velocity, on the accepted altitude levels. The boomer would take almost half an hour to reach Boston, and Alice felt keenly every shred of frustration and deep terror that she had mused on, since Daniel had arrived at GOA, and his potential had become discussed. The possibility that he would go rampantly missing of his own accord had always been a big one, and Alice hated that the boy had proved her faith wrong. And yet she couldn't hold it all against him. She had seen what lurked in his mind, beyond even his ability to perceive. It had been something dark, not well-meaning, and it didn't bode well.

"Charlie!" she snapped, forcing Charlie to look at her again. His face was etched with worry, but his eyes sparked fire when he looked at Alice. She didn't care that he was upset about Daniel vanishing, she had demanded constant updating, even if it meant telling her that Daniel was enjoying the sights and sounds of suburbia.

"He's in the central city, a cathedral, or something like it." Alice nodded. There was no time to discuss Daniel's scan with Charlie now, although Alice knew something Charlie didn't. There was no telling how disturbing the info could be to Charlie, but she kept it to herself for the nonce. They had to concentrate on a strategy to capture Daniel, and that involved massive expenditure of GOA's resources. Alice watched the vid screen terminal open on her lap. Before the boomer had lifted off, she had informed the President of a potential threat, and had achieved his clearance to stage a bogus event that would cordon off the area where Daniel was. But that meant waiting for Daniel to stand still for more than five minutes, or else waste precious time relocating the joint effort of hundreds of police officers and specialists who would be called in to blockade the area. Alice had deemed it unnecessary for most of the people involved to know even limited details of the situation. The CIA and FBI had demanded – on a higher level – to be informed of whatever occurred, which was why Alice had opted to come with: Alexis could manage the less strong-willed officers and people there, but Alice herself had to enact persuasive coercion to blanket the stronger minds. She cringed inside at the thought of a mishap occurring now, then quelled the feeling with ruthless efficiency. There was no time for misgivings, and the protocols and plausible worst case scenarios had been prepared long before, making this a by-the-book exercise. As by-the-book as netting and subduing a monstrously powerful GenneY Changed could be.

"How long?" Alice asked the pilot. The cockpit door stood open, as Alice was in no mood to utilize any of her gifts for trivialities. The man turned his head to speak to her over his shoulder.

"Eighteen minutes," he replied. Alice looked to Charlie again. He gave her a look of long-suffering which she ignored completely.

"He's been stationary for five minutes," Charlie said darkly. Alice nodded, looked back down at the vid terminal and commandeered her people to initiate the systematic blockade of that area in the city, hoping against hope that Daniel didn't decide to move within the next minute or so. The minute she hoped against went by in the boomer in absolute silence, and still nothing from Charlie, except an unfocused stare. Alice wondered just how much he could perceive from Daniel's end, whether there was any conversation he could follow or not. She sent one more order to a far-off GOA contact within Boston's judicial precincts and leaned towards the silent empath before her. He started, and that look of irritation flashed in his eyes.

"What can you make out from the link?"

"He's talking to someone. I can't make out who – Daniel's confused himself – but nothing else is happening." He looked beyond Alice, eyes growing larger as his brow furrowed. "Wait, something's wrong..."

421

"What is it?"

"He feels threatened. There's something else in the room where he is." Charlie gasped as if in pain, doubling over, face contorting with pain. Alice rose quickly, dropping to her knees by his side, even as Alex and Jamie darted in to hover protectively, inquiringly. Charlie's face had gone white with strain, and he was clutching his stomach. He jerked upright again suddenly, eyes wide and terrified. "He's under attack," he managed, before doubling over again. Alice sprang erect, yelling.

"Make this thing go faster!"

Persephone snarled. Beside her, Amorphia rematerialized from the inky black haze and hunkered down beside her. The woman narrowed her slanted blue eyes, smooth face marred by concentration. And wariness. About them, the entire chamber shook. Persephone despised the fact that the other woman had less chance of suffering some massive, directed assault, prone to simply fading away as she was. Amorphia wasn't constantly darting from fallen statue to fallen statue, just to stay alive.

"What is Graven waiting for?" she griped angrily. Amorphia didn't look at her, calculation clear on her features. "He could crush this whelp within a flash!"

"Do not be so sure," Amorphia replied, almost calmly! It infuriated Persephone. "Either he is biding his time, waiting for us to soften the man up, or"

"Or what?" Persephone demanded imperiously.

"Or Graven is simply biding his time." The thought of such a thing, that Graven would allow the death of some of his most useful and powerful weapons, simply to watch and possibly admire some insolent – if mighty – little cur, twisted Persephone's mouth with disgust, and knotted her insides with sudden, icy fear.

Amorphia didn't wait for Persephone to start speculating, instead letting her body dissolve once more into that nauseating mass of smoky ripples, as she gravitated away from Persephone's current hiding place. Persephone, knowing she was no coward, but also in no mood to die, decided that she had no choice. She needed to escape to a safer location, and if she could use the others' conflict with the boy as cover, so be it.

Mentally she scanned the surroundings for the others' actions. Amal was nowhere to be found – he had vanished mysteriously the moment the attack had started – and Catherine was also missing. It galled Persephone, how someone like that woman could be so deviously cunning at seeing opportune moments, whether to hold back and observe or simply to not be where the most damage would be done.

She had a moment to deliberate when she realized her mental scan had been detected. She darted to the side on her precarious heels just as the large upper body of a statue came tumbling down from above her. She blocked the flying spray of debris that would have ripped her skin from her body, nearly screamed her rage and flew through the newly-risen screen of dust, using the lowest range of her abilities to navigate through the thick haze. She managed to get to safety before another reverberation shook the ground, and a cry of alarm went up from somewhere close by.

She looked out from behind the still-erect pillar she had ducked behind, hoping to see something other than obscuring fog. She drew back hastily, gasping. The boy – no other moniker would suffice to contain her contempt for him – floated in the middle of the room, a wild light in his flaring blue eyes. The floor had given way, pooling the depression created by the initial retaliatory strike with water from broken pipes. He simply floated there, wildly lashing out at anyone or anything that came at him. Persephone wondered at who had tried to land the first blow. It had to have been something offensive, or else the boy wouldn't have torn the ground to shreds below where he had stood. She cursed her own gifts suddenly, knowing that they were the reason she had to run so often. And she had seen, that night at that old Changed woman's mansion, what the boy was capable of. She had no intention of getting thrown through walls again, or having something slowly crush her to death because she could, for once, not hope to survive a direct mental face-off.

She heard a swift cry of rage – Clarissa – and dared a quick peek again. If the woman engaged the boy in a direct attack, Persephone knew the odds were she could escape. What she saw filled her with more trepidation. The boy was still afloat, but his face registered strain, eyes flaring vividly to counter Clarissa's assault. Persephone knew she herself could drive back the woman's fiery waves, but it took great effort.

The boy handled his defences well; the fire curled around an unseen bubble about him, held far enough away to ensure no singeing or excess heat reached him. From Clarissa's enraged screeching, it was clear she was throwing everything she had at him. Persephone found a moment to denigrate the woman: it would take more than just one of them to take the boy down, and there was no telling if it might actually require all of them. Cursing her unbreakable bond to Graven and her dedication to his cause, she ducked from behind the pillar and threw her most potent mental assault against the boy, broadcasting telekinetically and telepathically to try and unbalance him. His gaze turned to her suddenly, and the fire died down in the path of his vision. He shook where he floated, the impact of Persephone's blow catching him off guard. But not enough to break his defences. Persephone loosed wave after wave, hoping it would occupy him enough to ensure her own survival, and to make the others see that a conjoined effort would work better than single strikes. She smiled when she saw dark needles shoot jet bullets from somewhere. They rebounded off the shield, save for one which got through and snagged the boy's sleeve. He looked down, perplexed, and Persephone redoubled her efforts.

Fire filled the chamber, forcing Persephone to shield against the scorching heat. She wanted to yell at Clarissa to be careful, but she could see the effect. The boy was hard-pressed now, slowly floating downward under the combined onslaught. Now all they needed was something else.

The boy curled in on himself, decreasing the bubble with him. Persephone all but yelled triumphantly, before she realized it wasn't defeat. With a roar of fury the boy arched his body outward, and Persephone was thrown beyond the safety of her shield and against the wall, as a blast of monstrous strength ripped through the chamber, manifesting as a wave of sound that echoed like a tremendous gust of wind, blasting the fire into oblivion and no doubt forcing Amorphia into near-total dispersal. When the sound died down the boy was still floating there, but he was moving towards the chamber where Graven kept the ring. Let him, Persephone thought, and stepped clear of the debris pile where she had fallen. The others were nowhere to be seen, possibly having fled. The boy was horribly strong, and Persephone valued her own skin more than allegiances to even Graven. If he wanted the boy stopped, he could do it himself.

Dusting herself off, she trotted towards the exit.

The doors flew apart.

He floated through, borne up by the sense of power, and by the adrenaline of combat fuelling him forward. He hadn't expected to see that woman, Persephone, again, or that she would be stupid enough to face him again. Regardless, she had had help this time, and he had been hard pressed. There were moments, just moments, where he had doubted he would make it. Fighting the fire-wielding woman with the red hair had been as taxing, if only because she had made sure he focused on her only, or else suffer a mishap of breached defences. And there was the Oriental one too, the woman Luke had spoken of once. Her insidious assaults had been annoying, and he had taken a quick instant to study the thin black needles she had shot at him. Poison, possibly something vile and nasty to cause intense pain and loss of concentration. He had nearly fallen to the mercy of one of those. But they had fled after his last retaliation, a strike born of rage and desperation. The man who had called himself Eric, but was in fact no one of the kind, had disappeared with alarming speed, and Daniel didn't track the man's despicable presence anywhere within the building.

That left the central room, beyond the now-ruined chamber of statues. Daniel knew that was where the ring waited. A ring, but he had no idea what it did, or why it attracted him so. It still shone clearly in his head. Something told him he would have been able to find it even if he had sensed it from around the world.

Inside it was dark, and Daniel willed light into being, watching the chamber become limned in a silvery light. He gasped at what he saw. There on the floor waited a ring of solid stone, a creation of immense intricacy, carved all over with fine grooves and symbolic indentations. It was a masterpiece, and Daniel dropped to his feet, sinking to his knees beside the device. It seemed to croon at his touch, and he felt a slight twinge of pain when his fingers traced the edges. That, and a tug of something that felt strangely familiar. It defied logical explanation, but Daniel felt a sense of belonging, of being where he was supposed to be, at least for the moment. The ring was something that somehow belonged to him, he knew. But he had no idea of telling why he felt as he did, and why the object seemed to recognize his touch.

A brief flare of white light rushed to meet his departing fingertips, dancing off the runes and sigils and arcing over his hands. It did no harm, but it seemed to be a warning, as though the device demanded his touch. Rising to his feet, Daniel let his eyes roam across the device. He had to remove it from here, take it away. Possibly back to GOA, or anywhere where he could study it in peace, figure out what it meant to him and why it seemed to draw him to some inexorable end.

"You should guard your thoughts, boy. Any empath within a mile can read them." Daniel looked up quickly. A rawboned man stood there, a cruel but amused smile on his thin lips, narrow eyes minatory and cold. He pulled a hand across hair drawn back from his forehead, and stepped closer. Daniel frowned, identifying the small details. The man had a French accent, and he seemed, of all things, humoured by Daniel's presence. "I also wonder why the ring brought you here, and not…bah, c'est pas important. What I would like to know is why you've ruined my priceless collection!" The voice had gone suddenly from nonchalant querying to insurmountable rage, a cold and calculated gesture that seemed to draw the man's skin tight across his skull. "Well? Answer!"

"I had no intention of destroying anything until your people attacked me," Daniel replied evenly. He realized with a small surge of fear that he couldn't read the man at all. Where normally the presence of a mind waited, like a picture of doubled clarity emplaced over the visuals perceived by the eye, there was nothing, not even void. The man was like the absence of anything, and he knew it, judging from the way he smiled again. Daniel clamped down on his own thoughts, and the man chuckled.

"Yes, well, my 'people', as you call them, have their duties. I applaud your progress thus far, but it will gain you nothing. Where is your master? Surely he would not send a mere lackey to deal with me?" The demand was authoritative, and Daniel detected traces of command coercion therein. He forced himself to smile at the man's apparent displeasure.

"I came of my own accord," Daniel said. He erected as powerful a barrier against any mental assault as he could, in the event that the man's actions were as mercurial as his moods. "This ring, it drew me here." The man regarded Daniel for the longest moment, face inscrutable.

"You seem to be speaking the truth. I have killed for far less, but you may prove useful yet."

"I will go as soon as I've taken the ring," Daniel said, and took a step forward. The man's face turned cruel and contemptuous.

"You do not understand, you impudent little fool!" he snarled, and lifted a hand. Daniel didn't even see the blow that sent him reeling into the wall behind him. He retaliated instantly, hurling a combined assault of telekinetic and empathic transmissions against the man, marvelling at how deftly the complex assault came to effortless fruition. He gasped when the man peremptorily waved his hand again, a casual flick of the wrist, and Daniel shuddered as the directed mental blow was cut short and diffused, sending it clattering back into his skull with a dull echo. "You do not lie, but there is something about you. I must investigate further. Je deteste la mystere d'incomprehensible, and this bears looking into."

Daniel realized for the first time that he was outmatched. He couldn't defend against what he couldn't see, and facing this man was like fighting the sky, and having clear and indeterminate lightning strike back, without preamble or warning. He prepared to teleport, and was jerked short as the man spoke again.

"No, no, no, we cannot be having that! You will remain here, as my guest." The last word twisted the man's mouth into a menacing smile. Daniel stood rooted to the spot, unable to move or to cry out, immobilized by nothing he could see, touch or sense. "I have many useful people working for me, and they will relish unearthing whatever mysteries lie locked inside your head." From the shadows, the man who had presented himself as Eric before stepped, smiling knowingly. Even as Daniel watched, the man dwindled in height and build, until he was scant inches taller than Daniel, with as slight a frame. He had a light tan skin and curly dark hair, and a face that seemed both masculine and feminine, riddled with an indeterminate shift that at times seemed to deny gender specificity. With a start, Daniel realized he could talk again.

"What have you done to me?" he asked, clamping down on the terror he felt.

"I have made sure your behaviour is civilized," the false Eric said. That nasal voice fitted far better with that body, and it seemed to Daniel that the man – a Changed, beyond a doubt – had more gifts than merely altering his physical appearance and the sound of his voice. He stepped until he was close to Daniel, and snaked out a hand, casually taking Daniel's chin in hand and twisting his head to one side. "I fear you do not yet recognize your dilemma. I am about to let you continue unfettered, but you will engage none of your gifts. You will obey my every word, as well as his." The man tilted his head towards the Frenchman, who watched with unabated amusement, "and you will not leave to go anywhere. Is that understood?"

Daniel found himself nodding, and his face twisted into an appalled expression. The false Eric laughed.

"Excellent." He drew back, and the Frenchman stepped closer. "Yes, excellent. Now, get Enson, Alessandro and Catherine. I want him moved to the Ural Base. You may begin your ministrations there." The false Eric bowed his head, a strangely archaic gesture, and backed away, leaving the room. "First things first, though. You will call me Graven, and when you hear my name, you will feel this, every time."

Graven's eyes flared briefly, the first signal Daniel had seen the man display regarding the Changed gifts. Before he could think on it further, he felt something slice into his chest, seeming to miss his heart but pierce his lungs. He tried to scream, and a compulsion like sheer denial slammed home on the urge to screech like a wounded animal, even as the pain climbed to an unimaginable height. Face contorted and white, streaming sweat, he regarded the Frenchman before him through manic eyes, aware through the all but blinding haze of pain that he was laughing.

"You will not scream, when Amal has you under his eye. But for me, you will always scream." Daniel shuddered, and Graven leaned back slightly. The pain redoubled, and Daniel felt as though his head would explode, before Graven's oily voice sliced through the pain and the desire to shut it all away: "Scream."

And he screamed, without end.

Alex's eyes were glazed with concentration.

More, they were also glazed with tears. Her face was caught up in an expression of fearful defeat, and while she was staring off into the distance brought about by deeper levels of focus, she was also taking in Charlie's looks of utter horror and pain, as Jamie and Chris held him down in his seat.

It had taken both of the latter to secure the man, once he had started screaming. Alice watched it all with an unreadable expression, but her face was ashen pale. Her thoughts were fuelling Alex's, who was in a state of scanning the area below them for whatever was happening to Daniel. When she had shaken her head, Alice had seemingly withdrawn completely from her stream of commands, her mouth moving silently as though she was calculating at a phenomenal speed. The boomer hovered several kilometres above Boston, waiting for whatever command she would give. Her thoughts raced cleanly and clearly through Alex's mind, but Alex could read none of them. Every now and then a stray musing seemed clearer, but there was no coherence she could discern. Whatever Alice was doing, it was beyond her ability to discern, or follow.

At length, when Charlie's convolutions and gasping drew to a shuddering halt, and the man sagged in his seat as though he had been rendered boneless, Alice looked at Alex.

"What can you see?" she asked quietly, so that none of the men could hear.

"He's gone." Alex replied distantly. "Whatever happened to him, I can't feel his presence anymore."

Alice nodded curtly, turning to Charlie. Alex all but saw the options taking form there. With a single glance Alice summoned Margaret to come closer. The old woman had remained quiet and watchful during the fast rush to the eastern seaboard, and she approached without preamble. Some unrecognizable signal passed between the two older women, and Margaret nodded once, a look of determination entering her eyes. She moved towards Charlie and placed both her hands on his head. He didn't respond at all. Mesmerized, disoriented, Alex watched as Margaret no doubt engaged her less known-about gift of imprinting. It was a gift, she thought, that was close to her own brand of coercion, only it was almost unstoppable, but also regrettably linked exclusively to tactile contact. Charlie stirred beneath her hands, eyes fluttering, and he mumbled something, before jerking awake. His skin was pallid, and he was sweating profusely.

His reaction boggled Alex, even though she knew it was some sort of backlash from the mental bond with Daniel. Whatever had happened to him, Charlie was feeling it keenly. Margaret withdrew slowly, her hands still poised uncertainly as though she expected failure of some kind. When Charlie gasped and began moaning again, Alice stepped forward resolutely.

"Where is he?" she demanded. Charlie's head lolled haphazardly, until Margaret's eyes flared brief blue, and Charlie seemed to regain coherence. His face was a mask of pain and loss, and the words were barely audible.

"I can't sense anything but the pain," he said. A quick indrawn breath, and he continued. "He has no control over anything. He obeys someone, but nothing else is coming through."

"What is happening to him?" Alice continued, as unshakable as a mountain.

"He's being tortured," Charlie gasped. A look of surprise passed between Jamie and Chris, and Alex heard herself gasp as well. "The pain rolls through the link in waves, and nothing else comes through."

Charlie's face crumpled, and he began sobbing. Whatever Margaret had ordered him to do through her touch still remained in place though, as he continued through the tears. "He's being moved now. He can't do anything. There's a woman with him, but it, aah!" He reared back, as if someone had hit him in the face. He hissed. "It's like listening to pure noise!" he protested. "Nothing gets through now." He leaned forward, breathing heavily, like he had run several miles in a flat sprint. He seemed calmer, but the mounting hysteria in his voice was growing. "I can't feel him anymore."

"What do you mean?" Alice asked.

"Either he's unconscious or he's dead!" Charlie snapped, and at the utterance of the last word, the horror spread across his already beleaguered features. "He can't be dead."

"He was there one second, and then he wasn't," Alex added.

"When an empath dies there is usually a sense of immediate severance which no field or external control can hinder," Alice said, voice monotone and no-nonsense. "You would have felt him die, if he had died."

Charlie's body shook with grief, and he was completely oblivious to the soothing gestures Jamie and Chris made, rubbing him across the shoulders and gripping his neck. "If what Alex detected is any indication, he was teleported somewhere else."

"Then why can't I feel him anymore?"

"He's unconscious, or drugged," Alex ventured, hoping that her input was helpful. Surprisingly, Alice nodded. Charlie didn't respond to their efforts, and Alice turned back to Margaret. She nodded, and again the older woman moved in, placing a hand across Charlie's forehead. He started – his faculties were back to normal, even if he was still upset – but he couldn't deny Margaret's touch, casually pinioned by Chris and Jamie. It was only a moment, and then his eyes rolled backwards and closed, and he sagged into a pose of complete and utter unconsciousness. Alice, efficient even when she knew her most prized employee and find was gone from her sight, turned from the scene and sat down at her console again. She tapped away at the keys, while the others watched with bated breath for what she was about to do. Margaret alone withdrew, taking her seat again far at the back of the boomer.

At length, Alice looked up. She seemed drawn and exhausted, but not enough so that she was completely drained. The boomer shuddered and suddenly veered away, rotating on its axis and jerking into high velocity again. Alex curbed her impatient desire to press the woman for any details, knowing she would get little or nothing, and she had to settle for silence. She realized that she would probably be the first one to be accosted by Luke, on their return to Headquarters. She bit her finger, frowning mightily. What would she tell him? They'd lost his brother? That Daniel was being tortured, somewhere out there, where not even Alice or Charlie could detect him? Suddenly she didn't want to return to GOA. Even if it meant staying from her newly beloved darling, she didn't want to face that eventuality, of seeing him laid low by the devastating development.

CHAPTER TWENTY SIX

Assessment

It was unthinkable.

Alice couldn't quite come to terms with what had happened. The loss was monumental, and she couldn't figure out in any way how the situation could have been avoided. No one could have stopped Daniel from leaving – his gifts were too great, and the disturbing terror of that unmentioned presence in his mind lurked behind his every action. Why else would he have simply vanished, pulled away by some unknown directive that summoned him hence? The scope of what he had done, of what he had accomplished, baffled everyone, and Alice didn't stand apart from those who marvelled at it. Now, he was in the hands of whatever evil she had thought waited on the outskirts.

There was no denying it: her theory had proven correct. Alex's abilities, though nowhere near fully trained, had proven useful; the girl could detect the strength of other Changed individuals, and watching her blanch on board the boomer, when she had first begun the scan for Daniel's presence in Boston had been enough indication of just what calibre of people had taken Daniel. The information had been sporadic and less than conclusive, but this much had been ascertained: Daniel was held captive by people who on various levels of aptitude equalled and surpassed anyone GOA could throw against them. Individually. Alice shuddered, thinking about it, that there were several other Changed just below Nth Prime level out there, and that they were collectively working to some end. And Daniel had unwittingly fallen prey to whatever designs these people were planning.

She looked down at the reports before her. They were relatively trivial, confirmation of the events she herself had set in motion in order to create a suitably mundane cover for going in and extracting Daniel from that cathedral-like structure in Boston. The police reported a bomb threat, and whatever had caused that monstrous hole in the floor, and the black scorch marks everywhere else within the structure had been identified – with a little help from the forensics contacts within the police force itself, loyal to GOA – as one of the bombs having gone off. Heaven knows there had been a sufficiently violent tremor that justified such an assumption, and no one had turned out the wiser, concerning what had actually occurred. Alice was grateful for the clout she managed with the higher-level government affiliates. To blow GOA's cover now would be monstrous, considering that everything would out, then, including the fact that a super-human being of incalculable power, actively employed by GOA, was on the loose and unmonitored. Daniel's recovery was paramount, and Alice had nowhere to begin looking for him. She had thought Charlie's intimate mental bond with him would serve as a beacon of sorts, but whoever held Daniel was either aware of the reverse possibilities of the link, or simply aware of it and capable of blocking it. Or Daniel was, in a strange twist of compassion, blocking Charlie from feeling whatever it was he himself was going through. From Charlie's reaction, the pain must have been incredible: the strictures of empathic bonding rarely turned out on an equality basis, as Daniel had proved. The most powerful empath in the bond had more control over the workings of the bond, and the difference between Charlie and Daniel's capacities was a marked inequality. Daniel was either withheld from making contact, or he was willingly subjecting the bond to a dead zone, in order to keep GOA away, or to spare Charlie the magnified effects of the pain travelling through the bond. Alice showed the possibility of distance from hand: a bond between empaths of such strength as Charlie and Daniel maintained could last on fullest capacity even if the two of them were separated by half the world. No, Daniel was being held against his will, and whatever managed to do so by physical force gave Alice pause. She wished there was a way to find out who they were dealing with. As it was, they had nothing beyond the profiler reports of past situations in the dead zone pockets in the nine major cities across the world, where other Changed of average and higher capability were summarily executed out of hand. It spoke of misanthropic megalomania on a massive level. The only conclusions Alice could draw was that these nine cities were dominated by nine individuals of immense power, working under the guidance or coercion of their strongest member or members, and these Changed were xenophobic and paranoid to extremes, suffering no one they thought could pose a threat to their supremacy.

The organizational ability of whatever non-Changed people worked for them was also enough to cause wariness. These Changed could not accomplish their schemes without muscle or workforce and still remain unnoticed, even by GOA, so there had to be some level of affiliation from their end within the higher ranks of governments. Alice doubted these people would pursue the exposure of the world's Changed, given the secrecy with which they went to work. Alice snarled in frustration. There had to be some way to trace these people, some loose end they could latch onto and work with in order to find out more. Until they knew more, there was very little GOA, even with its significant resources and power could accomplish. Wherever Daniel was, he was alone.

On a humane level the thought made Alice cringe inside. She, Charlie and some others had unwittingly trained a weapon that could possibly be used against them now. Daniel knew almost everything about GOA, and at the least he knew enough for these people to somehow begin pulling strings to undermine GOA's powerbases, to pull the rug from beneath their feet.

Alice thought back on the last time she had spoken to Alex. She had summoned the girl to her office to glean any information she could rack from the girl's mind, anything that Alex might have missed before. Under pressure the girl had improved, no longer resorting to outbursts of outrage or misery when emotionally driven to such a depth. Alice was proud of the change, and knew finally that Alex would make an exceptional agent. But there had been precious little extra to find out, save for one interesting bit: the small fragment she had managed to feel when Daniel had still been free and fighting against whatever these people had hurled against him had detected a mind as healthy and focused as always. Only when the fight had ended did Alex detect something invasive, before being cut off. Alice was unwilling to rule out coercion, but she refused outright to consider what kind of mind could coerce someone with a will as undeniably rigid and insurmountable as Daniel's, considering the mental array of gifts he had. That left one other possibility. One she had discussed with Margaret.

"Imprinting is forcing your will onto another. It requires touch, and the slightest touch is enough, if the imprinter is skilled, and manages to slip past the defences of the mind," Margaret had explained. Alice refrained from showing disgust at the thought of sundered will – empaths called it violation, and coercion, while sometimes necessary, was nowhere near as invasive. It had never bothered Alice that her oldest friend was a skilled imprinter, mainly because Margaret herself disdained the use of the gift, and had professed using it against one of her assailants when her mansion had burned that evening. Self-defence was acceptable, but when imprinting was used for controlling purposes it became something that even the most liberal of Changed frowned on. If Daniel had been imprinted, it meant he could by express command of whoever had imprinted him not react or respond in any way save what was specified. Mentally Alice tabulated the gifts of those they had encountered, of the Changed she deemed part of the group that held Daniel. She had four so far, taking into account all the data she had: a skilled psychic, the one who had attacked Luke; the Oriental woman who had accompanied her that night, who had attacked Alyssa and Margaret; the mysterious man, whom Alice attributed the imprinter status on, seeing as she had nothing else to go on, and a woman who had an unreadable field of mental imprecision guarding her thoughts, and who could probably teleport. Four Changed. Precious little to go on with.

Alice rose from her chair, placing one hand against the cold pane of glass behind the desk. Tonight the lights of Headquarters failed to draw her in, to remind her of clockwork precision and the inexorable motion of progress and a working organism. One of her biggest cogs was missing tonight, and it had happened even before she could fully integrate him. Like a floodgate, the more peripheral consequences of losing Daniel rammed home. Charlie was still asleep, and would stay that way until the empaths monitoring him could assure her that his mind was more or less stabilized, and that he wouldn't try to commandeer a boomer and launch himself like a shot into the dark, on some furious quest to retrieve Daniel. Alice still hadn't had time to go to Charlie's bedside herself, to show the simplest gesture of trust and commiseration to her second-in-command, and possibly to gauge his condition for herself.

Then there was Luke. Nathan had fled, beyond her immediate concern, back to his parents, but Alice doubted when he heard what had happened that his resolve to alienate Daniel forever would hold. But she couldn't risk Nathan's presence here now, nor Joanie's; they would no doubt join Charlie in some foolhardy attempt to find Daniel, and if the three of them were lost, GOA would lose one of its finest employees, and the human race would no doubt get to see the world of the Changed, so casually but carefully merged seamlessly and unwittingly into their own, blown apart and out in the open, if GOA had to admit that they had lost two non-affiliated Changed. No, Nathan and Joanie would have to remain in the dark. Let Nathan grow accustomed to his anger, and with a little time, he would start healing by himself.

But Luke was another story. Alice had expected tears of rage, anger, frustration and an outpouring of vengeance, but instead, she had been surprised when Alex had told her Luke was disturbingly quiet, but not withdrawn. He seemed focused, and had demanded his immediate inauguration into GOA as a full employee.

Considering the circumstances, Alice would have denied the request, but she couldn't refute his claim to aid in looking for Daniel, and as a member he could play an active part, even serve as a mediator between his family and GOA, to soften the blow of Daniel's second kidnapping. Keeping Luke close at this stage was crucial, and GOA's field agent division was woefully short-handed, even inept, considering what they would possibly have to deal with quite soon. Alice looked over her shoulder, at the solitary sheaf of papers lying to one side of her desk. They would secure Luke's position in GOA, and begin the process of systematically eradicating his connections to the outside world, inasmuch as documentation could be considered a way of tracking someone. Secretly Alice welcomed his presence. He was a calming influence on Alex's usually rampant rebellions and childishness, and Margaret, having gotten to know him better in the month or so he had accompanied Alex to New York, had given Alice a glowing report of the older Hirsch brother's skills and personality.

She looked at the clock standing on her desk. Three-thirty. If Margaret had still been awake at this hour she would have chivvied Alice into going to bed. There was little time for that now. Though Alice had no idea really where to start solving their current problems, she felt it would appear less than calming, were she to give the outward appearance of being flustered or indecisive. Sighing, she dimmed the lights and left her office. Sleep eluded her now, no doubt a by-product of inner turmoil, but she distanced herself. Leaving the command level of the building, she took an automated tram outside and made her way to the hospital. She weaved her way through the narrow corridors, nodding politely at the late night nurses and doctors, finding her own way to the section reserved mainly for the Changed. In spite of the world in general being ignorant of the Changed, Alice harboured a deep-seated resentment, that even where non-Changed and gifted fraternized and worked together, there was a level of segregation. Still, it was to be expected; the Changed were more volatile, and prone to more pitfalls than the average human.

Charlie's room faced south, and the lights were relatively low, but, Alice saw, to her astonishment, Charlie was awake. He was staring fixedly at the eastern wall, brows faintly furrowed in a frown of mild concentration. He didn't pay Alice any heed as she entered, and she had a few more moments to study his face. The kidnapping had left him appearing more worn than before. His youthful face had several new lines, around eyes and mouth, and his eyes themselves appeared glazed with dark thoughts, practically swimming in the luminous grey-green depths. Alice pulled a seat closer and sat down beside his bed. She waited a while longer before breaking the silence, and when she did, his face didn't turn to her.

"How are you feeling?" No answer. "A remarkably dense question, considering." Still nothing. Alice sighed. "You must get some sleep, if you can."

"Why?" he asked softly. His voice quavered as if from disuse. "It's all I've done for the last two days."

"With good reason," Alice cautioned, detesting the motherly streak necessary for the occasion. "I need you rested and well."

"For what?" he cracked, derision clear despite the hoarseness.

"Do you really think I will let Daniel go that easily? The fate of the Changed hangs in the balance. Finding him is paramount, before all else. I need you by my side."

"I can't do it," he whispered, and his eyes pooled with moisture, glistening even in the low light. "I can't find him. There's a faint hint of something, far to the east, but that's it." Alice gasped, but hid the effort. She nearly rose to her feet. As it was, she calmed herself and schooled her voice to equanimity.

"You can still feel him?" she asked. He swallowed, and nodded very slowly, eyes widening. "What do you feel?" He shook his head from side to side with equal slowness. His face almost crumpled beneath another barrage of welling emotions, but he bit down on his lower lip and closed his eyes.

"If it is him, then that's all. A faint sense of him. Or maybe it's just what I hope for." He lowered his head. "How did you deal with losing your husband?" Alice had half expected a query of this kind, considering the sense of hopelessness. "Even when he was unconscious, or asleep, even when he had blocked me, I had always felt something from him, even if it only meant knowing he was still around. But this…"

"Daniel isn't dead, Charlie, that much is certain. Like I've said before, you would have felt the loss keenly, irrespective of distance or outside efforts to shut you out. Keep that in mind."

"I can't do anything when I'm like this," he replied at length, scrubbing the heel of one hand across his eyes. He sniffed and opened his eyes, and regarded her pointedly for the first time since they had started speaking. "The worry eats at me. I keep feeling as though I'm losing my brother and father again, and once again, there's nothing I can do about it."

"Focus your intentions and thoughts," Alice said soothingly. She knew the situation, knew what it felt like to stand on the brink of loss, and knowing that, when and if the actual loss occurred, the foreboding that preceded it would still not be enough preparation for the actual happening. She had dealt with her husband's death in a manner she had thought fitting, going through all the motions and rending her soul apart with his death, as all who grieved did. But when she let herself dwell on it, the dull echo of that well-remembered communion of mind and soul still resounded, and she had to fight the tears. She fervently hoped Charlie wouldn't have to go through what she had. But she would also not indulge his behaviour, considering that Daniel wasn't actually dead. Still, the least she could do was give him some time. She knew the resolution was supported greatly by the fact that he had just admitted to knowing that Daniel was out there, somewhere east, and with time, he could possibly begin discerning in more detail where and how far

441

exactly Daniel was. Time was a precious commodity, but when you knew nothing and had to deal with everything, even time had to take a back seat to necessity and the course of the moment. It galled Alice, not knowing the rules of whatever engagement they were about to enter, but like every astute and experienced leader, she knew that the best course of action was patience, when nothing else was forthcoming. "I'm keeping you here for a while longer, until the doctors have given you the all-clear."

"Then what?" he asked.

"Take some time off. Gather your thoughts, occupy your mind with something different than usual. In the meantime I will do all I can to find Daniel." He didn't protest. He knew she wanted Daniel back as badly as he did, if for completely different reasons. "I would advise against returning to the Vancouver house, though. And try not to cast off on some pointless quest that might only get you killed." She saw a vague hint of recognition in his eyes, followed by the obvious rejoinder of discovery. He looked away, and Alice let a little insistency into her words. "I mean it. No heroics."

"I won't promise anything," he replied moodily.

"If you don't, I will keep you under lock and key and neuronull field," she threatened, meaning every word of it. His expression turned mulish. "Promise me."

"I promise," he said at length, sounding like a scolded child. It was enough for Alice, though. She rose, smoothed her slightly rumpled suit and nodded.

"Now, get some rest. I will probably drop by again later during the week, see how you are holding up."

And she left him to his thoughts and musings. She felt strangely elated, that not all contact with Daniel had been lost. Even if it was sporadic and imprecise. She marvelled anew at the extent to which a mental bond could be taken, and the age-old humane rules such things followed, even in this day and age.

As she climbed back onto the tram and prepared to go home, her thoughts dwelled one last moment on the nettlesome topic of the